Christmas with the Variety Girls

Christmas with the Variety Girls

TRACY BAINES

EBURY
PRESS

1

Ebury Press, an imprint of Ebury Publishing
20 Vauxhall Bridge Road
London SW1V 2SA

Penguin
Random House
UK

Ebury Press is part of the Penguin Random House group of companies whose addresses can be found at global.penguinrandomhouse.com

First published by Ebury Press in 2020

www.penguin.co.uk

A CIP catalogue record for this book is available from the British Library

ISBN 9781529103816

Typeset in 11.5/13.5 pt Times LT Std
by Integra Software Services Pvt. Ltd, Pondicherry

Printed and bound in Great Britain by Clays Ltd, Elcograf S.p.A.

Penguin Random House is committed to a sustainable future for our business, our readers and our planet. This book is made from Forest Stewardship Council® certified paper.

FSC
www.fsc.org
MIX
Paper from
responsible sources
FSC® C018179

To Ant, Nick & Nelly
for all the love and happiness you brought my way

And the little stars of the show:
Elsie, Huxley, Hadley and California

Chapter 1

Cleethorpes, Sunday 3 September 1939

Frances O'Leary lay on top of her bed in Barkhouse Lane, watching the shaft of light grow stronger through the gap in the blackout curtains. She'd left them like that when she'd arrived home from the theatre with Jessie in the early hours, choosing to let her eyes adjust to the darkness of the room – practising in case the eleven o'clock deadline brought a declaration of war. She hadn't bothered to undress, unable to sleep, and it had been a blessed relief when dawn broke.

As she lay there, the light became brighter, creating a path along the floor, picking out the colour of the small rug by her bed. She eased herself up onto her elbows and twisted, punching at the pillow behind her. There were noises in the alley; footsteps, a gate, someone calling out. It was all so normal. Was this the last day it would be? How safe would it be, here in Lincolnshire, for Imogen? Her mind was racing, so full of questions, but at least her darling child was away from the sea, from the docks that were sure to be a target. She forced herself to think of the good things, the things she had done well. The light was stronger now, slicing through the gloom just as her child had when the rest of her life was darkness. If there was to be war, none of them would be safe, would they? Not this time, for they would bomb them all, men, women and children.

On that thought she sat up sharply, snatching up the photograph on her bedside table, tracing her fingers over her child's sweet face. It had been taken on Imogen's third birthday earlier that year – a double celebration because Frances had secured a long contract at the Empire Theatre only days before. She had been thrilled to finally get work close to Patsy Dawkins and her family, who cared for Imogen when she had to tour. She couldn't drag a child around the country, a different place from week to week – and what's more, she wouldn't. It wasn't what she wanted for Imogen, no matter the cost – financial, and otherwise. The Empire had offered them stability after the last few years of struggle and she prayed that it would last a little while longer. She leant back against the pillows.

Why did they have to make the announcement on Sunday? It was the only day of the week she could spend with Imogen, play with her, bath her, tuck her up tightly in bed, kiss her goodnight. What would happen to them now? She shook herself, knowing this thinking wouldn't get her anywhere. She would get through this, just as she had overcome all the other obstacles in her life. 'For heaven's sake, Frances, pull yourself together,' she chided. 'Wait for the announcement and then go. You can still have precious time with her.'

She heard the back door open, voices down in the yard, and she opened her eyes again, swinging her legs over the bed, padding over to the window. She pushed back the heavy black curtains that now covered the bright yellow ones she'd hung when she'd taken lodgings here at the end of June. Geraldine, her landlady, was in the backyard, slicing beans from the stalk with her ivory-handled penknife, dropping them into a white enamel pan on the path. They would be the last, for the green tendrils weaving along the trellis on the dividing wall were almost bare.

As though sensing she was being watched, Geraldine turned, looked up at the window, saw Frances and smiled.

Frances put her hand up to the glass in greeting, watching as Geraldine replied to Grace, Jessie's mother, and then bustled back inside. How wonderful it would have been to have Imogen here, but she'd left it too late to say anything to Geraldine, waiting too long for the right time, the right words. She should have been braver – but what would Geraldine say about having an illegitimate child under her roof? Wasn't it enough that Frances was Irish, and a dancer in a variety show to boot? But then, so was Jessie, and this wasn't like other places she'd stayed. It had all seemed too perfect, and now she knew it was. If war came at eleven o'clock, everything would change. A wave of nausea washed over her and she pressed her hand to her stomach, breathing slow and steady until it passed.

Enough of that, she told herself and drew the curtains wide. She heard a quiet tapping on the door.

'Frances, can I come in?' Jessie peered around it. Her eyes were puffy and red, her face blotchy. 'I waited until I heard you walking about.'

'Of course you can.' She moved back to the window and Jessie joined her, the two of them looking out over the rooftops. 'I haven't slept anyway.'

'I don't think any of us have been to bed. Not properly. Mum and Geraldine have been in the sitting room since six.' Jessie sighed and Frances linked her arm through hers. She tried not to think of Imogen and her own worry, her fears, pushing them back into the darker recesses of her mind. It was the only way she knew how to keep up the pretence – pushing things into dark corners and keeping them there. She turned to her friend.

'I suppose Harry's gone?'

'Hours ago. He had to get back to his training camp for seven.' Her voice faltered and Frances squeezed her arm, pulling her closer. They would all have to be brave, if the news was bad … Harry had joined the RAF and Jessie, though proud, was afraid for him. Loving people was hard, letting them go more so. She found a smile for Jessie, wanting to disrupt her melancholy thoughts.

'At least he was there to hear you sing in front of Vernon LeRoy. Imagine, a grand impresario like him in Cleethorpes! Who would have thought it?'

Jessie nodded mutely and Frances pulled her closer still. It must have been as hard for Jessie to say goodbye to Harry as it had been for her to say the same to Imogen. And once, long ago, to Johnny … She stiffened, blocking out any thought of him. It was how she coped. Johnny Randolph, she told herself, was the one who had lost out in the end. Frances stared blankly through the window, trying to shut off the memory of Imogen's father, who she saw whenever she looked at their child – in her smile, her eyes. If she told her friends, would it help? Keeping secrets had brought misery; she had been trapped by them. But bitter experience had taught her it was better that way.

'I hate goodbyes,' Jessie said.

'We all do.' Jessie's words stopped Frances's train of thought and she was glad of it. 'But we need to keep chipper, don't we? You don't want Harry to be worrying about you. He needs to be concentrating when he's soaring about the skies.' She pulled her shoulders back. It always helped to stand tall. 'We need to look to the future,' she said firmly, smiling, hoping to encourage the younger girl.

'But what kind of future will it be, Frances? War or peace?'

'Peace,' Frances said, her voice soft. 'Let's hope it's peace.' It had to be, for the thought of the alternative was too chilling to contemplate. They leant into one another and watched the ginger tom from next door slink along the wall and drop into the yard. 'At least we're together – and eleven o'clock might come and go, and nothing will happen.' Frances made her voice brighter, like the light as the sun rose before them. 'It will have been a false alarm, and we'll put on our dancing shoes and smile, just like we always do.'

Jessie sighed so heavily that Frances turned and gripped her friend's shoulders, gave her a bit of a shake, hoping to dislodge the despair. 'He will be back before you know it, Jessie.' Jessie shrugged, despondent, and it irritated Frances. They had to be strong, for who knew what lay before them. Frances didn't have time for weakness. If she'd been weak she would have lost Imogen long ago and any thought of life without her darling child, no matter how difficult things had been, was intolerable. She changed tack. 'I didn't get much chance to talk to you much last night, there was so much going on and I am *desperate* to know how it went with Vernon LeRoy.'

Jessie smiled then, a proper smile that reached her eyes. 'Oh, Frances, always turning your face to the sun, looking for the good! What would I do without you?'

'You'd manage.' Frances grinned. She couldn't have Jessie losing her spark. It was what Frances loved about her. It would be what she would miss most if Vernon LeRoy whisked her away to fame and fortune. 'Come on, tell me what he said?'

'Mr LeRoy?' Jessie said. 'Oh, he was so enthusiastic about my performance, Frances. I couldn't believe that someone as famous as him would come to Cleethorpes. I was so excited, so nervous, I can't remember half of what he said. And Harry had just proposed, and—'

Frances moved her hand up and down.

'Slower, slower. Take a deep breath.' Jessie did as she was told and fiddled with the strap of her wristwatch.

'He was lovely, Frances. And Madeleine Moore, the star of the show, was so gracious, so ... ' She searched for the word. 'Kind. Oh, it seems such a small word for how generous she's been to me these past few weeks.'

'It might be a small word but without it where would we be? Look how kind the—' She stopped herself just in time, sensing this wasn't the right time to tell her of Imogen, of the Dawkins, even though she longed to, wanting to release the lie that stood between them. Their friendship was new and Jessie was naïve; she might think differently of her. Instead she said, 'How kind people have been.'

Jessie lifted her head, her chin jutting out. 'Oh, Frances, you're right. I'm so sorry, going on like an idiot. We'll perhaps have worse things to worry about soon. I'm being selfish.'

Frances shook her head. 'Don't take any notice of me, I'm just tired, and what I really want is to hear what Mr Big Shot LeRoy had to say to my friend Jessie. So, get on with it, for pity's sake.' They were both laughing now. Jessie clutched her hand. 'He said …' She paused, and when she spoke, her voice was light with happiness, 'He's going to make me a star, Frances. Me. Jessie Delaney from Lowestoft. He's producing a new show in the West End and he wants me in it.' Happy tears filled her eyes. 'Can you believe it?'

'I can. And you deserve it,' Frances said, hoping that it would be all Jessie dreamed of, that it wouldn't be the disappointment it had been to her. 'It's your big chance.'

Jessie squeezed Frances's hand more tightly. '*Our* big chance, Frances. If I go to London, then you must come too.' Her tone was more serious. 'I'll insist.' She grasped at Frances's arm, pulling her close as they turned back to the window. 'I want us to be together, Frances.' She paused. 'I've never had a friend before, not like you, one I can share all my happiness and my fears with. My secrets.'

Guilt pierced Frances. Secrets. Should she tell? Jessie's eyes were bright with expectation. No, not yet. This is her moment, she told herself, don't spoil it. She nudged Jessie's shoulder. 'Don't be daft. What about your mum? And your brother?'

Jessie rested her hand against the window frame, thoughtful. Her mother, Grace, had been so ill when Jessie brought her to stay at Barkhouse Lane, rescuing her from the neglect of Grace's sister-in-law, Iris, and nursing her back to health. Her brother, Eddie, had been set to inherit the family legal firm – not that he wanted to for he was mad about engines – but all the same, it was lost opportunities so Jessie had her own guilt to contend with and Frances didn't need to burden her with any more.

'Mum's still not well enough, though the fresh air here is doing her the world of good, and the medication, of course. And Eddie,' she smiled. 'Eddie is thriving too, isn't he?' Frances agreed and Jessie went on, 'Do you know, Frances, when I first brought them here, I thought I'd done the worst thing; that I'd been rash and made a mistake. But it was the best thing, wasn't it? It all turned out right in the end. Things do, don't they, if we have courage?'

If only courage was all it took. Frances looked at the younger girl, her freshness, her innocence. At eighteen, Jessie's age, she had been innocent too, and life full of expectation. Then it all changed. Not everyone was kind ... She looked out into the yard, the alley beyond, the back of the houses in the next row, a mirror image. All the curtains were open. Had anyone slept last night? Or had the whole world lain awake, waiting and hoping, as they had here? Praying for peace, almost certain those prayers had gone unanswered. And yet, sometimes it helped, gave comfort when there was none. She pictured Imogen, eyes closed, small hands pressed together, and a lump swelled in her throat. She turned away, reaching past Jessie for her wash-bag, which lay on the chair at the bottom of the bed. When she turned back, she made sure she was smiling. 'Let's go downstairs. I need to freshen up. We have no idea what the day will bring and I want my best face on to greet whatever comes.'

In the back sitting room Grace and Geraldine were sitting at the oak table, stripping and slicing runner beans. An old copy of the *Grimsby Telegraph* was spread over it, a growing pile of ends and strings in the middle, the sliced beans mounting in a metal sieve. They looked up as the girls came in.

'Morning,' Frances said, omitting the usual good, because how could today be good when such a dark cloud hovered over them all?

'Morning,' Grace replied, making short work of the last bean and deftly wrapping the paper around the scrapings. Geraldine got up and took it from her, along with the sieve, and Frances followed her into the kitchen.

'Let me get rid of these and we'll get on with breakfast. Same as we always do, eh?' Not waiting for a reply Geraldine put the sieve on the side and went out to the dustbin. Frances picked up the kettle and the gas popped as she placed it on the stove. The pans for lunch were on the side, the potatoes scraped, carrots chopped and now the beans would sit alongside them. Everything prepared in advance. It was the same every Sunday, she presumed, for she was always up and out, heading for Waltham and Imogen, no matter how late they got back from the theatre the night before. She should tell them. It would be easier, wouldn't it, if they knew? She waited for the water to boil for her wash. How could she start the conversation?

Through the door that led into the sitting room she watched Jessie rummaging along the dresser, pulling out scraps of paper and envelopes, scrabbling about for a pencil, then sitting down next to her mother. Grace was gazing into the middle distance, her thoughts elsewhere for a moment, and then she got to her feet and picked up a newspaper. She yawned, patting her hand to her mouth and Jessie shortly followed suit.

'No one got any sleep, then?' Frances called through, her voice cheery despite her churning stomach.

Grace shook her head. 'It seems not.' She glanced at the crossword. When she looked up again, she smiled. 'Perhaps it will be different tonight and we will sleep safely in our beds, after all.'

Frances leant against the door frame. 'At least we'll know one way or another what it's to be.' She felt the draught as Geraldine entered from outside. Frances moved to let her pass and said to Grace, 'It's the indecision that's wearying. Not knowing one way or another.'

'Rather the indecision than war, Frances.' Geraldine was brisk. She went back to her chair, looked out of the side window, banged on the glass and shouted, 'Shoo! Wretched cats. Doing their business. Shoo!' Only then did she sit down at the head of the table.

'Yes, of course.' A small voice was telling Frances to be brave, to have courage. 'It's just that I can't forget the children I saw on Friday, standing in little crocodiles, being led towards the station, evacuated to heaven knows where.' So many mothers would be feeling as she did every time she had to leave Imogen. She shuddered. 'I couldn't bear it.' The image had stayed with her. Mothers trying to be brave, children clutching teddies, labels tied to their coats. The innocence of them ... and no idea of where they were going. Or when they would be coming back.

'It's good that you don't have to, Frances. I wouldn't wish it on any mother,' Grace said quietly.

Frances folded her arms, tucking them away, searching for the strength that had threatened to escape her. But only for a moment. Imogen was safe with the Dawkins, that was what she must hang onto. There was a thump from up above, then she heard Eddie, Jessie's young brother, thunder down the stairs and into the hall. He burst into the room, briefly stilling the conversation. He was in his pyjamas, his wavy brown hair in disarray, and he yawned, rubbing his hand over his face and grinning, his teeth white against his tanned skin. Jessie looked up from the list she was scribbling on the back of an envelope. The girl was always writing lists.

'Ah, we were wrong,' Frances said as he pulled out a chair. 'At least one person in the house slept.' The tension in the room seemed to break as the boy settled himself at the table, his back to the kitchen door. The moment to speak of Imogen had slipped away from her. The kettle began to whistle, and she went back into the kitchen, poured hot water into the bowl, then ran some cold into it.

'Refill it, Frances. I'll make some tea,' Jessie shouted through. Frances did, then stripped to her slip and washed. Jessie came in and busied herself behind her. The smell of bacon filled the kitchen and the fat sizzled when Jessie cracked the eggs into the frying pan. Frances's stomach felt hollow, but she wasn't hungry. Were any of the others? Or was Jessie simply going through the motions?

When Frances was finished, she dressed, poured the water away and cleaned everything down. Jessie filled the teapot, Frances sliced the bread and took it into the room along with butter, plates and cutlery. The two of them went back for the bacon and eggs. Eddie reached across for a slice of bread and Grace slapped his hand.

'Wait.' Her tone was light but firm and Eddie sat back and did as he was told.

Geraldine started pouring the tea as the girls sat down, side by side, at the table. Frances tried not to look up at the clock over the mantelpiece but couldn't help herself. Half past eight. Surely, it must be later than that. Had it stopped? Grace gestured to Eddie that he was now allowed to help himself. The boy grinned and Grace smiled back at him as he took a slice and placed it on his plate. Frances watched Grace as she studied her son, the worry clear in her eyes. She caught Frances looking and they exchanged a smile. Grace would understand. Any mother would.

Jessie cut a slice of bread in half, scraped a little butter across it, lifted it, then put it down again. 'Surely Chamberlain will be able to resolve things peacefully? He said it was peace with honour not so long ago. Hitler *must* keep his word.'

'People say lots of things,' Geraldine said. 'It's what they do that counts.' Frances nodded her head. Johnny's words had been empty promises. If only she'd been so wise.

'And the Germans have already moved into Poland,' Eddie said, taking a tug at the crust then dipping it back into the yolk.

'But we have to hope for the best, don't we?' Jessie was almost pleading for the others to agree with her. Geraldine sliced through her bacon while Grace reached across for the salt and sprinkled it over her egg. Frances looked down at her plate. She should eat. She should tell them. She picked up her fork.

'We do, darling,' Grace said. 'And you have so much to look forward to. You're on your way, now. Before long you'll be down in London, your name in lights.'

'Not in a blackout it won't, Mum,' Eddie said. 'It won't be allowed.' Grace glowered at him and he shrugged. He reached for a cup and ladled in three spoonfuls of sugar. Grace raised an eyebrow. 'What?' He quickly stirred the tea, took a quick gulp. 'I'm caddying for Mr Archer; I need the energy. It's a long walk around that golf course.'

Grace replaced her cup on the saucer. 'Surely Mr Archer won't be on the golf course, today of all days.'

Eddie nodded, hurrying to finish another mouthful of food. 'He said he would. He told me that he wasn't going to spoil a good round of golf for something he couldn't influence.'

Frances watched the boy. What could any of them do? If it was war, everything would change, for every one of them. They would all have to carry on as best they could.

'I suppose we can't really argue with that.'

'I agree with you, Frances; Mr Archer is being very practical,' Geraldine said. 'But mark my words, it will affect us all. As it did the last time.'

Grace briefly closed her eyes. Was she remembering her husband, Davey, who had fought in the Great War? He had returned a broken man, as so many of them had. Frances tried a piece of bacon. It was salty and her mouth watered. Grace picked up her knife and fork. 'We will all have influence when we get called to action.'

'Well, anyway, I'm going, Mum,' Eddie said with his mouth full. 'And listening to the radio won't change things. I don't want to miss out on the half-crown he pays me. If he doesn't turn up, I'll come home. It's easier now I have my bike.' His words were almost lost in his chewing and he caught a crumb before it fell to the table.

'He's right, of course, Grace,' Geraldine said with authority. 'Life will have to go on, no matter what the outcome. We must all be thinking ahead, like this young man.' Frances saw him grow a little. He would be fifteen in a couple of weeks, still a boy but almost a man. Almost. If it was war and it went on and on, then Eddie would be called up. Frances shivered.

Grace said, brighter now, 'I hope he's right.' She leant forward and ruffled his hair, smiling at her boy. 'Better get yourself dressed. Unless you're thinking of going around the golf links in your pyjamas.' He grinned, pushing back the chair and getting to his feet. He took another swig of tea and rumbled up the stairs. Frances saw the fear return to Grace's eyes as soon as he was gone. They were all putting on a face, weren't they? She wasn't alone in that. It was a scrap of comfort and she snatched at it.

'Sounds like a herd of elephants,' Jessie said.

Frances finished her tea, replaced her cup carefully in the saucer as worry enveloped her again. The waiting was interminable, the tick of the clock suddenly ominous. She glanced at it, was cross with herself, looked away. 'Life will have to go on, won't it? For us all.'

Geraldine sipped her tea. 'Unless they close the theatres, of course.'

Frances twisted in her chair. 'They won't do that, surely?' They had to keep the theatres open. *Had to*.

Geraldine held her saucer mid-air, her little finger pointing upwards. 'They closed them in the last war. Didn't they, Grace?'

Jessie turned to her mother, her list forgotten. 'Did they, Mum?'

Grace sighed. 'They did. That's when your father signed up. He thought they would be closed for good. They weren't, of course. They opened again a few weeks later.' She paused; when she spoke, her voice was quieter. 'Who knows what will happen this time?'

The silence was broken only when Eddie trundled down the stairs and stuck his head around the door. He was wearing his smart trousers and shirt, his hair tidy, and he kissed his mother and looked around at them all, puzzled. 'What have I done?'

Grace took his hand, rubbed at his arm. 'Nothing, my love. Off you go. Best not to let Mr Archer down.'

He shook his head. 'Not a chance.' He slipped out of the back door, calling, 'See you later!' They heard the clatter as he took hold of his bike, the rattle of the gate as he left.

Frances pushed her cup and saucer away and glanced at the clock. Ten minutes to nine. Time was grinding away. She *must* speak of Imogen. She glanced at Geraldine, then at Grace. Grace knew the theatre and the theatre was as good a place to start as any. She clasped her hands in her lap, took a deep breath. 'Do you miss your dancing days, Grace?'

Grace sat back in her chair. 'Sometimes, but not often.'

'What did you do, Grace? You never said.' Geraldine was curious and Frances relaxed a little. There hadn't been time for them all to chat easily because Geraldine worked long hours at the dock offices in Grimsby and when she returned, the girls had already left for the theatre. Grace had only been at Barkhouse Lane for a few weeks and had been too ill for much conversation. It had been a slow recovery from walking pneumonia and it was still early days. No one had wanted to tire her more than necessary.

'I was a ballerina,' she said with pride, 'and Davey was a renowned violinist. This was all before the Great War, of course.' She paused, remembering. 'The life is different, the discipline different.'

'More respectable,' Jessie offered.

Grace frowned, her dismay showing on her face. 'Not at all. I'm not saying that what you girls do is not respectable.'

'But it isn't, Mum,' Jessie countered. 'If Aunt Iris knew I wanted to dance with the corps de ballet, she'd have treated me differently. You can't say she wouldn't.' Jessie folded her arms across her chest and Frances wondered how Grace would answer. Her sister-in-law was a condescending snob, sour and pretentious. Frances had met her only briefly but once was enough. Over the past few years she had realised there were many people like Iris. The problem was you never knew who they were until it was too late.

Grace was reluctant to answer. 'Possibly.'

Geraldine said, 'Well, you can't entirely blame your aunt, Jessie. Variety is the child of the Music Hall and so many of the big stars have succumbed to drink and depravity, squandering their fortunes. It hasn't earned a reputation for loose morals for nothing.'

Frances was shocked by Geraldine's remark. This wasn't going the way she had wanted, and she straightened herself, wanting to stay calm, but her response had unnerved her. 'That's a tad unfair, Geraldine. There are plenty of people who behave like that, it's not linked only to the theatre. Or movie stars, for that matter.'

The older woman was picking at crumbs on the table and placing them on her plate with a sprinkle of her fingers. 'I agree, it's merely an observation, not an opinion. But it seems more prevalent. The excess, the drama,' Geraldine countered. 'And young girls' heads are easily turned by the lure of the bright lights and the glamour. More so than boys. Why, only last week there was the story of that young woman from Louth, a girl who had everything. Beauty, a private education, a good home ... Off she went to London in search of stardom and ended up dying from some botched —' She broke off abruptly, then continued, 'Operation. Such a waste.'

'But that could happen to anyone, Geraldine.' Frances's voice was high and she could feel her neck and face reddening. 'She had dreams.' Dreams that had led to disappointment, as they had done for her. The memories flooded in thick and fast, the pain of them intense, and she couldn't bear it. Jessie turned and looked at her; Grace too. She was breathing too fast. She looked down and realised she was wringing her hands; she released them. It was all going wrong.

Geraldine remained calm. 'Her expectations weren't realistic, Frances. And you have to keep your wits about you. We've all heard stories like this. Charming young men who only have one thing on their minds.' She turned to Jessie, eyebrows raised.

'I won't end up like that,' Jessie snapped, affronted. 'Harry's not like that.'

How it irritated. Harry wasn't like that, but Jessie had almost lost him, hadn't she, flattered by the cocky comedian, Billy Lane, who had been second top of the bill during the summer season.

'You have no idea how you'll end up,' Frances said, sharply. The girl was naïve. Frances had had to steer her clear of danger on more than one occasion. She'd had a lucky escape; Frances hadn't been so fortunate. 'Look how easily you fell for Billy Lane's charms.'

'Frances!' Jessie was horrified, her mouth open, her hand to her chest, her face registering her disbelief.

Frances could have bitten off her tongue. Jessie hadn't deserved that; she wasn't that kind of girl – but then, neither was she. People would make up their own minds about her, whether she liked it or not. 'I'm sorry,' she said, gently. 'I shouldn't have said that. I'm truly sorry. You did nothing to lead Billy on. Billy is one of life's chancers.'

'My point exactly,' Geraldine said. Frances held her gaze, fighting to hide her disappointment, feeling the hollowness in her stomach grow. She wouldn't understand; life was too black and white for some people. And Geraldine was one of them.

Grace reached across and pressed at Frances's arm. 'It's all right, Frances. We're all feeling jumpy and out of sorts today.' She leant back in her chair again. 'None of us can know what lies ahead of us. Not now, not ever, really; we just have to make the best of it.'

Grace's words didn't help, didn't soothe; words were empty, they gave Frances nothing to hold on to. She clutched the side of her chair. It was if the whole world had tilted and she was sliding off the edge. 'Please forgive me, Jessie?'

Jessie shook her head, reaching out to take Frances's hand, offering a sympathetic smile. 'Nothing to forgive. Like Mum said, we're all feeling rotten.'

Frances relaxed, but only a little. She had been shocked by Geraldine's attitude and, even though she'd said it was merely an observation, Frances felt the imaginary metal armour she protected herself with clamp shut. She wouldn't speak of Imogen here, not ever. She pushed back her chair and stood up, picking up her cigarettes and matches from the dresser and forced herself to smile, pretending that it had all been forgotten but her heart was heavy. 'I'm going outside for a smoke. Leave the dishes. I'll come back in and clear up, then I'll give the kitchen a thorough clean.'

'Good idea,' Geraldine said, tapping the table with her palms. 'I was thinking these windows could do with a wash – although it will be difficult with the tape across them.'

'I'll give you a hand, Frances.' Jessie began stacking the plates. Grace got to her feet.

'In that case, I'll be at my sewing machine if anyone wants me.'

They were all trying to act as if her outburst had never happened, but it had, and it was awkward. Frances was glad to leave the room.

*

By eleven, Jessie and Frances had cleaned every nook and cranny in the kitchen and swept and dusted the sitting room. Tackling the task with more vigour than necessary had helped dilute her disappointment, if nothing else, but Geraldine's words dominated her thoughts. The girls had tried to sing as they worked but it had been half-hearted and they soon fell into a quiet rhythm as they scrubbed and mopped. As the clock chimed the hour, Geraldine removed her apron and hung it on the hook by the pantry door, patted her hair into place. The girls downed tools, washed and dried their hands. It was all so very ordinary. The same as it was every Sunday, she supposed, for she was always with Imogen then. She forced herself to picture her child playing in the garden, smiling. It helped her to keep her life in boxes. Separate, uncomplicated. Imogen was happy and that was all that mattered. She unfastened her apron and followed Jessie into the next room, where sunlight streamed through the window, catching the dust motes as they swirled and settled. The pair of them sat down and Frances was solemn as the two older women took their place at the table. One last glance at the clock. The Prime Minister was due to speak at a quarter past. *Peace, please, let it be peace*. Geraldine reached out and turned the dial on the wireless. Jessie was nibbling at her nails and Frances touched her shoulder. 'It might not happen this time.'

The small room became unbearably stuffy. Geraldine got up and pushed the sash as high as it would go. The breeze was slight but welcome, the sun bright as it moved higher into the bluest of skies. Geraldine had picked up her book, but not turned a page. Grace had gone back into her room and returned with her embroidery, the light catching the steel of the needle as it moved in and out of the cloth. Frances looked at the clock and, as the hands moved around to the quarter hour, the familiar voice of the BBC announcer broke the uneasy quiet.

'This is London.'

Geraldine marked her page, closed the book and placed it on the table. Grace lowered her sewing into her lap, Frances sat more upright in her chair. Jessie put down her pencil.

When Neville Chamberlain spoke, he sounded the old man he was, tired and weary. She knew it was bad news. They all did. And when he said that they were indeed at war, no one moved, no one spoke, but sat in the small silence as he continued to talk. War. It was war.

Frances glanced out of the window; the cat was stretched out on the wall, basking in the warmth. She saw the slight flicker of Geraldine's eye as she acknowledged it. Frances tried to concentrate, but her thoughts were starting to tumble in her head. Harry would have to fight. Would Eddie? She looked at Grace's face. It was rigid, as was Geraldine's.

'When I finish speaking,' Chamberlain continued, 'certain detailed announcements will be made on behalf of the government. Give these your close attention.'

Would they close the theatres as Geraldine had said? No, they mustn't. They had to keep them open. She had to provide for Imogen. She must listen.

'... it is of vital importance that you carry on with your jobs ...'

Yes, that was good. They must carry on. She caught snatches, but not all of it, her thoughts too busy.

The silence as the speech ended was followed by the peal of bells. Small tears glistened on Grace's cheeks and she reached in her sleeve for her handkerchief, rubbed briskly at her eyes and under her nose, returned the handkerchief.

'How very silly of me.' Jessie reached out, but Grace pulled herself upright. 'Don't fuss, Jessie. I'm perfectly all right.' Frances admired her inner steel. Grace might be weakened by ill health but she was a strong woman. Frances would be strong too.

Geraldine stilled her with a finger to her lips as the BBC announcer spoke again.

'This is London.'

Geraldine leant closer to the wireless.

'Closing of places of entertainment.' The announcer's voice was crisp and without emotion. Frances gasped, her hand to her throat; she turned to Jessie, who was staring at the wireless.

The announcer continued. 'All cinemas, theatres, and other places of entertainment are to be closed immediately, until further notice.'

Jessie sprang to her feet, but Frances tugged at her arm and pulled her down again.

'Ssh,' Geraldine hissed, but the words went over Frances's head and out through the window. What else was there to know, she had lost her job, Jessie too, and any hopes of being with her daughter gone with it.

Chapter 2

At the end of the notices there was another silence before they played the National Anthem and all four of them got to their feet for it. Geraldine appeared taller than she'd ever been, her shoulders back, her head erect. Jessie knew that she'd lost her brother and her fiancé in the Great War; their pictures held pride of place in her room, forever young, captured in sepia, framed by silver. So many women had been left to fend for themselves after the conflict and now it would happen again. She said a silent prayer, that Harry would be safe, that they all would, for he would have to fight now, like so many others who had already answered the call. The thought made her shudder. Her mother was glassy-eyed, and to Jessie, suddenly small and frail, and a shiver of fear shot through her. She was still recovering and not yet returned to her old self; would this set her back again? And what of Eddie? Would she be left with photographs, like Geraldine?

When the anthem ended, they sat back down, somewhat revived because of the music, the call for king and country. Geraldine lowered the volume on the wireless. Jessie sighed heavily and turned to Frances. 'That's both of us out of work. I'll not hear from Mr LeRoy now.'

Geraldine shook her head, tutting loudly. 'There will be worse things to worry about, young Jessie.'

Jessie's cheeks burned. 'I know, Geraldine. I'm doing my best to be practical, not at all like me, I know. But I'm thinking of our immediate problem – and that will be paying the rent.' She turned again to Frances, who had remained motionless throughout the broadcast. Her face was pale; it made her dark eyes darker still. There had been something different about her this morning and she hadn't been able to work out what it was. Was it because of Vernon LeRoy? Was she jealous? No, it wasn't her way, not Frances. She was usually so encouraging. And her earlier outburst, about Billy – it was so odd, and she'd been so quiet afterwards. 'We need to go to the theatre, don't you think, Frances? Find out what's going to happen.' They couldn't just sit here. She had to do something to distract herself from the fear that had settled in the pit of her stomach.

'Nothing will happen, Jessie,' Frances stared at the wireless and when she spoke her voice was measured, flat. 'The theatres are closed.'

'Yes, but not the churches,' Jessie huffed. 'How ridiculous is that?'

Geraldine shook her head. 'People need their faith, Jessie,' she said, firmly. 'We all need to believe in something – especially when we face so much uncertainty.' Irritated, Jessie got up, stood behind her chair then pushed it under the table. Still Frances did not move and it unnerved her.

'So, we can get killed praying, but not enjoying ourselves. Is that because it's sinful? How old-fashioned!'

Geraldine was sharp. 'Did you not listen, Jessie?'

Jessie scowled. 'Of course I listened.' Did Geraldine think she was entirely stupid? 'The theatres are closed, no large gatherings in case we're bombed.'

Geraldine stood up and looked out of the window, rapped again on the glass. 'Blast that cat!' She turned back to Jessie. 'And?'

What was the matter with the woman? What did she mean? 'To take our gas masks with us everywhere,' Jessie offered. It was like being back at school. Harry was at school; training, learning to fly. He would have to learn faster, to keep safe. She mustn't give in to fear. Her head felt as if it would explode.

A slight smile played on Geraldine's lips. '*Until further notice*. That's different to forever, Jessie. He also said that they would open again in some areas. Possible. And probable, wouldn't you say, Grace?'

Grace gave her a weak smile. 'Without a doubt.' So, there was already hope then. Jessie was quiet. 'Remember what your father used to say, Jessie. Music gives people comfort.' Grace glanced across at Geraldine, who had sat down again. 'Not only that, it inspires. Look how the National Anthem made us feel. How everything changed when we heard it. They won't be closed for long – have faith, girls.'

Frances cleared her throat but didn't speak. Geraldine pressed her hands on the table in front of her, looked directly at Jessie.

'Now, more than ever, you need to listen, Jessie, so that you don't go off half-cocked and get yourself in a mess. No doubt those instructions will appear in the newspapers tomorrow and you can read them for yourself. But you must stop and listen. It's crucial.'

Jessie felt her shoulders soften: Geraldine was right, she so often was. She held onto the back of the chair. 'I'm going to the theatre.' Frances seemed lost in her thoughts and Jessie touched her shoulder to elicit a response. Frances moved, looked at her, but almost through her. 'I'm going to the Empire. Coming?'

Frances shook herself a little and got to her feet. 'Of course. We need to find out what's going on.' Her voice was weak. Was she thinking of her family back home? Would she go back to Ireland? That must be it. Of course, she would be worried about them, so far away.

'Are you all right, Frances?' Grace was concerned.

'Yes, I'm fine.' She pushed back her chair, smiled at them all. 'Let me do my hair and get some lipstick on first. Can't go out without my best face on, can I now?' She squeezed Jessie's shoulder. 'Give me a minute.'

'That's the spirit,' Geraldine urged. 'Business as usual.'

Jessie felt cheered. That was the Frances she knew so well. She was shocked, they all were, but they had to carry on, didn't they? She mustn't lose sight of her goals, not for war, not for anything. She was going to buy Grace her own home. To do anything else would be to admit defeat – and she was never going back to live with Aunt Iris, she'd rather die.

Geraldine smiled at her. 'All is not lost, Jessie, unless you believe it so. The show must go on, must it not?'

'Absolutely,' Jessie said, her spirits already revived.

When they were ready, they picked up their cardigans and bags and Frances hung back while Jessie kissed her mother goodbye. 'We won't be long, Mum. I'm sure Jack Holland will be at the theatre and we can find out where we stand.'

'And say goodbye,' Frances added. Jessie twisted, why was Frances being so miserable? They had to be hopeful, as Geraldine had said. Frances explained. 'A lot of the cast will head for home. There was only three weeks left of the show, so no point them hanging around now.' She walked over to the door. 'It might take a lot longer than that for the theatres to reopen. And we might not be in the right area when they do.' Jessie pushed her lip forward and Frances grinned at her. 'Well, I'm not going anywhere, Jessie, but the others might.'

That was what she'd wanted to hear from her friend. Frances had taken care of her all summer, given her courage when she had none of her own. Jessie went to stand beside her, linked her arm through hers. 'That's the best news I've heard all day.'

Geraldine came through from the kitchen. 'Don't be too long, girls. I'll delay dinner as long as I can. In the circumstances. Otherwise, I'll put yours on a low heat in the oven.' She paused. 'And girls ...' Jessie tilted her head to one side. 'Gas masks.'

Jessie squirmed and Frances laughed, pressing Jessie's arm. 'I'll get yours.' She dashed upstairs and quickly returned, handing Jessie the small brown box and putting her own over her shoulder.

'Listen, as well as do.' Geraldine said.

'We will,' they called as they stepped out into the street.

They walked up the small incline to the top of Barkhouse Lane, where a gaggle of boys were fiddling with the wheel of a battered cart they had cobbled together and further down, a bunch of girls were skipping. They rounded the corner onto Humber Street, which opened out, giving them a glimpse of the sea. The sun glistened on the water and boats moved along the horizon, just as they always did. Seagulls screamed overhead, swooping, diving. Was Imogen frightened? No, of course she wasn't; she wouldn't understand, and Frances thanked heaven for it. She lifted her head; she mustn't weaken. She had to be strong. She led the way across the road so that they could look down onto the promenade where life continued as normal, because, despite the news, people were out enjoying themselves. Cars trundled past as they headed down the hill, towards the Empire.

Jessie sighed. 'It's hard to imagine that all this will end.'

'But it will,' Frances said. 'Things will change and we need to change with them.' Already, shopkeepers were putting boards over their windows, paper signs declaring it would be Business as Usual fixed on the wooden planks. Their doors remained open and people drifted in and out as they walked along. She needed to get another job as soon as she could. Imogen's keep had to be found, and her own. And how many others would be out looking for work? There would be no more holidays, no more summer seasons by the seaside and her savings were not what she had hoped. She inhaled the sea air. *Lord, let Grace be right, let the theatres reopen soon.* She ran her fingers through her hair; too much thinking was no help at all. Her stomach was churning and she wanted it to stop. Wanted the world to stop.

'Who will want to send postcards now?' Jessie said, wistfully and Frances tensed. If only postcards were all she had to think about.

'People will still write to each other; they'll want to cheer each other up.' Her voice came out sharper than intended and Jessie looked hurt. She softened her tone, smiled to encourage her. 'You'll want Harry to know you're thinking of him. There's not always time for letters.' Who knew what time there would be for any of them? Jessie nodded dumbly and they were quiet as they walked the rest of the way, drinking in the last images of life as they knew it.

When they reached the theatre, they saw that posters had been pasted on each of the glass entrance doors, stating that the Empire would be closed until further notice. She pulled on the brass handle, waited for Jessie to go first, then followed. The door to the box office opened and their friend, Dolly, the usherette, came dashing out to greet them, her blonde hair a halo.

'I'm so glad to see you both. Isn't it just the worst news? I thought them in London with all their big brains would sort it out, didn't you?'

Jessie agreed. 'I've had my head in the clouds this last week. I didn't notice how close we were to war.' Frances briefly closed her eyes, wanting to shut out the words as the girls prattled on about things they couldn't control. Empty words. She was sick of them. She felt sweat prickle at her temples.

'What did it matter what we thought, Jessie?' Frances snapped. 'It wouldn't have changed anything. *We* can't change anything.' The two girls stared at her. She was only five years older than them, but twenty-three felt a lifetime away from eighteen. She tried to remember what it had been like to be so unaware of the harsh realities of life, a life without Imogen. Every minute now was taken up with how she could keep her child safe, away from people whose words cut like knives, whose looks made you shrink into the shadows. War would complicate everything. They were still staring at her. She must get a grip.

'I'm sorry, girls. I don't know what's the matter with me. It's just that, well, if we go over and over things it will drag us down. And we need to keep ourselves looking up.' Dolly and Jessie were quiet, and she took a deep breath, hoping to calm herself. 'Isn't that what the theatre is all about?' The girls nodded but didn't answer. She couldn't blame them; she was as confused by her outbursts as they were. It was awkward until Jessie spoke.

'How long have you been here, Dolly?'

'Since ten. Mr Holland asked Dad to open up and bring the wireless down from his office and put it in the bar in case anyone came. A lot of the acts have already come and gone.' The doors to the stalls had been weighted open and voices drifted into the cool of the foyer. 'I'm manning the box office in case people want their money back. Such a shame when it was all going so well.'

Jessie grasped Dolly's hand. 'But it's only temporary, Dolly. Remember that.' Frances smiled to herself. Geraldine's words were already having their desired effect.

She must remember that too. Temporary. There was a clatter of metal from inside the auditorium.

'We need to find out what's going on in there.' Frances tipped her head towards the inner doors. 'Catch up with you later, Dolly.'

'You're not leaving, then?' The girl's face brightened.

'Not for the time being,' Frances said, for where would she go?

Jessie shook her head. 'Cleethorpes is home to us all now.'

The house lights were on in the auditorium and members of the cast and staff were trudging up and down the steps at the front of the stage with boxes and bags, packing away props and instruments until such time they could be used again. And who knew when that would be? The atmosphere was flat and a palpable sadness punctured the air. Even the grand, deep red and gold boxes either side of the stage looked like open mouths, as if they, too, were taking in the shock of it all.

A cluster of cases straggled the aisles and on stage, props and equipment that belonged to the variety artistes were being dismantled, ready for them to be put onto a train along with their owners. Mike, the stage manager, was holding a timetable in his hand and talking to Arthur Trott, the old-timer who played the musical saw and could get a rousing tune from a kettle and a pair of spoons. The old man was scratching his head and, as she walked nearer, she heard Mike advise him that the best thing he could do was to go to the station and wait.

The scenery and props had already been taken down and stood ready to be returned to the hire company. Mary, the wardrobe mistress, small and round with tight grey curls, was standing beside two sturdy metal clothes rails. Sally,

Kay and Rita, three of the dancers who comprised half of the Variety Girls, were handing over their costumes and Mary was checking them off a list that she held, pushing her glasses up the bridge of her nose and frowning. Frances and Jessie walked down the aisle and Mary smiled as they made their way up onto the stage.

'Hello, ducks. When you've a minute can you bring me your bits up?' She sighed. 'Who'd have thought it, eh? I prayed me ruddy socks off, I did. Hoping for better than this. But there you go. At least we know what's what, don't we? Instead of all this buggering around.' Mary tried to sound cheerful, but her voice was edged with sadness and Frances clasped her shoulder, gave it a gentle squeeze. She'd thought the same herself. There was strength in knowing where you stood. Even if it was alone.

'Yes, all this buggering around has done for us all, Mary. But they've picked on the wrong ones this time, eh?'

The woman laughed. 'Too right, lovey.' Jessie had gone on ahead and Frances watched her disappear into the wings as Mary continued with her inventory. The ending of a good run was always tinged with sadness, but she'd never felt as she did today. She hurried down the stairs, eager to help Mary finish her task, and found Jessie and Ginny in the dressing room, whispering, their heads together. They stopped when Frances came in and looked awkward.

'Hiya, Frances.' Ginny was wary, subdued. She adjusted the costumes that were draped over her arm, took down the last one and placed it on top, grabbing the hangers. Her glorious red hair was pulled back into a bun at the back of her head and it made her look harsher than usual. The other girls had already packed away their make-up, which normally cluttered the long table that ran the length of the room. The bulbs around the mirror were lit, but the many photos, greetings cards and notes had been taken down, small patches of tape and pin holes left as reminders. Only Frances's mirror remained decorated with words from well-wishers. Jessie stepped back to let Ginny escape. They heard her tread heavily on the stairs. Yesterday they had all been light on their feet, rushing up and down the corridor, ready for costume changes, the excitement of a full house, the presence of a grand impresario, the nervousness and uncertainty of the audience, waiting for news of war. Well, it had come, and they had to get on with it. Frances put her bag down on the dressing table, peeled off her cardigan and laid it over the back of her chair.

'What's the matter with Ginny?'

Jessie shrugged. 'Upset. We all are.' She quickly turned her back and began removing her own costumes from the rail. 'I'll take yours, Frances.'

Frances looked at her through the mirror. Why was Jessie acting so strange all of a sudden? She began to peel away her cards from the mirror, taking time to read each one as she did so. They brought bittersweet memories, each one precious. Cards from her brothers, the words sparse; others from her two sisters, full of news and love. *Love.* She chewed at her lip. How she missed them! She held the one from her parents, read her mother's words, her precise hand so familiar. Dear Mammy and Daddy ... She closed her eyes, the thoughts painful. She'd been sixteen when they'd waved her off at the station, the day as clear to her as if it had happened yesterday. Her mother's tears, her father's fears for her; their pride. She wanted to weep for the girl she once was ...

Jessie returned with her vanity case in one hand, clutching her own treasured photographs and cards to her chest with the other. Last night she'd had a dressing room of her own, to celebrate the fact that she had her own solo spot in front of Vernon LeRoy. The girls had tried to make the moment special for her, but the celebrations had been brief – as was their happiness.

Frances took down the photo of Imogen with a heaviness in her heart, knowing that there wouldn't be time to be with her today. Jessie put her cards down on the dressing table.

'Pretty girl, your niece. Imogen, isn't it?'

'Imogen. Yes. Yes, it is,' Frances said, her voice softening at the mention of her daughter's name. The weight of her lies was unbearable. Jessie trusted her, looked up to her. She caught the girl's reflection in the mirror. Would she understand? Jessie leant over her shoulder.

'Gosh, doesn't she look like you! Is it your sister's child? Or one of your brothers?'

Frances swallowed. 'Jessie, she's—' She stopped as the rest of the girls trudged into the room.

'Jack's going to be ages, apparently. Still on the phone. We might as well wait in here.' Rita settled herself in the armchair and Kay and Sally rummaged around the room, picking up the last remaining hairgrips and rubber bands, putting them in a pile on the dressing table.

'Sorry, Frances, what were you saying?'

Frances shrugged. The interruption had unsettled her. 'I can't remember. It can't have been important.'

Rita took out her cigarettes. 'Gasping for a fag.' She held out a packet of Woodbines. 'Want one?' Frances declined and Rita adjusted herself in the chair, crossing her long legs and fiddling with her matchbox.

'Are you going to hang around?' Frances asked, not that she was bothered. Rita had been a good head girl, disciplined and fair but not the sort of woman you'd want as a friend. She'd probably bump into her again, sooner or later, so it was best to keep on the right side of her; she would need work and the more people you knew in this business the better. Rita shook her head and her blonde ponytail swung from side to side.

'Nope. Already packed most of the stuff at the flat. Going to get the first train back to Manchester in the morning. Pointless hanging about here. If I can't get work, I'll sign up.' She put her cigarette to her lips, lit up, tossed the spent match into a tin ashtray. 'What about you?'

Frances leant against the dressing table and watched Ginny take down a photo of Rita Hayworth that she'd torn from a magazine, screw it up and toss it in the waste bin. 'Not sure. Stay here. Find work.' The thought depressed her. It would mean being apart from Imogen again. 'Any work will do for the time being.'

'Well, we can't sit about waiting, Frances. We've got to get out there first, before anyone else. You know what it's like.' She puffed out a long plume of smoke. Frances watched it drift upwards. 'I'm not going to be back of the queue, are you?'

'Not if I can help it.' She couldn't afford to dither about. The rest of the girls were young, they would perhaps go home until things changed but she didn't have that luxury.

Kay picked up an old copy of *The Stage* and was about to drop it into the waste basket.

Frances stopped her. 'Mind if I have a look?'

'There's nothing in it,' Kay said, handing it over. 'Nothing that matters now, anyway. It'll all be cancelled.' Frances wasn't bothered; there would be news of where other friends had been working, what theatres were open and hadn't been converted to cinemas. It was temporary, she told herself, just like when the film jammed at the flicks and the audience moaned. The second reel would kick in and they'd be back in business. She needed to be ready when it did.

She turned the pages, not really taking anything in until she read a short paragraph in the Variety Gossip column. 'Oh!' she gasped, putting her hand to her neck. The girls stopped what they were doing and when she looked up, they were staring at her. She flushed, embarrassed, but her heart was thumping wildly as she tried to compose herself. Her throat was tight, her voice croaky when she spoke and she coughed to clear it. 'The Randolphs are back.'

'Johnny and Ruby?' Rita asked.

'I saw that.' Kay twisted towards Rita. 'Do you know them?'

Rita shook her head. 'I thought they were making it big in the States. Wonder what they've come back for? Surely not because of the war.' She drew on her cigarette. 'If it is, their timing's off.'

'That'll be the first time ever,' Kay gushed. 'Those two are amazing! Have you seen them dance? Sublime. Must be the bond between brother and sister that does it. They probably know what each other's thinking all the time.'

'It makes a difference.' Rita leant on her elbow and looked across to the rest of the girls. 'They must have been over there, what? Three, four years? More.'

'Four years.' Frances said. 'It's four.' Four years this month, the fifteenth. She'd never forget.

'I'm sure it's longer than that.'

Kay was staring at her and she felt pressured to say more. 'I was on the same bill. They toured, then the show went to London. That's when their agent came with an offer. They were thrilled.' She forced herself to sound as if it had been the most exciting thing in the world. At the time, it had. How soon it had all gone wrong.

'Lucky blighters,' Rita said. 'I'd love to go to America.'

'Wouldn't we all?' Sally said, dreamily.

Rita stubbed out her cigarette, and got to her feet, sweeping her hands over her skirt to smooth the creases. She leant forward towards the mirror, ran her tongue over her teeth, then her lips, touched her hair. Satisfied, she picked up her bag and slipped it over her arm. 'I'm off back to the digs.'

'Aren't you going to stop and find out what Jack has to say?' Frances asked, relieved that the conversation had been brought to an end. She put the paper to one side. It was bad enough that war had been declared, but to know that Johnny was back? She needed to focus on something else, something other than him.

'Write it down on the back of a fag packet and tell me later. He can't do anything and I'm not hanging around on a promise. Not my style.' Jessie dipped her head, biting her lip, and Frances had to look away in case the pair of them laughed. Rita had been through the band like a dose of salts. Ginny coughed.

Frances called over her shoulder, 'Got a pencil, Ginny?' The girl rummaged about in her bag and held it up.

Frances looked at Rita, her face deadpan. 'Right, all we need is a fag packet.'

Rita laughed then, and they all joined in, united one last time. Partings were difficult, more so in the circumstances they now found themselves in and it was best to part as friends.

Kay and Sally decided to leave with Rita. Hardly surprising since they had followed her about all summer like little ducklings. The remaining three girls finished clearing the dressing room and when they were done, took their bags upstairs, leaving them in the small office at the stage door.

Back in the auditorium they found the owner and manager, Jack Holland, on stage. He'd been a familiar sight throughout the production, totally hands-on and well liked by his staff on both sides of the curtain. What remained of the cast and crew were scattered about the stalls, waiting for him to speak. The girls skipped down the steps at the prompt side of the stage and he waited while they settled themselves before speaking. He had removed his jacket and stood in his shirtsleeves, the cuffs turned back; even from a distance they could see how tired he was.

'He must be devastated,' Jessie said, pushing down her seat next to Frances. 'I know it's difficult for all of us, but he's put all his money into this place. And everything was going so well until today.'

Frances wriggled, making herself comfortable. 'I suppose he'll lose his shirt if the theatres don't reopen sharpish.' It was a sobering thought, but one that many theatre owners would be facing. The Empire had been closed for months, the previous owners running out of money, unable to keep the doors open. The same had been happening elsewhere and so many of the grand old theatres had been given over to cinemas. Jack hadn't settled for the easy or, it had to be said, more profitable option, but had risked his arm on a variety show. It had been his baby and he'd wanted to see it grow. Frances pushed her legs out in front of her and conversations stilled as Jack cleared his throat and began to speak.

'I've already said goodbye to a few of the cast and crew.' He paused and Frances looked about the rows to see who had stayed. Not many. Mike, the stage manager, was sitting on a wicker hamper at the side of the stage, his arms folded across his wide chest. A couple of the cleaners had seated themselves in the back row, along with Dolly and her dad, George, who was the stage doorman. Dolly wiggled her fingers in a wave. Frances turned back to hear what Jack had to say.

'Thank you to those who have remained.' He was sombre as he looked out into the auditorium, the flat of his hand above his eyes, to see who was at the back. He brought it down again, slid it into his trouser pocket and paced to the right, stared down at the stage thoughtfully, then up again. 'Many of you will be eager to get home, back to your families, so I'll keep it brief.' He paused again. 'War has brought our happy show to a rather abrupt end, but it was good while it lasted, wasn't it? You did me and this town proud.' People shuffled in their seats, lifting themselves a little higher. It was bittersweet, to leave in the middle of success, but what was the end of a show compared to what everyone faced once they walked out of the theatre? Frances thought of Johnny. He and Ruby should have been opening at the Coliseum in November. How would she find him now … if she wanted to? She wasn't sure she did. She closed her eyes, listening as Jack went on.

'I can't ask you all to wait and see what happens, because I can't afford to pay you a retainer, no matter how small.' Frances opened her eyes. It was hardly Jack's fault. It was no one's fault, was it? People had done what they could, but a line had to be drawn and they had to make the best of it.

'I will, however, pay the wages you were due this week. I feel it's the very least I can do.'

'That's kind of him,' Jessie said. 'He didn't have to do anything, really. He's probably worse off than any of us. A building like this doesn't come cheap.' Frances shushed her, directing Jessie's attention back to the stage.

'The theatres *will* open again; I have no doubt of that,' he continued. 'And we need to pull together if we are to get through.' He took a deep breath. 'And win this ruddy war.'

He was quiet for a time and people became uneasy. He looked up again, smiling. 'What I want to say is: keep steadfast.' He clasped his hands together and shook them fiercely. 'This world will be a sadder place without song and laughter.' His voice wavered and he paused, composed himself before he spoke again. When he did, his voice was strong. 'We'll be leading the charge, my friends, because I'm going to make sure that the Empire is entertaining the crowds again. Twice-nightly.' There was a ripple of applause from around the theatre and Frances joined in. His words had given them hope – and things being as they were, hope was needed as never before.

Chapter 3

The following day Frances left the house early and caught the bus to Waltham. Monday was washday in the Dawkins' household and she knew Patsy would appreciate the help. Finding work was a priority but she told herself that one day wouldn't make much difference if it meant she could be with Imogen.

Frances watched the children through the kitchen window. Imogen's skipping rope was around Colly's waist and he was holding onto it, pretending to be a horse, galloping around the lawn, Imogen jiggling the reins. The pair of them were racing around in the dappled sunlight that filtered through the fruit trees towards the bottom of the garden. The neat white bungalow in Waltham was heaven, Patsy and Colin Dawkins her angels. She would never let her thoughts linger on what life would be like for herself and Imogen without them, for they were far too dark. Patsy came and stood beside her.

'And the world keeps turning.' She put her hand to Frances's shoulder. 'What they don't know can't hurt them, thank the Lord.'

It didn't comfort her. 'If only that were true.'

Patsy ran the tap and washed her hands, flicking off the excess water before drying them on the towel that hung over the range. 'Don't worry yourself needlessly, Franny. I know they'll use the airfield, but I reckon we'll be safe enough out here.'

'I wasn't thinking of the war, Patsy, I was thinking of the future, Imogen's future.' Frances turned away from the window, leant with her back against the sink so that she could see her friend's face and gauge her reaction. 'Johnny's in England. It was in *The Stage*. The pair of them are back.'

Patsy hung the towel over the rail, her back to Frances. 'Ah, so that's why you came in looking like you were ready to take on Hitler single-handed. I knew something had upset you. I thought it was Chamberlain.'

Frances folded her arms. 'Was it that obvious?'

Patsy turned. 'Well, they were bound to come home eventually.' She pursed her lips. 'So... What are you going to do?'

Frances shrugged. Talking about Johnny made her anxious and she hated it. 'Nothing. I didn't sleep a wink again last night, thinking about it.' She gave her a wry smile. 'It caught me off guard.' It had reignited the anger, a strong flame which she had previously let die, not giving it air so that it had almost been extinguished. Angry with him, at her herself. Had she really been so stupid? But after the anger had come curiosity. Had their love been a lie?

'You must want to do something,' Patsy said, choosing her words carefully, 'or you wouldn't have said anything.'

'I need to talk about it – and I can't talk about it with anyone but you.' For that she had no one else to blame. If only she'd spoken to Geraldine when she first moved in it could all have been so different. 'I was so ruddy angry, all the old feelings coming back of ...' She shook her head. 'How could he turn his back on me? After promising so much?'

Patsy came and stood beside her. 'I don't know, my love, I never did.' Patsy leant across the windowsill and pulled the dead leaves from the begonia that was doing its best to keep blooming. She tossed the dry leaves into the bin, brushed her hands together, pressed Frances's arm, held her gaze. Frances chewed at her lip. She was desperate to undo the knots in her brain. 'You have to write to him,' Patsy said. 'Let him know where you are.'

Frances looked down at her feet. The toes of her shoes were almost worn through, they wouldn't last much longer. 'Why?' she asked, looking back up at her friend. 'What makes you think he'd reply this time?'

'I don't, but you have to try. Imogen is his child. She's his responsibility as much as she is yours. He should support you. *Both* of you.'

'I am not going to use Imogen like that. Never!' She was surprised by the venom in her voice as well as her heart and she stopped, not wanting the poison inside her to take hold again. 'I'm sorry, Patsy. I don't want to argue with you but I'm so damn tired – and knowing he's back, well, it's brought everything up to the surface again. All of it. The good and the bad.'

'It will. It's bound to.' Patsy picked up her wicker washing basket and settled it on her hip. 'It's been tough and it's going to get a whole lot tougher.' She held onto the back door and looked out into the garden, speaking over her shoulder to Frances. 'Anyway, he should be made to pay something.'

Frances stood away from the sink and walked towards Patsy. 'It's only ever the women who pay. And the children. Imogen will be paying the price for the rest of her life.' She could hear her daughter's giggles and craned her neck to see over Patsy's shoulder. It was Imogen's turn to be the horse and she was pounding her foot to the ground, neighing and tossing her head, her dark curls moving about her sweet face. Frances's heart pinched. Imogen didn't deserve the shame that would follow her around. It was her mother's mistake, but she would be the one who suffered most.

Frances followed Patsy outside into the garden. The sun was high, the breeze warm and the washing they'd done earlier had dried in no time at all. Patsy removed the prop so that the line was easier to reach and the pair of them started pulling at the pegs, folding the clothes and dropping them into the basket at their feet. They slipped into an easy routine and Frances wondered if that was where the comfort was, in routine. Patsy had been her one constant, her rock. Her generosity – and Colin's – had allowed Frances to keep her child and she would never be able to repay their kindness. She looked away, blinking back tears. Over by the vegetable patch Bobby was on his knees, lifting leaves, searching for caterpillars and grubs. He called out and the skipping rope was abandoned as Imogen and Colly ran over to help.

'Have you been mulling that over all morning?' Patsy asked. 'Why didn't you say something sooner?'

Frances tipped her head back. 'I don't know. I don't understand myself. I can't bear it. If it wasn't for Imogen, I could forget him.'

'Ha.' Patsy raised her eyebrows. 'Could you? Really?' She rested her hands on the line and looked at Frances, who was facing her, the pair of them moving along seamlessly as they had done on stage so many years ago. Patsy had been the head dancer, keeping a chorus of twelve girls in line: a big sister, a teacher, but most of all, a friend. Frances had been fresh off the boat from Ireland and had arrived in Blackpool with her head full of dreams, wanting to make her Mammy and Daddy proud, their sacrifices worthwhile. It was Patsy she'd turned to when she fell in love with Johnny, Patsy who'd held her close when he abandoned her, Patsy who put a roof over her head when she was pregnant.

And after. 'What about Imogen? One day she's going to want to know who her father is,' Patsy said, her voice low. 'She might go searching.'

Frances looked to her child. Imogen was crouched with her hand outstretched and Colly was gently placing an earwig on her flattened palm. She didn't want to think that far into the future. It was how she coped, not thinking. She looked back at Patsy, whose green eyes showed her concern. 'That's not going to happen for a long time, Patsy. Perhaps never. I might be enough.'

'It's not about being enough, Frances.' Patsy rubbed at her friend's shoulder. 'She'll be curious. Kids are.'

Her heart felt leaden. Patsy gave her a gentle smile. 'He would fall in love with her the moment he saw her. Who wouldn't? She's such a darling. And so like him.'

'Don't,' Frances begged. She bent down and picked up the basket that was piled high with the children's clothes and the two of them went back into the house. Frances pulled out a chair, put the basket on it and began sorting the clothes into piles on the table while Patsy busied herself making drinks for the children. Dandelion and burdock fizzed into three small beakers and Patsy pushed the cork back in the bottle with the flat of her hand.

'You can't walk away from it forever, Franny. Or turn your back.' Frances pulled a face but Patsy ignored her. 'You'll have to confront it one day, whether you like it or not.'

Frances tried to block out the words. Why did life have to be so complicated? Patsy pushed the three mugs into a triangle. 'You need to write to him. Again. And if that doesn't work, find him. Confront him.'

'I don't know if I can. If I'm brave enough.'

Patsy frowned. 'Oh, darling! I don't know anyone braver. Keeping Imogen was the bravest thing you've ever done.'

'I couldn't have done it without your help.'

Patsy was quick to disagree. 'Yes, you could. You'd have found a way. It's who you are.'

She didn't argue. Patsy was right: she would have kept Imogen, no matter what it cost. 'Well, that's beside the point. I'm never going to set Imogen up to be rejected. Never!'

'But she's the image of him. A fool could see it.'

Frances clasped Imogen's small blue cardigan to her chest. Each thought of Johnny disturbed her. She put the cardigan on top of Imogen's little pile of clothes. 'He would deny it. He wouldn't want anything to damage the Randolph name. His mother would turn in her grave. I don't want to be his dirty little secret and I certainly don't want to be beholden to anyone. Least of all *him*!'

'It's not about being beholden, it's what's right. And his mother is gone now.'

'Ruby hasn't.'

Patsy shrugged, she wasn't going to let Frances wriggle out of the conversation. 'He's a grown man, Franny. Life's knocks will have changed him, as it has changed you.'

Frances didn't comment. She knew she had lost her softness, saving it only for Imogen. Everyone else she kept at a distance. It was safer that way.

Patsy shook her head. 'Good God, you're so damned stubborn, O'Leary! It was always hell trying to keep you in line and you haven't changed at all.' She took hold of Frances's hands. 'You have to try, Franny, for Imogen's sake, if not your own. It's no good putting it off, girl.' She let go of her hands, picked up the beakers. 'You know, something doesn't add up about all this. Johnny was besotted with you. If it hadn't been for his mother, I'm sure he would have taken you with him from the very start.'

'I can't blame his mother for everything. He was a grown man, he knew what he wanted.' She thought he'd wanted her. He had proposed, asking her to keep it quiet until he found the right time to tell his mother and Ruby. She smiled, ruefully. She understood that now, when she hadn't before: finding the right time wasn't as easy as she'd thought. She heard Imogen's laughter. 'Was I a fool, Patsy?'

'Not at all, my lovely girl. And he's not married or engaged, that's for sure. We'd have seen it in the papers. He might be waiting for you just as much as you're still waiting for him.'

Frances gave a hollow laugh. 'I am *not* waiting for him.'

Patsy didn't hide her wry smile and Frances hated knowing her friend was right. 'He loved you, for heaven's sake!'

'Loved? Perhaps. I thought he did, but perhaps he just didn't love me enough.' The pain was coming again, up into her chest and her ribs hurt. 'I was wrong. I was wrong about so many things. I'll never trust another man again.'

'I hope I'm not included in that lump of humanity.' Colin, Patsy's husband, ambled into the kitchen. He put his baccy pouch on the table and looked about him for an ashtray. Patsy directed him with a nod of her head and went outside with the drinks.

'Never!' Frances laughed. 'You're the one exception, Col. Give me a minute to put the clothes away and I'll make you a cuppa.' When she returned, he was sitting down, his back to the wall, chewing on the stem of his unlit pipe. He was a big man with a large, open face that was ruddy and weather-beaten from a lifetime at sea. His hair was thick waves, his eyes dark, and it was easy to imagine him in command of his ship and his men. Frances poured a little water from the kettle and warmed the pot, swirling it around, looking out into the garden. Imogen's dress was green with grass stains and she told Colin, as she spooned the tea leaves into the pot, 'She'd be better wearing the boys' hand-me-downs. Much as I want her to have pretty things, I don't think she's interested.' The words pained her. She had thought Imogen would have wanted the dresses and ribbons that Frances worked so hard to pay for, the sort of things that she'd yearned for herself when she was a child.

'As long as she's happy, lass. That's all that matters.'

She brought the teapot and set it on the table, went back for the mugs and sat down with him.

'It's the only thing that matters, Colin. Thanks for reminding me.' As if she could ever forget. But sometimes things tipped her off course. Like Johnny.

He reached across and patted her hand. 'Now, who's this beggar getting us men a bad name, our Franny?'

Frances told him of the Randolphs.

'Happen our Patsy's right, don't you think?'

She rubbed at a mark on the table. 'I don't know if I can put myself through it again, Col. Waiting for a reply when nothing comes of it? And if I had to take Imogen to prove my point?' The thought made her shudder. 'It's too much of a risk. I couldn't do it.'

He opened his baccy pouch, pressed strands of tobacco into his pipe. 'Sometimes we have to take a risk. It's how we make a better catch.' He looked up, grinned, tilted his head towards the open door. 'That's how I caught my mermaid. Catch of my life, that one.'

'Well, I must admit, not everyone goes to an end-of-the-pier show and comes back with a beauty like Patsy.'

'It was worth the long wait at the stage door, especially with that north wind coming in over the Humber.' Colin chuckled. 'She took the bait in the end.'

'She did. You're one lucky man, Col.' He smiled and Frances envied them their love for each other. Patsy had indeed for fallen for her Colin, hook, line and sinker and had given up the stage without a backward glance.

'And don't I know it.' He rummaged in his pocket for his matches, struck one and drew on his pipe. 'Anyhow, enough of us. What about you and Johnny Randolph? Mebbee he didn't get your letters.'

Frances puffed out a breath. 'One or two I could understand, but not the number I've sent.' She'd been desperate when he hadn't responded after promising her so much. 'I wrote every day to begin with, then every week. Then …' She looked up, anger hardening her heart again. It made her feel strong. 'No, he had his chance. If he'd really loved me, I wouldn't have had to write at all. He knew where I was.'

She leant back in her chair, stretching out her long legs, folding her arms. They heard Patsy talking to the children in the garden. Colin drew on his pipe and she closed her eyes, the familiar smell taking her home to Ireland, to her daddy sitting by the fire. How disappointed they would all be if they knew the truth about her life. She wrote home often, telling them of the shows she was in, the auditions, the rejections. The good and the bad – or most of it. She wanted them to think she was living the life of her dreams, but they knew nothing of Imogen. What they didn't know couldn't hurt them. It wasn't that she thought they wouldn't forgive her, or take Imogen to their hearts, it was the lies she would have to weave to go back. And she couldn't do it.

Colin spoke, interrupting her thoughts, 'As I see it you have two choices, you can forget about him altogether …' She looked up at him, waiting. He studied her eyes, smiled gently, reached out for her hand and took it in his. 'I was wrong. You have *one* choice, lass. I can tell from your eyes that you'll never forget the man, no matter how much you want to.' He squeezed her hand. 'Not knowing is eating you up inside. Patsy's right, you must write again.'

She looked away from him, unsettled by his truth. The love was still there whether she wanted it to be or not. 'I can't, Col.' She sat up, tipped her head back. 'I'm not going to let him reject me again – and I'm certainly never going to let Imogen go through it.' Her heart was twisting, still bruised after all this time, so full of pain and nowhere for the pain to go. She pushed the thoughts away, deeper still, where they couldn't hurt her. He didn't comment.

'How's things at the theatre?'

She told him of Jack giving them a week's wages. 'When I leave here I'll go looking for something, bar work, waitressing – anything to tide me over until the Empire reopens.' *If* it reopens, she thought.

'Why don't you come and stay here until you have something firmed up? It'uld save you going hither and thither.'

Frances shook her head. 'I'm not putting the boys out of their beds, Col. Besides, it's cheap enough where I am and I've more chance of getting a job in Cleethorpes. I'm certainly not going to put on you and Patsy more than I have already.'

'It works both ways, lass.' Colin took the pipe from his mouth, checked the bowl, pushed down with his thumb. 'I know you're here for her and that gives me comfort when I'm at sea.' He paused, drew again on his pipe, moved his head up and down while he organised his thoughts. He said, 'Do you think you might go back home to Ireland, Franny? Now that it's war?' The pair of them had obviously given Frances's situation a lot of thought; it must have been on their minds almost as much as it had on hers.

There was a commotion outside and she twisted to look out into the garden, glad to be distracted. When times had been at their bleakest, what she wouldn't have given to walk back down the old familiar lanes, to the warmth of her life?

'I couldn't go back, Col. We'd be meat and gravy to the gossips for years to come. I'm not letting my girl suffer that.

'I know we've said it before, but couldn't you pretend her daddy had died? That you're a widow.'

'I can't, Col. I can live my lie here, away from them. But Mammy would know. Perhaps I will, one day. But not yet.' She doubted she ever would. She imagined the hurt in her daddy's eyes. No, this was her punishment.

Colin leant back in his chair.

'You know what's best for the pair of you, lass.'

Frances let out a long sigh. 'I don't know if I do, Col, but I can only keep trying to do my best.'

'That's all any of us can do,' he said quietly.

After lunch Patsy and Frances stayed in the garden with the children, picking the last fruit from the trees. Imogen dropped an apple into the basket her mother held. Frances looked about her. Flowers were still blossoming in the beds, bees hovering, butterflies flitting among the blooms.

'It's hard to think that things are any different from what they were last week, Patsy.' War seemed a long way away.

'I suppose that's because it's not, for most of us. For the time being. Monday's still wash day, Wednesday baking day.'

'And Colin?'

The smile left her face. 'Waiting for his call-up papers. The Naval Reserve are full of fishermen manning the minesweepers.' She was quiet. Colly dropped another apple and it fell off the pile; he picked it up and it balanced, fell again. The children giggled. He gave it to his mother and ran around for more, checking for grubs. 'I thought he might have been too old.' Patsy held the apple to her nose, sniffed it. 'Whatever happens, he'll be at sea, fishing or fighting, perhaps both.' She sat down on the garden bench and Frances sat beside her. 'Does it feel like a dream to you, Franny, because it does to me?'

Frances took her friend's hand. 'It does. A bad dream at that.' The two of them sat back and closed their eyes against the sunshine, letting it warm them, and Frances hoped the heat would melt away the fear that kept catching at her heart.

Later, when it was time to leave, she gathered her things and popped her head around the sitting room door. Colin was settled in his armchair by the window, smoking his pipe and reading the paper, the wireless on low.

'I'm off, Col. I'll see you next week, maybe.' His pipe was quickly placed in the ashtray that balanced on the arm of the leather chair and he got to his feet, opened his arms. Frances gave him a squeeze, taking in the smell of tobacco. Memories of her father erupted again and she squeezed harder, treasuring the familiarity. What it was to be held, to be loved …

'Take care, my lovely.'

She pulled away. 'And you too, Colin. Be safe. Have a good trip.'

Patsy was waiting for her in the hall. Imogen was sitting on the chair at the side of the front door, her knees green, her socks wrinkled about her ankles. It broke Frances's heart every time she had to leave and today Imogen seemed unmoved, which upset Frances even more.

'Are you going to give Mummy a kiss goodbye?' Imogen slipped off the chair and threw her arms around her mother, who had squatted down on her haunches to hug her. She planted a kiss on Frances's nose.

'Sorry, Imogen, Mummy has to leave early this week, but I'll be back on Sunday, the same as always.' She tried not to let despondency get the better of her. 'Be good for Auntie Patsy.'

Patsy smiled benignly. 'She's always good, aren't you, Imogen?'

Imogen's curls bounced as she nodded her head. 'Can I go back in the garden with Colly, now?' Frances was disappointed and Patsy pressed her arm as she stood up again.

'Don't take it to heart, Franny. It's just kids, they're all the same.' Frances forced a smile. Were they? Or was Imogen growing away from her? She reached for her bag, which she'd left in the hall, and took out her purse. Patsy put out a hand to stop her.

'I don't need the money, Frances. Please keep it.' Frances ignored her, taking out the ten-bob notes and pressing them into Patsy's reluctant hand.

'She's my responsibility, Patsy. Not yours. It would be taking advantage.'

'But things are different now. You don't know when you'll get work again.'

Frances was dismissive. 'I can get work. Any work will do. Something will come up, it always does.' She slung the box with her gas mask over her shoulder. So much more to think about already. She took coins from her purse for the bus fare.

Patsy put a hand to Frances's shoulder. 'It'll work out, love. Be brave. Be bold.' They shared a smile. It was what Patsy had said every night to her dance troupe before the curtain went up. Colly ran in and Imogen followed him into the sitting room. It made her feel better, that the kids were doing what they always did, brought a sense of normality. It was what she wanted for Imogen and that she couldn't be a part of it was only temporary. She smiled, that word again. Yes, it was all temporary; one day she would have a home with Imogen, but this was the best she could do for now. She stepped out onto the path; Patsy stood in the doorway and Colly and Imogen waited at the window in the sitting room, then the three of them waved until she could see them no more.

Chapter 4

Johnny Randolph placed the black coffee on the low mahogany table in front of his sister. Ruby was wearing a red satin negligee and had sunk into the generous armchair, her long legs over one arm of it, her back against the other. She was wearing a black velvet eye mask, her long brown hair hanging almost to the floor, her hands to her head.

'Sit up,' Johnny said, taking the chair opposite her. He spread his feet, interlocked his fingers and leant forward, waiting for her to do as he'd asked. She groaned. He asked her again, frustrated, his voice sharper this time and she slowly pulled herself around, lifted a corner of her eye mask, grinned at him and dropped it down again.

'Ruby, for God's sake! Take that damn thing off and drink the coffee.'

She pouted, swung her legs down, pushed the eye mask to the top of her head, blinking against the light of the room. She cupped her hands at her brow, squinting at him. Her mascara had run and her eyes were smoky black. He waited for her to rouse herself.

She leant forward, picked up the cup, put it down again. 'What time is it?'

He looked at his watch. 'Twenty past eleven.'

She screwed her face. 'Far, far, too early.' She got up, wobbled, sat down again. 'I should be in bed.'

'You should be working. We both should.' He stuck out his hand towards the cup. 'Drink the coffee.'

'There is no work, darling brother.' She smiled, sweetly sarcastic, sipped at the coffee, pulled a face. 'That's not coffee. It's horrid.'

'It's the best you're going to get, probably for years. We're not in America now.' He sat back in the armchair, relaxing a little, watching her drink. The small sitting room reeked of her cocktail cigarettes and he'd opened the window to freshen the air. The sound of traffic and people shouting drifted in, English voices, reminding him they were home. Had he done the right thing, not taking up the new American contract? Their agent had been furious and cast them off like dirt on his shoe when they turned down Broadway; he couldn't blame him. He looked at Ruby, the blankness in her eyes. No, he'd definitely made the right decision. Much longer and he wasn't sure he'd have a sister to bring home.

'Better?' He softened his tone. He wanted to be tender, but Ruby would take advantage. He must stay firm.

She mumbled, non-committal, pulled the eye mask from her head and threw it on the table. He crossed his legs. 'We need to rehearse, Ruby, keep in shape, develop new routines.'

'What for? The show's cancelled.' She made a sweep with her arm. '*All* the shows are cancelled.' She slumped back in the chair and put the flat of her hand to her head. He half wanted to laugh at her dramatics, would've done in the past, but not now.

'We have to keep at it, Ruby,' he said, hoping to encourage her. 'It's an interruption, not an end.' He tried not to get angry with her. 'Where's your discipline?'

She picked up a cushion, looked behind it, put it back, leant forward, wafted her hand under the chair. She sat up, holding her head, obviously dizzy, bent her arms at the elbows, splayed her hands. 'Lost it. No idea where it is.'

She tucked her legs underneath her, reached forward for the coffee, then stared into the cup.

He couldn't be too irritated with her, understanding her disappointment, her boredom, but he was doing his best to put things right. He glanced at his wristwatch. 'I've got to go out, sort a couple of things. You have a bath and get dressed.' He stood up, looked about him. 'Perhaps tidy up a bit?' She'd been untidy since she was a small child, but this was different; she really didn't care. The expensive clothes she'd once cherished were dropped anywhere she pleased and things had been lost – jewellery, handbags. He knew she'd have a bath but, as for anything else, his expectations were low. 'I won't be long. We'll go out for lunch.' She brightened a little. 'Then we'll talk about what we're going to do next. OK?'

She ignored him. He picked up his hat, his wallet, slipped it into his pocket. When he turned, she'd shrunk back into the chair, her back to him, the eye mask shutting out the light.

He called goodbye and she stuck her hand up, wiggling her fingers as he closed the door.

He chose the stairs over the lift, enjoyed the burst of sunlight as he came into the lobby and stepped out into the fresh autumn air. He raised his hat in greeting as an elderly woman walked by. It was good to be home, to familiar streets and sounds – even if the circumstances had not been as he'd wished. America had promised so much and delivered so little. Not that they hadn't done well, it was timing, that's all. Of the worst possible kind. He wondered if Ruby would ever get over it. He checked his watch. Half an hour with their new agent, Bernie Blackwood, would leave him enough time to get back over the bridge to Waterloo.

He walked down the Strand. The Adelphi and the Vaudeville were showing closed notices. They couldn't have come back at a worse time for work, but there was more to life than work, wasn't there? And there was the conundrum. How could he help Ruby without it? He waited at the kerb, watching the red buses and black cabs go by, stood for a few minutes at Trafalgar Square. Nelson was still standing guard, lions at his feet, and he suddenly felt comforted by the permanence of things. He tilted his face to the sun. Would the sky soon be filled with planes, ours, or theirs? Trucks were rumbling down towards Whitehall, the pavements patched with khaki uniforms. He would have come back anyway, work or not. He couldn't stand by and watch his country from afar, not now it was at war. It was ironic that he felt Ruby was safer here. He put his hands in his pockets, quickened his pace to make up time. As he rounded the corner he saw the queue and hardly needed to lift his head to see the sign on the wall, Bernie Blackwood Variety Agency. He squeezed past the line of people on the stairs to Bernie's office on the first floor. What little light there was filtered from the door on the small landing that was permanently open and dust motes swirled above the heads of the eternally optimistic. A woman wearing heavy-handed make-up was smoking under a sign that said No Smoking.

'Hey, Johnny, old thing. Good to see you back.' He didn't recognise the tall thin man with the sharp jaw. 'Mickey Harper. We met at The Piccadilly?'

'Good to see you,' he replied cheerfully. He had no idea who Harper was, but that was normal these days. The Randolphs were names, headliners. Many people knew who they were, wanted to make themselves noticed. It was how you made your way, connections, but you had to have the talent and the work ethic. He thought of Ruby again. Would she have moved from the chair yet?

The waiting room was packed with old-timers; some he recognised and he touched his hat to acknowledge them. He and Ruby had left hanging around agents' offices waiting for work behind them. People asked for them now. Bernie had taken them on gladly, securing them a place in a London revue at top money – a fresh start and a chance to leave all the bad memories on the other side of the Atlantic.

Bernie's private secretary, Shirley, was manning the desk and switchboard, keeping the mass of humanity crowded into the small office at bay. She was fierce but kind – and guarded Bernie like a lioness. She beamed when she saw him, stopped typing and got up and walked towards him, opened the small gate that kept the acts the other side of the counter.

'Mr Randolph, hello. Bernie's expecting you.' She closed the gate, batting her hand as the crowd surged forward a little, pressing on the counter. 'Wait your turn. *He's* got a long-standing appointment.' Johnny tried not to smile. His long-standing appointment had been made yesterday.

'Please, call me Johnny, Shirley.'

She inclined her head. 'I will, Johnny. Thank you.'

He still felt uncomfortable with fame. He knew many who worked just as hard as he and Ruby had but they hadn't got the breaks. Success was still partly luck, and they had been lucky. Lucky, but not happy. Perhaps you couldn't have both.

Shirley knocked on the half-glazed door that bore the legend Bernie Blackwood Agent in bold black letters edged in gold. 'Johnny Randolph is here for you, Mr Blackwood.' She opened the door wider, stepped back to let him in.

Bernie was seated behind his broad desk, publicity photos and yellow contracts spread across it. He got to his feet, placing his oversized Cuban cigar in the silver ashtray. He was shorter than Johnny, his thick, silver-grey hair combed back from his face. His brown eyes twinkled and creased at the corners when he smiled and Johnny was glad he'd agreed to take them on. Unlike many of the theatrical agents, Bernie had a good reputation and their deal had been done by telegram followed by lunch at The Ivy. A handshake, that's all it was. 'Then, if you don't like what I do, you're free to leave whenever you want.' It was an unusual way of doing business and Johnny liked it, knowing that Bernie scrutinised every line of the contracts that secured his acts' time and talents in theatres and clubs around the country. He was a kind man and fair – but woe betide anyone that crossed him.

He gripped Johnny's hand and shook it vigorously, slapping him on the back and showing him to the chair opposite his desk.

'Si' down, my boy. Si' down.' He stretched out his hand towards a chair. Johnny did as he was asked, removed his hat and placed it on his lap.

'Tea? Coffee? Something stronger?'

Johnny put up a hand. 'Not at this time of the morning, Bernie.'

'Glad to hear it, glad to hear it.'

Shirley left them to it and Bernie went over to a small table on which was a carafe of water and glasses. He held up the carafe and Johnny assented. As Bernie poured the drinks, Johnny looked about him. The dark blue walls were covered with bills from variety shows at the Empires, Palaces and Hippodromes; with photos of Bernie with the King and Queen at a variety performance, with The Crazy Gang, Gracie, Formby … Bernie was well liked and Johnny could tell from the photos that the stars were genuinely smiling and not forcing it for the camera. It was all in the eyes. Always the eyes.

Bernie set a glass down in front of him and went back to his own seat. He shuffled the papers on his desk into an untidy pile and pushed them to one side. A silver-framed photo of his wife and another of his children took pride of place. Bernie adjusted them, smiling as he did so, then gave Johnny his full attention.

'No news from Whitehall, Johnny, my boy.' He took a quaff at his water, Johnny did likewise. Car horns and police bells drifted in through the open window. Johnny ran his finger around his collar. It was already stifling in the small room.

'Something's in the pipeline but nothing confirmed, of course.' He sipped again and put his glass down. 'I haven't heard from the Coliseum. Not sure if they'll still go ahead with the show. If the investors lose their nerve …' He leant back in his leather chair, interlaced his fingers and rested them on his stomach. 'And if they reopen, there'll be restrictions. Will we get bums on seats?' He splayed his hands. 'It's all down to bums on seats.'

Johnny acknowledged the fact. 'I didn't come to you about that, Bernie. I don't expect many of the shows will reopen anytime soon.'

Bernie agreed, waiting for Johnny to go on. Something in his gut told the younger man he could trust Bernie – the man had built his reputation on it. Johnny had been reckless, turning down the Broadway contract. Their old agent, Cookie Porter, had called him a madman and maybe he was. He wasn't used to handling that side of the business. Their mother, Alice, had taken care of everything: contracts, where they performed and who with. He and Ruby had been small children when their father was killed and Alice had poured every ounce of her energy to making sure the Randolph name would headline theatres again. It felt as though he was going against everything his mother had wanted for them – but Ruby had been very different, then. Johnny drew a deep breath, exhaled. 'I was wondering if you could get us something out of town?'

'The provinces?' Bernie frowned.

Johnny rubbed his jaw. 'I know the money won't be great, and your percentage of the take will be less, so we'd be happy to pay more. Fifteen?' Bernie must think him an idiot. Perhaps Cookie was right, he was a madman. He certainly wasn't a businessman.

Bernie wafted the suggestion away with a wave of his hand and a small shake of his head. He leant forward, his hands flat on the desk. 'For you. Or for Ruby?'

Johnny grasped the arms of his chair. 'The two of us. The Randolphs come as a pair; always have done, always will.' Bernie smiled and Johnny had a feeling that he wouldn't have to explain. 'You know why?'

'I had heard.'

Johnny sank in the chair. 'Already. And from America?'

Bernie was sympathetic. 'Don't worry too much, son. The time to worry is when they're not talking about you.'

Johnny clasped his hands, his knuckles white. 'Even so, a spell somewhere quieter would give us the chance to work on some new routines, take the pressure off somewhat.' Bernie opened an expensive inlaid box and offered a cigar to Johnny. 'No thanks, Bernie. I don't smoke cigars.'

'Very wise. Although I have to say I don't smoke much either – mostly it burns away in an ashtray.' He smiled. 'An expensive habit.' He picked up the cigar from the ashtray, lit it and blew out a long plume of smoke. It reminded Johnny of New York, the parties and bars, the long lunches. He tried to relax.

'I have to say, my boy, you're probably the first act I've ever had that didn't want town first. What if the show goes ahead at the Coliseum?'

'Are we tied into the contract?' It had been the first thing to cross his mind when the rumblings of war had grown louder.

Bernie shrugged. 'Hard to say in these circumstances. Does war make all contracts null and void? I don't know.' He leant back in his chair. 'Early days.'

'Bloody contracts, I hate being tied to them.'

'It gives you security, my boy. A long contract is a good thing.'

'Not when you're thousands of miles away and your mother's dying, it isn't.' Ruby had been hysterical. Not that they'd found out from Alice; she hadn't wanted them to know. Their Aunt Letty had sent a telegram, against her sister's wishes. If only she'd sent it sooner. The ink was barely dry on the dotted line of a contract that would send them coast to coast when they got the news. Ruby had started drinking when she'd barely touched alcohol before and it had been a slippery downward slope ever since.

Bernie puffed on his cigar. 'It must have been hard. The show must go on and all that.'

Johnny stared out of the window at the buildings opposite. Pigeons clung to the sills, shuffling along, making room. 'I doubt Ruby will get over it. We couldn't afford to buy ourselves out of the contract and they held us to it. Biggest mistake of my life.'

He looked back at Bernie, who moved his head from side to side.

'These things happen, my boy. If you'd been in Liverpool or London you still might not have got back in time.'

'We would have been able to do *something*.' Johnny got up, went to the window, his hand resting on the wall above him. 'Ruby lost heart.' How they had ever managed to finish the tour he had no idea. The strain had been terrible. She wasn't fit to perform some days, but he'd pushed her through it and she'd hated him for it. They'd had their differences before, but never as they had those last few months. The relief when they'd got on the boat to come home had been enormous. He turned back to Bernie. 'We'll take anything.'

'And Ruby?'

'Will do as I tell her. Don't worry about it, Bernie, I can handle Ruby.' Even as he said it, he doubted he could. He was in charge of their career now, their lives – and he'd better start making a better job of it.

Bernie got to his feet, walked over and put his arm on Johnny's shoulder. 'I'll do what I can, son. Leave it to me. As soon as I have something, you'll know.'

He couldn't recall the last time he'd been able to trust anyone. He drew himself more upright. 'Thanks, Bernie. I appreciate it.'

'That's what you pay me for.'

Johnny grinned, wryly. 'We haven't paid you anything yet.'

'I can wait,' Bernie said. 'I believe in you.'

Johnny nodded, not having the words, feeling that at least he'd done something right. Maybe he wasn't so mad after all.

Bernie walked with him to the door, his hand resting on Johnny's back.

'Next time we must do lunch, my boy.'

Johnny put his hat back on. 'We will.' He found himself looking forward to it.

People were still queuing on the stairs and he hurried down, anxious to get back to Ruby. He felt someone grasp the top of his shoulder and turned. The same man, Mick Parker? Harper, was it?

'See ya around, Johnny.'

Johnny stopped. 'Yes, see you around.' He hurried out into the street, blinking at the brightness of the sun. He still had no idea if he was doing the right thing; he only knew that he had to go forward and take Ruby with him.

Chapter 5

Frances and Jessie walked along the Kingsway; the boarding houses that overlooked the promenade and beaches were all showing Vacancies signs and the promenade was virtually deserted, just a handful of dog walkers and kids running along the pathways. The flower beds were still in their glory and it seemed such a waste without the crowds to enjoy them.

'Feast your eyes, Jessie,' Frances said as they crossed the road. 'We might as well, because they'll be dug up soon and we'll be looking at turnip tops and cabbages in future.'

Jessie grinned.

'Do you think they'll be planting them in rows, or stick with the display?'

The pair of them stood by the rail, looking over at them. Frances made a shape with her hand.

'Oh, yes, I can see a lovely anchor there, the carrot tops blowing in the breeze. And leeks would make a splendid backdrop, don't you think?' It was good to have something to be cheerful about, knowing they had to take the joy when and where they could. Only a week ago they would have been getting ready for what was to become their final appearance at the Empire.

'So much has changed, hasn't it, Frances? And yet nothing has really.' They'd left the house early, searching for the smallest indication that things were moving forward. The Café Dansant and the Olympia were showing signs similar to the Empire, letting customers know that they were closed until further notice, but that they hoped it wouldn't be too long.

'How long is too long, Frances?'

Frances leant on the glass and peered in the window. The inner doors had been wedged open and the dance floor was littered with paper streamers and confetti, the tables still full of glasses and ashtrays. 'It looks like the *Mary Celeste*. As though the world froze and the people disappeared.' She turned away, wishing she hadn't looked in the first place.

It was odd, living in such strange limbo. Places had closed, people had left, but there had been no threat, no attack.

They strolled along the promenade, heading towards the pier. The tide was coming in and the rush and suck of the waves was soothing. Gulls soared across the water, screeching and calling, and Frances wanted to join in, feeling a good scream would be a welcome release. All but one of the shops along the walkway were boarded up, save for a small cabin that had opened its front and was selling hot and cold drinks and snacks. A couple of old blokes sat outside, each with a mug of tea beside him on the wooden table, and they removed their flat caps in unison as the girls passed by. The one on the left was smoking a pipe and it reminded Frances of Colin. She stared across to the horizon and the boats going in and out of the Humber estuary. Was he at sea? Had he been called up? She would find out tomorrow when she went to see Imogen. The wind blew her hair across her face and she pulled it away with her hand, fighting a losing battle. They would all be fighting soon. She turned to Jessie.

'Have you heard from Harry?'

Jessie's face shone with warmth at the mention of his name. 'A letter in the first post. He has exams again. He's busy, but he found time to write.' Jessie ran her hand along the metal railings, lifting her hand over the bumps where the posts linked to the rail as they went along.

Frances stared back at the sea. Loving Johnny had made her feel that way. Once … She closed her eyes, felt the cool wind on her face, her hair billowing behind her. In her dreams he'd come back to her, told her that he loved her. A happy ending. She opened her eyes, turned to Jessie.

'When did you know you loved Harry, Jessie? I mean, *really* loved him?'

Jessie looked up to the sky as Frances noticed she did whenever she thought of him. Her Harry was up in the air, in his plane, soaring among the clouds.

'I suppose when I thought I'd lost him forever.' She wrapped her hand over Frances's and leant closer. 'I loved him, but I wasn't sure I was *in* love with him. I was desperate to escape from living with my aunt and uncle. Uncle Norman wasn't too bad; he gave me a job at his office and he paid for my secretarial training so I could have stuck it, I suppose, but Aunt Iris was such a witch.' She thought for a moment. 'If I hadn't been there I would never have met Harry, would I? So that's another good thing.' She paused again. 'I was confused. My heart ached for my dad. I missed him so much, Frances, and I so wanted to make him proud of me. I thought I loved the theatre as much as I loved Harry, but it's not the same.' She looked at Frances, their eyes meeting, understanding passing between them and Frances wanted to be in love again, to have her eyes shine as Jessie's did when she talked of Harry. She smiled.

'No, it's not the same at all.'

They crossed at Brighton Slipway, down towards the pier that stretched way out into the sea. It was odd, walking so freely, when normally they had to weave their way among the crowds that flocked to the seaside, all wanting to breathe the fresh, clean air.

'I suppose the pavilion is closed too.' Jessie was glum.

'Everywhere will be shut, Jessie. Anywhere that crowds gather to enjoy themselves. It's not just the theatres but the sports grounds too. No football season, no cricket come next summer.'

'It's sensible, I suppose,' Jessie said, 'but such a shame.'

Frances agreed. 'There's nothing like the sound of people enjoying themselves to give you a lift.'

Jessie leant on the railings again. Frances joined her and the pair of them looked down onto the beach. A gang of kids had dug a big hole and scooped a channel down to the water's edge. As the tide rushed in, water ran up and filled the hole before disappearing into the sand, leaving a dark wet patch and the kids disappointed. Life was full of disappointments.

'What if the theatres don't reopen?' Jessie said. 'I'm not talking about work, I'm thinking of morale. An escape. We all need it, don't we?'

'We do,' Frances agreed. The theatre had been her escape as it had been for others. You didn't have to be in the audience to want to forget your troubles. She checked her watch. 'Let's call in the Empire and see if there's anyone about. We've time before we meet Dolly and Ginny at the café.'

They were delighted to find the entrance doors to the Empire unlocked. Frances pulled on the brass handles and they went inside. There was no sense of abandonment evident here, as there had been at the Olympia; the tiled floor was spotless, the mirrors without smears, and the brass rails that led to the dress circle were buffed and gleaming.

'It looks as if we could open tonight!' Jessie's eyes were bright. 'It's good to know that Jack's not given up.' Frances looked about her. The photographs of the summer show were still in the glass cases by the box office, even though boards had been placed in front of the arched eyes of the pay desk, rendering them blind. Frances opened the doors to the stalls and heard voices. They discovered Jack sitting in the back row with Mike, the stage manager. The two men stopped talking and turned when they saw them.

'Morning, girls. How are you getting on?'

'Fine thanks, Jack.' Jessie was cheered already. 'We only popped in to see if there was any news?' Her friend sounded so hopeful and Frances felt a stab of regret. Once, she too would have felt hopeful, but she had given that up when she'd found herself pregnant and alone. It wasn't that things got better, they didn't; it was that she learned to cope. But hope, that was something else entirely.

'A little here and there, Jessie. Nothing solid, but I'm optimistic. I can't say any more than that at this stage.' Jack got to his feet. He looked tired, the bags evident under his eyes, but he smiled encouragingly at them. He put his hands in his pockets, leant against the back of the seat in front of him.

'We understand, Jack,' Jessie said, her voice bright. 'We just wanted to let you know that we're still here should anything change. And Ginny's here too.' Jack smiled and, encouraged, Jessie went on, 'We're willing to do anything.' She turned to Frances. 'Aren't we, Frances?'

'Well, not quite,' Frances said and grinned. Jack laughed and Mike got to his feet. He'd had a haircut and his red hair was almost stubble on his head.

'I'll be out back if you need me, Jack.' Jack lifted a hand, gave him a short nod.

'See you later, girls,' Mike said. 'With any luck it won't be too long before you're cheering us all up again.' He strode down the aisle and his feet were heavy as he walked up the steps at the front of the stage. There was no rush about anything these days, it was simply a matter of eking things out until something started to move.

'Are you still at Barkhouse Lane if I need to get in touch?'

'We are,' Jessie said quickly. 'And we can get hold of Ginny.'

Frances raised her eyebrows, puzzled by Jessie's sudden concern for Ginny. It wasn't as if the two of them had been close, more that they had tolerated each other. Six girls squashed in a dressing room had to rub along as best they could and Ginny had taken up with Billy Lane although he still had Jessie in his sights. It had caused friction between the two girls which hadn't been there before.

'That's good to know.' He stood away from the seat. 'I'll make sure I get a message to you as soon as I know things are starting to move.' He paused. 'I can't promise anything, girls. There might be restrictions if we do open, but ...' He smiled at them both, lifted his hands, spread them out. 'When I need my Variety Girls, I'll know where you are.'

The two of them walked around the corner to Joyce's Café, where there was always a warm welcome, a mug of tea and Joyce's generosity waiting for them. The café was on the corner of Dolphin Street, which ran along the back of the Empire and the gift shops, and it had become their regular haunt since they'd started at the Empire in July. Ginny and Dolly were already waiting at their usual table at the window and they waved when they saw Frances and Jessie. Jessie hurried forward and held the door open; Frances caught it and stood back while a couple walked out into the street and linked arms. She watched them go, wistful while Dolly moved round a chair and Jessie sat down.

Behind the counter, Joyce, the owner, was slicing a doorstop of bread, her head down. The café was surprisingly busy. Frances had expected it to be quiet but a few of the regulars were sitting at the back with their toasted teacakes and egg butties. Winnie, one of the theatre cleaners, was with her hubby, neither of them speaking to each other, and although she put every effort into a smile when she saw the girls, it looked like something between a grimace and a sneer; knowing Winnie as they did, it probably took a huge amount of effort. It had been a good summer; they had made so many friends and it would be wonderful if the theatre did reopen soon. Joyce's daughter, Vi, was sitting to the side of the counter, nursing her baby, Frank, and chatting to her mother as she worked. Joyce turned and held her knife aloft. 'Hello, you lasses. Good to see you.'

'Tea, Jessie? Milk?' Frances asked. She turned to Dolly and Ginny. 'Can I get either of you anything?' The girls shook their heads, pointing to the cups in front of them. Jessie took out her purse. 'Put it away, Jessie,' Frances said. 'You can get the next one.'

Jessie returned her purse to her bag.

'In that case I'll have a glass of milk.'

Frances leant on the marble counter, watching Joyce flip bacon in a pan thick with hot fat. She pressed it with a metal slice, then turned to the counter, wiping her hands on her apron. 'Tea for two?' She smoothed her black hair back from her forehead with the back of her hand, sniffed and smiled broadly, her brown, pencilled eyebrows moving alarmingly high as she did so.

'One. Jessie will have a glass of milk. I'll wait to save you bringing them over.'

'Bless ya, Frances.' Joyce took a saucer from the pile at the side of the metal urn and placed a cup on top then drew a glass from under the counter and poured Jessie's milk. 'Did you manage to get any work, ducky? I know the other lasses have found themselves bits and bobs, and Jessie was in here the other day, telling me her news that she'd got a job at a solicitors. She didn't look too thrilled about that, neither, but work's work now, isn't it?' She twisted, gave the bacon a cursory glance, and turned back to Frances. 'And Ginny's got a job at the Little Laundry down by you, Barkhouse Lane way.' She wrinkled her nose. 'Not ideal – ruddy awful in hot weather, but nice in the winter, I should think.' Joyce turned back to the bacon, jiggled it onto the metal slice, slipped it onto the thick bread, stuck another round of bread on top and cut it in half. She put the plate on the counter, leant forward and bellowed. 'Ernie, your sarnie's ready.' Ernie left his table with the newspaper spread out on it, shuffled up to the counter and took it. He gave Frances a gappy smile.

'Best bacon butties for miles.'

Frances agreed, watching him shuffle back, wondering how he would eat it with so few teeth. Joyce placed the milk and tea on the counter.

'There you are, ducky.' She frowned, 'Did I ask you something?' She flapped a hand, 'Never mind, can't have been important. If I remember, I'll call ya.' She switched her attention to the man standing next in the queue. 'Yes, flower, what can I get ya?'

Frances took the glass and mug and headed back to the table. Jessie was grumbling about her work at the solicitors.

'Honestly, with all the hassle it took me to get here and now I'm almost back where I started. I suppose I should be grateful for Uncle Norman really; at least I've got some work and the pay's not too bad – although Miss Beaky Bird is a miserable old so and so. Not a patch on my old boss, Miss Symonds.'

'Is she really Beaky Bird?' Ginny asked, holding her cup halfway to her mouth, looking at Jessie.

'Not really. She is Miss Bird, though. We call her Beaky 'cos she has her nose in everything.' She put her hand to her mouth, glancing about the café. 'Me and my big mouth! She might have been sitting behind me.'

Dolly laughed. 'I think you're safe in here. Joyce would soon sort anyone out.'

Frances handed Jessie her milk and sat down.

'Well, now I've spoken to Joyce I don't need to ask you what you've all been doing this week. I got the full rundown while she served me and everyone else.'

Dolly grinned. 'You don't need to buy a paper, that's for sure.'

'How are you finding it at the laundry, Ginny? I didn't know you'd started there?'

Ginny pushed her cup away. 'It's hard work but I really can't do anything else. I've never worked in a shop or office and it's simple enough.'

'I said she should call in to see us – we're only down the street,' Jessie said. 'If I'm not there, Frances is, or Mum. You're always welcome, isn't she, Frances?'

'Of course. We Variety Girls have to stick together.' Ginny seemed encouraged and Frances felt for her. Rita, Kay and Sally, the other Variety Girls, had left the day after war had been declared, leaving Ginny alone in the flat they'd all shared so she would be lonely, but at least her rent had been paid to the end of the month. It would give her time to look for something else.

'I wish I was a Variety Girl.' Dolly was wistful. 'It sounds so glamorous.'

'It might sound like it, but it isn't, you know that, Dolly,' Frances said, laughing. 'But you're welcome to be an out-of-work Variety Girl. Or "resting" as we say in the business. No skills required.' Jessie reached over and rubbed Dolly's arm. 'You can be an honorary Variety Girl, can't she, Frances? Ginny?'

'Of course. I always think of you as one of us anyway,' Frances said, because it was true. Since they'd first come together for the summer season Dolly had been part of their lives, just as much as her lovely dad, George, was when he greeted them at the stage door each evening. 'Have you found work, Dolly?'

'With my sister. Her boarding house is now an official billet. She's already full of people from the army and I help with the breakfasts and then the evening meal, making the beds, doing the laundry.' She looked across at Ginny. 'Proper little Widow Twankeys, aren't we?'

Jessie started to sing 'Chinese Laundry Blues', playing an imaginary ukulele, grinning and tilting her head in an impression of George Formby.

'Sing up, Jessie love,' Joyce called from behind the counter. 'We all need a cheering up, don't we?' Customers at the other tables called their encouragement and it was all Jessie needed. She got to her feet and went to the front of the table. The bell over the door rang out and a sailor in uniform came in. Jessie waited while he squeezed past and then started from the beginning. Ginny and Frances got up beside her, dancing and stepping in what little space there was, joining in the chorus with Jessie, along with everyone else. When they came to the end of the song, everyone applauded. How good it was to see smiling faces!

'Eeh, that perked us all up good an' proper, you lasses.' Joyce came out from behind the counter. 'We'll have a bit of that every day, if you please. Won't we, folks?' She turned to the customers, who voiced their agreement. 'Nowt like a bit of George Formby to make you smile, eh?' She stacked cups and plates and put them on the counter, chatting to Winnie as she did so. The girls sat down again, Dolly's eyes shining at them.

'Oh, it's a crying shame that you aren't doing what you've worked so hard for! How quickly everyone changed when you started to entertain them. I know it's only a café, but it's almost like magic, isn't it?'

'That's exactly how I feel, Dolly,' Jessie said. 'And now I've done that, I feel I can suggest something.' She grinned. 'It was what we were talking about the other night, Frances.'

'Shall we get another drink first?' Frances offered. 'I feel like this might take a long time.' She got to her feet, but Jessie pushed her back down with a light touch.

'My turn this time, remember?' She took their drinks orders and went to the counter.

'What's Jessie up to?' Dolly asked.

'You'll find out soon enough,' Frances said. 'I don't want to step on her toes and it was her idea. I don't think she's willing to accept that the show is over.'

'You can't blame her,' Ginny said, quietly. 'Everything was looking so good for her. I wonder if she'll go to London now?'

'I doubt it,' Frances said. 'If they start a bombing campaign, London will be top of the list so I shouldn't think any of the theatres will reopen there.' She leant back in her seat, waving at Ernie as he left. 'I don't think her mum would be happy about her going, either. Grace is in much better health, but I don't believe Jessie's ready to leave her yet.'

'Leave who?' Jessie said, setting a tray down and handing over the drinks. Dolly slipped the tray against the wall behind her.

'Your mum, Eddie, Cleethorpes. Us.' Frances said, stirring in a spoonful of sugar, the spoon clattering on the cup's sides. Ginny sipped at the hot tea, coughed and spluttered. Jessie was all concern.

'Are you all right, Ginny?' The girl nodded, putting out her hand to keep Jessie back.

'My own stupid fault. Too hot.'

Frances stared at Jessie, who looked away from her. Jessie was a warm, affectionate girl, who was quick to her emotions, but this concern for Ginny? What was it about? The pair of them had been at daggers drawn for most of the season, Billy Lane the cause of it, as he was of so many things. Frances wasn't the only one who was glad that he'd left when he did, before he did any more damage. The agent Bernie Blackwood had come to see Jack Holland, and Jessie too. He had been her father's agent and had seemed a kindly sort, not like other agents she had come across. Billy had lingered around him like a bad smell when he found out Bernie had contacts in the BBC. He hadn't cared one jot about any of them, leaving the show before the end of his contract and haring off to London. Well, good riddance!

'Please don't fuss, Jessie.' Ginny caught Frances's eye and flushed with embarrassment. She stared down into her cup, fiddling with the handle, and in that instant, Frances understood. The girl was pregnant. And Jessie knew. It explained everything, the whispering, the sudden closeness. The three of them were quiet until Dolly said, seemingly oblivious, 'So, Jessie. What's your plan?' She leant across the table, eager to join in.

Jessie was hesitant at first, her words measured. 'I was thinking, you know. Well, when I was younger my dad played in social clubs and pubs. I haven't ever done it on my own and I wouldn't want to, I'd be too scared. But we could do something together and share the money, couldn't we? Our weekends are free.'

'Not for all of us, Jessie.' Frances stopped her. 'I'm working in the Fisherman's Arms and the landlady said she might need me the odd Saturday and I said I'd help when I could. It's on a rota.'

'I thought you were working at Grant's sweet shop?'

'I am. I'm doing both. We don't know how long we're going to be out of work, Jessie; theatrical work anyway. I want to save as much as I can.'

'OK, but most Saturdays. Evenings?' Frances nodded and Jessie carried on, gaining confidence. 'And some places have entertainment on a Sunday lunchtime.'

'Not for me, Jessie.' Frances interrupted again. 'Sunday evenings, but not lunchtime.'

'Not ever? Not just the once?' Jessie's mouth turned down at the corners.

'Not at the moment, Jessie. I'm sorry.' If she could tell them about Imogen, they might understand. She looked again at Ginny. God, life was full of secrets – and pain.

Jessie was deflated. 'I thought we could make some extra cash *and* do what we're good at.' Her shoulders sagged. 'It was a daft idea.'

Frances reached out and touched Jessie's arm. 'It's a great idea, Jessie. It needs more thought, that's all. Perhaps we need to find places that will take a booking first? We won't know what we'll need until we know what's available.'

'Frances is right,' Ginny agreed. 'It's OK to stand up and sing in the café and get a great response, but we need to put more effort into it if we want to make money. I'm all for that. Any extra cash will be welcome indeed.' Frances smiled; the girl smiled too and she could only guess at what turmoil she must be in. The girls continued to talk but Frances's thoughts were in the past; the terror of finding out, of it being too late to tell Johnny. And when he'd not replied … the pain was still raw. In her distress, she'd turned to Patsy and she and Colin had welcomed her into their home with open arms. They were family as much as anyone else ever could be. Who would Ginny turn to? One thing was certain, she wouldn't be able to manage alone. Jessie's insistent voice broke into her thoughts.

'Can we do that, Frances?'

'I'm sorry, Jessie. Do what?'

Jessie was impatient and Frances couldn't blame her. It wasn't that she didn't want to support her – heavens, the money was bound to be helpful to all of them, but they needed to be professional in their approach.

'Rehearse, today. Jack might let us use the piano. It's not as if we'll be in the way.'

Frances bucked up. She needed to get rid of some energy and to have the whole stage to dance as she wished would be such a treat, for when she danced she could let go of her jumbled thoughts and her worries, and that could only be a good thing.

'I'm sure he would; shall we go and ask? He might still be there.'

Jessie beamed. 'Drink up,' she urged. 'The Variety Girls are going back to work! That means you too, Dolly.'

Chapter 6

To Jessie's delight the front doors were still unlocked and the girls hurried into the auditorium to find Jack sitting alone. He was leaning forward, his head in his hands as though he was praying. As well he might be, thought Jessie. She'd been praying too, for so many things.

He lifted his head, surprised to see them, and sat back in his seat, somewhat uncomfortable, as if he hadn't wanted anyone to see him despondent. Jessie thought he looked drained, his earlier enthusiasm having deserted him. His shirt collar was undone, his tie loose about his neck. For a moment she was wrong-footed, knowing that they had intruded, but he smiled, and she felt her confidence returning.

'Could we use the stage to rehearse, Jack? It's OK if not, you only have to say.'

Jack put up a hand. 'Careful, Jessie, you'll be talking me out of it before I've given it any thought.' She grinned, flustered.

'We wanted to try a few things. Work on a routine, or an act we can use when the Empire opens again.'

He stood up, punched his fist across his body. 'That's the attitude. I'm glad you're optimistic, Jessie, girls. Let's hope it's not too long, eh?' He made a sweeping arc with his arm. 'The stage is yours. Do you know where the working lights are?' He picked up his jacket, laying it across his arm.

'I do,' Frances said.

'Good, that's good.' He was forcing himself to be positive, but it wasn't working and Jessie wondered if he'd already had bad news regarding the theatre. She felt a shiver run through her. If the Empire didn't reopen she would have to go elsewhere, leave Barkhouse Lane and start again. Jack wouldn't give in so easily, would he? He cleared his throat.

'I'll be up in my office for a while yet. Mike's already gone, so if you need to stay longer, I only have the one key.'

Dolly leant forward. 'I can ask Dad. He still has the stage-door key.'

'Perfect.' Jack said. 'I'll lock up the front when I leave. If you get the key, Dolly, you girls can come and go as you please.' He looked about him, to the circle, the boxes, the stage with such sadness that Jessie wanted to hug him and tell him it would all be better, even though she had no idea that it would – none of them did – but it didn't mean you stopped trying. He patted the top of the seat. 'I'll leave you girls to it.'

They watched him walk away, the doors banging behind him, echoing throughout the auditorium.

'I'll put the lights on,' Frances said, making her way down the aisle and up the steps onto the stage. She disappeared into the darkness of the wings and suddenly Jessie felt deflated, all the energy from the fun she'd had in the café deserting her. Ginny noticed and rubbed at Jessie's back. It comforted her, reminding her how lucky she was to have friends.

'Don't lose heart now, Jessie. It's still a good idea.'

'It is,' Dolly encouraged. 'And starting anything is always the hardest part.'

They heard the thump of the lever as Frances threw the switch for the lights and the stage was illuminated.

Something inside Jessie shifted. Frances walked out onto the stage, her fists on her hips.

'What are you waiting for, Delaney? Get your backside up here!' The three girls grinned and dashed up the steps to join her.

'Give me a shove to get the piano on stage,' Jessie called over her shoulder, racing up the steps to the stage, her energy returning. Dolly and Ginny followed her into the wings, but Frances stepped between them.

'I'll do that, Ginny.' Jessie froze, looked quickly at Ginny and then to Frances. Had she given the game away? Ginny reddened again. Frances didn't appear to have noticed. She stood one end of the piano, ready to push, and Jessie hurried to the other side. 'You bring the chair,' Frances said. 'The maestro needs to put her big bottom somewhere.' Dolly giggled and it broke the tension.

When the piano was where they wanted it, Jessie sat down and made a performance of wiggling her fingers, cracking her knuckles.

'Save it for the paying punters, Jessie,' Frances said. 'We have work to do.'

Jessie began to play anything that came into her head, songs from the summer show, songs her father had played. How she longed for him, to feel his arms about her once more, to feel safe. She was trying not to be fearful, to keep chipper for her mother's sake if not her own. It wasn't easy but at least music gave her strength and solace when so little else did. Dolly leant on the piano facing Jessie and rested her chin on her hands. Occasionally Jessie glimpsed the girls moving about the stage and when they stopped and came to lean on the piano alongside Dolly, she stopped too.

'Enough of enjoying ourselves, Jessie. We need to get to work.' Frances stepped back and walked across the stage.

'We should have brought our practice shoes, Ginny. It would've made it easier.'

Jessie twisted on the chair, holding onto the back of it. 'It was all a bit spur of the moment, but we'll be more organised in future. We can soon put things together.'

The door at the back of the auditorium opened, letting in a shaft of light from the foyer. As it closed, a tall, slender woman came sashaying down the aisle. She was dressed in an expensive navy suit and matching hat, a gold and navy clutch bag tucked under her arm. Jessie sprang from the chair as if she'd been electrocuted.

'Good afternoon, Mrs Holland.' Frances smiled and Jessie blushed, feeling as though she'd been caught out at school.

Jack Holland's wife looked along the empty seats. 'Where's my husband?'

Jessie stepped forward. 'He's in his office on the first floor.'

'I know quite well where his office is,' she snapped. 'Has he asked you to rehearse?'

'We asked. Ja-Mr Holland said we could use the stage,' Jessie explained. 'We're putting an act together. For when the theatre reopens.' The woman raised one perfectly shaped eyebrow and Jessie felt like a small child.

'*If* it reopens.' She looked the girls up and down and, by the expression on her face, found them wanting. Jessie put her hands behind her back, standing more upright. She didn't like being inspected by anyone. It was how Aunt Iris had made her feel. That no matter how hard she tried, she would never quite be good enough. The woman looked all around her then turned back.

'I hope you won't be too long,' she said, firmly. 'All those lights are expensive. I needn't remind you of the cost of the electricity.' She spun on her heel and they watched her walk back down the aisle and out of the door.

'Cow!' spat Frances.

Dolly sighed. 'He's such a lovely man. I can't imagine how he came to marry her.'

'Once she dug her claws into him I doubt he could escape.' Frances said. 'And I bet he wanted to, poor sod.'

Jessie was disappointed. 'Perhaps we should turn off the lights, go home.'

'Don't you dare,' Frances said. 'Jack was delighted when you asked. Poor bugger looked like he'd got the world on his shoulders until you walked in. We need to support him too. If we have an act, that'll help. And we'll be cheap.'

'But not *that* cheap,' Jessie countered.

'That's the spirit.' Frances rubbed her hands together. 'Right, let's get down to work. What are we going to do first?'

They found more chairs backstage and brought them into the light. Dolly went off in search of some paper and a pencil, came back and sat herself down facing the girls, pencil poised. Frances said, 'You can be the producer, Dolly.'

'And the director,' Jessie added.

Dolly's eyes sparkled. 'Ooh, I do feel important! Does this mean I'm in show business at last?'

Frances winked at her. 'You're an honorary Variety Girl, remember? You're already in show business.'

They spent a happy couple of hours selecting songs, working out routines, and the fact that the country was at war and the theatres closed seemed to fade into the distance. They put their heads together and worked amicably, selecting first the songs and then the harmonies.

'You have a lovely voice, Frances,' Jessie said. 'Really lovely. You should sing more.'

Frances smiled. 'Thanks, Jessie. It's nothing like yours but I can hold a tune well enough. I used to sing a lot.'

'When?' Dolly asked.

'I suppose the nearest I came to success of any kind was as understudy for Ruby Randolph in *Lavender Lane*.' She paused, wondering whether she had said too much. It was odd talking about her past, she usually avoided any conversation that might lead there. The girls were giving her their full attention, waiting for her to go on. She didn't have to tell them everything. 'When they left for America, I took the lead for a while.'

'Wow, that's amazing,' Dolly gushed. 'That was a *huge* success. Wasn't it a record-breaking run?'

'It was. Still is, I believe.'

'And you worked with the Randolphs?' Dolly hadn't been there when she'd spoken of them last week. She didn't want to keep talking, but you could never mention working with the Randolphs and hope to keep the conversation short. Everyone was fascinated by them.

'What were they like, Frances? I've heard she's fun.'

Frances stared into the darkness of the auditorium and considered her answer. 'She is, most of the time.' It didn't hurt to blur the lines a little. How best to describe Ruby? One word would never do. She could be enormously generous one minute, mean-spirited the next. 'There's an enormous amount of pressure being that famous. It makes her a bit volatile.' There was no need to go into details. 'Their mother was very ambitious for them. She pushed them so hard, was the driving force.' That was a nice way of putting it. The woman was dead now and she wouldn't speak ill of her. 'But it worked. They *did* get to the top – and still so young. She's a little younger than I am, almost twenty-two, and Johnny will be twenty-six. They've done well.'

Dolly was star-struck. 'I can't imagine what it must be like to be on stage with all these huge stars.'

'You're such a dark horse, Frances. You never speak of what you've done in the past. I thought you'd stayed in the chorus.' Jessie leant forward. 'You must tell us more, mustn't she, girls? We want to hear all about it.'

Frances was torn. Talking usually helped her marshal her thoughts, helped unknot the mess of her head. But not now. Perhaps if she and Jessie had been alone. They were kind, sweet girls, but they had no idea of what could happen to a woman. And that was the difference. She was a woman and they were still girls. Except for Ginny. If she was right, and she had no reason to doubt her suspicions, Ginny had a hard and difficult path to walk. She was putting on a brave face but Frances could see through it, just as Patsy had seen through hers.

'Enough,' she said, getting to her feet. 'We've plenty of time to talk and the lights are burning money. We can't make Mrs Holland more sour than she already is.' She pushed her chair back. 'Jack has been generous. Let's make the most of the time we have and talk later.'

At four thirty Frances stopped them working. 'I've got to go. I have to be at the pub for five and I need to have a quick wash and freshen up beforehand, grab something to eat. See you at home, Jessie.' She sprang down the steps and headed outside, glad to be going to the fresh air, albeit for a short time.

Jessie turned to the other two. 'At least we've got some songs, some routines. We can work more on the harmonies. We don't need the theatre for that.'

'I'll pop and get the key from Dad,' Dolly said.

Jessie and Ginny put the chairs back in the wings, leaving the piano where it was.

'I think Frances knows,' Ginny said, her voice hardly more than a whisper. Jessie was quick to reply.

'I haven't said anything, Ginny. I promised – and I wouldn't dream of breaking it.'

Ginny threw the switch to kill the stage lights. They stood in the pale shadows and walked towards the stage door to wait for Dolly. 'I know you haven't. I just got a funny feeling in the café. And then she wouldn't let me move the piano.' She touched Jessie's arm. 'I know you noticed it too.'

Jessie looked down at her hands. 'Maybe you should tell her.' It would make it easier for both of them. She hated keeping secrets. 'Frances is older. She'll ... Well, you know, she might know things, know what to do.' Jessie was frightened for Ginny. Since the girl had confided in her, she'd been anxious, feeling overwhelmed by a rising sense of panic, wanting to help and not knowing where to start. She wanted to tell Grace, wanted to fix things, but Ginny had asked her not to tell and she couldn't break her promise.

'Please, don't say anything,' Ginny pleaded. 'It might not be anything at all. It's been so unsettling. War. The show ending. The girls leaving. And worst still, Billy going without a backward glance. I already feel used and stupid, and I know Frances disapproved of him.'

'Of him, yes. But not you, Ginny. You haven't done anything wrong.'

Ginny sighed. 'Not many people will see it like that, Jessie. They'll think I got what I deserve for letting him have his way.' She shook her head in despair.

'You're just one of the unlucky ones, Ginny.' She rubbed at the girl's shoulder. She was painfully thin, her soft features made sharp with fear, and Jessie wished she could do more. 'I want you to know you're not alone. I'm going to help. If it is,' she fumbled for the words, 'what you think it is.'

'Thanks. But I shouldn't think your mum will be too pleased, you keeping my company.'

Jessie pulled her close, hoping to give her some comfort. 'My mum has been in show business for almost all of her life in some way or another. She's much tougher than you think, than anyone thinks.'

The door opened and Dolly breezed in, all smiles. 'The key to the kingdom,' she said, dangling it in front of her.

'Or queendom,' Jessie said, letting Ginny go in front of her. The two of them stood to one side as Dolly locked the door and tugged at it. She slipped the key into her pocket.

'Tomorrow?' she said, encouragingly.

Jessie agreed. It wasn't as if they had anything else to do. 'I don't see why not. Frances is too good not to pick it up later.' She looked down the street. 'Who'd have thought it? The Randolphs ... That girl's full of surprises.'

Chapter 7

Frances opened the back door of the Fisherman's Arms, pulled the blackout curtain aside and went in. It wouldn't be dark for at least another couple of hours, but Lil, the landlady, had taken to leaving it permanently across. She'd told Frances she had enough to do without fannying around with whether curtains were open or not. The back door was rarely used and it seemed sensible. Lil ran the pub on her own and it was long hours, seven days a week, so Frances imagined any shortcuts would be welcome.

'Is that you, Frances?'

Frances stepped into the private sitting room at the back of the bar, where Lil was having a last cigarette before opening up. 'No, Lil. You've got it wrong. You have to say, "Is it yourself?"'

Lil took a drag then twisted her ciggie in the ashtray on the mantelpiece behind her.

'I haven't got the voice for it, flower. Or the charm.' She adjusted her bra straps and her bosom welcomed the lift. Lil was a well-upholstered woman and went out as much at the front as she did at her backside. She was in perfect proportion and had plenty of padding.

Frances draped her coat over the back of one of the two easy chairs that faced the gas fire. The room was cosy but chaotic. A small table was up against one wall, one of the flaps permanently out, old copies of the *Grimsby Telegraph* were piled high, and a stack of buff envelopes and letters had accumulated beside them, while a tin can held numerous pencils that Lil used for her crosswords. The furnishings were old and heavy, too big for the room, but Frances reflected that it was like Lil herself: warm and welcoming and built for comfort, not beauty.

'I see your filing system is under control,' Frances said, grinning at the clutter on the table.

'It works for me, so don't knock it until you've tried it.' She turned to the mirror over the fireplace and checked her appearance, picked her lipstick up from the mantelpiece and slicked some on, smacked her lips. 'Eeh, them chaps out there don't know how lucky they are! I look just like Mae West tonight.' She patted her bleached blonde hair that was set in tight curls about her broad face. 'Come up and see me sometime.' She turned to Frances. 'Do you think I can carry it off?' Frances grinned.

'If anyone can, you can, Lil.'

The older woman smiled and pressed Frances's arm. 'You're a good lass, Frances, I like you. I reckon Him upstairs sent you my way in this darkness.'

'Him upstairs?' Lil pointed to the ceiling. Frances was puzzled. 'Do you have a lodger?'

Lil roared with laughter. 'I meant God, lovey. Upstairs. Hell, if I had a man upstairs, I wouldn't be down here with you!' She rubbed her hands briskly, 'Let's let that rum lot in, shall we?' She led the way like Boadicea and opened the door that led to the back of the bar. The tea towels were quickly removed from the pumps, the drawer to the till put in place. Frances lifted the flap of the bar, quickly checking that every table had an ashtray and a selection of beermats as Lil had instructed. When that was done, she pulled aside the curtains that covered the front door, twisting her head to look at Lil, her hand reaching up to the top bolt.

'Shall I let them in?'

Lil bent her neck and looked up at the big brown clock over the bar that told customers when they could drink and when they could not. The woman stood rigid as the second hand clicked round and finally fell on the hour.

'Right, let's 'ave 'em, then.' She turned back to the bar, one hand on the bitter pump, the other on the counter. Frances unfastened the top and bottom bolts and unlocked the door.

A tall, thin man was waiting on the doorstep, newspaper under his arm, his Jack Russell terrier, Fudge, at his side. He let the dog go before him and Fudge immediately took his regular place on the seat by the fire. As the dog's owner came up to the bar, Lil placed a pint of bitter in front of him. 'Evening, Artie.' He handed over his coins, took his pint and sat in the corner next to Fudge. Frances took her place beside Lil.

'Does he ever speak?' she whispered.

'Never. Probably be nowt but tripe if he did. Still, he comes in here, regular as clockwork, has two pints, reads the paper and off he trots. I could do with a few more like him. No trouble.'

Frances took up a duster that was tucked behind the till and began wiping the shelves. Lil laughed. 'You'll not have time for that, I hope. Best put that back where it came from.'

Frances did as she was told. She had no idea how busy they would be. When Lil had taken her on she'd hoped that things would stay as they were, war or not, but she wasn't certain and so hadn't been able to offer Frances a regular shift. But people started to drift in, haphazardly, mostly elderly regulars who were not going to let Hitler dictate their habits.

A short man wearing a suit and a bowler hat came in, his body rolling from side to side. 'Used to be a fisherman,' Lil said from the side of her mouth. 'Tell 'em a mile off.

Roll around like they're on the bloody water all the time. Makes my head spin if there's a few of 'em come in all at once.' She called out as he swayed towards them, 'Now then, Charlie, missus let you out for a bit?'

'I hope I get it, Lil,' Charlie said cheerfully. He leant on the bar and tossed his coins onto the beer towel.

She tilted her head. 'He says that every time, Frances.'

'Cos you ask me every time, Lil.' He nodded at Frances. ''Ow do.'

'Evening,' Frances said, unsure how to respond. Should she say ''ow do' too? Or would he think she was mocking him? Lil reached to the shelf under the bar and pulled out a half-pint glass, handed it to Frances. 'Bottle of stout in there, Franny.' Frances reached for a bottle of Mackeson, flipped the top and poured, filling the glass halfway as Lil had shown her, then put both glass and bottle on the bar in front of Charlie. Charlie looked at her approvingly.

'That'll do nicely, darlin'.'

Lil patted her back. 'You'll do, lass. You'll do just fine.'

The door swung open again; there was a rustle of the curtain and a man appeared, who almost filled the doorway. He was over six feet tall, smartly dressed, his thick sandy hair brushed back off his square forehead. He reminded Frances of a B-movie actor, John Wayne, only not as rugged, but definitely the strong silent type. From his walk Frances guessed he was a landlubber and she grinned at the thought. Lil was teaching her well. He looked about him, tipping his head in a slight nod to the other men in the room, then came to the bar, pulled out the stool by the corner and took a seat.

'Pint of the usual, Malc?'

'Aye, if you please, Lil.' He gave Frances a half-smile. 'Hullo, lass.'

'Evening,' Frances offered, playing it safe.

Lil took a tankard from the back shelf. 'Watch,' she said to Frances. She poured a pint of bitter, tilting the glass then slowly bringing it upright as the tankard filled, leaving a foamy head about half an inch thick. She placed it in front of the man, who put his hand around it but didn't lift it straight away. 'This is Big Malc,' she said. 'That's *his* tankard and that's how he likes his pint pulled. Got it?' Frances wondered what Big Malc would do if she didn't. Lil threw back her head and laughed, her generous bosom wobbling. 'Only teasing.' Big Malc grinned. 'This is Franny, Malc. She's like an angel from heaven, come just at the right time.' Malc put his hand across the bar and Frances took it. His hand was big, his grip firm but warm. Up close, he had a kind face, but Frances wondered how many people ever got that close.

'Glad to hear it, Lil. Sorry that Ted left you in the lurch, but I suppose it's same for everyone. Some 'as got their call-up papers already.'

Lil put one hand on the bar, leaning forward, the other on her hip. 'I know. I hope it don't last as long as last time. Can't be doing with that, can we?' Malc shook his head, supped his beer.

Customers came in a steady stream after that and there was no time to chat, the bar three-deep with blokes holding out their glasses to be refilled. The bar curved round and a partition divided the snug from the smoke room. It seemed pointless to Frances, for the noise as the place filled up was unavoidable and smoke from pipes and cigarettes created a hazy fug which rose slowly towards the mustard-coloured ceiling.

As the night progressed, someone sat down at the piano and started to play. Frances couldn't see who it was, but they played a string of oldies that some people sang and others hummed along to. The refrain of 'Danny Boy' took her back to home and left her feeling odd for a few moments, but it was too busy to dwell on home and she was glad, just then, to be too busy to think.

When the rush died off, Frances refreshed the sink with hot water and the two women dealt with the glasses that had accumulated at the end of the counter, Frances washing, Lil drying. She stuck a tea towel in the glass and rubbed with efficiency born of years of practice, twisting and replacing the glasses on the shelves with economy. Some of the men were the worse for drink, their laughter louder, their smiles broader. Women with heavy lipstick and large cleavages leant in, talking close to the men, and Frances looked on impassively, glad she didn't have to do that.

'Don't judge 'em, Franny,' Lil said, looking in the same direction. 'Some of them get knocked about a bit but they don't know no better.'

'I wasn't judging,' Frances said, disappointed that Lil thought that of her. And as she thought it, she realised that Lil was right, she *had* been judging in a way, being glad she wasn't one of them. Lil began wiping the bar down with a damp cloth.

'Not all of them are drunks, you know. And when they're at sea, by gum, what a life that is! Only home a few days and they don't have to drink much to get merry. Some of 'em overdo it, but then there's them that's on land don't fare no better – and *they* don't have to contend with big seas and sleeping where they stand. It's a rum old life. People judge 'em wrong. They don't know the 'alf of it.'

'Lots of people judge harshly, Lil.' She'd had to contend with enough people passing judgement on her these last few years. Bad enough that she was Irish, that held enough problems in some quarters, and she had only added to her problems.

'Born out of ignorance, flower.'

'My friend is married to a trawler man. A skipper.'

'Then you'll know exactly what I mean.'

Frances nodded. Not that Colin talked much about his time at sea. He'd talk of the catch and the times he'd seen the aurora borealis, the colours of the skies, the seagulls, the whales and other sea creatures. But he didn't speak of the seas and the life too much and now she wondered whether it was not to frighten Patsy. He'd mentioned that she wasn't used to this life on more than one occasion, but did you ever get used to your husband being away so much? A young lad, who looked barely old enough to be served, squeezed himself to the front of the bar. Lil stepped forward.

'What can I get ya, sonny?'

'Can the dark-haired one serve me?'

Lil winked at her. 'He wants the pretty 'un to serve him. No taste.' She moved further up the bar and got busy with another order.

'You're not from round here, are ya?' the lad ventured as Frances poured him a bitter shandy. He was fresh-faced, his cheeks ruddy, and she wondered if he was even old enough to shave. He reached forward, his change in one hand, accepting his pint with the other.

'No, I'm from Ireland.'

'Long way from home.'

She was suddenly overcome with longing. 'I am.' He was a sweet lad. He blushed as she answered, at a loss as what to say next. 'Are you?' she asked, wanting to put him at ease.

'Round corner. Barkhouse Lane. D'ya know it?'

'I know it well.' Other people were coming for orders and she had to break off to serve them. 'I live there, with my friends.'

'Knew I'd seen ya before.' He beamed with satisfaction. 'You one o' those girls what was in the show at the Empire?'

She nodded an answer, taking money from the customer she had been serving, ringing it in the till and handing over the change. As she worked, the boy, Wilf, waited for his answer, then his turn to speak. She didn't recognise him but then she'd spent most of the time in the theatre or with the girls. He was quiet, supping his pint as Frances continued serving. Through the mirror that ran along the back of the bar she could see him watching her. Lil stood next to her, waiting for Frances to count out the change so that she could ring in another order.

'He'll be in every night now, looking out for you.'

'He doesn't look old enough to be in here.'

'Probably isn't, flower.' She rang in her order, slipped the ten-bob note in the drawer and counted out the change, handed it back to the customer. The pair of them leant against the back of the bar, watching the show before them. Big Malc was still on his seat at the corner of the bar – he'd only moved to go to the lavatory. He chatted briefly to other customers but mostly watched the goings-on, nursing a pint which he drank at a slow, steady pace.

Wilf was still at the bar. Occasionally he turned to lean against it, watching the banter of the crowd, the ones that spoke too loud, the raised voices, the gentle words, the steady sigh of the room as different groups got up to meander out of the bar and onto the streets. Frances went from behind the bar to collect glasses and bottles, weaving between the tables and the wandering hands, glad that she was supple and they were slowed by alcohol. They were mostly a friendly crowd, respectful, and if they said something too forward, the more sober of their friends put them in their place. There were kind words and apologies in abundance and she felt at ease under the watchful eye of Lil. One word from her and they behaved.

They had another stint of washing glasses.

'That lad hasn't moved all night.'

'You'll see a lot like him, Franny, young and old. They're lonely. You're here to cheer 'em up.'

'Not too far from what I usually do.' Frances drained the dirty water. 'That's what Jack calls it.'

'What?' Lil hung a damp tea towel over the open bar flap.

'The theatre. He calls it the cheer-up business.'

'Well, he's right. They don't come here to hear your troubles, they come to get away from everything for an hour or two, or as much as their pocket can stretch to.'

Frances picked up a cloth to give Lil a hand with drying and stared out across the bar. 'I'm glad they never shut the pubs.'

'Shut the pubs!' Lil spluttered. 'There'd be a ruddy riot and no mistake.'

Lil leant back, looked up at the clock and rang the brass bell underneath it, shouting, 'Last orders!' There was a rush for drinks and then she called time. Frances collected glasses as people drifted out, calling night to Lil, holding up a hand and making sure Frances was included, whether they knew her name or not. Some of them walked perfectly well, others swayed and staggered. Lil called, 'Do be nice!' and the last couple of drinkers supped up and left.

'Will I see you here tomorrow?' Wilf asked Frances.

Lil interrupted. 'Monday, lad, she'll be here Monday.' She pressed Frances's arm. 'That all right with you, Franny?'

Frances's shoulders dropped with the relief, knowing she had met with Lil's approval. Lil hadn't made any promises other than to take it shift by shift to see how it went. It had been hard work, but Lil was fun, she paid cash in hand and the tips had been good. A half-pint glass that Lil had told her to put by the till had filled with coppers and thrupenny bits. It would all help. As Wilf went to the door, Big Malc got to his feet.

'See you tomorrow, Lil.'

'Aye, thanks, Malc.'

He said goodnight to them both. 'Lock up after me, Lil.'

She put up a hand. 'Right behind ya.' Frances heard the bolts slide into place as she cleared the remaining glasses. The two of them went around emptying the ashtrays and wiping them with a damp cloth.

'Have you got time for a nightcap before you go?'

'A quick one.' Frances was tired but her brain was fizzing. She finished washing the glasses and Lil wiped the counter. When she was done, she took the money drawer from the till and passed it to Frances.

'Take that in the backroom for me, will ya, love? While I turn off the lights.'

Frances went through, pushed aside a few papers and put the till drawer on the table. Lil followed soon after, carrying a bottle of whisky and two glasses that she squeezed onto the table, shoving the drawer aside with her elbow. 'Want a drop of water in yours?'

'That would be grand.'

Lil fetched a small jug of water from the kitchen and put it on the table, putting the papers on one of the dining chairs.

'Move that coat and sit yourself down, you can help me tot up.' Frances picked up the red coat and placed it on the easy chair, alongside her own while Lil poured the drinks. 'Be quicker with the two of us.' Lil took an envelope from the pile and a pencil from the tin. She scooped the shillings from the tray, pushing them across the table. 'Add that up and tell me how much.' They worked their way through the coins, the half-crowns and the coppers. Lil licked the pencil nib, totted it up in her head, and wrote the total, picked up her glass and smiled at Frances. 'Not a bad night at all.' She took a small sip of her whisky. 'So, what d'ya think then, Reckon you can stick it out with me?'

'If you want me, Lil, I'm here.' Lil counted the change out of the takings and pushed it in Frances's hand. 'And don't forget your tips behind the bar. You can take 'em now or leave 'em until you've got a few bob.' She sipped her whisky. 'I don't know how long I'll need you, lass. I'd thought I might be a bit light this week, but it's not been much different. Most of the regulars are old 'uns and too old for service. Although Artie and Charlie are ARP now.'

Frances took a sip of her whisky, added more water.

'What about Big Malc?' As the words came out, she wished they hadn't. Lil would think she was being nosey. Lil leant back in the chair; if she had minded, she didn't say anything.

'Malc used to be a friend of my hubby, mates since they were lads. I think he feels he needs to watch over me, since Jimmy died, like. I don't need it, but I appreciate it. He's a kind man.' Lil put her hand on the table, looked at her wedding ring. She became quieter, more reflective. 'Keeps asking me to marry him now and again.'

'Would you?'

Lil shook her head. 'No, lovey. Three's enough for any woman.' Frances raised her eyebrows. 'Oh, aye. I've never been short of admirers but I can manage on my own. I can't go through the heartache again.' She took another swig from her glass. 'Bend down and put that gas fire on, lovey. It's got a bit chilly now we've sat down.' Frances did as she was asked. 'Have you got to rush off?'

Frances sat back down. 'No. No one to rush home for.'

'Pretty lass like you? You do surprise me.' She felt as if Lil could see right through her, that the woman knew all her secrets. For once it didn't bother her.

'There was once,' was all she was willing to offer. Lil didn't press her.

'My first husband, Kenny, was killed at Ypres. Lovely lad, he was. I was full of hopes and dreams when we wed. Worshipped the ground he walked on. He was a dear man.' She closed her eyes, a smile playing on her face. Frances thought how tired she looked now that it was just the two of them. It was like coming down from the high after a show and Lil certainly gave a performance while she was out front. She opened her eyes. 'I wasn't the only one, though, so it helped. Lot of us women in the same boat.' She drank again. 'Then Bob, he was a good 'un. Laugh! He made me roar with his stories.'

'What happened?' She was nervous to ask.

'Accident. He worked down the docks. Looked up one day and a sack hit him in the wrong place. Killed outright. A blessing when you see how some people suffer, lass.' She added a splash of water to her glass. 'Jimmy suffered. He'd been in the trenches too. Never got over it. Filled his pockets with rocks and walked into the water last summer. I don't think he could cope with another war. He was such a kind, gentle man, tall, dark and handsome. You'd have liked him and he would have liked you.' She stared at Frances, who didn't want to look away from Lil's pain. 'I reckon he sent you along, lass. He was like that. Help anyone except himself.' She emptied the glass, thoughtfully. 'The damage the war did goes on and on.'

The clock on the mantelpiece chimed midnight.

'I better go, Lil. I have to be up early tomorrow.'

'Of course. I've kept you too long. Will you be all right walking home? Do you want me to walk with you?' Frances took her coat from beneath Lil's red one then picked up her gas mask and flung it over her shoulder.

'I'll be fine. It's only five-minute walk. I'm getting used to it now and the moon's still quite bright.'

Lil got to her feet. 'It's been nice talking to you, Frances. I think you and me will get along fine.'

Frances grinned, pulled aside the curtain over the back door, and repeated Big Malc's words, 'Lock up after me, Lil.'

Lil grinned too. 'Aye, I will.'

It was cool outside after the warmth of the small sitting room and she stood for a minute, letting her eyes become accustomed to the darkness before opening the back gate and stepping out into the street. Her feet stung and she reeked of stale ale and nicotine, but it had been a good night. Lil was grand to work for and even if Jack got another show going, she'd be happy to work the odd shift with Lil. Tonight she had felt closer to confiding in Lil than she ever had to Jessie and it saddened her. But Lil had lived, she would understand. She snapped the latch and stepped out, pulling the gate shut; as she did so someone came up close behind her and she froze, her heart thumping wildly. She turned quickly. If she screamed, would Lil hear?

'Sorry, sorry, Frances.' She recognised the voice. 'It's Wilf, s-s-s-sorry. I didn't want to frighten you.' He put his hands out but didn't touch her, awkward, embarrassed. 'It's so dark in the blackout and I didn't want you walking home alone.' He was agitated, shifting from one foot to the other.

She pressed her hand to her chest and could feel her heart hammering away.

'Lord, you half-scared me to death, Wilf! Have you been waiting here all that time?' As her eyes adjusted further, she could see his distraught expression and she felt for him. 'You daft thing, I'm perfectly all right. It's not far.' His face fell and she softened. 'But thanks, Wilf, that's very chivalrous of you.' She started to walk, her legs still trembling from the shock. 'You mustn't lurk about on corners, Wilf. You'll give someone a heart attack.' She adjusted the strap on her shoulder. 'I was about to batter you with my gas mask.' She laughed and he said again, 'Sorry, Frances.'

She nudged him with her arm. 'Don't let me hear you say sorry again. Let's get home, 'cos I'm shattered.' They walked along in silence because she was too tired to make small talk. 'This is me,' she said as she came to the house.

'Bye, Frances,' he said quietly, walking on down to the bottom of the street. He was a boy, not much older than Eddie, and she said a silent prayer that this war wouldn't last; that, unlike the Great War, it really would be over by Christmas. She watched him turn into the house by the alleyway, put her key in the lock and went inside, ready to fall into bed.

Chapter 8

The vans were already lined up, steam pouring out from the chimney of the Little Laundry on Barkhouse Lane. The air smelled of soap and coal from the hopper that heated the boiler and a steady stream of women and girls spilled into the entrance doors. Ginny hurried to join them. Alf Naylor was leaning against the back wall, having a last drag on his fag, and he lifted his hand in greeting, knocking the ash away with his finger at the same time. He winked at her.

'Here's our lovely dancing girl, bright as the morning.' It made her smile, even though she didn't feel much like it. He took another drag, flicked his fag end to the floor, ground it with his heel and kicked it alongside the others he'd smoked that week. It was only Tuesday and already there was a tidy pile in the corner. He rubbed his hands together. 'Better get in there before ol' droopy drawers gets stroppy.' He stood back to let her pass and Phyl came running up, her arms high, pulling back her hair and securing it with an elastic band.

'Made it!' she called, following Ginny inside. The overwhelming smell of soap made Ginny nauseous and she stepped to one side, closing her eyes for a second, wishing she'd eaten something. Phyl clocked in and Ginny took her card from the slot, waiting for her turn.

Edna Bowers was standing against the wall, looking as if she'd sucked on a lemon, pristine in her white overall and turban.

'Get your backside in sharpish, Thompson. We don't have time for prima donnas here.'

Alf closed the door, bringing with him the tang of nicotine, and Ginny tried not to breathe.

'Leave the kid alone, Edna. Poor lass has barely set foot in the place and you're on her back.'

Edna sneered. 'As well I might be. I haven't got time for slackers.' She disappeared into the laundry, the double doors banging behind her.

'Thanks, Alf.'

He winked at her. 'You don't have to thank me, lass. Take no notice of her. Her bark's worse than her bite.'

Phyl grabbed her arm. 'Come on, Dolly Daydream. She'll be barking again if you don't get a shake on.' Ginny followed Phyl into the cloakroom, where they hung their coats and left their bags. Women were hurrying into the main laundry room, the doors held open, the warm air flooding into the cloakroom. Ginny quickly pulled on her blue overall, tucking her hair inside the matching hat. She tried not to think of the heat, which would worsen as the day went on. Betty, from the hand-ironing team, put a hair-grip between her teeth to stretch it open, then used it to secure her starched cap.

'You look a bit peaky, Ginny. Are you all right?'

Ginny nodded.

'I'm fine. Couldn't sleep, that's all.'

'Me neither,' the woman said, patting down her overall and sticking out her large bosom. 'I'll be glad when Eric buggers off back to sea. The sound of his snoring is like a ruddy foghorn when he's had a drink. I bet they can hear 'im at t'other end of our street.'

Phyl laughed. 'I heard him in mine. I thought it was an earthquake.'

Ginny grinned. It was a lot like the banter they had in the dressing rooms before they went on stage and she enjoyed the good-natured leg-pulling. If she didn't feel so bad she'd join in, but her head felt like cotton wool and her mouth tasted of rust.

'We'll see if you're still laughing when you're wed to our Terry and he's the foghorn!' Betty strode after the others and Ginny and Phyl followed. The room was beginning to hum with the sound of the washers, the whoosh of water and clatter of the wicker baskets being pushed along the floor once they had been sorted. Ginny had worked there for five days now and was beginning to get used to the overwhelming smell of soda that had burned her nostrils on the first day. At first it had seemed fresh and she'd associated it with cleanliness and her mother, but over time, as the building grew hot with toil, it only added to her sense of sickness and detachment. Over by the machines Vera and Sylv were on sorting, sifting through the linen and clothing that was piled high in wicker baskets, before being loaded into the machines. They would be moved into the dryers then on to the steam rolling irons. In the far corner was a row of ironing boards, where six girls stood pressing shirts and fine silk blouses.

Phyl and Ginny went to the flat steam roller and picked up a sheet, grabbing the four corners, folding it in half then half again before feeding it through the machine.

'By heck, my mum would've loved to have one of these years ago,' she called to Phyl. 'The hours she spent ironing, breaking her back.' Her mum been almost permanently bent over an iron, a pile of clothing behind her, but always finding a smile for Ginny no matter how tired she was.

'Aye, must be ruddy lovely to have the luxury of having your laundry done for ya. How the other 'alf live, eh?'

She reached down for another sheet, waited while Ginny found the corners.

'I keep worrying about our Dan and Kenny, gone off in the army,' Phyl said. 'We ain't heard from 'em yet. I wish they hadn't gone so soon.' Ginny tugged at the sheets and Phyl did the same. It made her think of her own brothers. All four of them had escaped, one by one, as soon as they could, taking whatever work that would get them away from their dad's fists. Would they have joined up too?

'It's early days,' Ginny said, trying to concentrate as sounds in the laundry grew louder, raising her voice. 'I expect you'll hear from them before long.'

Phyl tilted her chin upwards.

'Aye, just me being impatient.' She grinned. 'Never could wait, not even for the lavvy.' Ginny laughed and the two of them fell quiet as the noise grew louder and made conversation nigh on impossible. They worked quietly, using mime and their facial expressions to communicate. The room became much hotter as the steam presses worked their magic, the dryers and washers rumbling along in the background. Light flooded in through the doors that Alf had wedged open and 'Sticky' Sam went around with his pole and opened the top windows to let in some air. The room was lit by long lights high in the ceiling. It added to the heat and stuffiness and she felt herself stumble forward as she leant into the wicker basket for another sheet.

Phyl caught her hand and steadied her. 'You don't look well, are you sure you can manage?'

Ginny rested one hand on the basket, pressing her lips together as she felt bile rising again. She focused on the ground, not the noise of the machines, nor the heat.

'I drank some milk this morning.' She looked up, smiled broadly. 'I think it was off.' She took up another sheet but felt lightheaded and leant again on the basket, gripping the side to steady herself.

Edna strutted over. 'What's going on? You'll hold everyone up if you don't keep it moving along the line.' Ginny pulled herself upright but the sudden movement made her head swim.

'She's not well!' Phyl shouted above the noise.

'If she can't do the job, she needs to get another one.' Edna folded her arms across her chest. 'I knew it was a mistake, taking her on. I can tell by her hands. Not used to a hard day's work like the rest of us. Too busy pointing her pretty toes and showing her backside.'

Ginny wanted to laugh. If Edna saw her feet she would soon change her tune. The corns and blisters, the blackened nails and deformed toes. She hadn't come across a dancer yet who liked her feet.

'It won't happen again, Edna. I drank some iffy milk. It's upset my stomach.'

Edna scoffed. 'Your own stupidity then. I was—'

'Edna!' Mr Edwards, the manager, was leaning over the rail on the upper floor where the offices were and calling down to her. She looked up. 'Could I have you for a moment?' She went off, shaking her head, and Phyl pulled a face.

'Take no notice of misery guts. *She* looks like she drinks sour milk all day long!'

Ginny took up the sheet, ready to start again, glad that Edna had been called away. 'I'll try not to.'

The machines tumbled and turned and the sound was like thunder in her head as it grew hotter, and each time she checked the big clock on the back wall, the hands seemed to be in the same position. She looked up again, back to the press, leant down into the basket, tugged at a sheet with Phyl, stood up again. Her head spun, the windows seemed to tilt on the wall, and she heard Phyl call out, 'Catch her!' as she fell backwards onto the floor.

Her vision was blurry when she opened her eyes; someone was hauling her to sit upright, supporting her back. Phyl held a glass out and put it under her lips.

'Try and sip it, Ginny.' She tried to focus but Phyl's face looked odd and misshapen and she blinked until her face became normal. She did as she was urged and sipped. The water was cool and she wanted to gulp it down, but Phyl kept drawing the glass away. Ginny shuffled more upright.

'I'm absolutely fine. It's the heat, that's all it is. It's taking a bit of getting used to.' She couldn't lose this job, for where would she find another, and she still had to find somewhere to stay. There were only two weeks more left on the flat.

Edna came back as Ginny got to her feet and took up a sheet. Her neck was hot and her forehead was burning, but she forced herself to keep going.

'I knew it was a mistake taking you on. Only fit for prancing about the stage, showing what you've got to all and sundry.'

'That's unfair, Edna.'

'You can keep your trap shut an' all.'

Phyl glanced at the clock.

'Time for our break anyway, Edna.' She flipped the switch that stopped the rollers and turned her back on the woman. Taking the sheet from Ginny, she dropped it into the basket and leant in close to whisper in Ginny's ear, 'She's an old sod, been here years. She's never like that with the blokes, only us lasses – and that's all there is left, mostly.'

'I can't blame her, Phyl. Theatricals don't have the best of reputations, unless they're famous. I don't take it personal.'

'She's still an old sod.' She put her hand under Ginny's elbow. 'Come on. Let's get outside while we can.'

The girls sat or leant along the low wall as vans came and went with their loads of dirty or clean laundry. Being out in the fresh air was bliss and a cool breeze blew in off the sea, reviving her a little. Kath held out one of her potted beef sandwiches.

'Get that down ya! Ya need something nourishing, there's nothing on ya. Ya look like a filleted earwig.'

Ginny put her hand up, shook her head.

'I'm fine, thanks, Kath. I must have caught a sickness bug – or it's something I've eaten.' She hadn't eaten much for days, mostly from worry, partly to save money.

'Yeh, course you 'ave,' Sylv chipped in. She was leaning against the higher part of the wall and she pushed her bottom lip forward. 'If you need any help with that sickness bug,' she said, pointedly, 'I know someone who can help.'

Ginny felt her face burn. Phyl flicked her cigarette end over the wall and slipped onto her feet, brushing down the back of her overall.

'Take no notice of her, neither.'

It was a difficult afternoon; her back was aching like the very devil but at least the sickness had gone and for that she was grateful. She carried on with Phyl, bending, tugging and turning, folding and threading the sheets through the press. Her mam would weep if she could see her now.

'When did you start dancing, Ginny?'

'When I was a kid, three, four. My mam took in washing from thc theatre folks to bring in extra money. She took me with her, whether I wanted to go or not.' Phyl smiled and she carried on folding the sheets, feeding the machine. 'She got me free dance lessons, acting, singing – whatever she could barter. She didn't want me to be stuck doing laundry like her.' She blushed. 'Oh, that sounds awful! I didn't mean—'

Phyl laughed.

'Don't apologise. Christ, if I could do summat else I'd be off like a shot! I'd be sticking two fingers up to Edna and singing as I went.' She looked over to the other girls. 'Some of us have already been talking about signing up ourselves. A ruddy regimental sergeant major will be a doddle after Edna.' They looked over at her. 'Atten-shun!' Phyl saluted and the woman turned away. She reached in the basket for another two corners and took hold of them while Ginny found hers. 'I hope you get back on stage soon, Ginny. I'll come an' see ya. We all will.'

They carried on and Ginny thought of her mother, pushing her forward, setting her on a path that she would never have for herself. No, she couldn't stay here much longer. It would be as if her mother's life had been worthless. She had to get back on the stage, she owed it to Mam and nothing was going to stop her, not women like Edna, or men like Billy Lane.

'You've got a bit o' colour in your cheeks now,' Phyl shouted over the noise as they came together over the linen and picked up another sheet. 'Feelin' better?'

'Tons. Whatever it was must have gone through me. I'll be fine.' She felt Edna's eyes on her as the woman moved about the room and she steeled herself to keep going. Phyl was not convinced and she glanced to where Edna was, checking she was far enough away not to hear.

'You still look iffy. Perhaps you should switch to sorting for a bit. It's not so hot and you'll be nearer the doors. I'll work it so you can. You'll get more of a rest while they wait for a delivery.'

Ginny was brisk. 'Don't worry about Edna. She's a pussycat compared to some of my old dance teachers. I've danced all day and all night with blisters and corns on my feet, with torn ligaments and broken toes.' Nothing was easy but you had to make it look as if you were just floating along with the breeze.

When the whistle blew at four, they hurried off to the cloakroom and collected their things. Phyl pulled on her coat and woolly hat, checked herself in the mirror.

'Why don't you come back with us for a bite to eat? Me mam won't mind.'

It was kind but she felt too vulnerable, too exposed. They would ask questions and she was tired; she might slip up. She might cry. She mustn't be weak.

'Thanks, Phyl, but I'd best get back. I think I need an early night.'

Phyl rubbed at Ginny's shoulder. 'Course you do. Another time, then? When you're feeling more chipper?'

Ginny buttoned her coat, pulled her beret from the pocket and put it on. 'I'd like that.'

She walked out of the yard and onto Barkhouse Lane, lingering on the pavement as the other women streamed past her, back to their homes, their families. She looked down towards the house that Jessie and Frances shared. Jessie had invited her for tea on the Monday the other dancers had left and they'd all been so warm and welcoming ... Oh, she longed to go there now, walk in and be part of their home. She shivered, wrapped her arms about herself and made her way to the end of the street, started to walk home then stopped, turned, looked down towards the sea. What was the point in rushing back?

She made her way towards the Empire, knowing it would be locked but wanting to feel attached to something, feel that she mattered. She hurried past the shops, all shuttered, and arrived at the theatre. The photos of summer were still there, and she wished for a moment that she could roll back the days and start again. There was a picture of the star, Madeleine Moore, photos of the girls in their various costumes. She moved to the showcase at the other side of the door. The comedian, Billy Lane, was smiling out at her. How easily she'd fallen for his charms, eager to be loved. She touched the glass. Her fingertips were grubby with dirt and she spat on them, wiped them on her skirt. If only everything could be cleaned away so easily.

The sky was overcast, the clouds thick, and she made her way down towards the pier, the wind on her face. The iron gates at the entrance were locked and she held onto them, peering along the walkway that stretched ahead. All the laughter and happiness of the summer seemed to cling to her shoulders and she wanted to hang onto it but the wind was lifting it away, carrying it up, up, up to the grey skies. She moved away. The tide was out, the edge of the water so far away that it looked as if it would never come in again. How long would it take to walk out that far? More than the energy she had. She leant on the railings and watched seagulls waddle about on the ridges that had been left as the tide receded, pecking for shrimps in the rock pools, drilling down with their beaks for worms. Hunger was tearing at her stomach but she mustn't eat. It wasn't a baby, just a seed – and seeds needed nourishment.

She began walking again, enjoying the feel of the salt air on her skin, tightening, tightening, and crossed the deserted road, started walking up the steps below the Cliff Hotel. The treads were wide and broad. A fall could trigger loss ... Auntie Beryl had lost *her* baby when she fell down the stairs. Could she do that here? She stopped, her hand on the rough concrete of the wall, turned and looked again at the tide, so far, far away. She moved up the steps again, her footsteps heavy. At most she might break her ankle. She would need enough to live on while it mended, but it wouldn't take too long to heal. Yes, yes, there were things she could do …

She kept her head down, focused on each wide tread until she reached the top. She stopped, turned back to look at the sea, then lowered her eyes, slid one foot forward; it wouldn't take much. It would look like an accident. She put her hand to her face, longing to feel her mother's hand there, gentle, protecting. How Mam had loved to watch her dance, her pretty little flame. She leant forward a little further, closed her eyes, wanting to let go of everything, the rail, the world …

She felt a hand on her shoulder and staggered forward, but the hand gripped her firmly, another one at her elbow. The shock of it made her scream and the hands clung tighter, pulling her back, leading her away. When she opened her eyes she saw that it was Frances, her dark hair flying in the wind, her red lips so vivid, everything about her so sharp and wild – alive. She moved her hands to either side of Ginny's shoulders.

'I'm sorry, so, so sorry, Ginny. I didn't mean to startle you.' She was leaning into Ginny. 'I called but you didn't hear me.' Frances held onto her, slowly releasing her grip as Ginny moved away from the top of the steps, guiding her onto the pavement. Her heart was pounding so loudly she couldn't make sense of what Frances was saying. She tried to focus on the shape her friend's lips made.

'How stupid of me! I shouldn't have startled you like that. I've given you a fright. Here, sit down.' She led her over to the shelter by the ornamental gardens and made her sit down on the bench inside it. Ginny put her hand to her throat, her mouth opening and closing. Tears sprang at her eyes and she couldn't hold them back. She could have fallen, so easily. But she knew now that she didn't want to. Cars went past, people on bicycles, the world seemed louder that it had before. And there was Frances, beside her, talking to her. She forced herself to concentrate although she was trembling now and she couldn't stop.

Frances was still apologising, filling the silence, fussing about her, her words a jumble. Blood was coursing through Ginny's ears, a thunderous waterfall, making it difficult to hear.

'Oh, Ginny, you're white as a sheet.'

She must stop this. She must get home.

'You took me by surprise, that's all. I-I'll be fine in a minute or two.' She tried to smile but her teeth were chattering. 'I'll just sit here until I calm down. I'm fine, truly I am.'

Frances shook her head, pushed her dark hair away from her face.

'You are not OK and it's my fault. I saw your red hair and your green beret and I knew it was you. I should have waited for you to turn but I didn't want to make you fall.' She took Ginny's hand in hers. Her fingers were long, her nails perfect ovals, painted red to match her lips. Frances was always so put together. Her hands and arms were expressive when she danced, Ginny had noticed how deeply she felt the music. But it wasn't like that for her. She could dance, but she didn't love dancing, did she? Not like Rita, not like Frances. There was a difference. It was just something she could do, something she'd worked so hard at to please her mother. She swallowed, pressing hard on her lower lip, holding back the tears. She must not think of her mother.

'I'm fine.' Ginny got up, sat down again, stared at the pavement. She was cold, her trembling more violent.

Frances pulled at her arm, gently this time, patted her hand.

'You're coming with me. I can't let you go like this. You're in shock.' Frances took Ginny's hand in hers, her voice softer now. 'Come and meet Lil and I'll get you some hot sweet tea. It's the very least I can do.'

Chapter 9

It was three minutes past six when Frances led Ginny through the front doors of the Fisherman's Arms. Artie was sitting in his usual place, reading the *Telegraph*, Fudge the dog at his side. He raised his eyes when he saw Frances, his wagging tail beating against the leather seat. Lil was pouring Charlie's stout into a glass and she looked up when they came in, her eyes flicking over Frances, then Ginny.

'Sorry, Lil. I'll make the time up.' She pulled one of the empty stools up to the bar flap and made Ginny sit down. 'This is my friend, Ginny. I gave her a fright, nearly knocked her down the stairs, so I did.'

'And you call ya'self a friend.' She passed the half-filled glass and bottle to Charlie, took his money and held it in her hand. 'Friends like that, who needs enemies?' She winked at Ginny. 'Looks like she's frightened you good and proper, you're like death warmed up. Get a drink, Franny, and I'll have one with ya.'

Satisfied that Ginny was not going to move, Frances lifted the flap and went behind the bar and into Lil's sitting room. She hung her coat and gave her hair a quick brush, made herself presentable. Ginny wasn't the only one who had been frightened, for when she looked in the mirror, she could see that she too was pale. A second later and Ginny would have stepped out and thrown herself down the steps. She'd considered it herself not so long ago – and all the alternatives. If it hadn't been for another girl dying from the effects of a backstreet abortion, she might have gone the same way. It had happened that first season in Blackpool and she'd been terrified. The girl had collapsed in the dressing room, blood running down her bare legs. Patsy had taken charge and done her best, but it was all too late. And it had been Patsy who comforted the girls. No wonder she was glad to leave it all behind for Colin; her life was settled now, no longer the dramas, on stage or off, and she knew that was exactly how Patsy liked it. Frances pinched her cheeks which brought a little colour to them and slipped back behind the bar. Lil was already gassing to Ginny and the girl appeared calmer, her cheeks a little flushed. She was nursing a small glass of brandy.

Lil said, 'I reckon Ginny here could do with a hot sweet tea. I'll have one too, Franny. And bring a pie, there's one in the larder. Looks like she needs feeding up.' Ginny protested but Lil was having none of it and Frances was so grateful to the woman for just being her kind-hearted generous self. 'It's left over from lunchtime and I'll not sell it now. Nice to see Franny's friends, lass. I hope we see a lot more of ya.'

Frances went into the backroom, leaving the door from the bar open so that she could hear Lil chatting to Ginny and Ginny laughing, quietly. Poor girl. Frances didn't have to imagine how she'd be feeling – she knew only too well – but what was the best way to help her? She stirred sugar into the tea, took out the pie that Lil had probably saved for her own supper, put it on a tray and went back into the bar. There were a few more customers but not many. Big Malc had arrived and Lil was introducing him to Ginny.

'So, Malc, I reckon my luck's in with these Variety Girls, don't you? I'll have the fellas beating the door down when they see I've got these beauties here.'

Big Malc agreed. 'They're no competition for you, though, Lil.'

'Ah, go on with you!' Lil batted her hand at him. Frances shared out the tea, pushed the pie in front of Ginny and placed a fork beside it.

'I couldn't,' Ginny said.

Lil insisted, 'Course ya can. You look like you could put away a few more an' all. But that'll do ya for now.' Frances sipped at her tea in-between serving but it was quieter on Tuesday, too far away from payday, and the nights were darker, the moon less full, keeping people at home. Ginny was quiet as Frances served and the older girl took every chance she could to watch her through the mirror that ran along the back of the bar as she rang the money in the till. Ginny still looked like a frightened rabbit, but a bit more at ease, and Big Malc was being kind to her. At half past seven she slipped from the stool and took out her purse but Lil waved a hand at her.

'Ya can put that away for a start.'

Ginny became agitated. 'I must pay my way.'

Lil placed her hand on Ginny's. 'Next time you're in, ya can buy me a small one. That OK with you?' Lil smiled and Ginny did too. Frances lifted the flap of the bar.

'Will you be OK going home, Ginny? You still don't look well.'

'I'm fine, now.' Ginny pulled on her coat, looking considerably better than she'd been when Frances had found her. She called goodbye and Charlie and Artie held up a hand, as did Big Malc. He put down his pint, stood away from the bar.

'See you again, lass. Would you like me to walk with you?'

Ginny shook her head vigorously and raised her hand. 'No, please. You've all been kindness itself. I'll be fine. There's still enough light if I go now.' She was smiling, but she looked so small and delicate and Frances wondered whether she should let her go home alone, to that big empty flat. She walked with her to the door.

'Why don't you stay a little longer, Ginny? You could come home with me.'

Ginny wrapped her coat tight around herself, kept her arms across her chest. Her neck was bare, her bones sharp angles. 'I'm tired, Frances. I just want to go home to bed. To sleep.'

Frances tried not to show her alarm. Should she force her? But then Ginny would understand that she knew of her predicament. She had to be careful not to embarrass the girl, she'd already frightened her witless. Frances watched her walk down Sea View Street then went back into the pub. Lil was wiping down the bar that was already clean. There wasn't really enough work for the two of them, but Lil had insisted she come in. Back behind the bar she ran some hot water and started washing the few glasses that had accumulated. Lil picked up a tea towel.

'Your little friend is troubled.'

Frances stared down into the water. Troubled enough to want to end it all? Should she go after her?

'Man trouble?' Lil put the glass on the bar; it had little specks of lint on it from the tea towel.

'You could say that.' Frances didn't look up, finished the glasses and dried her hands on the bottom of the tea towel Lil was holding.

'Good job you brought her back, love. Looks like she needs a friend. I wouldn't want her to do anything stupid.' She fixed her eyes on Frances. 'Only one reason a girl looks that troubled. Only one.'

Ginny walked down the streets, tears coursing down her face. She had a feeling Frances knew what she was about to do and had stopped her in the nick of time. Now she didn't know whether she was glad she'd been saved. It had been warm in the pub, the people kind; they hadn't asked questions and Lil looked a cheery sort. Big Malc had been gentle, they all had. She pulled her coat tighter and started to cry, a quiet keening that she couldn't hold back. She wanted her mum, to hold her hand, to tell her it would all be OK. As she walked down Mill Road, curtains were being drawn and she caught small glimpses of families reading newspapers, settled for the evening. She'd never known that softness of life. Nothing had been cosy, save for the times she was at her mother's side, folding washing. She put her hand in her pocket and counted her change.

In the off-licence near the flat, she waited while the man behind the counter served a woman with straggly brown hair, scattered with grey. It was matted in places, thick clumps of hair that looked like the wire wool her brother had used to get the rust off his bike. Her jacket was thick with grime and the hem of her skirt had unravelled, hanging awkwardly in places, and Ginny questioned why life was so unkind to some people and not to others. The woman's head was bent low as she counted her change with grubby fingers, her nails black with dirt. She cast a furtive glance Ginny's way and Ginny, awkward, studied the bottles that lined the shelves. The man behind the counter looked at her and shrugged his shoulders as the woman handed over her money and he passed her a bottle of port. When she turned, Ginny saw her face, haggard and worn, her skin red and blotchy. She hugged the port and slunk past Ginny, her head down. The man shook his head as she went out, the bell ringing emptily behind her.

'Didn't know you girls were still here. Having another party?'

She nodded. He'd got to know all four of them since they'd taken the flat. He wouldn't know that the others had left last week. It gave her a little confidence. 'Sort of,' she said, not wanting to invite conversation.

'Gin again, is it?' he said, reaching behind him, his hand hovering over the Beefeater Gin on the shelf. 'Or d'ya fancy a bit of something else this time?'

'Gin will be fine.' She placed her coins on the counter.

'One or two?'

'One.' One would be enough.

'You lasses drank the last lot, already? I suppose you're waiting for the show to open again?'

'Yes,' she said and handed over her money. What did the truth matter when all was said and done?

Chapter 10

Johnny leant over the balcony of the Café De Paris, searching among the crowds. The band was playing and Joey Miller was crooning into the microphone. Waiters weaved among the table with bottles of champagne and fine wine and people ran up and down the stairs on either side of the stage, or squeezed themselves into the crowd dancing to 'Jeepers Creepers'. Cigarette smoke drifted up and caught in this throat. It was hopeless. If he couldn't see her straight away, he knew she wasn't there, for Ruby had never been a girl to blend into the crowd. He heard a loud burst of laughter from underneath the balcony and moved further around the circle, peering underneath. Someone slapped him on the back and he turned, confused.

'We meet again, Johnny.' It was the man from Bernie's office, Mickey Harper; his brown hair was oiled back and he was wearing an evening suit that had seen better days. Johnny wanted to turn back and dash downstairs but he mustn't be rude. One wrong word and something would find its way to the gossip columns. He nodded politely and tried to give his attention to Mickey, but Ruby was his priority.

'Good to see you, Mickey. It's getting to be a regular occurrence.' There was no time to chat, he could miss Ruby and she would move on, leave with God knows who. He looked over the man's shoulder.

Mickey smiled again. 'Looking for Ruby?'

Johnny brought his attention back to him, trying to sound relaxed, as if his only intention was to buy her a drink, not drag her away from it. 'Have you seen her?'

The man smiled, or was he smirking?

'Everyone's seen Ruby. She's the star of every party since you came back to England.'

Johnny couldn't make the man out. Was he being offensive? No, it was his fault. He was too jumpy. He asked again. 'Have you seen her?'

Mickey took a drag on his cigarette, tilted his head back and blew out smoke.

'Downstairs. She's with Alex Pardoe's party. What circles your little sister moves in, Johnny! But then, everyone wants to be with Ruby. She's quite a gal.'

He *was* being offensive; Johnny clenched his jaw.

'Nice catching up with you again, Mickey.' He wanted to get as far away from the man as he could. Mickey put up a hand.

'You too. Bound to bump into each other again.'

They wouldn't if he saw him first, Johnny thought. He pushed himself into the crowd and made for the stairs. The band had switched to a softer tempo and the crooner was taking a break, sipping an amber-coloured drink as he chatted to a couple of older women who were staring at him with dreamy eyes. Johnny weaved between the dancers, following the sound of laughter to Ruby. Her eyes were glittering brightly – too brightly – and he knew he had to handle this carefully, seeing her sway from side to side. How could he get her out without any fuss?

'Ruby!' She glowered, then her face brightened and she threw her arms about Johnny, excitedly introducing him to her friends. He shook hands, exchanged what pleasantries he could above the noise without shouting.

Joey Miller came back to the microphone and started talking. 'Ladies and Gentlemen, we have those huge stars, The Randolphs, here tonight. We all know Ruby, but Johnny is here too. Where are you, Johnny?'

The spotlight searched among the crowds and Ruby stepped onto a chair, waving. The crowd burst into applause and Johnny bowed, then took her hand, turning his back to the light. 'Get down,' he said, his jaw tensing. 'If you break your ankle, you won't dance for weeks.'

She leant down to him, smiling sweetly, aware all eyes were upon them.

'But it won't matter, darling brother, will it? Nothing matters any more.' She stood tall again, smiling, waving, enjoying the attention.

He took hold of her upper arm, her hand, and guided as she stepped down onto the floor. She twirled out and away from him as she had done so many times before, sweeping a low curtsey, and he stood back to let her take the applause. The people around them cleared away to give them the spotlight and, before Johnny knew what was happening, she was dragging him onto the dance floor. He smiled through gritted teeth.

'Dance for us, Ruby!' someone called from the balcony. The pair of them looked up. He saw Mickey waving. Ruby blew him a kiss. There were more calls, louder now. Johnny stared at Mickey, who was holding onto the gold balustrade, grinning back at him. What was his game? Ruby twisted and called to the band, '"Anything Goes".' Johnny gripped her hand.

'No, Ruby. Not now, you're too drunk.'

Ruby leant into him as the band started to play.

'Only a teensy-weensy bit, Johnny, darling. I can do this in my sleep and you know it.' There was nothing he could do but follow the music and dance to the routine they knew so well. Ruby was right, she *could* dance this in her sleep, but she faltered, wobbled and hammed it up, making her mistakes appear intended. The crowd loved her for it. When they'd finished, the applause was deafening and Johnny saw his chance. He swept her up into his arms and carried her up the stairs, knowing how much Ruby would enjoy the spectacle of it. She waved and blew kisses and he managed to smile as they made their way through the club towards the entrance. He stopped a waiter and asked him to fetch her bag and bring it to them at the door.

'I'm not going home, Johnny. It's far too early to leave.' She tried to wriggle free but he gripped her tighter until they got to the door. The doorman hailed a taxi and Johnny bundled Ruby into it, leaning back to avoid her flailing arms. The waiter arrived with her coat and bag and he tipped him then got into the car beside her.

'You spoil all my fun!' She slapped at his arm.

'That was so damned unprofessional.' He could barely speak. He'd spent half the night wandering in and out of her usual haunts in search of her. It was getting harder, but it seemed there were plenty of people who were going to party the war away – and Ruby was always able to find them.

'It was wonderful! We're meant to dance, aren't we? Entertain. It's our life. It's all we have left.' Her voice faltered and she brushed at her cheeks with the back of her hand. He took the handkerchief from his breast pocket and held it out to her. She snatched it from him, leant into the window, sulking, and he stared ahead as the taxi drove slowly down the darkened streets, the emptiness of life gnawing at his insides. Ruby was right: if they didn't have dance, they had nothing at all.

*

In the morning he left her sleeping and went out to meet the ten thirty at Waterloo. The station was a sea of khaki as men poured down the concourse, kitbags on their shoulders. He needed to be in uniform too. The quicker he got Ruby settled, the better. Porters weaved through the crowds, shouting, calling, their trolleys stacked with cases. He searched the board for the Bournemouth train and hurried down the platform, stood back to let a family pass and then slipped between the swarming mass as they surged forward. He craned his neck this way and that over people's heads, peering into carriages until he saw a blue velvet hat with an extravagant peacock's feather fastened in the band around it. The eye of the feather shimmered and glistened as it caught the light. A young airman was helping the wearer of the hat with a voluminous carpet bag. As he moved aside, Johnny caught sight of Aunt Letty, who was oblivious to her nephew, giving profuse thanks and further instruction to the airman. Johnny grinned. What a charmer the old girl was! He watched her, talking the whole time, the boy's face animated as he responded, smiling broadly. It would do him good to be the object of such attention, for Aunt Letty had a way of making anyone feel they were the most precious being on this earth. Johnny walked towards them and her face glowed when she saw him.

'Aunt Letty.' He held out his hand and she took it. The airman placed her bag at her feet.

'Lovely to meet you, young man – and remember what I told you.'

'I will,' he called, hurrying down the platform to join his comrades.

Aunt Letty brushed at the shoulders of her dark blue suit. It was belted at the waist, which was almost as wide as her generous bosom.

'Johnny, my sweet boy. How tired you look.'

'That wasn't the welcome I was expecting.' He took her bag.

'Come now,' she smiled. 'You haven't asked me here to pay compliments, have you? For you'll get none.'

He laughed. She bent her arm at the elbow and he linked his through it. 'You must tell me all about America.' She paused. 'After you have told me about Ruby.'

He offered to hail a taxi but she opted to walk. 'I'd rather walk and talk. Ruby will be all ears and I want to know what the little minx has been up to.'

Johnny suddenly felt able to breathe deeply, taking the air into his lungs and letting it go again. Aunt Letty wouldn't pander to Ruby, who was the nearest thing to Mother they would ever have, and who still possessed the softness their mother had lost when their father died. He had forgotten.

They strolled over Waterloo Bridge in the sunshine, Aunt Letty stopping as they went, leaning over, watching the boats slide underneath them. 'Good to see familiar sights,' she said. 'Like old friends. You can see so much from the bridge. On the streets it's all hustle and bustle, but here you have a bit of clarity.' They started walking again and he felt lighter, less troubled being with her, enjoying the slower pace as they talked. His thoughts slowly strengthened, along with his spirit.

'I'm so glad you agreed to come, Aunt Letty. I'm at a loss how best to help Ruby. She was distraught when Mother died and I didn't handle it very well.'

'Well, she would be, wouldn't she? A girl away from her mother, so far from home? But that's not your fault. You had work to do and I doubt *anything* you might have done would have helped.' He pulled her closer, adjusted the bag in his other hand. That was exactly how it had felt.

'I tried sympathy, cajoling, anger, threats. Nothing seemed to help.' He could do it, so why couldn't she? He had compartmentalised it, put it to one side to do the work, but it didn't mean that he felt the loss any less. 'It's not that I didn't care.'

She stopped, turned to face him and looked into his eyes. He felt as if she could see inside his head. People hurried around them and the traffic spat out fumes. 'You don't have to explain to me, Johnny.' She rubbed at his arm and it was comforting. He touched her hand. How lonely he'd been these last few years ... They started walking again.

'We were so excited to get the chance, Aunt Letty. America! The big time. Mother was *thrilled*. When we sailed across the Atlantic I thought it was the beginning of everything. But it was mostly a disappointment.'

'Dream fulfilment is a disappointment in general, I find. Nothing ever matches up to the dream.' They turned onto the Strand and a little further along she stopped outside The Savoy and Letty read the poster on the board out front. 'Opening soon.' She turned to Johnny. 'Positive news, my boy. The quicker you both get back to work, the better.'

As they walked along he told his aunt of the night at the Café de Paris. 'I'm not sure it's the dancing that she lives for, more the attention.' It was awful talking about his sister like this, but it was what he thought. He knew Aunt Letty would understand.

'But of course it is. It's all she's ever known. And it's a way of proving to herself that she exists.' She moved her head to indicate the Lyons Corner House. 'Shall we go in there? You can treat me to a bite to eat and we can talk some more. Will Ruby be all right on her own a little longer?' She was smiling as she said it, and he knew that she was well aware that Ruby would still be sleeping off the effects of the night before.

'I have to get her away, Aunt Letty, before she ...'

'Before she what? Gets worse? Causes a scandal? Gets pregnant? Kills herself?' He looked at her and she raised an eyebrow. She smiled gently. 'Perhaps you have things you don't feel able to tell me. Well, I can guess. Ruby will tell me if she wants to.'

He stepped ahead, opened the door into the tea rooms and found a table. He pulled out a chair for Aunt Letty to sit down and tucked her bag underneath the table. The Nippies, as the waitresses were called, weren't called so for nothing and a petite blonde took their order and soon returned with a tray bearing tea and scones. Aunt Letty picked up the teapot and reached out for his cup. He handed it over.

'Now, America. Start at the beginning.'

He told her how they had arrived, wide-eyed. It was hard to tell who was more excited – Ruby or their mother. Ruby was eighteen, the world was opening up for her, but to Alice it was the culmination of her plans. Although their father, Bruce Randolph, had been a headliner in England, he had never been able to conquer America. Alice was determined that Johnny and Ruby would. They had travelled from state to state; small theatres, large ones, half-empty houses and standing-room only. Alice had set up newspaper and radio interviews wherever they went, wangled invitations to the house parties of the great and good, haggled for spots further up the bill, more pay, a percentage of the box office. There had been no time to think, no time for romance, no time for anything but what their mother laid out for them. Day after day life was a blur of rehearsals, performances and meetings. That's all there was.

'No time to play?' Aunt Letty spread a generous amount of butter on her scone, took a bite.

He splashed a little milk in his tea. 'Never has been, Aunt Letty. Not much, anyway.' He thought of Frances, the dancer he had fallen in love with in the last show they'd appeared in before they sailed for America. They had kept their love a secret, knowing Alice would disapprove because it wasn't part of her plan. He wondered where Frances was now.

'Your mother was a strong woman, Johnny. Determined,' Aunt Letty said, interrupting his thoughts. 'But she didn't start out that way. She was much like Ruby until she met your father.' She touched at the corner of her mouth with her napkin. 'She loved the glamour of his life, the after-show parties, the travelling, mixing with people of power and influence.' She was quiet for a moment, considering her words. 'He left her in a parlous state when he died.' Johnny nodded, remembering. He'd found her once, sprawled out on the bed, crying, her empty purse open in her hand, a few coins on the counterpane. It must have been frightening, a woman alone with two children.

'She did her best,' he said. 'She wanted a better life for us. What mother wouldn't?'

'I agree, my boy.' She finished her scone. 'Personally, I think she went too far, but who am I to judge?'

He wanted to agree with his aunt, but it felt disloyal. 'She should have told us she was ill,' he offered. 'That she was dying.'

'She should.' Aunt Letty was thoughtful. 'More tea?'

He shook his head. 'I wouldn't have signed the contract if I'd known. We would have come home.'

Aunt Letty gave him a sad smile. 'That's exactly why she didn't tell you. She died knowing she had done her best by you. You were her life.'

'Her entire life,' Johnny agreed. 'It's not a good thing though, is it? To set your sights on success to the point where there's nothing else.' The emptiness of his life gnawed at him again.

'It's not, darling boy. Indeed, it is not.'

By the time they arrived at the flat he'd given Aunt Letty a full description of Ruby's behaviour, both in America and since they had arrived back home. Only it wasn't home, was it? He didn't feel they belonged anywhere, and he could understand that Ruby would be feeling the same, more so; for she had loved to go home to Mother, sought the security of her forgiveness when she'd misbehaved.

Johnny opened the door and stood back to let Aunt Letty enter. She strode into the middle of the sitting room, looking about her as she did so, taking in the furniture, the lighting, the oak fire surround, the gas fire. She walked over to the window, rubbed at the cloth of the curtains, peered down into the street.

He placed her bag on the chair by the door, waiting for her verdict.

'Very nice,' she kept looking about her. 'Very nice indeed. Pleasant.' She drew the pin from her hat, which she took off and placed on the small table at the side of the easy chair. 'You rented it furnished?'

'For a year. I got an agency to sort it for us before we arrived back in England so that we didn't have to live out of a suitcase. We've done enough of that.' It had been the perfect find, but now he only saw the downsides; it was too close to The Savoy, to the clubs. Now that there was nothing to keep Ruby busy, what had seemed like heaven was now a hell. He slipped off his jacket and draped it over the back of the chintz armchair. 'Can I get you a drink, Aunt Letty?'

She shook her head. Her long grey hair was curled into a neat bun at the back of her head and he was fleetingly reminded of his mother. He looked up as the bedroom door opened and Ruby shuffled out, bleary-eyed, rubbing at her face with her hand. Her hair was a complete mess and she padded forward, oblivious to her surroundings. Last night so glamorous, today this. That was show business for you.

She yawned, opening her mouth wide.

'Hand to mouth, Ruby. You weren't born on a farm. Manners.'

Ruby froze on the spot and looked across to where Aunt Letty was standing, selecting books from the shelves beside the fireplace.

'Aunt Letty!' Her face crumpled. Aunt Letty opened her arms wide and Ruby ran into them. Their aunt enfolded her, her bosom a cushion for Ruby's head. When Aunt Letty deemed that Ruby had been comforted enough, she grasped her niece's hands and held her away from her, her eyes reflecting sadness, not disappointment.

'My dear, darling girl, what *have* you been doing to yourself? You've lost too much weight and it doesn't become you.' She touched Ruby's cheek and Ruby grasped at her hand. 'Dull eyes, dull skin. This will never do, Ruby Randolph! We need to take you in hand.'

Ruby fell into her embrace again and started to cry, little sobs that were the beginnings of a torrent. Aunt Letty consoled her, leading her to the small sofa that faced the fire, peeled her off and sat her down. She lifted Ruby's legs and made her lie on the sofa, plumping the cushions. 'Now then, madam. You're going to behave yourself while I'm here, aren't you?'

'You're going to stay?' Ruby flashed Johnny a grateful smile.

'For a few days. Yes.' Aunt Letty looked at Johnny – he obviously hadn't told Ruby, who would have asked too many questions of him. Aunt Letty rolled up her sleeves. 'I'm going to make you something nourishing for—' She broke off and pursed her lips. 'Your breakfast, although it's well after lunch.' Ruby was about to protest but Aunt Letty stilled her with the flat of her hand. 'Now, now! I know the ways of the theatre as well as you do, young lady, but you're not working in the theatre at the moment and this is no time to be getting out of bed. Dearie me, it's not!' She smiled and it gave her face such luminosity that Johnny could almost swear she was an angel. He felt his shoulders relax and he stretched his neck from side to side, releasing a little of the tension that had built up these past months. Ruby would be safe with Aunt Letty. He could leave her for a few days, knowing that she would still be in one piece when he got back.

Aunt Letty bustled into the kitchen and he followed her. She began opening cupboards and drawers, familiarising herself with the contents, took eggs from the refrigerator, then milk, sniffed it, rummaged for butter. 'Scrambled eggs on toast. Can you get some bread, Johnny boy?'

He leant over and kissed her cheek. 'I will get you anything your heart desires.' He jangled his hand in his pocket for change. 'Thank you, Aunt Letty.'

She cracked an egg into a bowl, reached for another. 'Off with you.'

Ruby had gone into the bedroom and pulled on her silk dressing gown before brushing her hair and wiping her face with cold cream. She came back out into the sitting room as Johnny came out of the kitchen. Aunt Letty was right, he thought. Ruby's skin and her eyes *were* dull – and so was Ruby herself, inside and out. Oh, she was good at faking her smile. They had been doing it most of their lives, after all, but Aunt Letty had sliced through to the truth like a knife and Ruby was the better for it. His sister wouldn't take it from him, they were too close, and he felt he couldn't save her without making a huge change. Aunt Letty would give him the time he needed. Bernie had suggested he come look at an investment and possible venue for a show, way out on the east coast at the end of the train line. Ruby wouldn't like it – but then she never liked what was good for her.

If it all worked out as he hoped, they would have a good income because he planned to put on a revue and rehearse an understudy to take his place. Ruby would have work; she would have focus and she would get well. Eventually. But it wasn't fair to burden Aunt Letty for more than a few days. It was good of her to come at all. He made for the door and Ruby hurried to him, standing on tiptoes to kiss his cheek.

'Thank you.'

He smiled. 'For what?'

'Aunt Letty. It's like having a little piece of Mother with us.' Her voice was soft, sad, and the bitter-sweetness of their aunt's being there lay heavy in her words. He pressed her shoulder, gave it a squeeze.

'I'll be back in two ticks. Behave yourself.'

'I daren't not.' It was the first time in weeks they'd shared a civil word and he closed the door behind him, a spring in his step, raced down the stairs and out into the street.

He could smell the food cooking as he dashed back upstairs, the loaf balanced on top of a white box tied with a black and cream ribbon. He'd picked up a couple of cakes from the patisserie as a treat. Ruby was setting the table, the bathroom door was open and he could hear the bath running, the smell of perfumed oil mingling with the smell of eggs. She turned, smiled and it all seemed so normal that he hoped he wasn't being too optimistic. Aunt Letty could only stay a few days before she had to return to Uncle Jim and her work with the WVS. Would Ruby then resort to her earlier habits? He had to hope she wouldn't. And with any luck they would be away from temptation before she could do more damage to herself.

Chapter 11

The flap at the end of the bar was open and Frances stood in the gap, playing patience. It had been a quiet morning, the regulars in their usual places. She was getting to know many of them, if not their names, what they drank. Lil was at the other end of the bar, checking the shelves for stock and working out what she would need.

The door opened and Eric, a dour Scotsman, came in with his Alsatian. 'Two pies and a pint of the usual, please, Frances.' Frances put down the cards, poured his pint and put it in front of him, passed him a clean china ashtray from under the bar.

Eric handed over his money, put the ashtray on the floor and poured some of his pint into it for the dog, who noisily lapped it up. He then fed him the pie. Frances gathered up the cards from the counter, her moves exhausted, and shuffled them. She put her hand across her mouth and yawned.

'Tired?' Eric asked.

'Not sleeping.' Frances yawned again. Her mind had been busy with things she had no control over.

'Don't know that many of us are, these days.' He looked into the top of his glass. 'I thought, if they were going to bomb us, we'd have had a bang or two be now.'

Lil agreed. 'Making us all jittery. Ruddy sods.' She sighed. 'It's all right working out what I need, it's whether I can get it. The brewery wagons have been requisitioned and can I get a delivery?' She blew out her cheeks. 'It's a right caper. All right if I go and put me feet up for an hour? You can manage, can't you, love?'

Frances said she could and Lil went through to the backroom. Lunchtime dragged on and Frances pondered on why Lil employed her when it was so quiet. Any profit must be going on her wages. The dog started breaking wind and Frances wafted a hand in front of her face. 'Don't you think you should stop giving Duke the ale, Eric? I can't think that it agrees with his stomach.'

'I only come in for him. I can't stand the stuff myself.'

Frances laughed, then started taking glasses from the shelves and polishing the mirrors behind them. In the corner, four old boys had the domino board out and were playing a game of fives and threes. The silence of the bar was punctuated with the rattle of the tiles on the wooden board, the occasional rapping when someone had to forgo a turn. She had climbed up on the small stool to tackle the shelf with the bottles of liqueurs when the door was pushed ajar. She watched through the mirror, her hand on a bottle of Drambuie as a familiar face appeared around the door, furtively searching the room until she caught sight of Frances. Jessie beckoned with her finger and Frances beckoned back. Jessie squirmed, pushed the door wider and crept forward, blushing a deep crimson.

Frances put the bottle back on the shelf and came down the steps.

'Don't be shy, Jessie. No one will bite. Well, Duke might.' She leant over the bar and pointed to the dog. Jessie froze and Frances grinned. Eric peered at her over his glasses.

'Pay no attention; the dog might look fearsome but he's as soft as grease.' Jessie gave the dog a wide berth as she came to the end of the bar. She had a newspaper in her hand and she tapped the front page, holding it out towards Frances.

'Have you seen the *Telegraph*?' Her voice was high with excitement as she handed it over.

'I have now,' said Frances, taking the paper and reading the headlines.

'Not there,' Jessie said, leaning forward and whispering. Frances bit her lip, trying not to laugh at Jessie's discomfort. 'Page four, in the middle.' Frances made great labour of turning the pages. Duke growled and Jessie squealed. Eric tugged at the dog's lead. The air around them became rank.

Frances spluttered with laughter.

'Sorry, lassie. It's his guts. He's got a touch of bellyache.'

'A bit?' Jessie wrinkled her nose and moved closer to Frances, which set Frances off again but Jessie was getting irritated. Frances reached out and squeezed her hand.

'Sorry, Jessie. It's your face. You look so – so *uncomfortable*.'

Jessie winced. 'That's because I am.'

'No need to be, gal.' Eric was apologetic. 'The dog can't help it. I'll take him for a walk.'

'No, please don't.' It was Jessie's turn to apologise and as another smell hit her nose, she laughed too. The pair of them were still giggling when Lil walked back behind the bar.

'What am I missing?'

Frances wiped the tears from her eyes with the back of her hand.

'Sorry, Lil. It's Duke's bellyache.' Jessie giggled again and Frances stepped out from behind the bar and put her arm about Jessie's shoulder. 'This is my friend, Jessie. She's a Variety Girl too.'

'Another one?' Lil said, putting out her hand in greeting. 'Got me a ruddy hat trick, Eric. Three gorgeous girls.' Frances grinned, pulling Jessie tighter.

'Jessie came to tell me something, it's on page four but I can't read it. My eyes are full of tears and the writing's gone all blurry.' Frances reached in her pocket and wiped her eyes with her hanky.

'It's the theatres!' Jessie said, her eyes alight. 'They can reopen. All the places of entertainment will be opening again.'

She turned about her and Frances did too. The old boys playing dominoes moved their heads slightly, which Frances explained meant they were thrilled to bits. Eric pushed his pint glass across the bar to Lil.

'Worth a celebration I'd say, Lil, wouldn't you? Let me get you a drink, girls. What are you having?'

'Oh, I couldn't,' Jessie said, getting flustered. 'I only came to let Frances know. It means we can dance again.' She looked at Frances. 'It changes everything.'

Frances gripped her hand, squeezed it. Hope, they had hope.

'It does. Stay and have a drink – a lemonade, anything; let's mark the moment.' It didn't really change everything, but it was a definite step in the right direction. If the theatres reopened, she could save instead of simply managing and her plan to get Imogen and herself stable was back on track. Jessie paused, then nodded.

'Lemonade it is.'

Frances went behind the bar and poured two glasses of lemonade while Lil poured Eric another pint. Jessie saw the piano against the wall and Frances caught her looking. 'Have a go. It's all right, isn't it, Lil? If Jessie plays the piano?'

'Could I?' Jessie felt her fingers flex involuntarily, ready to touch the keys.

'Course it is. Play something lively – happy music, seeing as you've had happy news, eh?'

Jessie moved quickly to the piano, running her hand across the top. It was beautiful rosewood, inlaid at the front with leaves and acorns. She lifted the lid, ran her fingers over the keys, played a few notes. It was in tune and, delighted, she pulled out the stool and started to play. She started with 'Roll out the Barrel', which seemed appropriate given the setting, and moved on to 'Peg o' My Heart'. Lil began to sing. Her voice was robust, not bad at all, and Jessie turned to see Frances grinning and cheering her on. She played 'Mother Kelly's Doorstep' and Lil came out from behind the bar, lifted her dress as if it were a crinoline and danced about the floor, singing, using her arms to bring in the other customers. The four old boys carried on with their dominoes, oblivious, but didn't complain and Jessie wondered what Lil would do if they did. She seemed happy and encouraged Jessie to go on, not that Jessie needed it. The theatres were opening again and she would take up where she left off, war or not. Eric leant on the bar, watching Lil with a smile on his face. Lil was having fun, taking off Fred's cap as he played dominoes, draping it over his eyes so he couldn't see. The other old boys laughed and paused their game, watching Lil in full sail.

When Jessie finally stopped, the customers applauded. Lil placed her hands on Jessie's shoulders.

'Oh, that were grand, my lovely. What a boost to have someone come in who can play that ol' Joanna properly. Not a bum note in sight.' She pulled out a stool and sat beside Jessie. Her cheeks were flushed and her grey-green eyes were shining with happiness. She pressed her hand to her chest until her breath steadied. 'Perhaps you could come back tonight and play for half an hour?'

Jessie wasn't sure Grace would approve. She hadn't liked Jessie's father playing the pubs, but as his health had failed it was the only avenue open to him. It was a far cry from the grand concert halls he'd played in when he was a young man, before the Great War damaged him forever.

Music had been so important to her father, and it was to her. And she knew she could make people forget, even for just a short time. It didn't do to dwell on sadness, they would all have enough of that before long; that was perhaps the only certainty they had.

'I can't pay you, lass,' Lil said. 'But you can put a glass on the piano for tips. Will that do ya?' Frances was smiling, her eyes almost pleading for Jessie to agree. 'It'll help my business no end, having you girls here. And that other beauty with the red hair.'

'Ginny!' Jessie jumped up from the seat. 'We need to tell her too.' She turned to Lil. 'Yes, yes, I will, Lil. I'll come back later, all three of us will, but we need to tell Ginny, don't we, Frances?' She'd meant to come in and tell Frances and then find Ginny at the laundry on her way home. It had been a half-day at the solicitors and she'd bought the paper to take home to Grace.

Lil got up, put her hands to her back, and bent backwards slightly. 'Think I've done myself a mischief.' She placed her hand on Jessie's arm. 'Thank you, lovey. We need cheering up in these dark days and any little we can do to add a little lightness to proceedings will be a blessing. So get off, the pair of you. It's almost time for last orders anyway.'

'Are you sure, Lil? Don't you want me to help clean up?'

'Nope, I feel like a twenty-year-old since I've had a sing and a dance. Don't know where I'm gonna find one.' She laughed. 'Off you pop. I'll see ya later.'

Jessie waited while Frances grabbed her jacket and bag and the two of them left by the front door.

'Did you call in at the Empire, Jessie?'

'Not yet. I thought it would be better if all three of us went. I shouldn't have played the piano, Frances; I should have gone to Ginny and told her. She hates working in that laundry and she'll be so glad.'

'I can't see the Empire opening straight away, though. We'll still have to keep working at the jobs we've got.'

'Yes, but we have hope now, Frances. I'm glad we've got work, but it's not what we're meant to be doing, is it?'

They hurried into the laundry yard. Vans were arriving and linen was being taken in through a loading bay. Jessie opened the door and a few girls turned when they saw them but kept working. An older woman hurried across to them.

'We haven't got any vacancies if you're looking for work – although we might have one. Someone didn't turn up today and if it happens again, I'll have a slot – but not for both of you.'

Jessie kept searching the room, leaning from one side to the other, seeking her friend but finding only unfamiliar faces. 'We came to get a message to our friend Ginny Thompson.'

The woman folded her arms. 'Well, she's the one who's not here. And when you see her you can tell her that if it happens again she'll be getting her cards.'

Jessie was shocked. 'She's probably ill. She wouldn't let anyone down on purpose. She's on her own.'

'We're wasting time.' Frances was pulling Jessie's sleeve, almost dragging her towards the door. Jessie scowled at Frances, tugged back her arm, rubbed at it. 'She wouldn't be able to get a message to you,' she said to Edna. 'She's not a magician.'

'And neither am I, Miss Clever Clogs.' She turned her back on them. 'Stop gawping!' she shouted to the girls who were smiling at Jessie and Frances. 'Get back to yer work.'

They fumbled their way out of the laundry, Jessie furious. 'You made me look an idiot in there, Frances. What the hell are you playing at?'

Frances strode ahead. 'I'm worried about Ginny.'

Jessie hurried to keep up beside her. 'I'm sure there's no need to hurry. It's probably just a stomach upset. Slow down, Frances.' She stopped and Frances turned back.

'I haven't had a chance to tell you.' She grabbed Jessie's arm again, started hurrying down the street. 'Ginny was about to throw herself off the steps last night.'

'*What*?' Jessie stopped again, making Frances stop too.

'I took her to the pub and Lil gave her something to eat.' She bit on her lip. 'I should have brought her home with me.'

Jessie felt her stomach tighten and hurried next to Frances, the two of them tearing down Cambridge Street, dashing between cars and onto Mill Road. They pushed on the gate and hurried up the path, praying the door was open. It was, and they pounded up the stairs, two at a time. 'I should have stayed here with her. She shouldn't be here on her own,' Jessie said and Frances raised an eyebrow. Frances knew, Jessie thought. She knew – and she knew that Jessie knew too. Jessie chewed at her bottom lip. Would she still want to be friends? Did friends keep secrets from one another? Frances hammered on the door, shouting Ginny's name. A door opened and the landlady appeared at the bottom of the stairs. Her dark-grey hair was in curlers, a floral overall covering her dress.

'She's in,' she called up, holding onto the newel post. 'I heard her walking about, up and down all night, she was. Although it's been quiet for the last couple of hours. But she hasn't gone out. I'd have heard the door.'

Jessie leant over the banister. 'Have you got a spare key?' The woman disappeared and Jessie could feel the blood pummelling in her ears. This was her fault. She knew Ginny was vulnerable. If only she'd have let her stay … Frances was quiet, squeezing her fists open and shut, then she was banging on the door again, calling Ginny's name.

They heard a jangle of keys and the landlady hauled herself up the stairs. Jessie wanted to tell her to move her ruddy arse but instead she bit her tongue, willing the woman to move faster. She ambled up, her round body rocking from side to side as she sorted through the keys. Jessie wanted to snatch them from her, but her hands were shaking, and she wouldn't have any idea of which key it was. Time seemed to be slowing and galloping at the same time, and with every second she felt more knots grow in her stomach. Please, please let Ginny be safe. She would never keep another secret ever again, not as long as she lived, as long as Ginny was safe. Oh, let her be safe! Frances moved away from the door and Jessie walked two steps up to the next floor to give the woman access.

'I can't say as I like doing this,' the woman was muttering as she put the key in the lock and clicked it over. 'It's not right, opening the door when she's in. Invading her privacy.'

Jessie blustered forward. 'But she's our friend and we're worried about her.' The woman stepped back and Frances swiftly pushed herself into the gap and took hold of the handle, blocking the way.

'Don't worry, we'll take the blame,' Frances said as she closed the door.

Jessie dashed in and Frances followed her into the sitting room. Everything was neat and tidy, apart from a pillow and blanket on the sofa and a bottle of gin on the floor. Frances picked it up.

'Full.' It was a relief.

'The landlady swore she hadn't gone out.' Jessie was trying not to panic, looking into the empty bedrooms. Perhaps they were both mistaken. Ginny wasn't really going to throw herself down steps. Frances had got it wrong. Please

God she had got it wrong and Ginny was out somewhere, had got another job.

'The bathroom?'

Jessie paled and Frances led the way. The door wouldn't open. It wasn't locked but the door wouldn't give. Frances leant against it with her full weight and it shifted a little. She could see Ginny's glorious red hair and she barged at the door again. The smell of vomit and worse filled her nostrils and she pressed her lips together, trying not to inhale. 'Ginny, it's Frances – are you all right?' The girl moaned and Frances pushed herself around the door and managed to climb over Ginny, who was curled into a foetal ball. Frances squatted over her, straddling the toilet pan that reeked of illness. Jessie was pushing her head and shoulders around the door.

'Is she . . .?'

'She's alive, if that's what you mean.' Jessie let out a long sigh as Ginny moaned again. Frances moved behind her, put her hands under the girl's arms and pulled her up, propping her against the bath panel. 'Have you taken anything, Ginny?' The girl was a leaden lump and there wasn't space to manoeuvre gently so Frances pulled her as best she could until Jessie could open the door wider. Together they dragged Ginny into the narrow hall and once she was safely out, Frances pushed open the small window in the bathroom and flushed the lavatory. The sink had remnants of vomit and the whole place needed a good clean – but that would be later. She looked about her, found a clean flannel and towel and ran some water in the bath. She soaked the flannel and went out into the hall, wiping Ginny's face and hands, trying to remove the residue from her hair. Ginny's eyes rolled back in her head and Frances said again, 'Ginny, what have you taken?'

Ginny mumbled incoherently, tried again.

'Ppp,'

'What?' Frances leant closer, tugging at her to get her back into consciousness.

'Pp.' Ginny started moving, attempting to revive herself, but her head flopped around and Frances couldn't make out what she meant.

'Poison?' Jessie gasped. 'Oh, no, no. She's taken poison.'

Ginny shook her head; it was only slight, but it was definitely in disagreement. They were wrong. She tried again.

'Pp ff.'

The two girls looked at each other, none the wiser. 'Help me get her onto to the settee,' Frances said, taking her arms.

'She looks awful.' Jessie clasped her hands round Ginny's ankles. Frances agreed but at least they weren't too late, and she could live with that. She should never have let her go home, knowing she was in a fragile state – and she knew how that felt, for how many things had she tried in the early days of her pregnancy? And yet now, to be without her darling Imogen didn't bear thinking of.

They managed to get Ginny onto the settee and Jessie found a bowl and ran some hot water into it while Frances fetched soap, refreshed the flannel and towel. Ginny was still wearing the clothes she had on yesterday and the two of them undressed her to her slip. As Jessie gently ran the flannel around her neck, Ginny started to respond and they talked to her, quiet, soothing words, until she was able to tell them what had happened.

'Food poisoning.'

Frances bit down on her lip. Surely the girl wasn't going to carry on with the pretence?

'The pie ...' She closed her eyes, put her hand to her mouth. Let it drop again. 'At the pub. I think it was off.' She opened her eyes as Jessie adjusted the pillow behind her and dropped back onto it, half smiling at Frances. Jessie tucked the blanket under Ginny's armpits and laid a cool flannel on her head.

'Better?' Jessie asked.

'Much. Thank you.' Ginny was more alert. 'I think it was the food and,' she paused, trying not to gag, 'the br-the drink Lil gave to me. And the hot sweet tea.' She shuddered. 'I thought I was going to die.'

Jessie said briskly, 'Well, you didn't. And you're not going to. We're here to look after you.'

Ginny gave her a wan smile but didn't say anything more. Frances yearned to offer Ginny the freedom that truth would give her, the openness of sharing her burden, but how could she? What a hypocrite she'd be, forcing Ginny to air her dirty linen and keep her own locked away. But Imogen was not dirty, was she? She was pure and innocent, like the daisies that scattered the gardens and verges, cheerful and unexpected. She mustn't think of herself, she must think of Ginny. If the girl was trying to get rid of the baby, what would she attempt next? She might not want to die now, but if she wandered further down the path it would lead her to the backstreets – and whatever way you looked at it, that would never end well. She took hold of Ginny's hand and looked up at Jessie. Jessie's eyes grew round in anticipation of what Frances was about to say. Frances was going to speak up at some point and it might as well be now.

'You're not alone in this, Ginny.' Jessie was shaking her head, her mouth had dropped. She mouthed, 'Don't', but Frances felt she had to. In Ginny's state of mind, she might do anything. She'd already contemplated a fall and the gin wasn't there for social reasons. The next thing she tried might kill her. Jessie was squirming and Ginny looked at her, then her eyes flashed with fear.

'I *know*,' Frances said. Jessie let out a squeak and Ginny struggled to sit up, but Frances held up her hand and made her lie down again. Frances squeezed her hand tighter. 'Jessie didn't betray your confidence. I guessed.' She leant in closer, passing Ginny a handkerchief from her pocket as the girl began to cry.

Ginny had looked so frail and weak before the sickness and now she was more gaunt than ever. Her eyes were dark hollows and her breath stank. How long since she had eaten anything before the pie was anyone's guess. The pie might very well have been off but even if it wasn't, Ginny was right: the combination of alcohol, sweet tea and the pie would have upset her stomach and she might have hoped that it would do the trick. If only she could reassure the girl.

'Whatever happens, we are with you. The two of us,' she said. Jessie pressed her hand on Ginny's shoulder, removed the flannel and dropped it onto the windowsill. The girl was crying now and Frances wished with all her heart that she could make this easier. Jessie was kind-hearted and determined but she was naïve. Being kind wouldn't help Ginny; the girl needed to have some practical advice – and she could give it. But could she tell her everything?

'I prayed to God, night and day,' Ginny sobbed. 'I prayed and prayed and still nothing came.' Frances clasped her hand in both of hers. Ginny's fingers were thin, like the rest of her. She was a beautiful girl, but the shine had gone from her.

'And the gin?'

'For if the prayers didn't work.' Frances squeezed her hand again, hoping to give Ginny some strength. 'I tried to fall down the steps by the promenade, but I couldn't do it.' She looked at Frances from beneath her lashes. 'I know you pulled me back – but I wouldn't have done it anyway. I'm a coward.'

'You're not,' Jessie butted in. She opened her mouth to say something else, but Frances glanced at her and she stopped, perhaps knowing that platitudes would be of no comfort. Frances rested the back of her hand on Ginny's forehead. It was still clammy.

'I don't think you should be on your own,' Frances said. 'You don't look at all well.' A small exaggeration given the circumstances, but being alone would give the girl more time to think and she knew herself that overthinking anything only led to misery.

'I'm fine,' Ginny said, her voice feeble. 'A good night's sleep and I'll be back at work tomorrow. If I still have a job.'

'Oh,' Jessie gasped, her voice taking on a brighter tone, 'that's what we came to tell you. It was in the paper.'

Ginny looked at her blankly.

'The theatres and cinemas can reopen. We'll be in work again.'

Ginny sank back into the pillow. Frances got up and brought a fresh glass of water and she held the bottom of it while Ginny put her hands around it and sipped.

'I suppose that will be all right for a while, but who will want to give me a job later? I won't be able to dance.'

'You will.'

Ginny sighed. 'Don't keep trying to make me feel better, Jessie. I have to be realistic.' Jessie sank a little, but Frances was firm.

'Ginny's quite right, Jessie, as are you. So the three of us need to stick together and work something out.' She was trying to convince herself as much as she was Ginny. And if they could help Ginny, then perhaps the two of them would help her in return. The very thought prompted a twist of guilt. It was something to consider, but for the time being, Ginny's situation was the most pressing. Imogen was safe, Ginny's problems were just beginning.

Ginny looked down at her hands. 'It's not your responsibility. I was the stupid one.'

Frances rubbed at her shoulder. 'Nothing stupid about it, Ginny. You were one of the unlucky ones.' She considered for a moment before speaking again, making herself sound cheerful. Could she give Ginny hope without revealing too much of her own situation? She had managed, Ginny might manage too. 'I knew a girl who danced until the week before her baby was born. The head girl put her at the back of the chorus.'

'She must have looked like an elephant.' Ginny tried to smile.

'She was neat and the baby, when it came, was small.' Imogen had been a little over six pounds, so tiny in her arms …

'See, it's possible. Other girls have managed and so will you.' Jessie got up and drew the curtains. 'I'll go back and get my work clothes. I'll stay with you tonight.'

Ginny pushed herself up on her elbows. 'There's no need.'

'Jessie's right,' Frances said. 'You're already looking a lot better than when we first arrived but you're still weak. We'd take you home with us, but I don't think you'd make it to the bottom of the stairs, let alone the bottom of the street.'

They would brook no argument and Jessie went off to get her clothes while Frances ran Ginny a cool bath. 'It will all seem so much better in the morning.'

'Really?' Ginny said, sadly.

'Really,' Frances said, hoping she sounded convincing.

Chapter 12

When Jessie returned, Ginny was resting on the settee. Frances had found her some fresh clothing then helped her dress, brushed her hair and tied it away from her face. When she heard the front door she came out of the bathroom, the smell of disinfectant in her nose infinitely better than what it had smelt of before. She was wearing a headscarf tied at the back of her neck, her sleeves rolled up to the elbows, a small tablecloth fastened about her waist for an apron, her face almost as red as the gingham squares.

Jessie put her bag down on a chair by the wall and took out a packet of arrowroot biscuits. She opened it and offered them to Ginny. 'Mum sent them. Said it's the best thing for an upset stomach.' Ginny took one, her eyes cast down. 'Don't worry,' Jessie said, sitting down beside her and rubbing at her forearm, 'all I said was that you were sick. They didn't need to know anything other than that. No one does.'

'Not yet, anyway.' Frances leant on the doorjamb. 'You won't be able to hide it forever, Ginny – and you need all the support you can get.' She flinched at her own hypocrisy.

'Frances!' Jessie was shocked.

Ginny shook her head. 'Frances is right. I'm not so stupid as to think I could hide it forever.'

'That's if you *are* pregnant,' Frances said, bustling over to the kitchen. She took off the apron and headscarf and dropped them on top of the pile of dirty sheets that included Ginny's clothes and towels. They could drop them at the laundry. How ironic it all was. She washed her hands and went back into the sitting area. 'Hopefully, this is just down to shock from Billy dumping you like he did, the bastard!'

'Frances!' Jessie exclaimed again.

'Well, it's the truth. He was. Is.' She took a deep breath, let it out with a sigh. 'Then the theatre closed and you were left on your own, here. It could all be a false alarm.'

Ginny released her hands from Jessie's. 'And if it's not?' She paused. 'I know it's not.'

Frances sighed.

'Let's hope for the best, Ginny,' Jessie encouraged.

'But plan for the worst.' She twisted to face Jessie, gave her a small smile. 'I have to be realistic. I can't exist on wishful thinking.' Her lip trembled. 'I've been terrified. I've no idea what to do. How I'll be able to work. And what then? After . . .' A tear dropped onto her cheek. Frances was glad that she was talking about it. Talking helped, she knew that. Patsy had made her talk and it had saved her on more than one occasion – but only because she trusted Patsy.

'It's early days. We'll help,' she said firmly.

'Yes, yes, we will.' Jessie was enthusiastic, her voice eager, but Ginny looked at Frances, the weight of her worry clear: she would need more than enthusiasm in the days ahead.

'The best thing you can do is to take one day at a time,' Frances said. She looked about her. 'How long have you got left on the flat?'

'Until the thirtieth.'

'Have you asked if you can get anything back if you leave earlier?'

Ginny shook her head. 'I can't think straight. All I can think about is this.' She pointed to her stomach, which showed no signs of her problems. Not yet, at least. Perhaps she would be neat and get away with it. Some girls did. If she was lucky, she could keep dancing until she dropped as Frances had done. She tried to be encouraging. 'Should we ask?'

Ginny shrugged. 'I don't see the point. I'll have to find something else and I'd need another deposit.'

Jessie was about to say something but looked at Frances and closed her mouth.

'What?'

Jessie reddened. Ginny looked at her. 'I was thinking . . .'

Frances half knew what was coming next. It would be typical of Jessie, trying to solve everyone's problems without thinking too much of the consequences. 'Yes?'

Jessie frowned. 'You know what I'm going to suggest. I saw when you looked at me.'

Frances tilted her chin. 'I have no idea *what* you're thinking.'

'That Ginny should come and stay with us at Barkhouse Lane. I could share with you and then Ginny could have my room.'

'Oh, no, Jessie! I wouldn't dream of it. And I wouldn't want to. What would your mum and Geraldine think? And Eddie. How embarrassing for him. For them all. No, I couldn't do it.' Ginny became quite agitated and Jessie reached for her hand.

'They wouldn't think anything. They would help.'

Ginny was tearful. 'You have no idea, Jessie. No idea at all.' Jessie was offended and let go of her hand, thought better of it and took it in hers again. 'I'm sorry, Jessie. I don't mean to be harsh, but people will judge me by the mess I've got myself into.'

Frances leant forward.

'And Billy will go on living life his own sweet way, regardless.' It made her sick to think of it.

'But if he knew? What if we contact him?' Jessie got up. 'My agent, Bernie, will know where he is. He was going to get him a job on the wireless. I can write to Bernie, send a telegram.'

Ginny reached up and tugged at her sleeve, pulled her back onto the settee. 'It's a nice thought, Jessie, but it's not going to happen. It's my own stupid fault. I should've said no.' She wiped her nose on her sleeve. 'I just wanted to be loved ...'

Frances was quiet. She had loved Johnny and he her, or at least, she'd believed he had. She hadn't felt soiled or abused. Not then. She closed her eyes, remembering stolen kisses in the darkness of the wings, away from the ever-watchful eye of his mother. What had gone wrong? She'd known what she was doing and had wanted to be a part of him, and he her. They had belonged together. It was different. She considered Ginny and how best to offer solace, knowing it wouldn't make things better, no matter what she said.

'Perhaps Lil will know of lodgings. I'll ask.' Frances checked her watch, stood up. 'I need to get back. I have to be at the Fisherman's before six.'

Jessie sighed. 'I'd forgotten. Oh, we must find out if Jack's going to open the Empire again. Will you call in and check if you have time, Frances?'

Frances said she would. She picked up her jacket and Ginny shuffled to the end of the settee. Frances put out her arm. 'Stay where you are. Hopefully, you'll be back to work tomorrow.'

'I will. Thanks, Frances. For everything. Cleaning, everything.'

Frances put on her jacket and flicked her hair from under the collar. They had done so very little. 'It was nothing. Rest. It will help.' She gave her a small smile and walked towards the door.

Jessie got up. 'I'll come out with you.'

*

Jessie followed Frances down into the hall. They heard the click of the landlady's door.

'All right, is she? Your friend?'

'She is, thank you,' Frances said, her smile false. 'Eaten bad food.' No need for more information than was necessary. The two girls stepped out into the street.

'I couldn't tell you before, Frances. I promised Ginny I wouldn't say anything.'

Frances adjusted her jacket. She smelt of sickness and sweat and needed to get freshened up before she went to work.

'No need to apologise, Jessie, you did it for all the right reasons. Keeping secrets isn't easy.' Her duplicity made her squirm. Jessie was a good kid and kind, but most of all she was loyal. Would she ever forgive Frances for holding back? What did it matter? If the theatres were opening, Jessie would be off to London; they would all move on in time.

'I'll say,' Jessie said, her shoulders sagging with the relief. 'I hated not telling you, but a promise is a promise. And it wasn't mine to tell.'

Frances pressed Jessie's arm. 'Exactly.' She looked up at the window of the flat. 'Poor, poor Ginny. What a state she was in.'

'But it will be better now. Now that we can help her,' Jessie said eagerly. 'A trouble shared and all that?'

Frances smiled. 'Let's hope so.'

Chapter 13

Jack Holland often questioned the choices he'd made in life, but buying the Empire had never been one of them. It had given him a sense of purpose and direction that had otherwise been lacking. If his wife could only see it from his point of view, things would be so much easier.

'Please, come with me, Audrey? It will be good for the staff to see us as a united front.'

She was leaning into the ornate mirror over the fireplace, running her index finger over her brows, smoothing them into place, standing back to check the symmetry.

'But we're not a united front, are we, Jack? I loathe the place. It will be the ruin of us.' She gripped the mantlepiece, staring down at her hands. 'What will be left for our children? For us?'

She turned away from the mirror, picked up one of her magazines from the coffee table and sat down. 'Of all the places to invest! A damn theatre, for heaven's sake.' She flicked the pages, looking at them but not seeing. 'I tried to warn you against it, but would you listen?' She glared at him. 'When everything was uncertain, when the threat of war was the world's waking thought, you knew best and you went ahead.'

'It was a risk, Audrey – and it paid off. We've had a successful summer, the profits of which will keep us going for a while yet. And there are other opportunities already presenting themselves. It's the beginning of things for us, not the end.'

She sneered, pitying him, but he'd become immune to her disappointment; she'd been proud of him once, in his officer's uniform, but he'd returned a different man and he knew it was a man she didn't care for. He didn't blame her. War had changed him.

He turned his back and looked out of the window. Brooklands Avenue had been a good choice, a quiet enclave of private homes, all unique, and only a short walk to the promenade and seafront. The air was clean and fresh, the people welcoming. He'd thought to delight her, but nothing seemed to work, although he wouldn't give up trying.

'Why couldn't you invest in clothing, as my father did? We could be churning out uniforms. Or engineering.' She sighed. 'In God's name, why the theatre?'

They'd had this argument so many times. It was like the needle was stuck in a groove and she couldn't move on to another song, a brighter, happier one. Like the songs that Madeleine Moore and people like her sang in theatres each night. He couldn't invest in the tools of war, in armaments or uniforms – he would fight for his country another way.

'Because morale is important. *Happiness* is important.'

'Yours, perhaps. But not mine.' She slapped the magazine back on the low table and reached for the cigarette box, took out a cigarette. He hurried forward, picked up the silver table lighter and held the flame. She leant into it and he tried to catch her eye but she wouldn't look at him. He could see the fear behind the bitterness. He'd learnt a lot in the trenches, survival mostly, but about people too; how they reacted when they thought all was lost. How could he make her understand how important it was? 'I know I've asked a lot of you, Audrey, but trust me. Please.'

She blew out her smoke, licked the corner of her lips. She was still quite beautiful but the softness she once possessed was masked by disappointment; he knew he was the cause of it.

'Do I have an option?'

'Come with me?' he asked again.

'I don't think so, Jack. There's nothing I can say that will help anyone. They don't need my bitterness at a time like this.'

He wasn't going to push her; Audrey would have to come around in her own time. He leant forward and kissed her cheek but she didn't respond.

He took his hat from the oak dresser in the hallway, scarcely taking in his reflection, not wanting to be reminded of the scar that ran across one side of his face, close to his ear. His shoes clicked on the black-and-white tiled floor, the sun shining through the stained-glass panels in the front door throwing rainbows at his feet. Stepping out into the avenue he turned right and walked down towards the sea. It lifted his heart when he saw it.

On the main road people were out, defiant as he had expected them to be. Army trucks rattled down the road towards the holiday camps near North Sea Lane, fresh-faced lads staring out at shops that had been boarded up. Buckets and spades and tacky holiday ornaments had been hidden from view – but they were still there, waiting, just as the theatre was. He checked his watch, quickened his pace.

Despite his words to Audrey, a small part of him knew she was right. It was a huge risk. He'd had no experience of theatre before he bought the Empire, but he loved it and believed in it with a passion that he no longer felt for anything else. All his life he had done what was expected of him, but for some inexplicable reason he'd made a rogue decision. The looming approach of another war had left him morose, his thoughts returning frequently to the Western Front, the horror of it. He'd survived when many of his friends had not, and those that did ... He sighed heavily. How damaged they were. Audrey would never understand. She was an only child and although loss was all around her, it hadn't touched her as it had so many families. He wouldn't be called to arms this time, his injured leg had seen to that. He was too old anyway, his sight not so sharp; but his mind was, and he intended to use it.

Jessie sat in the front row of the stalls, waiting for Jack to make his appearance. Dolly was on one side of her, Frances and Ginny on the other. The door to the stalls had been wedged open and cleaners, usherettes and anyone else who remained had gathered to hear what the boss had to say. Everyone had kept to their small groups, but they were all in it together. They all wanted the Empire to open its doors again. Jessie tried not to dwell on the fact that she should have been travelling to the West End for her debut. She thought how Aunt Iris would gloat over her failures, her inadequacies. Was she being selfish? Her mother might be safer in Norfolk, and Uncle Norman would be delighted to have Eddie back. They had no children and Eddie would inherit the thriving solicitors' practice. She balled her fists. She mustn't let doubts fill her head, not now. The theatres were opening. It might take time, but she would be ready for any opportunity that came her way. Bernie Blackwood would get her something. He'd been her father's friend – they had been in the same regiment – and he wouldn't forget her. Would he?

'Oh, gosh, Frances! I keep praying Jack'll put a show on. I don't think I can stick another week with old Beaky Bird.'

'He wouldn't have called us if he didn't have some sort of plan,' Frances said, her long legs stretched out in front of her. 'He'd have got Annie to type a letter and send a copy to everyone.'

Dolly agreed. 'Oh, yes, I'm sure he will. It means too much to him, doesn't it?'

Ginny pouted. 'God forbid I have to stick in that laundry.' She looked at her hands, chapped and raw, her nails short. 'Much longer and I'll have hands like my mother. She'd be so upset if she could see me.'

Frances nudged her. 'You're doing what you need to do. She'd be proud of you.'

Ginny shrugged. 'Perhaps.'

Jessie leant forward so that she could see Ginny's face. 'Have you had a chance to see your landlady yet, ask her about a refund?'

Ginny reddened. 'Not yet.'

'We'll come with you after we find out what Jack has to say. She might be a bit less scary if we're all together,' Frances said.

'As if you're scared of anyone, Frances!' Jessie said, leaning back.

'You'd be surprised what I'm scared of, Miss Delaney.' She gave her a nudge, but she was smiling.

There was a shift in energy and everyone turned to see Jack striding down the aisle, smiling at everyone, Annie, with her ever-present clipboard, following close behind. Jessie felt a tingle run through her body and sat up straight. Someone got up at the back and closed the doors; Jessie heard the soft bang as they shut. It seemed to make everything more intimate. Mike came out of the wings and sat down near what remained of his crew. Only the older men were there, the younger chaps conspicuous by their absence. Had they signed up? Were they in the RAF like Harry, or gone to sea like Pete, Dolly's fiancé? Dolly had confided her fears in Jessie. She was used to Pete being away at sea for days on end and fishing wasn't the safest of jobs – ships went down in heavy seas, men were lost overboard, some lost limbs when caught in the heavy rigging – but war brought other dangers and the dark waters of the North Sea left them nowhere to hide.

Annie stood to Jack's left, pen poised over her clipboard. Jack cleared his throat.

'Morning, everyone. I must say, it's good to see so many of you here.' He made sure he looked along the rows, making eye contact with them all, paused, smiled encouragingly, then was serious. He rubbed his hand around his chin. 'The good news is that the Empire will be opening again, I can assure you of that. But . . .' He smiled wryly. 'There's always a but, isn't there?' A few nodded, a few groaned. 'I don't have an exact date.' He put his hands out in front of him. 'Many of our young men who worked backstage have already signed up. Mike here, like me, is a bit past his best so we need to stay and make sure those men have something to come back to.' There was a call of 'Here, here!' from George and some of the older members assembled. 'Those young men are already filling billets and camps in Cleethorpes and Grimsby and they'll want to be entertained.'

'Cheeky!' Doris, one of the cleaners called out. 'I'll not be doing no entertaining, not with my bunions.' Everyone laughed and Jack stretched out his arm, holding out his hand towards Doris.

'Thank you, Doris. That illustrates my point perfectly.' He looked along the rows, making sure they all felt included. 'Morale is important. Laughter is important. Sticking together is important.'

'By, it is love,' Doris called out again, 'it is.'

Jack grinned. 'Those of us who are older will no doubt have memories of the hardships of the Great War.' Again, there was a general rumble of agreement and Jessie clasped her hands and twisted them. She recalled her father, Davey, calling out into the night, the sudden screams, their mother comforting him. Then again, when he was ill, dying. She looked up at Jack. Could it make a difference, laughter and song, when all was said and done? Davey had believed it could.

'I intend to do the very best I can to provide entertainment for the people of this town, the soldiers and sailors, the airman who may come to be with us in the coming months. But …' He paused. 'I need to make money too or we'll have to close, regardless.' He thrust his hands in his pockets, suddenly uncomfortable. 'So, even though I am fighting to keep variety live in this theatre, until I can get something more solid, I will be showing films.' There was a general groan and Jessie sank into her seat. There would be little chance to perform. She tried to keep positive, but it had been a blow. A quick glance at Ginny and Frances told her that they felt the same. Dolly would have work, but even her mouth was turned down. She loved live entertainment as much as the girls loved performing.

Jack paced the stage. 'I know, I know it's disappointing, but I can compromise. We'll do Cine Variety. We'll have a film then an act. A singer.' He took one hand from his pocket. 'Dancers.' He smiled at the girls. 'Comedians.' Jessie flashed a look at Ginny, who screwed her lips. As long as it wasn't Billy Lane. 'It will give me peace of mind to know that I'm halfway there. And Cyril. Cyril, are you there?' He put his hands to his eyes and they turned to where George was sitting. The man next to him got to his feet. 'Ah, this is Cyril, our projectionist.' Cyril raised his hand and they turned to check on the newcomer, then back to Jack. 'Cyril has checked the projection equipment left by the last owners and he should be able to get it all shipshape in a couple of days. Films are booked and on their way. That means we need to get the theatre up and running.

Front of house staff?' They sat up. 'Let's get things in place as soon as we can. Annie?' She stepped forward and he touched her shoulder. 'If you take our wonderful team into the foyer, you can give them the information they need to get the Empire open on Monday.' There were gasps of delight and Jessie clapped her hands. Frances shook her head, grinning at Jessie's enthusiasm. Jessie didn't care. Something was happening at last, something good. Annie stepped down into the auditorium and there was a clatter of seats as people got up and followed her. Dolly wiggled her fingers at the girls. 'That's me,' she said in a loud whisper, 'see you all later?'

'Joyce's.' Frances said.

'Usual table by the window.' Dolly hurried along the aisle and caught up with her colleagues. As the door banged shut, Jack came down into the stalls and walked in front of the girls. 'I can't give any dates yet, but I hope you'll be willing to take part and I'll be putting on a pantomime as planned. The scenery is already on hire, acts being contacted, bookings made. I'd like to give you girls something. Could we work together on it, do you think? I'm thinking especially of you, Jessie.'

His words warmed her. He had kept his promise. When the acrobatic act had had to leave suddenly in the summer Jessie had been given a solo singing spot to make up the timings. It had been Billy who put her forward, Billy who suggested they do a duet. She had thought it the first step up the showbiz ladder until Jack had cut her solo with as much speed as he had allowed it. She had blamed Madeleine Moore at the time; put it down to professional jealousy: the old hand keeping the fledgling performers where they belonged – at the bottom. She had been wrong. That had been down to Billy too. She looked up at Jack, hoping her commitment was evident. He had let her down gently when he didn't have to. After all, he was the producer and what he said was final, no argument. To smooth things over he'd promised her something in his next production and here it was. It might not be star of the show – she couldn't hope for that, not having built a name for herself yet, but it was better than nothing. And it was early days. Her head filled with pictures of being on stage, performing. They'd sung at Lil's pub a few times, but it wasn't the same as being on stage, with lights and costumes, a band.

Jack continued, 'We need to fill in the gaps until the beginning of December. We're looking at a couple of months' cine variety. We can work it on minimal staff and that will give Mike time to find more crew. OK with you, Mike?'

'Aye, Jack. I already have a couple of youngsters I can call on. What they lack in strength they'll make up for in speed. Leave it with me.'

'And George will keep us all in order, won't you, George?'

George pushed his glasses up the bridge of his nose and jiggled the arms of them over his ears. 'That's what I'm here for.'

They laughed. 'Any more of that and we'll be putting you on the stage,' Jack said.

George put up his hands. 'No, not me. I'm happy where I am.'

'We are too, George.' Jessie said. 'You're the first happy face we see when we come to the theatre and the last one when we leave. It wouldn't be the same without you.' Jessie was glad she'd spoken up. George had been almost like a father to her. She would never forget his kindness, nor Olive, his wife's, for when she'd arrived in Cleethorpes with nowhere to stay they had taken her in without a second thought. Such kindness had been overwhelming, especially after Aunt Iris's meanness.

'It wouldn't be the same without any of you,' Jack continued. 'I feel we're more than a team; we're a family, now.' There were nods of agreement because that was exactly what Jessie felt too.

Cyril coughed. 'If you don't need me for anything else, Jack, I'd prefer to go and get started.' He got up and George left with him. The stalls were empty but for the three of them and Jack.

'Girls, it's good to have you here. You have my word that there'll be something for you each week, even if it's only a couple of days. We'll have to see how it goes.'

It was a small consolation for having to keep their day jobs for a while yet.

'Do you know the subject of the panto, Jack?' Jessie asked, wondering if she'd be Cinderella or Dick Whittington, certain Jack would make sure she got a good part.

'Yes, we decided on Aladdin. All those colourful silks and jewels will look good, don't you think? Bright baubles, a lamp to light the darkness.'

'We all need one of them,' Mike chipped in. Jack laughed and leant against the rail of the orchestra pit, his hands behind him. 'Keep rehearsing, girls. Perhaps put something together for when Bernie Blackwood arrives? That way, if we can't stay open, you'll at least have something for the future.'

The girls walked through the foyer and out onto the street. The wind was blowing up from the sea and their hair flapped about their faces. Jessie pulled hers back and fastened it with a ribbon from her pocket. Ginny was still pale and gaunt, and she tugged her cardigan about her and held onto it, hunching her thin shoulders forward. Jessie had been staying with her, afraid to leave her on her own. Frances checked her change. 'I've got enough for a cuppa.'

Dolly was at their usual table in the window. It was cloudy with condensation, save for a patch she'd rubbed away. 'It's good news, isn't it? At least we have work again,' Dolly said, as they wriggled into their seats. 'Our kind of work. And the theatre is open. Jack will make it a success.'

'I hope so,' Ginny said flatly. 'We'll just have to make the best of it.'

Jessie didn't want to be despondent; this was good news for them all; she wanted to grasp at anything that gave her the feeling that things were moving again, however slowly that might be. She grinned at Dolly. 'He will. We can keep going. And we have the panto to look forward to.' It was months away, but it meant that Jack hadn't given up. And if he hadn't then neither would she.

'Do you know which one it will be?' Jessie was grateful for Dolly's enthusiasm. It must be difficult for Ginny to look forward to anything in the circumstances, but she mustn't let it drag them all down.

'Aladdin. Genies and magic lamps. It'll be such fun. Something to throw ourselves into.' Hopefully, they'd play to full houses again as they had in the summer and the thought of this lifted her again. Things were getting better slowly but surely, and she had to hold onto it for there would be darker days ahead and people would need to escape them – if only for two hours in the red velvet seats of the Empire.

'Oh, my favourite!' Dolly was delighted.

'Not mine,' Ginny said. 'Seems I can't escape the laundry.'

Jessie nudged her. 'But this is better than the Little Laundry. It will be fake bubbles and custard pies.'

'And Bernie is coming,' Frances said, reminding her that things were indeed more positive. 'He might bring good news.' Jessie wasn't sure whether it would be such good news, now that they were at war.

'Will you stay, Jessie?' Dolly asked. 'I mean, if the Empire is ready to open again, Vernon LeRoy might go ahead with his show after all.'

'I don't know.' Jessie glanced down at her hands. That excitement had long lost its shine. Would it have done the same if they had been at peace? But at least, if she went away she knew her mother and Eddie were happier now. Would she be safe in London? It hadn't been bombed so far, but it was expected. 'It might be really dangerous and I'm not brave. And Harry is nearer if I'm here.' It sounded ridiculous. So near and yet so far. He could've been a million miles away, for letters were slow, his leave brief.

'When will you see him again?'

She shrugged. 'I don't know.' She tried not to think about it too much, rereading his old letters until the new ones came just to keep him close – her longing for him a dull ache that never left her.

Frances got to her feet. 'If Bernie Blackwood's visit is imminent, we need to get cracking on something. He'll want us to audition. Let's order some drinks and then we can work out when we can rehearse.'

Frances waited at the counter for Joyce to reappear from the kitchen. Mention of auditions had brought back thoughts of Johnny – not that he had been far from her mind. And Patsy wouldn't let the subject drop, nagging at her to make contact. It would be easier now they were back in the country. Their appearances would be noted in *The Stage* so she would know where to find him from now on – when she decided that that was what she wanted. The Randolphs had been due to appear at the Coliseum but whether the shows would resume in London was anyone's guess.

Joyce bustled behind the counter carrying a Victoria sponge covered with a glass dome which she placed in the gap between the scones and a treacle tart.

'How are you lasses doing? Any news?'

'A bit. The Empire will reopen on Monday,' Frances replied. 'They're going to put films on.'

'Oh, that's a damn shame. What are you girls going to do?'

Frances leant on the counter, fiddling with the container of spoons Joyce kept on one side, twisting it this way and that. Joyce watched her. 'I'll carry on at the pub. Jack'll put a spot of variety here and there between the films, but mostly we'll have to juggle things until the panto in December.'

Joyce rubbed her hands. 'Oh, that's marvellous. Christmas would be bleak without a few bright, shining stars. I do love a panto. Oh, yes, I do.' Frances laughed and Joyce spread her hands on the counter. 'At least we'll have something to look forward to, lovey. And my God, aren't we going to need it? She picked up a tea towel, ran it over her hands. 'I know it seems like nowt's going on at the moment, but it is.' She was sombre. 'There's always something going on we don't know about. There's gonna be more dark days ahead of us, you mark my words, winter or not.' Frances had tried to shut those thoughts out of her head. The noise of the café sounded as if it was coming from somewhere else. Her only thought was Imogen, the two of them in the darkness when all she wanted was the light. Joyce broke into her thoughts. 'What can I get you, lovey?' Frances gave her order and when the drinks were ready, took them back to the table.

'Can you rehearse on Sunday, Frances?' Jessie was writing on the back of a paper serviette. 'We could get a full day in before they start putting the films on.'

'I can't do Sunday, Jessie.' It irritated. How many times would she have to repeat herself? 'You know I can't.'

'You did the other week.'

Frances felt her skin prickle. 'That was different. We were waiting for news of war.' The events of that day erupted in her head. The interminable waiting, the ticking of the clock, Geraldine's condemnation of the girl from Louth. Of girls like her. She swallowed the thoughts down. 'I needed to know where I stood. We all did.' She lifted the cups from the tray and placed them in front of her friends.

'But just once,' Jessie pleaded. 'Surely your friend won't mind?'

'No, Jessie, I'm not changing it.' She looked at her watch. 'I can do a couple of hours now, then I have to open up for Lil.'

'But it's *important*.' Jessie wasn't going to give up.

'Paying bills is important.' Frances sat down, sipped at her tea. Joyce was right. The bombs hadn't come as expected but they would, in time. Hitler was lurking in the background, waiting, and it was making everyone uneasy. Jessie was persistent.

'*This* will help pay the bills, Frances. I'm being realistic, like you're always telling me. You should be happy.'

'I am.' She was cheered by Jessie's ebullience but wouldn't let it sway her. Anything could happen between now and December: the panto might get cancelled, she might have to find work elsewhere, leave Imogen with Patsy for longer. If the bombs fell … No, it was out of the question. 'I can't give up paid work, Jessie. I have to fit it around my commitments.'

'But visiting your friend is not a commitment.'

'It is,' Frances snapped. 'I don't want to discuss it.' She was aware her voice was sharp. 'Sundays are out for me.'

The girls were silent.

'But ...' Jessie said, softly.

'No buts.' She stirred sugar into her tea and the only sound was the clatter of the spoon as it hit the side of the cup. It was awful not being to explain further but this was neither the time nor the place. When would it be? She picked up her cup, took a sip, swallowed, looked at the girls. She smiled to dispel the awkwardness that had settled between them. 'Better make the most of the two hours if you want me.'

When the two hours were up, Frances gathered her things and left. It had been enough to move them forward and their routine was slowly taking shape. Jessie and Ginny sat at the edge of the stage and Dolly came to join them from where she'd been watching from the front row.

Jessie was sulky. 'I wonder why she has to go to her friends every Sunday. It's a bit odd, if you ask me.'

Dolly sat down with them. 'Have you ever met her friends?'

Jessie shook her head. 'No. But she goes there every Sunday, religiously.'

'Maybe it *is* religious,' Ginny said, idly. 'Perhaps she goes to church all day and is too embarrassed to say anything.'

Jessie laughed. 'Embarrassed? Frances? No, Frances is never embarrassed about anything. There's something she isn't telling us.'

Ginny was quiet. 'We all have secrets, Jessie. If Frances wanted to talk about it, she would.' Was she talking about herself or Frances? No one would understand better than Ginny. Dolly was tracing circles on the floor with her finger and Jessie bit at the inside of her cheek. They were supposed to be friends but they were all keeping secrets ... She put her hand on Dolly's shoulder.

'Have you heard where Pete is?' She berated herself for not asking sooner. Dolly was always the first to ask about everyone else.

Dolly stopped, sat back, her hands on her lap. 'On the convoys going over the Atlantic as far as I can guess. I have to work it out from the letters, the parts that aren't blacked out. He gives me clues, like "Tell Dick I've been at the old place", then I ask my brother-in-law what he means and we work it out between us.' For once the smile disappeared from her face. 'The troops might be doing nothing much in France but the war's pretty real for men like him, out at sea.'

Jessie took her hand. There were no words of comfort were there? They just had to pray – and hope.

Chapter 14

Johnny yawned and stretched his arms out as wide as he could. The journey seemed endless, the hours ticking by as they headed north, and he leant back in his seat, staring out of the window. The landscape had changed from the hills and valleys to the flatlands of Lincolnshire. They were almost there but still a few miles yet to go.

'Had a snooze, young fella?' Bernie had the window open, his elbow resting on it, his hand on the wheel. Johnny eased himself upright.

'I must have nodded off. It was that fry-up we had at the service station on the Great North Road. Made me drowsy.'

'It'll put a good lining on your stomach, my boy.' Bernie tooted his horn at a passing army truck and waved to the boys. Johnny yawned again, wound down his window and leant his shoulder towards it. It was good to breathe in the fresh air as they moved along, to see the green fields, hedgerows and winding lanes that were so familiar to England. He hoped he would always be able to see the beauty of it.

'It's good to be home, Bernie. I was thinking of all the miles we travelled in the States. Wide open spaces that stretched for miles, mountains, dust bowls, trees that seemed to touch the sky. Bigger than you could imagine, if you hadn't seen it for yourself.'

'Bigger and better?' Bernie looked away from the road briefly and at him. There were few cars, unlike the wide, busy freeways of America. The cars here had all seemed so small when he'd come back – everything had seemed smaller, cosier, more comforting. Well, to him, if not to Ruby. He wondered if anything would ever be of comfort to her.

'No, different. But it's good to be home.' They'd loved America in the beginning, feeling as if something wonderful was within touching distance. And it was. They'd worked hard to make it so. But it had soured and there was nothing he could do about it. He'd tried. Johnny folded his arms and adjusted his legs. Bernie's car was luxurious but after a hundred miles even the luxury of a Daimler waned. They'd stopped once or twice but Bernie was eager to get to Grimsby in daylight. He didn't want to be driving along unfamiliar roads in the blackout and he wanted Johnny to see the place in good light.

'Well, at least you get to see it in its autumn glory. It's a good job you could join me. When petrol rationing comes in, we won't have the luxury – or the freedom.'

'When will it come in?'

'Any day, my boy. Any day.'

Johnny grinned. 'One of your many "ears"?'

Bernie smiled. 'One of many.' Johnny looked back out of the window. Troop trucks were rattling by in the other direction, heading down south to the coast. They had passed so many of them, kids looking out of the back of the trucks. Because they were just kids, these new recruits.

Bernie pulled a cigar from his top pocket and stuck it in his mouth but made no attempt to light it.

'Thinking of joining up at any time, Johnny?'

'As soon as we get this bit of business sorted, Bernie. It would set us up, keep things ticking along for Ruby until it's all over. It'll be good for her, to have a purpose. And I think she'll be better out of London – and safer.'

'From the bombs? Or the parties?'

'Both.'

Ruby was out of control and they had their reputation to think of. Yes, she'd had her dalliances, a polite way of putting it, but she wasn't the only one. They had learned just how much was covered up from the public when they were in the States. The silence of the press could be bought; everyone, it seemed, could be bought – and everything. It all had a price, if you were prepared to pay it.

'What happened? She was always such a sweetie. I mean, she still is. Don't mind a fumbling idiot with his words, my boy. I didn't mean to insult your sister, she's a sweet girl.'

'She is. And don't worry, Bernie, I know what you mean.' Bernie was being kind. Ruby was not the girl she was when they'd left for America, but he couldn't tell Bernie everything. Johnny trusted him as much as he trusted anyone, but the work could dry up. The theatres were able to reopen but many of them were being cautious, especially in town. There were more people fighting for fewer jobs. If Ruby got a reputation for letting people down it would affect them both and he couldn't let her throw away all that they had worked so hard for.

'Didn't she want to go?'

He smiled, remembering her eagerness. 'Couldn't wait to get on the boat at Southampton, she was so excited. Mother came out with us for the first year and everything was great; we got a terrific reception from all the towns we played.' It was exciting but exhausting, hours and hours travelling state to state; checking into lodgings then out again; brief stops when their days were empty, their nights full. They had been lonely but had jollied each other along and he'd kept Ruby busy working, rehearsing. It hadn't been as glamorous as it was made out to be. Many times he'd yearned for the simple things, for home.

'So I heard my boy. Everyone heard. The reports in *The Stage* followed your journey. Quite a name you were making for yourselves out there.'

'We were. But it's not home, is it? And then Mother died. And well, I've told you all this before.'

Bernie took the cigar from his mouth and returned it to his pocket. 'Sounds to me like Ruby's still grieving badly and partying her way out of it.'

Johnny sighed. 'She is, Bernie, but that's not the way to do it, is it?'

Bernie shrugged. 'We all grieve in our different ways. Good job she's got you.'

Johnny looked out of the window. He was grieving too. If only he could have talked to his mother … She would know how to deal with Ruby, she always had. And Ruby had listened – eventually. He was afraid for her more than he had ever been. She was reckless, adrift. At least Aunt Letty was with her and perhaps a few days of them being alone would help. Aunt Letty wouldn't suffer any nonsense – and with that thought he eased back in his seat again.

The landscape changed as they drew nearer to Grimsby, past fine houses, a church, then along the main shopping street lined with jewellers and department stores. It wouldn't impress Ruby, but it might pique her interest. He felt a pang of guilt. Perhaps he should have enlarged on his plans, but would she have listened? He decided not. After all, he might not like it himself. Grimsby, what was he thinking? It had been a suggestion from Bernie. A suggestion, that's all. It was up to him to work out whether it would be suitable.

'Damn good job I've been here before,' Bernie muttered. 'I'd have no ruddy idea where I was, otherwise.' The shops became warehouses. Johnny took in the high, smoke-covered walls and different smells that emanated from the dock area:

coal, hemp, fish. Mostly fish. He grimaced. It was grubby, industrial – he could almost smell the sweat of the toil – but the variety and number of shops indicated there was money to spend. They passed the bus station and neared the docks on which Grimsby had built its empire. Bernie pulled the car onto the opposite side of the road and pointed to a building slightly ahead so that Johnny had the better view. 'There she is, my boy. The Palace Theatre. Whaddya think of her?'

Johnny leant forward and peered through the windscreen. It was ornate, over the top, with pointed roofs, domes and cupolas. A statue presided over the centre entrance and a long canopy covered the frontage. It seemed that the architect had taken his favourite features and given them all to the Palace. It looked large enough to make a profit, if the houses were good – and so far, the indications were that they would be. There was a warehouse and flour mill to the right of it, a pub to the left. A large iron bridge went over the river. Oh, Ruby would hate it. He didn't care for it much himself.

'That's the Palace Buffet on the corner – see it? Does good business. All part of the deal.' Bernie drove slowly down the road, pointing out the other theatres that had gone to cinema.

'Lot of competition, Bernie.'

'It's a big town, Johnny, my boy. Prosperous. Smell that money.'

Johnny laughed. 'I can smell fish.'

'Like I said, money.' He drove into the dock area. Even though it was late in the day there were still signs of activity; people came and went, wagons passed, and trawlers were lined side by side in the docks, packed in like sardines. 'Lots of 'em have gone, converted to minesweepers,' Bernie explained. 'But they'll be back. And boats are out there still, catching fish. We'll always need food, whether it's from the sea itself, or cargoes from other places.'

They paused at the crossing while a train with numerous wagons rattled past. The gates were swung back and Bernie drove on, past a gentleman's outfitters and furniture shops. They came to a crossroads that had a large pub on one corner.

'We're in Cleethorpes now,' Bernie said as he changed gear and picked up a little speed. The road was long, filled on one side with small shops such as fishmongers and greengrocers, with houses along the other; nice houses they were too, with small front gardens, trees and hedges. Bernie drove up a small hill, lined on either side with guest houses, past a library and cinema, pubs and shops. The road curved around, showing the sea to the left and leading on to a long road that had ornate gardens to one side, a fancy hotel and a parade with shops on the other. It was much like many other seaside towns they'd worked in – a different one each year. He smiled, remembering the fun of them, being in one place for weeks on end, making friends, relaxing. It had been the best of times, he realised now, if he hadn't known it then. Perhaps that was what Ruby needed.

'Your little sister will prefer this.' Bernie said as he stopped the car opposite a theatre, the Empire, and left the engine running. Johnny looked down towards the sea and the pier. It was lovely little place. He liked it.

'My good friend, Jack Holland, is the proud owner of that little beauty. We'll call and see him tomorrow. He's putting on a bit of cine variety to get going again; testing the waters.' He started driving again and Johnny looked at the resort as Bernie gave him a rundown. 'It's all going to be a bit of a risk, isn't it, these early days? But where there's risk, there's reward. And the bigger the risk—'

'The bigger the reward,' Johnny finished. The two men smiled.

'I wanted you to see it for yourself. See what you think. It's all about the gut, my boy. All about the gut.'

He pulled up outside an open-air bathing pool and they got out and walked around the frontage. Johnny stretched and bent, trying to ease the discomfort of the last few hours. He rested his hand on his hips and looked about him. On opposite sides of the road in front of them were two buildings built for fun and entertainment. He walked to the Café Dansant, peered through the windows, and crossed over to the Olympia. A sign on the door proclaimed that the Olympia Dance Orchestra would be there at the weekend, would be back in business. They all had to bounce back, didn't they?

Bernie stood on the pavement, took out his cigar and turned his back to the wind to light it. He puffed and blew out the smoke. 'Far enough away for you? And Ruby?'

Johnny put his hands in his pockets. The wind was sharp. What would it be like when winter came?

'It could be. I don't know, Bernie.' He didn't want to commit himself to anything that would tie them up long-term. Although, now that they were committed to war, everything was liable to change at any time and he sensed that what Ruby needed was stability. Would this offer it to her? He wasn't convinced. 'Could we look about the theatre?'

Bernie put his hand on his back as they walked back to the car. 'Sure we can, sure we can.' They stood in the fresh air for a few more seconds and Bernie said, 'I don't mind what you choose. And I mean that, Johnny.' He opened his door. 'Let's go back to the Palace and you can have a good look around. I wanted you to see what was on offer, that was all. There's more to this area than fish.'

They drove back down the long road, leaving Cleethorpes behind them, and Bernie parked his car outside the Palace. He checked his watch.

'We've made good time, my boy. Stan Simms should be here. He's the manager. I asked him to open up and show us around.' They walked to the front of the theatre and Bernie pushed on the door and walked in. A light was on in a small office to the right of the foyer and a tall man with neat white hair came out. His posture indicated a military past and he had a tidy moustache and black eyes.

'Mr Blackwood. Good to see you again.' He put out his hand and Bernie gripped it, pumping it vigorously. It seemed to Johnny that Bernie didn't hold back on anything. He let go of Simms's hand and turned to Johnny. 'Johnny Randolph, Stan Simms.' Johnny reached forward and shook the man's hand.

'Good to meet you, Johnny. I hope I may call you Johnny?'

'Of course.' He would make certain Ruby was addressed as Miss Randolph, though, if they came. She needed boundaries. Stan stretched out his arm.

'Let me show you around?'

'That would be great, Stan. I'd like Johnny to get an idea of the place, inside and out; the clientele we can expect. I'd like your take on it as much as anything.' Stan opened the door into the stalls.

'Follow me.' He led them down the aisle and up onto the stage. The safety curtain had been flown out and the three men stood looking out into the rows of empty seats. 'Room for one and half thousand when we're capacity,' Stan informed them.

Johnny moved about the stage while Bernie and Stan remained where they were, talking quietly. He had to get a feel for this. Bernie had already spoken of his ideas for the theatre. In normal circumstances they would turn up wherever they were booked and make the most of it; and for a few months more they would have the luxury of being able to choose. Perhaps the war had been a good thing for them – if ever anything good could come from war. It had certainly bought them time. If the show had gone ahead at the Coliseum, Ruby could have partied even harder. He knew he needed to get her away, but not on a whim and certainly not to the first opportunity that presented itself. Bernie had been as good as his word, finding something that was mutually beneficial, but Johnny needed to see more before he made a commitment. He wandered into the wings.

'The lights are on all over, Johnny. Take your time,' Stan called out.

He went backstage and checked the dressing rooms, the back access, the stage door. A rat scuttled into a hole. That was nothing new. He made his way up into the gods, looked down on the stage, at Bernie and Stan, sat down on the banked seats, leant on the rail. Would it be enough? He rested his chin on his hands. He could put up with anything, go anywhere – it didn't matter to him, but he owed it to Ruby to take care of her. More than that, he owed it to their mother. He was glad he'd spoken to Aunt Letty. He understood now, more than he had before. His mother must have been so afraid when father died, alone and grieving, with two small children to care for. No wonder she was so driven, so determined to make sure they were a success. Secure. Ruby was young, she wanted fun, but an excess of fun was leading to her ruin. Would this be too brutal? He walked back down to the stage. Bernie and Stan were sitting down at the back of the stalls.

'Seen enough, my boy?'

'I have. Thanks, Stan.' The two men stood up.

'My pleasure,' Stan said, standing back.

Bernie put out his hand and Stan shook it. 'Thank you, Stan. I appreciate you staying on for us. I'll be in touch tomorrow if we need to call in before we go. Otherwise I'll be in contact from my office when I'm back in town.'

'Right you are, Bernie,' Stan said.

Bernie led the way into the light of the foyer, Johnny and Stan bringing up the rear. It was hard to tell what time of day it was inside with all the windows blackened in the foyer and as Bernie and Johnny stepped out into the street, daylight was fading. The traffic had slowed but the road was still busy with buses and bicycles as people went about their business.

'The hotel beckons, my boy. Shall we get freshened up? Have a rest? I don't know about you, but my backside feels numb.'

Johnny laughed. 'I don't know why – you've got enough to cushion it.' Bernie slapped his back and the two of them crossed the road to the car. Three kids were running their hands over the bodywork, peering into the windows and admiring the motor. They leapt away when Bernie got to the door.

'A beauty, isn't it, boys?'

'It is, sir.'

They stood back while Johnny got into his seat and raced after the car as it moved off down the road. Johnny could see them in the wing mirror, their faces bright with nothing more than admiration. What it was to be happy with the simple things.

The dining room of the Royal Hotel was quiet. Staff were attentive and there were a few looks and quiet comments as Bernie and Johnny were shown to a table. Bernie picked up the menu. 'Has to be fish, doesn't it? Can't come to Grimsby and not have the fish.' He leant back in his seat to get nearer the waiter. 'What do you recommend, old chap?'

The elderly man leant forward, his hands behind his back, and directed them towards the plaice and they were happy to go with his recommendation. Wine was brought over to Bernie to taste and approve while they waited for the meal to arrive. Bernie touched the ends of the silver cutlery. His hands were big, practical.

'I suppose I should give you more details, now that you've seen the theatres, and there's a third one we need to look at on our way home. We'll do the Empire in the morning and see the Royal on the way back through Lincoln.' He took his glass and quaffed a little of his wine, sat back in his chair. 'Jack Holland owns the Empire outright and he's stepping up to purchase the Palace and the Royal. I'll be looking to find other theatres to add to his stable.'

Johnny frowned.

'Isn't that madness? When the theatres have been closed and no one knows if they'll change their minds and shut them again?' The waiter placed the wine bottle on the table and disappeared.

'They won't; believe me, they won't. Jack and I saw action in the Great War. He's younger than I am but we played our part, although I remained in England. They shut the theatres then. You would have been far too young to notice, but it was a big mistake. A *big* mistake.' He eased himself forward. Conversations carried on around them, peppered by the occasional bout of laughter. Glasses tinkled and plates were removed as waiters moved discreetly about the room.

'This is the time to buy, Johnny. People are nervous; they want out and they'll lower their price to do it. Now is the time to hold your nerve. You can't panic and throw it all in the air when something doesn't go as you'd expected.'

He thought of Ruby. *He* had to hold his nerve too. Bernie continued, leaning as close as he could, lowering his voice, 'We'll all need a break from the horrors to come, because come they will and people will be looking for lightness and laughter and a chance to leave it all behind, to fall into someone else's story and have a happy ending. We all want a happy ending, don't we, my boy? It's what we yearn for.'

Johnny smiled ruefully. He had lost all hope of a happy ending for himself.

'Jack's proposing to buy. He wants to build an empire to rival that of the Stoll Moss chain and I want to help him do it. We wondered if you'd be interested, if you worked for a percentage of the take at the Palace and shares? With a name like The Randolphs, we could guarantee packed houses, two shows a day, three on Saturday. If you would be up to that?'

Johnny laughed. 'It's less than we did in the states. Vaudeville is continuous, six shows a day, morning to night. We didn't do it often, but you have to have the stamina of an ox to get through it.'

Bernie interlaced his fingers over his stomach. 'It's a lot to think about, my boy. But we don't have to rush into anything. This is a reconnaissance exercise, nothing more because I wouldn't want to offer you something you knew nothing about. It's not my way.'

'I know that, Bernie; I appreciate it.'

Bernie shook out his napkin, draped it over his lap. 'Any ladies in your life other than Ruby?'

'Only my Aunt Letty. She's with Ruby at the flat.' He leant back as the fish arrived and the plates were placed in front of them. 'There was, once.'

Bernie cut into his fish and put it in his mouth. 'Fabulous. Good choice.' The waiter smiled and left.

'Only once?'

Johnny started to eat. The fish was mouth-wateringly delicious. 'Only one that meant anything, Bernie.'

'The one that got away?' Bernie drank more wine. 'Not like this fish, eh?'

Johnny agreed.

'What happened?'

He shook his head. 'I have no idea.' He gave an empty laugh. 'No idea at all.' He wondered where she was now. Was she happy? He hoped she was. If only he'd stood firm – his mother would've come around in the end because they couldn't be children forever. At the time he hadn't realised the extent of her control over them. He loved her, she loved them – but to the exclusion of all else and it wasn't healthy. Aunt Letty was right – their mother had gone too far. No wonder Ruby was rootless. She'd never had to think of anything but the theatre, and their mother had kept it that way. Ruby's recklessness was grief – and it was also bewilderment; neither of them knew how to live.

He slept well for the first time in months. The bed was soft and he sank into the feather mattress, relaxing because he didn't have to worry about Ruby. On waking, he felt refreshed, more alert than he had in days, and he got up and went to the window, the sounds of industry and enterprise outside growing stronger with the daylight. Below him the streets were thick with people, trains and wagons moving steadily along tracks in the distance, carrying fish, he assumed. He dressed and met Bernie in the dining room, where they ate a hearty breakfast before heading for the Empire.

Bernie parked opposite the theatre. Above them the sky was thick with clouds that rolled quickly through the sky, showing patches of blue here and there. Bernie put his homburg on and tugged at his cuffs as they crossed the road. Inside the theatre a young girl with a mass of soft blonde curls smiled at them from the box office.

'Can I help, gentlemen?'

Bernie went to the arched window. 'Is Mr Holland here? Bernie Blackwood for him.' The girl was looking past him and straight at Johnny, her eyes growing rounder by the second. In the end he had to smile, even let himself laugh a little, and she blushed.

'Mr Randolph, Johnny Randolph?'

'That's me,' he said as she came out of the box office. He could see that she was nervous and he felt bad. She looked embarrassed.

'I'll let Mr Holland know you're here.' She almost curtseyed as she passed them and they heard her run upstairs.

'Quite a powerful effect you have on women, my boy.'

Johnny smiled. 'It's not me. It's who they *think* I am that has the effect.' He looked at the photos in the display cases and recognised the top of the bill, Madeleine Moore. He pointed to her photo. 'Madeleine was here? Headlining?' Bernie stood beside him, admiring the photos.

'She was. Very successful summer season. Packed every night. These people got to see a big star.'

'What was she doing here? She could top the bill anywhere.'

'Much the same as you and Ruby. Taking a step back, letting go of the pressure for a while. I believe she enjoyed it. And it was successful enough for Vernon LeRoy to come out of his way to see it.' Johnny whistled through his teeth. Bernie slapped him on the back. 'It was a special season, it really was. There's a certain magic about the place. And here's another little girl of mine, Jessie Delaney.' He tapped the photograph. 'She's going to be a big star. A *big* star. Yes, she is.' Johnny saw a girl with long brown hair, attractive, but not a beauty by any means. They were about to look in the other display case when they heard footsteps on the stairs and turned to see a man with black hair, peppered with grey. He came forward, the girl from the box office close behind him. Jack stopped in front of them while the girl went back to her position, watching them from behind the glass front of the ticket desk.

'Jack,' Bernie said, pushing Johnny gently by the back towards the man. 'My good friend, Jack Holland. Johnny Randolph.'

'Good to meet you.' Holland looked a nice chap. There was an immediate warmth about him and he had a firm handshake. As he moved, Johnny noticed his slight limp and when he smiled, Johnny could see the scar to the side of his face. Bernie had said they'd been through the Great War. At least they'd both survived, although he was well aware that scars on the outside were only a glimpse of the scars on the inside.

'Glad you could make it. Do you want to join me in my office?' They followed him upstairs to the first floor and he led them to a room where a woman with short brown hair was on the phone. 'Annie, my secretary.' Annie put one hand over the mouthpiece and said a quiet hello then returned her attention to her caller. 'She's much more than that, really. I couldn't do without her.' He led them into his office and Johnny looked out of the window across the gardens, then onto the sea. The pier was empty of people and he imagined that only a few weeks ago it would have been filled with holidaymakers enjoying the long warm evenings of summer. It made him desolate. There was nothing so sad as the seaside in winter, with only the echoes and ghosts of happiness remaining. He shuddered and turned back to the room. Jack had found another chair for Johnny and the three of them sat down.

'Can I get you a drink?'

Bernie put a hand up. 'Not for me, Jack. We had rather a substantial breakfast.' Johnny shook his head.

Jack clasped his hands in front of him and rested them on the blotter on his desk. 'Glad you could make the journey. I expect Bernie has talked over what we're proposing to do?'

Johnny sat back, crossed his legs. 'He has. It's given me plenty to think about.' They chatted about shows Johnny had been in and Jack was eager to hear of their experience of America.

'Have you ever been?' Johnny asked.

'Never. I'd like to go someday. I know my wife would and I think the lifestyle would suit her.'

'It doesn't suit everyone.' Johnny got up and walked to the window, rested his arm on the frame. Seagulls gathered along the rooftops. Would Ruby like it? 'What do you have planned for the winter, Jack? Would we be better suited here, at the Empire? If we decided to go ahead?'

Jack picked up a pencil, twisted it in his hands. 'We don't have the capacity to make it work, Johnny. Much as I'd love to have you and your sister appear here. The Palace is more than three times our size and, in the end it's all down to the numbers.'

Johnny sighed. 'It's always down to the numbers.' Numbers had trapped them. Numbers in their bank account that, although handsome, were not enough to free them from their contract. Not then – and what did it matter now? Their mother was gone. He turned his back to the window, leant against the sill.

'When do I have to let you know by?'

Jack glanced at Bernie, who turned in his seat to look at Johnny. He squinted against the light from the windows, moved so that he could see Johnny eye to eye. Johnny liked that about him. Bernie never looked away.

'Next week. I'd like to get on with the publicity. We have the pantomime in the final planning stages for the Empire. Like everyone else, we put all our plans to one side when war was declared, but now we're taking back the reins with a vengeance. Christmas will be here before we know it and

I want to make an extra effort this year. I feel we'll all be in need of it.'

'We will, Jack. Dark days ahead of us.'

Jack dropped the pencil into a leather tray. 'It should all be shipshape by the end of the week. I'd then like to put our energies into the Palace and the Royal.'

Bernie got to his feet. 'OK with you, my boy?'

Johnny came away from the window and shook hands with Jack. 'I'll let you know by Friday at the very latest.'

'I appreciate it, Johnny. I'm sure we can make it work and make money as well. But it's what you feel comfortable with. Would you like to look around the place?'

He didn't see the point. 'No, I'm fine. It's a theatre, beautiful as she is. But as we won't be appearing here, I don't want to spoil myself wishing I was.' It would make him long for the days when life was simpler, when they had so much to achieve. They had reached the top, but it hadn't brought the happiness he'd thought it would. The top was a lonely place if you didn't have anyone to share it with. If he'd known that, would he still have worked so hard? Johnny chewed his cheek. It was a huge risk and he wasn't sure he wanted to take any more. Not with Ruby as she was.

Jack led the way downstairs. The doors to the stalls were open and a piano was being played, a girl singing. Bernie turned to Jack, who was behind him on the stairs. He took his cigar from the breast pocket of his camel coat.

'Is that little Miss Delaney?'

Jack smiled. 'It is. She's rehearsing with two of her friends. A couple of the dancers stayed over from the summer and I'm putting on live entertainment between films, just to keep something going. They're going to be great, working hard, all three of them.'

'Admirable. Admirable,' Bernie said. Johnny was intrigued. He left Bernie and wandered down the aisle, sat in the back row. It was dark, the house lights off, and the girls were moving about the stage in the brutal glare of the working lights that bleached the colour from everything. The girl he assumed was Jessie Delaney was playing the piano and singing, and a stunning redhead with a great figure was working on a dance routine instructed by a girl with long black hair who had her back to him. He leant back in his seat, watching them rehearse, envying the fun they were having. When had he and Ruby last had fun? When had it not been work? Bernie and Jack stood in the doorway and he twisted towards them and gave a nod of approval, turned back to watch the girls. The girl singer was good. Very good. When she stopped playing the three men applauded and Johnny got to his feet. As he did so the girl with black hair turned around. He froze. The three girls leant forward, peering out into the darkness at them. Frances? He walked down the aisle. My God, it was her.

'Frances. Frances O'Leary!'

Chapter 15

The girls remained where they were as Johnny came towards them. He stopped by the orchestra pit, uncertain of how Frances would react. He gripped the brass rail, the metal cool beneath his fingers, and looked up at her. Her skin was milky white and she wore the same red lipstick that only made the darkness of her hair and eyes more so. Those eyes; those dark, dark eyes. She didn't look away and it gave him a little courage. He smiled but it was not returned. She had grown more lovely over the years they had been apart; there was something about the way she held herself that was tougher, harder, but he could see beyond that. She was still the same inside – he didn't know why he knew, he just did.

'Frances … It's been a long time.' He glanced briefly at her hands, the merest flicker – and there was no ring. He felt a surge of hope. He took a chance, skipped up the stairs and onto the stage.

'Frances.' He walked towards her and couldn't stop smiling, even though her face was set against him. Her eyes flashed a warning; he had no idea why. What had he done but love her? He went to embrace her, but she stepped away and he let his hands drop. The two girls came closer; were they protecting her? 'Forgive my manners, ladies. Johnny Randolph.' He bowed his head slightly, put out his hand and they took it in turn, Frances reluctantly. He gripped warmly, wrapping both hands around hers, wanting to take her into his arms. Her hand was limp in his and he couldn't for the life of him work out what he'd done to receive such a cool reception, so he held back, even though he longed to take her away, talk, find out what had made her change her mind. Had she met someone else? He looked again at her hand. No, it had to be something else. He was certain she'd loved him. Did she love him still? He couldn't tell.

'I won't keep you.' He tried to look at the other two girls, but his gaze stayed on Frances. It was hard to take in. 'It was great, what you did was great.' The red-haired girl smiled. What a beauty. The one he knew was Jessie grinned as if her face would split in two, but Frances looked ahead, past him, away into the darkness. He stood back. 'Good to see you, Frances.' She didn't respond and he turned and walked back down the stairs and into the aisle, feeling awkward, yet the blood was pumping about his body as if he'd danced for hours. Bernie and Jack were still by the door.

'All right, my boy?' Bernie tilted his chin.

Johnny put a hand on the man's back as they followed Jack out of the auditorium. 'Fine. Just fine.'

The blonde girl in the box office was smiling broadly as they came back into the foyer and she gave him a small wave. He waved back. It all felt rather odd, standing here in the little theatre, the likes of which he and Ruby had not appeared in for years – and yet for the first time in ages he felt as if he was standing on solid ground. He had found her. Part of him wanted to rush back into the theatre and run up on stage to Frances, pull her into his arms and kiss her like a corny B-movie, but common sense told him to be cautious. She hadn't spoken a word, but he'd seen something in her eyes, and that was enough. He turned to Jack and Bernie.

'About your proposition. I've made up my mind. I'm on board for the shares. The Randolphs will appear at the

Palace for the winter season. You have my word on it.' He held out his hand. Jack was taken aback, as was Bernie. The two men looked at each other.

'Are you quite certain, my boy?' Bernie removed the cigar from between his teeth.

'Absolutely. We can discuss the finer details over the telephone.'

Jack shook his hand with vigour, clasping his other over the top. 'You won't regret it, Johnny. I'll make sure of that.'

'I know you will, Jack. We'll be in touch, won't we, Bernie?'

Bernie's eyebrows were still at the top of his head and he pushed his homburg back onto it.

'You can be assured of it, Jack.'

Outside, the wind was picking up and the trees were bending in the wind. Johnny crossed the road to where the car was parked. He sat on the low wall looking up at the Empire. Bernie sat beside him.

'What was all that about?'

Johnny pressed his hand on Bernie's arm and couldn't stop smiling. 'That, Bernie, was about the one that got away.'

'Seriously? Which one?'

Johnny nudged him. 'Do you have to ask?' He folded his arms, shaking his head, grinning. Of all the places to find her. 'The one who didn't react, the one who didn't speak.'

'The tall, dark-haired girl? Frances?'

'It is, it is, Bernie. Frances O'Leary.' Just to say her name again was heaven itself. He looked up to the sky, to the clouds scudding by, and said a silent prayer. Someone up there loved him.

'So, let me get this straight. You made a business decision based purely on seeing a girl. A girl who didn't speak. A girl who didn't react.'

He laughed, patting Bernie on the shoulder. 'I did, Bernie. And I reckon it will turn out to be the best decision I ever made.'

The older man shook his head. 'I'm not going to disagree, my boy. With you on board, things will be easier.' He paused, looking back at the theatre. 'She must be some girl.'

'She is.' He could hardly believe it. A second chance. He couldn't stop smiling. What were the odds of finding her again – and here? He longed to stay, to talk to her, find out what had happened, but it was enough to know she was here and the quicker he got things finalised with Bernie, the sooner he would be back.

Bernie got up and went to the car. Johnny did likewise, taking one last look at the ornate balconies of the theatre, the long windows that ran the length of them, before he opened the door. He'd found her. All he had to do now was find out why she'd stopped all contact, why she'd never used the ticket he'd sent. He didn't need to write and have nothing come in return. It was only a matter of time, now.

Bernie started the engine. 'What about Ruby?'

Johnny settled himself in his seat for the long journey back to London as Bernie made a U-turn in the road. 'Leave Ruby to me.' She wouldn't like it one bit, but this booking, this place, would suit both of them. He had to help *her* break away from the downward spiral she was in – and he would get a chance to rekindle the love of his life. Throwing themselves into something new would be just the ticket. He took one last look at the theatre as they passed it. There was a chance they could find happiness after all.

Frances couldn't move. She could only watch as Johnny walked away from her.

'Did that really happen?' Jessie was shaking her head. 'Did Johnny Randolph really walk into this theatre and tell us we were good? And he remembered you, Frances, after all this time. Not everyone does. People can be flakes.'

'He's not everyone,' Ginny said. Jessie twisted to look at her and Frances turned away, moving back towards the piano. It felt as though her legs would go from under her and she needed something to lean onto. 'I've never had anyone look at me that way. Billy never did. Not once.' Frances sat down on the piano stool. 'You were more than an understudy, Frances; it's obvious from the way he looked at you.' Ginny leant on the piano.

'Never!' Jessie was incredulous. 'You said you worked with The Randolphs, that you understudied his sister. You never said anything about the two of you being together.'

'There's nothing to say.' Frances didn't want to remember because it would bring back happier times and that would lead her to sadness and pain and she hadn't time for it now, to be dragged back through it all. 'We should be rehearsing. Time's running out and I have to go to work.' She got up, sat down again.

Jessie sat next to her, held her hand. 'You're white as a sheet, Frances.' Ginny hurried over to her bag at the side of the stage and brought back a bottle of water, pulled out the stopper and handed it to Frances, who took a sip, and then another. It was so confusing. She'd never expected Johnny to turn up. Not ever. She'd thought that she would have to go looking if she wanted to tell him about Imogen, that he would avoid her. But he hadn't. She sipped at the water again; she was beginning to shake uncontrollably and she fought to steady herself.

'What happened, Frances?' Jessie's face was etched with concern. Frances took another sip of water, rested the bottle on her legs.

'We were in the show, in London. Johnny asked me out and I liked him.'

'Who wouldn't?' Ginny said and Frances looked across at her and smiled.

'Yes, he's good-looking, and yes, he's a wonderful dancer – but he's also very kind and quiet, really.' She thought back to that year, a year of perfect happiness. 'I was chosen to understudy Ruby and so we got to rehearse more. He asked me out to dinner and, well, you know ...' She forced herself to stand. 'His mother didn't like me. I didn't take it personally; she didn't like anyone who came close to Johnny – or Ruby, for that matter. It was sad, really, how she controlled them both.' Oh, she mustn't say more. She couldn't think. Would he come back? What would she do if he did? And Imogen? She shook her head to try and stop the thoughts. 'I need to go to work. Lil needs me.' She picked up her bag.

'We'll walk with you,' Jessie said. 'You look a bit wobbly.'

'I'm all right.' She pulled herself more erect. 'Honestly, I am. I'm tired. We all are. It's hard juggling jobs and rehearsing as well. Please, don't fuss.' Her voice was firm now and the girls knew her well enough not to press the matter. 'I'll see you at home after I've finished at the pub.' She walked down the steps, feeling their eyes on her, glad to get out into the natural light of the foyer. Dolly rushed out of the box office, her face glowing with excitement.

'Did you see Johnny Randolph?'

She nodded, pulling on her jacket and Dolly leant in close. 'Don't tell anyone – well, you can tell Jessie, of course, or I will. But I overheard him talking to Jack. You'll never guess!' Her brain was a jumble; she needed to walk, to think.

'Never guess what, Dolly?'

Dolly took a deep breath, her eyes glittering. 'The Randolphs are going to do the winter season at the Palace. Can you imagine?'

She gripped Dolly's arm. 'Are you sure?'

'I saw them shake on it.' She clapped her hands with delight. 'We'll have to go and see the show, won't we? All of us.'

Frances bit down on her lip. She wanted to smile for Dolly's sake, but she couldn't find it within her. 'We will,' she managed to say, letting go of her arm and striding towards the door. She needed light, she needed air.

Lil was outside the Fisherman's Arms when Frances arrived. The draymen had delivered the barrels and were closing the hatch that led to the cellar. The older of the two men got up onto the front of wagon, the younger lad on the back, his legs dangling as the horse moved forward. Lil turned to wave them off, caught sight of Frances and rushed towards her. 'Good grief, lass, what's happened to ya? Ya look like you've seen a ghost.'

She tried to smile, relieved to be away from the theatre, from the girls, from questions. 'I have, Lil.' She pushed open the door to the main room and Lil bustled behind her. 'I have.'

'Sit yourself down and I'll get you a drink.'

'I'd rather have a tea, Lil.' She got up. 'I'll make it.'

'You'll do no such thing! Let me put the kettle on. Two ticks.' She disappeared through the door behind the bar and came back quickly. 'I'll leave the door open till I hear it whistle. Now then, lovey, what's upset you?'

Frances wrung her hands in her lap. 'Nothing. *Everything*.' She looked up, gave Lil a rueful smile. 'I don't know where to start.'

'Beginning is as good as anywhere, Franny.'

But where *was* the beginning? She glanced at the clock. Almost eleven. Lil saw her. 'Aye, I know. My bottle man let me down this morning an' all. Still got me shelves to fill.'

Frances got to her feet. 'Let me help. That's what you pay me for.'

Lil sighed. 'If you must. We can talk while I bottle up.' The two of them went behind the bar. Crates were already upended behind it, set in front of the shelves. 'I'll make a start on the pale ale.' Lil picked up a cloth, sat astride the crate and pulled the bottles out one by one from the gap between her knees. Each one was given a quick wipe before being placed in neat rows along the wooden shelves, the labels facing forward. 'There's a satisfaction in bringing order to chaos, Franny. Suits my simple mind, filling the shelves, making it all look nice.'

'Taking pride in your work is what sets people apart, Lil.' Frances began laying out the bar cloths on the counter, smoothing them out with her hands.

'Now then,' Lil said, 'what's upset you this morning?'

It was somehow easier to talk with Lil's back turned to her. It made Frances smile. She was a clever old thing, she was sure Lil knew that. Frances told her of the rehearsals, of Johnny Randolph turning up out of the blue.

Lil turned. 'Johnny Randolph? Of *The Randolphs*? Here?' She turned back to the shelf. 'Ruddy hell! What was he doing in Cleethorpes?'

'I don't know, Lil. But . . .'

'It's the "buts" that get ya every time, isn't it, lovey? But?'

She told Lil of their relationship, Lil moving along, stopping here and there while she listened to Frances. 'What? And he left without another word?'

Frances nodded even though Lil still had her back to her. 'He said he would send me a ticket, my passage to America, but it never came.' Lil got up, moved the crate and went to the next one. Fran picked up the empty and took it through the back way. She came back carrying two mugs of tea. Lil got off the crate, bent her knees a few times.

'By, I'm ready for that. It's been non-stop all morning.' She wrapped her hands, rings on almost every finger, around the mugs. 'Didn't he let you know why?'

Frances sipped, the warmth of the drink making her feel less shaky.

'I wrote letters, cards, a telegram. Not one reply. Nothing.'

'Ever?' Lil's face was contorted. Frances shook her head. 'How long?'

'Almost four years.'

Lil blew into her mug. 'Well, I know America's a long way, but hell, letters get through eventually. He coulda *walked* back with a letter in that time.' Lil looked piercingly at Frances over her mug and Frances felt her neck redden. 'And what else? Listen, Franny, I've been around the block a few times, as I've told you. And I know man trouble when I see it. Like your little friend, Ginny whatsit. You're not like her, so ...' She patted the counter with her hand. 'What's the "but"?'

Frances sipped at her cup, wanting to hide her face. Should she tell Lil about Imogen? It would be a relief to tell someone else; Lil wasn't a gossip, she knew that, and she had a good heart.

Frances put her mug down on the counter but held onto it, needing an anchor. She took a deep breath and stared directly at her boss, her friend. Lil held her gaze, her grey eyes soft and kind, and it gave her courage.

'I have a child. A daughter – Imogen.' There, it was out, the words seeming suspended in the ether. The door opened and Artie walked in with Fudge.

Lil said, 'I'll get this.' She poured the pint and as always, Artie took it wordlessly, handed over his cash and sat down, the dog at his side. Lil lowered her voice. 'His child?'

Frances nodded.

'Does he know?'

'No one does.'

'Where is she?'

'With friends.'

Lil came and stood close to her, rubbed her back. 'How have you managed, lovey?'

Frances shrugged, her throat thickening so quickly she felt she would suffocate. 'I had one good friend, Patsy. She's been everything to me. Everything.' She put her hand to her neck. 'It's been tough, really tough, Lil, but somehow I've survived. And I still have Imogen. She's my world.' Was she so different to Alice Randolph after all? Her children had been her world too. She understood now how that felt – but not to let them have a life of their own? Not find love?

Lil picked up her mug. 'Well …'

'Not what you were thinking of me?'

'Now don't you start that, madam! I'll have none of you telling me what I'm thinking. You should know by now that I'll come straight out with it, whether you like it or not.'

'I'm sorry, Lil. I didn't mean to insult you.'

She flapped a hand. 'You can't insult me. It'll take more than that.' Lil leant on the bar, the bottles forgotten. 'You poor little bugger.' She was thoughtful for a moment, then stood up sharply, put her hands on her hips. 'So, what's he ruddy doing, coming here, lording it about? The rat!'

Frances looked to Artie but he was oblivious, his nose in his paper, the dog sleeping.

'That's just it, Lil. He didn't. If he'd have breezed in as if nothing had happened, I'd have been furious, but it wasn't like that.'

'Well, what was it like?' Lil was angry on her behalf.

'I think that's what upset me the most. He looked puzzled. As if …' She thought about it, now that she could talk about it, now that someone else knew about Imogen. It gave her strength that she'd somehow lost these past few weeks, worrying about the war, the consequences of not doing the right thing. All the old insecurities had come rushing to the fore, that Imogen might be in danger and Frances unable to be with her now, when it mattered most. But then hundreds of children had been separated from their parents and sent away to strangers. And Imogen wasn't with strangers, was she? She was with friends; good, kind friends. 'He looked as if it was me who had let *him* down.' She paused, seeing his face in her mind's eye. What had his expression said to her? 'He was puzzled, confused. Much as I am.'

Lil calmed a little, leant back on the counter. 'Hmm … did you ask him?'

'I didn't get chance. Not this time.'

Lil raised an eyebrow. 'You think you'll get another?'

Frances bit her lower lip, lowered her voice again. 'I think they're set to come to the Palace for the winter season. Dolly overheard Jack talking with them.' Talking about it made her heart race. No matter how many times she'd imagined confronting him over the years, it hadn't been like this. She had expected anger, denial – even violence. His reaction had left her confused. She sipped her tea and Lil slapped her hands together then brushed them side to side.

'Well, if they do, you'll have to tell him.' She made a start on another crate. 'So, do you get to see your little lass, Imogen?'

Frances tried to focus on what Lil was saying. It wasn't easy, her mind racing with what might happen in the future. 'I see her Sundays and, if I get time, in the week.'

'Where is she then? Close?'

'Waltham.'

Lil paused, a cloth in one hand. 'And that's why you can't work Sundays?'

Frances nodded.

'Why haven't you got her with you?'

'I couldn't, Lil. I've got to work to keep the both of us. Sometimes that's meant travelling away for weeks at a time, rehearsing all day and working all night. I can't drag her around with me, relying on strangers.' She didn't want to. Not everyone was kind or could be trusted. 'She's in a good place. Patsy has two boys and is wonderful with her.' She smiled, thinking of how well they all got on. 'More importantly, there's no one asking questions, no one judging. As far as anyone's concerned, she's staying with her Aunt Patsy and that's all people need to know.' Artie rustled the newspaper as he turned the pages and the two women watched him then turned back to each other. 'I was so thrilled to get this summer season and tie it in with the panto. It meant I could be with her more.'

Lil rubbed at her arm and Frances reached across and held her hand. 'She's safe, Lil, she's with a family, she has stability.'

Lil looked at her from under her eyebrows. 'But not her mother.'

Frances chewed her lip. 'I want what's best for her.'

'And it's breaking your heart.'

Frances looked away. It was less painful if she didn't think too deeply about it. The door to the bar opened and Big Malc walked in. She tapped the pump and picked up his tankard.

'Aye, you've got it, Frances. But just a half if you will.'

She put the tankard back and picked up a glass. Her heart had been broken long ago.

Chapter 16

Ruby sat among the bubbles, rubbing them over her shoulders, breathing in the heavy rose perfume. Her dark hair was piled on her head and she sank down into the warmth of the water. The room was cloudy with steam, the windows heavy with condensation. She should have opened them – Aunt Letty would nag – but she hated the sounds of the city spoiling her bath, preferring to imagine that she was somewhere else, anywhere else. The door was ajar and through it she could hear Aunt Letty bustling about the flat as she brought it all to order. She closed her eyes. It had been heavenly to have Aunt Letty here and not have to share her with Johnny. A wonderful two days when she'd been almost able to forget the misery of everything. Of losing her mother, of being back in England with its greyness and drabness, and war. But Aunt Letty wouldn't stay … no one stayed. They all left in the end.

She sank deeper still, her chin in the water, her ears, her mouth, her nose and closed her eyes, submerging herself, opening her eyes. If she stopped breathing …

The soap suds stung and she burst out of the water, blinking and gasping for air, and Aunt Letty, hearing the noise, dashed in.

'Ruby! Are you all right?' Aunt Letty was holding Ruby's fur cape.

Ruby grinned, pushing strands of wet hair from her face, rubbing at her eyes. 'Perfectly. Are you?'

'I heard a commotion and thought you'd fallen in.' Ruby knew it was nothing of the sort, it was the reason her aunt insisted she leave the door open. She tried to look suitably apologetic.

'Sorry, Aunt Letty, couldn't find the soap.' She felt around the bottom of the bath and held it up. It was clear Aunt Letty didn't believe her.

'Isn't it about time you got out and got dressed? You've been topping it up for over an hour.' She held out Ruby's cape, brushing it smooth with her hands. 'And it's about time you started sorting your room out, young lady. What a mess it is. All your lovely things just left where you've dropped them!' She smiled encouragingly. 'Get out and come and help.'

Ruby pouted.

'All that eye flashing and fluttering your lashes won't wash with me, Ruby Randolph! Get your backside out of that bath!' She handed Ruby a towel from the rail and Ruby reluctantly took hold of it. Aunt Letty pulled out the plug.

'Such a shame to waste the water.'

'Such a shame to waste the day, my girl.' She put Ruby's cape over her arm and pushed up the sash window, tutting as she did so. 'Out you come.' She waited for Ruby to step out of the bath before leaving the room and Ruby wrapped the towel about her.

Aunt Letty had flung open the large mahogany wardrobe in Ruby's room and was unpacking one of her two trunks. Ruby sat down on the bed, rubbing her hair with a small towel.

'You should have done this yourself, Ruby. Days ago. You can't go on living out of a trunk.'

'Why not? We've done it for years.' She let the hair towel drop to her shoulders.

Aunt Letty slipped a black cocktail dress onto a hanger, smoothing the shoulders so that it hung correctly. Ruby pushed out her lip. Henry Longman had bought it for her in Illinois. Nice boy. *Too* nice. Boring ...

'It's not good for you, Ruby. It's unsettling. You need structure. Roots.' She bent down and picked up a long chiffon dress in baby blue. Eye-wateringly expensive, bought for a party at the Hollywood Roosevelt.

'Stick that one at the back, Aunt Letty. It's hideous.'

Aunt Letty held the gown higher so that the fabric draped as had been intended. 'Why, it's beautiful.' She looked at Ruby, puzzled. 'It must have cost a fortune.' She caressed the fabric, admiring the cut.

Ruby pouted. 'It did.'

'Ah, the dress is beautiful – the memory hideous. Is that it?'

Ruby looked away. 'Something like that.' Aunt Letty pushed it to the back of the wardrobe.

'Come on, darling girl. Buck up.' She sat on the bed next to her niece, clasped her hand and Ruby leant on her shoulder, glad of the closeness. Letty smelt like Mother, the same powder, the same comforting shoulders – but it wasn't Mother, was it? Tears brimmed in her eyes and she let them fall. Aunt Letty rubbed at her hand.

'It will get easier, darling. It will.'

Ruby brushed the tears away. How lovely to be able to believe it, but she couldn't ever imagine that the pain would go. And she didn't want it to, for while she felt it the memory of her mother was as vivid as it would ever be. She bit down hard on her lip to invite more pain, to take her thoughts away from her heart that felt so heavy in her chest.

'Sometimes it's just too hard to breathe, Aunt Letty. Too much effort.'

Aunt Letty moved her arm and put it about Ruby's shoulder, holding her tight, and Ruby sank into the peace and comfort offered.

'I know, I know. But time will heal. Some days will be better than others and then, one day, you'll find that you're able to think of your mother with happiness, instead of the heaviness you carry with you now.'

They sat quietly until Ruby's tears stopped and Aunt Letty got up and found her a handkerchief. Ruby wiped her face, blew her nose. Her aunt put her hand under her chin, tilted her face up towards her. Ruby tried to look away, but she couldn't, Aunt Letty wouldn't let her, moving her chin until she looked into the old woman's eyes. 'Your mother was so proud of you, Ruby. It's what she lived for. You both made her so happy.'

Ruby swallowed. Her throat hurt, her eyes stung and she felt ugly. 'But we can't make her happy any more, Aunt Letty. It all seems pointless.'

'What does?'

'Everything. Dancing ... Living ...'

Aunt Letty put her hands on either side of Ruby's shoulders and shook her gently. 'Now, we'll have no more of that. My goodness, action, no matter how small, is the key. Even if it's something as simple as hanging up your clothes, it will bring a sense of order to your thoughts. It all helps.' Ruby hung her head. Aunt Letty took hold of her hands and pulled her to her feet. 'Chop, chop,' she said, briskly but not unkindly. 'Get dressed in something sensible and help me sort out this jumble.' She bent over the trunk again, scooping out a heap of clothes, dropping them onto the bed. 'All these lovely things, Ruby!' She could see Aunt Letty was trying not to look disappointed. How many girls would love to have what she had? She just couldn't summon the pleasure of them any more.

'Discipline, Ruby. Discipline gets you through the bad times, you know that.'

Ruby pulled on khaki pants and a sweater, tying back her hair with a silk scarf. It was a style she admired in Katharine Hepburn, that preppy casual wear that looked so effortless if you had the figure – and the money to afford a good cut.

Aunt Letty beamed. 'What a beauty you are without all that muck on your face.' She pinched her cheek.

Ruby gently batted her hand away. 'You make me sound like I'm five years old. And that "muck" is the finest muck a girl can buy.'

'And you don't need a drop of it, Ruby. It's what's on the inside that counts. You'll appreciate that when you get old, like me. I look like Ginger Rogers on the inside.' The pair of them laughed. 'That's better. A real smile is better than any make-up.'

Ruby started to tackle the cotton sweaters and silk blouses, folding them carefully, Aunt Letty placing them in the chest of drawers at the side of the window. Aunt Letty leant again into the trunk. 'Almost done. Only your shoes, now. Do you want me to take them out of the boxes?'

Ruby dropped the sweater she had been folding and dashed forward. The boxes! She'd forgotten. 'No!' she exclaimed. Then seeing her aunt's reaction said again, softer, 'No. It's perfectly fine. I can finish the rest.' She squeezed her aunt's arm. 'Thank you, Aunt Letty. It doesn't seem so overwhelming now.' She forced a smile. 'Shall we go out?' She glanced towards the window. 'The forecast is for showers later. We could pop along to Fortnum's, get something lovely for supper to welcome Johnny home.'

'He'll want more than a cake after that drive.' Letty folded her arms. 'I'm not leaving a job half done. Will you finish this, or will I have to come back with a big stick?'

Ruby smiled. 'I'll do it right now. It's my wardrobe and I shouldn't have left it to you to sort out. You've been too easy on me, Aunt Letty. And you're right. I do need to buck up. And I will.'

Her aunt raised her eyebrows. Did she believe her? She made a move towards the bedroom door and Ruby followed her. 'I'll be back to check,' she said firmly, then softened her tone. 'You'll feel so much better if you keep yourself busy. Let's hope Johnny's bringing good news with him. Lord knows we're all in need of it.'

Ruby closed the door as her aunt left and leant on it. It would have been difficult explaining things if she'd opened the lid on the wrong box. She hurriedly put the boxes into the bottom of the wardrobe, leaving one until last. She held onto it and sat on the floor, her back to the bed, concealing the box's contents in case Aunt Letty should come back in. They could easily be pushed under the bed if she did. She removed the lid, rifled through the envelopes, her brother's long, elegant handwriting on each one, and beneath them the ones from Frances. At the very bottom was the ticket for Frances's passage to America. Unused. Her mother had asked her to take care of all of it before she left for England, impressing upon her the importance of her task. Mother's words were so clear, as if she were in the room.

'Frances O'Leary is a nothing but a cheap gold-digger, Ruby. She has bewitched Johnny and he can't see it.' Her mother had placed her fingers under Ruby's chin, tilting her face to hers. 'She won't be satisfied until she has taken your place. She wants Johnny all to herself.'

Ruby touched her chin, wanting her mother's touch once more. To feel something, *anything*. It was such a relief when the letters had stopped coming. An overwhelming sense of her own badness swept over her. She hadn't opened them. Not one. She was protecting her brother, she told herself, then fear gripped her again. What if someone else came along and took Johnny away? What would she do then?

The last part of the journey home had been hairy. With only a slice of moon that night, Bernie had crawled along the last few miles. It would have been quicker to walk. They had swerved to avoid a man wearing dark clothes and for a moment Johnny had thought they were all done for. It had shaken them and he had stopped for a quick drink with Bernie then chosen to walk the last couple of miles back home. How bleak it all seemed, to come from the bright lights of New York and be plunged back into darkness. Yet, weirdly, he felt happy; more so than he'd felt in years and it seemed to override the weariness. At last there was hope; it was as if a window had opened and shone a brilliant light in his direction. He had found her. Fate was on his side.

He adjusted his overnight bag to his other hand. A door opened and someone called out, 'Mind the ruddy light!' A couple stepped onto the street and lit their cigarettes, the man extinguishing the match with a flick of the wrist and throwing it onto the pavement. Dark shadows of buses and trucks trundled by, moving slower these days. There had already been far too many accidents. There had been none of the expected bombing raids, but how long before they did come along? London, the seat of power, all that England stood for, would be the target. He was doing the right thing, he knew it, so why did he feel so uncomfortable? Because he had to get Ruby away and he had convinced himself this was the best way? Perhaps. She would be furious with him, but that was nothing new. She'd been angry for so long that a little more would be worth it, if it saved her from herself.

The lift opened and he stepped out, rummaged in his pocket for his key and let himself into the flat. The lamp was on in the small hallway and he placed his bag on the floor, slipped off his coat and hung it in the small closet, left his hat on the chair. In the sitting room Aunt Letty was sitting in her dressing gown and slippers, reading a book by the light of the standard lamp behind her. She smiled, removing her glasses. The room felt calmer, welcoming, and he wished that Aunt Letty could stay and work her magic for them both. She placed her book down quietly on the side table, her spectacles on top of it, and got to her feet.

'Bad journey?'

He nodded, removed his jacket and draped it over the back of the sofa. She kissed his cheek.

'Whisky?'

He sank into the easy chair.

'That would be wonderful.' They kept their voices low, Aunt Letty taking great care not to chink the glass of the decanter as she returned it to the silver tray on the long table behind the sofa.

'How did it go?'

He eased back into the chair. 'Good, good. Better than I thought.'

'Not a wasted journey?'

'Not at all.' She handed him the glass and he sipped. It warmed his throat and for a moment he closed his eyes, glad his journey was over. He opened them again. 'How has she been?'

Aunt Letty bent down and turned up the gas fire; the bricks began to glow a deeper red and she watched them for a moment before returning to her seat. 'A little brighter. Still very brittle. But I don't have to tell you that.'

He sat forward, nursing the glass in his hands.

'Oh, God, Aunt Letty, I hope I've done the right thing.'

'Of course, you have. Whatever you've done, you've done for the best. Ruby's not a child.'

Ruby stuck her head around the door. 'The wanderer returns.' She was wearing her cream sateen pyjamas and had pulled his black dressing gown over them, the sleeves rolled back. It made her appear tiny and vulnerable and for a fraction he doubted his decision. 'I thought I heard voices.' He rested his glass on the arm of the chair and got up and hugged her. When she pulled away, he rested his hands on her shoulders.

'You look much better, Ruby.'

'Do I?' She smiled at him, but it didn't reach her eyes. She was still playing the game and it saddened him. What had he expected? That Aunt Letty could wave a magic wand and make it all right again? He sat back in his chair and Ruby sank onto the sofa, curling her legs beneath her. When she saw his whisky, she got up and was about to pour herself one when she caught Aunt Letty's eye, put the decanter down and instead filled the glass with water. She sat down next to Aunt Letty.

'How did it all go?' He could tell she wasn't interested, merely going through the motions for Aunt Letty's sake. He sipped his whisky. How much should he tell her? There would be a row, but at least Aunt Letty was here. It would neuter her reaction to an extent.

'The Randolphs are back in business.'

'We have a show?'

Johnny took a deep breath. 'We do.'

'Which one is it? Let me guess. The Adelphi? The Vaudeville? Cabaret at The Savoy?'

'It's not in town, Ruby. I can't get anything in London, not yet.'

'Where, then?' She drank the water, placed the glass on top of her aunt's book. Aunt Letty leant forward and moved the glass onto a coaster, sat back.

Johnny rubbed at his lip. Aunt Letty looked at the clock, then at him. He had to get it over with.

'Bournemouth? No, it wouldn't be Bournemouth, not near the coast. I hadn't thought. Will you be safe down there, Aunt Letty?' She didn't wait for her to answer. He could tell by the high pitch of her voice that she had an inkling it wouldn't be to her liking. It didn't really matter where they went, did it? Not in the long run, so why shouldn't he be with Frances. 'Bath? Bristol?' She rattled places off the top of her head and he tried to stop her. Aunt Letty clasped her hands together, placing them in her lap, her cheeks red. The room had become hotter and she got up and went to the fire and turned it down.

'It's not any of those, Ruby.' He stood up, went to the window, inched through the slightest of gaps to open it, careful not to let the light escape. He gulped in the fresh air and slipped back behind the curtains. He turned to Ruby, who peered at him, trying to read his expression, something she'd done since they were children, trying to guess what he was feeling.

'Manchester.' Her voice was flat. 'I can tell you're not happy about it. Liverpool? That's not too poor, is it? I love the Empire and the people are fun. Is it Liverpool?'

Ruby's eyes glittered in the light and Aunt Letty sucked at her cheeks. It was best to get it over with. He stepped into the middle of the room.

'Ruby, it's a beautiful theatre, the Palace. You know that I've been working on something with Bernie Blackwood? Well, he had a business proposition and that's where I've been, to check it out. For us. You know things aren't brilliant and it's not just us, Ruby.' He didn't want to plead but he could feel himself placating her. He must be firm. 'So many theatres have closed, Ruby, and many of the

London ones might never reopen. Lots of acts have been called up and you can't put on a show without professionals.' He waited for what he had said to sink in. Was she listening or was she blocking him out? 'I'm going to join the RAF, Ruby, if they'll have me, once this show's bedded in. You should think about contributing too.' He glanced at Aunt Letty.

'Don't!' Ruby put her hands over her ears. Aunt Letty pulled them gently away, glared at Johnny to get on with it. He coughed to clear his throat.

'We're at war, Ruby. We have to think of the future. We will all need to play our part in keeping this country going.'

She sulked, picked at her nails. 'Manchester it is then. That's not too bad. I like Manchester, plenty of shops.'

Good God, she was selfish. Didn't she realise the gravity of the situation? So many people, people just like them, had already answered the call. Was she going to ignore it, as she did everything else that didn't meet her liking? She was still such a child in so many ways. Aunt Letty glowered at him.

'It's not Manchester, Ruby.' Her eyes were bright, and she twisted to her aunt and then back to Johnny.

'Where?'

He rubbed at his forehead. How many times had he gone over how he was going to break it to her on the long drive home? He knew all the reasons it would be the best thing for the pair of them, but whichever way he cut it, she would hate him for it.

'It's Grimsby, Ruby. A lovely theatre. You'll like it, I know you will.' He moved to the edge of his seat. 'We'll have part of the profits and shares. And there's two other theatres and—'

'Grimsby!' Her face twisted as reality sank in, then she sprang to her feet. 'Grims. By.' She gritted her teeth, her eyes flashing, and he got up, moved towards her.

'It's what we need. It's for the future. A future that's uncertain for all of us, Ruby. We're not living in normal times any more. We *have* to make different decisions. Decisions other than we are used to.'

'You've done this to punish me, haven't you? Why you dirty, rotten—' She lifted her hand to strike him and he caught it. 'I won't go, you bastard! I won't go!'

'Ruby!' Their aunt was on her feet. Ruby's eyes were black with hatred and she clenched her fists, then, taut with frustration, ran to her room, slamming the door so hard that the glasses rattled and the lampshade swayed above them, the crystal droplets tinkling laughter. He made to go after her but Aunt Letty pressed his arm. 'Leave her. She needs to cry about it. It will do her good.' He sank back in his chair and she fetched the decanter, topped up his glass and poured herself one. 'It wouldn't have mattered where you were going, Johnny, she would have hated it.'

'I have to get her away from temptation, Aunt Letty, and it seemed the perfect solution, so far away.' He should tell her about Frances, but what difference would it make?

'There will be temptation everywhere, my boy,' Letty said. 'She's looking to fill the hole your mother left in her life.'

'But—'

Aunt Letty held up her hand to stop him. 'You lost your mother too, don't forget that.'

He stared into his glass. 'It wasn't just Mother, Aunt Letty. America changed her – and not for the better. It should have been the making of us both. Professionally, success was there for the taking. Privately?' He shook his head. 'It was a disaster.'

Chapter 17

Dolly came down the aisle carrying a large bouquet of yellow roses. Jessie grinned.

'Another one. I wonder who on earth they can be from?'

Frances stomped down the steps at the front of the stage. 'Ha, jolly, ha.' Dolly held the roses out to her and Frances peered inside for the envelope, read the card, tore it in half and pushed it into her pocket.

'Do you want them, Dolly?'

'Oh, Frances, you can't keep giving them away.' She sniffed the flowers. 'They smell gorgeous.'

Frances took them from her and marched back on stage. 'Ginny?'

Ginny waved a hand. 'I don't have room.'

Jessie reached out to Frances, touching her wrist. 'I think you to have to face facts. Johnny isn't going to stop and we've all had our turn at being on the other side of your generosity.' Jessie held a bloom, admiring it. Each bouquet had been beautiful.

'I might as well leave them in the dressing room this week,' Frances said. 'At least it will brighten it up a bit.'

'It'll take more than the roses to do that.' Jessie sank down onto the piano stool. They could hear Mike walking about in the wings. He joined them on stage.

'You girls need anything for the next half hour?' He looked at Frances's bouquet but didn't comment and she flushed. It seemed everyone was getting used to them appearing. 'I need to pop out before the first showing. Will you be done by then?'

'Well before that, Mike. We're working out what we're going to do for the talent show.'

'Ticket sales have jumped because of it. Be nice if punters start coming back.' He rubbed his hand over his stubby red hair. 'It's been a bit dodgy lately, hasn't it, girls? Good job Jack stuck at it. They're going to start taking bookings for panto at the end of the week so let's hope people still want to spend Christmas at the theatre, otherwise I reckon I'll have to go elsewhere. I can't see Jack hanging on past Christmas, in all truth.' He pulled his cap onto his head, pushing his arms into his jacket as he walked out through the auditorium. Dolly came to join them on the stage and Jessie twisted on the stool, ran her fingers over a few keys, sighed.

'I'm only thinking as far as the panto anyway. I have no idea what to do after that.'

Frances leant on the piano, Ginny next to her, her cheek resting on her hand.

Jack had started the films, bringing in the girls two, and then three days a week. It had been hard work after the ease of the summer when being part of a bigger show had a different energy that gave them all a lift. They had to work harder to get a response. It had been worse when the moon was slight because people were nervous to venture out and road accidents were on the increase. How long Jack could sustain it was something they talked about, but not much.

'We're all in the same boat, Jessie. I think this is the first time in years when I haven't known where I was going or what I was doing.' There had been little time to rest after Imogen was born. She had danced to the last, hidden in the back row of the chorus, back to work in days. If it hadn't been for Patsy she would've had to give Imogen up. Thank God for friends, good friends.

'Me too,' Ginny added.

Dolly came beside the three of them and placed a hand on Jessie's shoulder.

'It will get better; I know it will. Ticket sales are good for the talent show. There are plenty of picture houses for people to go to but there's only one Empire.'

'You're right, Dolly.' Frances tapped the top of the piano. 'Let's get this pushed back into the wings and clear up so Mike only has to drop down the screen. We can chat in the dressing room – or go to Joyce's.'

'Let's stay here,' Ginny suggested. 'You can put your flowers in water and I can make some tea. It'll be cheaper.' Frances picked up her bouquet, held it so the roses' heads dropped down towards the floor. Jessie reached across and forced her to bring them upright.

'Don't, Frances. They're so lovely, it's like bringing the sunshine in.' Reluctantly, Frances did as Jessie requested and all four of them headed down to the dressing room.

Frances laid the flowers on the dressing table. 'Turn the lights on, Ginny, it'll warm it up a bit. It's going to be ruddy freezing in here, come the panto.' Frances pulled her cardigan about her.

Dolly lingered by the door. 'I'll go and find a vase.'

'Might be one in Madeleine Moore's old room. She always had flowers,' Jessie said.

It made her wistful. Had it only been a few weeks since the corridors were busy with cast and crew running up and down the stairs to the stage, George on the stage door? Now it was like walking around the library, with only the echoes of happier days. Frances sat on the table and eased out her chair, using it to rest her feet. She brushed at the toes of her shoes. Ginny settled herself in front of her mirror; she glanced briefly at her reflection then looked away. Jessie slumped down in the one and only easy chair. 'Did we do the right thing?'

'Which right thing?' Jessie pulled at the stuffing escaping from a hole in the arm of the chair. 'I don't know. It was different when everyone else was here. There was energy and life about the place and now it's flat.'

'It wasn't all good.' Ginny turned and looked at her through the mirror. The lights made her cheeks look hollow and she pulled at her hair, using her fingers as a comb.

'I wasn't thinking . . .' Jessie apologised.

Ginny shrugged. 'I know what you meant. When I came here I didn't count on being, well, you know. I wasn't really thinking of the consequences, was I?'

'So many girls don't,' Frances said. 'And they don't all get caught out.'

Jessie leant forward, pushed her hand to her cheek. 'It's all so depressing. And smiling takes so much energy these days. How does that work?'

Dolly came back with a vase of water, set it on the dressing table and unwrapped the bouquet. Jessie noticed Frances watch Dolly take each bloom and arrange it in the vase, pulling out the tallest in the middle to show them off to their best advantage. It was obvious that she loved the flowers, so why did she insist on giving them away? What difference did it make whether she kept them or not? Frances turned back to Jessie.

'To get back to answering your original question, Jessie, what thing did you mean? Coming to Cleethorpes? Forming our little act to fill in the gaps until the panto? Shall I go on?'

Jessie stuck out her tongue. 'All right, all right, clever clogs! I suppose I meant all of it. And none of it.' Frances threw up her hands. Jessie laughed, then was thoughtful. The last few months had been hectic and she'd made decisions without thinking them through. 'I suppose I'm thinking of Mum and Eddie. I've never had much time to think before, just reacted more than anything.' It was usually her downfall and she was trying to curb it. Dolly closed the door and sat next to Frances.

'There's nothing wrong with that, Jessie. It's all worked out. Look how well your mum is doing.' Frances was softer now, no longer teasing. 'If you hadn't acted when you did, it might have been a different story.' Jessie was grateful for Frances's reassurance. Grace had been sorely neglected and if Harry hadn't come to her rescue it might all have been too late. Dear Harry, was he safe? He'd written every day, even though the letters arrived haphazardly of late. There wasn't much you could rely on any more. She supposed it would get worse. 'We're all just doing our best, aren't we?'

'We can't do anything else, Jessie.'

She pushed out her lips. 'If we can keep going until panto we'll be fine. That's what we have to focus on. At least we won't be on our own down here. There's no atmosphere, no warmth.'

'Not much in the auditorium either. It's hard work going on when most of the audience have come out to see Greer Garson and Robert Donat. I can't help feeling we're a disappointment.' They were all quiet and Jessie knew it was because they agreed with her. There was nothing to defend. It was generous of Jack to give them work, but it was soul-destroying when you knew people weren't really interested.

'Well, at least the houses are getting better, now that everyone's getting used to the blackout,' Ginny offered. 'We're all getting a bit braver, aren't we?'

'We don't have an alternative.' Frances said. 'The people who do venture out to us are coming here to leave their troubles behind for an hour or two. When the lights are on, we can take them anywhere and we need to hold on to that. It's vital.' Jessie was once again reminded of her dad. He was with her, wasn't he, watching over her? Here in the theatre she felt his presence stronger than ever, a guiding hand on her shoulder that gave her courage.

'Dad always said music took people out of themselves, made them forget their worries, remember happy times. I hope we get the chance to do that.'

They heard footsteps coming down the corridor, a muffled rap on their door. Dolly got up and opened it and Grace came in carrying a bolt of red satin fabric. Jessie leapt to her feet and took it from her mother, laying it down on the dressing table. Frances budged up to make room and Grace smoothed her hand over the cloth, gave it a pat. 'Look at this, girls. What do you think?' Frances got down off the table and stood next to Grace, the girls crowded round.

'Lovely! So nice to have a bit of colour. What's it for, Grace?' Frances pulled out her chair, brushed her hand over the seat and made gestures for Grace to sit down, which she did.

'Thank you, Frances.' Her cheeks were pink and Jessie was gladdened to see her looking so revived. A little of her old energy was in evidence and she glanced away to see Frances smiling, an acknowledgement that she had indeed made good choices. Mary hadn't wanted to come back to the Empire and Jack had offered Grace the position of wardrobe mistress for the pantomime. It had given Grace a much-needed boost and the extra money was always welcome. Grace sat back, tapping her hand on the fabric. 'Jack let me have a rummage around upstairs in Wardrobe. I was looking for some odds and ends so that I could make something for you three girls. This was more than I hoped for, a little blessing. It was hidden under some old curtains.' She smiled at them. 'What do you think?'

Jessie got up and hugged her. 'Oh, Mum, you're a marvel! That will be wonderful. Red's such a jolly colour and we can use it for any Christmas shows we might get before the panto.'

'Just the lift we needed, Grace,' Frances agreed. 'Your timing is perfect.'

'I don't know about that, but I think we all need to cheer ourselves up as much as we can. It's going to be a difficult winter.' Ginny looked down at her feet and Jessie reached out and discreetly pressed her arm, hoping to imbue her with a sense of hope. She could do little else and it was awful to feel so impotent. Frances put her arm about Grace's shoulders.

'I know you'll work your magic, Grace. Thanks for thinking of us.'

Grace beamed. 'Don't mention it, Frances. I'm only happy that I'm feeling up to it and able to be creative again. We led such a dull existence at my cousin's. I hadn't realised how much I missed the theatre.'

'See,' Frances said, raising her eyebrows. Grace twisted to look at her daughter.

'It was nothing, Mum.' She glowered at Frances, then grinned. Her mother would hate to think Jessie was fussing. 'Is there anything else we need to bring down for you?'

'Not at the moment. This is enough to be going on with. I can measure you two later. Perhaps you'd like to come along and join us for tea sometime, Ginny, so I can measure you up? You too, Dolly.'

Dolly was quizzical. 'I don't need a costume, Grace.'

Grace flapped her hand. 'I meant for tea. And why not? The costume, I mean. You would look lovely in red with your gorgeous blonde hair to set it off.'

'I'll pass on that, but I can perhaps help with the sewing and cutting out.' She stood by Grace and smoothed her hand over the fabric, nodding appreciatively. 'Have you got a pattern?'

'I'll make one. We can work off that. Thank you, Dolly. It will be much easier with two of us.'

Ginny was noticeably quiet.

'Are you all right, Ginny? You look very pale, my dear. Are you eating enough? How are your new digs? Where did you go in the end?'

Ginny pleaded to the girls using her eyes and Jessie obliged.

'Mum! Too many questions.'

'Oh, forgive me, Ginny. I haven't seen you for a while so I'm curious.'

Ginny tried to smile. 'It's fine, Grace. My digs are … adequate, shall we say?'

Jessie stepped in, sensing Ginny was floundering. 'And Joyce is very generous, isn't she, girls?'

'Oh, she's a diamond,' Frances said. 'We gave her tickets to the talent show.' Jessie was relieved that, once again, Frances had swiftly diverted the conversation. Poor Ginny. Dolly was valiantly pretending that she wasn't aware of their silent signals between the three of them, but her expression told Jessie otherwise. It all felt so unfair that she should be excluded especially when, over the past weeks, they had all become so close. Grace got up.

'Leave the cloth here, Mum. Frances and I will carry it home to save you.'

'Thank you, sweetheart.' Her mother's relief was obvious and it pleased her. 'It's dire weather outside. The rain came in and the streets are awash. It can't run down the gutters fast enough.'

Frances sighed. 'Perhaps we'll leave it until tomorrow, then. There's no rush and it will save spoiling the fabric.'

'Exactly, plenty to be getting on with before then. We know we have it, so it can wait. I'll work out a pattern first. Do come for tea, Dolly, Ginny. You'll be most welcome. It will be lovely to swap ideas.'

Grace kissed Jessie on the cheek and Dolly picked up the bolt of fabric. 'I'll put this in one of the other rooms so it's out of the way. Dad will have some paper somewhere that we can cover it with, so it doesn't get it marked.' She followed Grace out into the corridor.

Ginny dashed to Jessie's side. 'Oh, Jessie. I can't have your mum measuring me. She'll be able to tell straight away.'

'She won't,' Frances said, looking to Ginny's midriff and then to the door. 'It's way too early to tell.'

'But my waist, my stomach!' Ginny ran her hands over her slightly extended belly then rested them at her waist, looking down at herself, then up at Jessie and Frances.

'Looks like wind, or bloating,' Frances said. 'Honestly, Ginny, you'll have to get tougher, darling. It's going to get a lot worse than this.'

'Frances!' Jessie was appalled. 'No need to be so harsh.'

'I wasn't being harsh, Jessie.' She softened her voice. 'I'm being practical. Ginny knows that, or she wouldn't have mentioned it.'

Ginny's shoulders sagged. 'Frances is right. I don't care what most people think. Not really.' She swallowed away her fear and Jessie knew she was being brave. 'But your mum has been very kind to me and so has Geraldine. You all have. I don't want them to think I'm …' She searched for the word. 'Cheap,' she said, sadly.

'They wouldn't think that.' Jessie went and stood beside her, put her hands on her shoulders. 'You might be worrying too much.'

'Or not enough.' Frances lowered her head. 'Not everyone is as kind as your ma, Jessie. There are some spiteful people about.' Jessie was reminded of her Aunt Iris. This was exactly the sort of thing she associated with the theatre, as if nice girls from middle-class backgrounds would ever dream of doing such a thing.

'I know that, Frances. I'm not simple-minded.'

'I never suggested you were. Not for a minute; but this isn't the movies.'

Jessie winced. What on earth was the matter with Frances? Sometimes she couldn't work her out. Since the moment war had been declared she had been angry and had remained so. While everyone else adjusted, Frances had held on to her rage and let it fester.

Ginny was getting agitated. 'Please don't fall out over me, you two. I don't want to spoil your friendship.'

'You won't do that, Ginny.' But even as she said it, Jessie wasn't so sure. Couldn't Frances find it in her to show more compassion? She checked the door and turned to Ginny.

'Do you think we should tell Dolly about ... y'know ... Ginny?'

'Jessie!' Frances was sharp. 'It's not for us to tell. It's for Ginny to decide who knows, and who doesn't.'

Jessie's cheeks burned. Would she ever learn to think before she spoke?

'It's all right, Jessie.' Ginny stepped in to defend her. 'I know you didn't mean anything by it.'

Jessie gritted her teeth, barely able to contain her frustration with Frances. 'I don't know what on earth's wrong with you, Frances. I was thinking that Dolly could measure Ginny and leave excess for letting the seams out. No one else needs to know. Not until Ginny's ready to tell. And we might have thought of something else to help by then.'

Frances sighed, shaking her head. 'I don't know what ruddy miracle you think's going to happen, Jessie, my love. Let's keep things realistic, shall we?'

'I think telling Dolly—'

'Telling me what?' Dolly said, coming through the door, and Frances glared at Jessie. Jessie felt sweat prickle on her skin, even though the room was chill; she clenched her fists.

'Not tell you, ask you, really,' Jessie said, thinking on her feet. Frances turned her back, scowling at her through the mirror, 'If you wouldn't mind measuring Ginny here; save her having to keep coming along to us at Barkhouse Lane.' She could feel her cheeks burning with heat and began searching for a tape measure, anything to avoid looking at Frances.

'Of course.' Dolly acted as if everything was perfectly normal when it was clear it was anything but. Ginny went over to her, took her hand, drawing her into the room.

'It wasn't just that, Dolly. Although I would like you to measure me and fit my costumes. It was an excuse. I should have told you earlier.'

'You don't have to tell me anything you don't want to.' Dolly's smile had disappeared, her blue eyes serious.

'I know, and I appreciate that,' Ginny said kindly, 'but we're all of us friends, aren't we? And you'll find out sooner or later.' Ginny took a deep breath. Exhaled. 'I got caught. With Billy.' She looked at Dolly under her eyelashes. 'I'm in the – the family way.'

Dolly stared at her friend then leant forward and hugged Ginny.

'Oh, Ginny! I'm so sorry, I really am. That's so unfair.' She drew back but held onto Ginny's hands. 'Of course, I'll measure you. I'll do whatever I can to help.'

Jessie glanced towards Frances, who shook her head and looked away, her disappointment clear.

Ginny sat back in the easy chair and the room prickled with tension until Dolly said, 'I know it won't be any comfort, but my sister got caught out. She married the bloke and she's very unhappy. At least you'll be able to have the baby adopted. If that's what you want, of course,' she said quickly, her neck reddening. 'Oh, I hope I haven't put my foot in it.'

Ginny reassured her. 'Don't worry, Dolly. Who knows what's best to say? Or best to do.' She stared down at the floor, picked at the stuffing of the arm as Jessie had done earlier. 'I *will* be having it adopted. I can't manage on my own and Billy won't want to know.' She let out a long sigh then looked up at them all, smiling sadly. 'I'd rather give the baby away to have a better life than I could provide. I don't want to struggle like my mam did. She wanted so much better for me.' Her voice wobbled but she took a deep breath and pulled her shoulders back. 'So. What are we going to do now? Rehearse? Go home?'

Frances pushed back her chair and picked up her bag. 'I've had enough for today. We might as well go home. No sense hanging around here because nothing's going to happen.'

Jessie was still mad at Frances, madder still at herself. It wasn't her secret to tell – but she hadn't told it, had she? And she'd managed to save the situation. It was Ginny who'd decided otherwise. Still …

'I'm sorry, Ginny. I was only thinking to save your embarrassment. I didn't mean to make things worse.'

'You didn't, Jessie. And I'm glad it was brought out into the open. I feel much better now that Dolly knows. To tell the truth, I was terrified of anyone finding out, but you're such good friends and somehow it makes this horrid situation feel less daunting.'

Jessie was uncomfortable. She didn't want to fall out with Frances, their friendship was too important to her.

Jessie put out her arm. 'Let's walk the long way home, Frances. We can walk Ginny to her new lodgings.'

They left by the stage door, Dolly crossing over the road for the short walk to her house, the girls turning down into Market Street with Ginny. The rain had stopped but large puddles had collected around the gutters and, as they passed the trees, the wind gusted, showering them with raindrops that had gathered on the leaves.

When they arrived at the bottom of Bowling Lane, Ginny bade them stop. 'I'll be fine from here, thanks, you two.' The light was fading and the narrow, cobbled street that ran into the darkness was bleak.

'Are you sure, Ginny? We don't mind going with you to your door, do we, Frances?'

Frances stood back but didn't comment.

'Thanks, Jessie,' Ginny said, kindly, 'but honestly, I'm fine. I don't need protecting.'

'Too late for that, eh, Ginny?' Frances said. Jessie turned on her heel only to discover Frances looking kindly at Ginny. 'Some of us learn the hard way.' It was a truth that couldn't be argued with and the two girls exchanged glances. Ginny turned and walked away and they watched her for a while before moving on again. Jessie stuffed her hands in her pockets, pulled them out again, smoothing the flaps down, her mother's words in her head, telling her it would spoil the line of her coat. Frances was silent as they walked down St Peter's Avenue.

'Aren't you going to speak to me?' Jessie said when she could stand it no longer.

Frances stopped and turned to look at her. Her dark eyes showed sadness more than anger and Jessie braced herself for whatever Frances decided to dish out.

'You shouldn't have done that, Jessie. You put Ginny in an awkward position. Dolly too.'

Jessie bit at her cheek. 'I know.' It had started to rain again. A boy on a bike rode through a puddle, making spray that splashed on her legs. 'Oi!' she shouted after him. He called 'Sorry' over his shoulder and carried on down the street. Frances chafed at the mess on her legs as she brushed it away and they walked on as the rain came down harder. 'I knew I was wrong, Frances, but it was too late.'

They hurried along to the house at Barkhouse Lane. The curtains had already been drawn and Jessie thought how hard it was going to be in the coming dark months with no light at all to welcome them home.

'It was all right in the end though, wasn't it?'

'This time.' Frances pushed the front door open and they stood in the hallway, shaking off the worst of the water from their coats before they hung them on the rack. 'You should think before you speak in future, Jessie. It could get you in a lot of bother, which is fine, but you'll have to deal with the fallout.'

Jessie tried to interrupt because Frances was being unfair. 'But—'

Frances put her hand up to stop her, then rested it on her arm. 'I know you were being kind, Jessie, but you can't solve everyone's problems for them. Sometimes you have to let them work it out for themselves.'

Ginny slowed as she reached the end of the street, wanting to delay the moment, wishing she had somewhere else to go. She turned and looked down towards the main road where she'd left the girls, envying them their closeness. She hitched her gas mask higher on her shoulder as she turned into Kew Road, fumbling in her pocket for her key. Inside the hall she made for the stairs but was too late. The door opened and Mr Blake came out. He leered at her and she shivered.

'Finished for the day?' He smiled, his mouth parting. 'I've just made a brew if you want to join me?'

'That's very kind of you.' He stood behind her and she gripped the handrail. 'But I've things to do.' She hurried up the stairs, her hands trembling as she put her key in the lock. Inside her room she closed the door and leant against it. She was hungry and thirsty and she wished she had gone with Frances and Jessie. Yes, they were all getting braver – but not brave enough.

Chapter 18

Johnny stepped out onto Cleethorpes station in the late evening and made his way to the Cliff Hotel. He stopped outside the Empire and read the posters. Suez starring Tyrone Power was showing, with live entertainment from the Variety Girls featuring Jessie Delaney. Their photographs were in the display cases at the front and he leant in close to look at Frances. What the hell was she doing here, in a small seaside theatre, when she danced like an angel? She should be in the West End, where she belonged. When he and Ruby had left for America Frances had been a rising star. She'd had to step in for Ruby when she had her appendix removed and although he'd been concerned for Ruby, it was a dream to dance with Frances, to hold her so close. She was sensational, and he'd been glad that she'd been thrust full centre into the spotlight – it was what she deserved. When she didn't come to America he'd thought it was because she'd chosen her career over him; so why was she hiding away in the provinces? It didn't make sense. He smiled to himself, glad that she *was* here, it didn't matter how or why.

Jack was waiting at the hotel and, after checking in and arranging for his bag to be taken to his room, Johnny joined him at the bar. He liked him enormously; Bernie had said to trust his gut and he had. If he had to be partners with anyone, it would be with men like Jack and Bernie.

'What can I get you, Johnny?'

'Scotch and ice.' Jack ordered it and Johnny pulled out a stool and sat down, leaning his elbow on the bar. The bartender placed his drink on a mat and he picked it up, sipped, the burn welcome in his throat. Johnny looked about him. The bar was busy with military personnel he recognised as coastal command. It had been difficult to get a room, but they had somehow squeezed him in. He felt uncomfortable, the only younger man not in uniform. Did they think him a coward? Jack cleared his throat.

'You said you had a proposition, Johnny, about the Empire?'

He looked at Jack, who was smiling, putting him at his ease. He'd noticed, hadn't he? Well, it wouldn't be like that forever. 'I did, Jack.' He'd spent the entire journey working on it. Was he mad? He took another sip of his whisky.

'I'd like to make a guest appearance, Jack, if that's at all possible. Sing, dance, a couple of numbers, a precursor to the season at the Palace. A sort of live advertisement – coming soon to the Palace, sort of thing.'

Jack's enthusiasm was evident. 'Absolutely. That would be wonderful, although it's only a three-piece in the pit – piano, double bass and drums; not great, not what you're used to.'

'That's fine. It doesn't have to be perfect.' He paused. 'And the girls will be there?'

Jack picked up the beer mat, flipped it on its side and tapped it on the bar. Johnny watched him.

'They will. Unless you don't want them to be.' He caught Jack's eye. He must have guessed there was more to his request, but he didn't let on, simply waited until Johnny was ready to enlarge on his idea.

'I don't want them to know.' Johnny rolled his glass around on its heel. 'It's complicated.'

Jack smiled, understanding. 'These things are.'

At ease with Jack, he told him a little of his relationship with Frances. 'I'd love to dance with her again. A bit of a surprise for the audience.'

'And for her.'

What could he say? How could he tell him it was about the magic? Would he understand that everything hinged on holding Frances, on dancing with her, creating that indefinable connection he felt when she was in his arms. She'd been reluctant to speak with him the other day and he had no idea what he'd done wrong. He'd seen the anger in her eyes. And pain. Was he the cause of it? If he knew what it was, maybe he'd be able to make it right. Women were so complicated. Jack laid the beer mat down, rested his glass on it.

'Listen, Johnny, I'm willing to give it a go, if you're sure it's what you want.'

He touched Jack's shoulder. 'Thanks, Jack. I'll make sure it's a success.'

Jack laughed. 'As if Johnny Randolph could be anything less.'

He spent the day at the hotel, resting, thinking, staring out of the windows across the estuary. Ships were moving in and out; there was a mock castle to the left, a tourist attraction. He liked the place more than he had done the last time he was here with Bernie. In the afternoon he went downstairs and found a room with a dance floor where he could rehearse and limber up. How long was it since they had danced in front of an audience, he and Ruby? He couldn't count the night at the Café de Paris when he'd told her she was unprofessional, and yet here he was, arranging to do the same. What was worse? Ruby's drunken impromptu performance or his intended ambush of Frances? Would she forgive him? He picked up his jacket and made his way to his room to shower. Well, Frances hadn't answered his letters, or acknowledged the flowers. He had nothing to lose …

*

Johnny and Jack chatted in Jack's office at the theatre while the film was showing and there was plenty to discuss. He hadn't been this nervous before a performance in years, but then he hadn't danced with Frances in, what was it, four years? It was good to be fired up about performing. But would she go through with it? Well, he could wing it if she walked off, crack a gag, win the audience over, dance one of his solos. But it wasn't the audience he wanted to win.

Jack led him through the pass door on the dress circle at the intermission before the girls went on. They remained hidden in a dressing room and Jack turned up the tannoy so they could hear the girls sing. Between them they had arranged for Johnny to come on at the end of their performance; Jack would introduce him. The band had been primed during the afternoon, arriving at the hotel at Johnny's request to go through the music, the timing. At Jack's signal he went up into the wings, stood in the shadows as the girls performed their last routine. His heart was pumping as it hadn't done in years and he leant forward slightly, watching Frances, singing the harmonies to Jessie's lead when she was more than capable of doing the same herself. Frances was a leading lady and he had no idea why she was holding herself back, making herself small. None of it made sense.

When the girls took a bow at the end of a song, Jack walked out on stage. The three of them were surprised and Johnny felt uncomfortable, springing this on them; but he had to know and this was the only way he could think of. She wouldn't kick up a fuss, not in front of an audience, not in front of her friends; she wasn't like Ruby, thank the Lord. He flinched. Ruby would hate it if she knew. Hate *him*, but then she did already, so what difference did it make?

The applause died down and Jack stepped forward.

'Ladies and Gentlemen, aren't these girls brilliant? Let's show our appreciation again.' He clapped, his hands high, leading them. The girls smiled, bowing and taking another call, then Jack quietened the audience with his hands and beamed. 'I'm delighted to announce that we have a special guest tonight,' he stretched out his hand and announced, 'Mr Johnny Randolph!'

There were gasps and cheers and the audience applauded as the male half of the famous Randolphs walked onto the stage, waving, smiling. Out the corner of his eye he could see Frances, the shock on her face, the excitement and bewilderment on those of her friends. He felt a sharp stab of shame again, but he had to go through with it. It was a test, not for her, but for him.

He bowed, taking the applause. 'Thank you, Ladies and Gentlemen.' He put his arm out to the girls, smiling. They smiled back but beneath her smiles Johnny could see that Frances was thunderous. He walked towards her, taking her hand and bringing her forward. Jack stepped back, taking his place between Jessie and Ginny.

Johnny stood centre stage with Frances. He could feel her nails digging into his palm. He didn't care.

'A few years ago, I had the pleasure of dancing with this young lady, Miss Frances O'Leary, in *Lavender Lane*. You may remember it.' There were shouts of appreciation. 'Thank you. Some of you may have seen it.' He sensed Frances's fury but he couldn't stop, wouldn't, not now. He wanted to dance with her. Longed to. He turned to Jack, gave a slight nod of his head, and Jack led Jessie and Ginny offstage. Johnny leant down to talk to the band, stood back again, all the time holding onto Frances. He wouldn't let her go, not this time.

He turned to her and she faked a smile at him, to the audience. 'We'd like to give you a small taste of our success. Gentlemen ...' he said to the boys in the band. He stepped back from the microphone and Frances tried to release her hand but he pulled her close. Her anger was obvious, her body rigid with fury, and a sliver of doubt shot through him. He ignored it. 'Go with it, Frances. Do you remember the moves?' It was a ridiculous question; he knew she would, and he was suddenly excited, her anger irrelevant. The band began to play and he swept her into his arms. To his delight, she moved with him. The audience disappeared, everything and everyone melting away because, at last, it was just the two of them. She was light and deft and he felt such joy within him, a feeling long forgotten. He put his arms to her waist, lifted her, and her body was beautiful lines, her hands expressive, sweeping out and then to his face, touching him and then away.

Johnny grasped her hand and she twirled away from him, then he pulled her back, wrapping his arms about her, and it felt so good to have her close again. God, how he loved her! Their bodies matched, they were meant to be together, as one. The complicated knots of his life unravelled as they danced. He put his cheek to hers, feeling her skin, the smell of her hair, as she leant against him and he wanted it to go on forever. It was nothing like dancing with Ruby. Frances was light and beauty and he could express movement with her that he couldn't with his sister. This love was different, all-consuming. The music came to an end and she was in his arms, their cheeks touching, staring out into the audience. 'Damn you, Johnny,' she whispered as they took the applause. 'Damn you.'

He held her hand and put out his other hand towards her for the audience to appreciate her. She dropped her knee to a low curtsey, smiling out to them. He let her fingers go and she rushed into the wings. He called her back and she came to the side, not to him, gave a little bob with her head, glaring at him with such pain that he felt suddenly ashamed, the joy of the moment dissipated. My God, what had he done? He could see the tears glistening in her eyes.

Jack came back on, exchanged a few words with Johnny and announced the intermission. Johnny took the applause and rushed into the darkness of the wings, racing down to the dressing rooms to find her. He knocked on the door and Jessie opened it slightly.

'Can I see Frances?'

'She doesn't want you to see you, Johnny.' She kept the door tight so that he couldn't see into the room.

'Please, Jessie. It's important.' The girl hesitated, stared into his eyes, then slowly opened the door and stood back. Frances was sitting shaking, her breath coming in quick bursts.

'Jessie!' she hissed, looking away from him. Ginny turned, awkward, and he felt truly ashamed at what he had done to the three of them.

'I'm sorry, girls.'

Jessie stepped back against the wall. Frances got to her feet.

'Are you? Are you *really* sorry, Johnny Randolph?' She folded her arms, trembling, and he knew it was with rage, not fear. 'That was cruel. Cruel.' She was close to tears. 'But then, that's you all over. There's nothing new there, nothing I didn't already know.' He tried to step into the room.

'Please, let me explain.' Oh, God, this wasn't how he'd expected it to go at all. He thought she felt as he did, that she would know. He stared at her, seeing the pain.

'What if I hadn't remembered the routine?'

'I knew you would. We had something special, Frances.'

She lunged at him, screaming, 'Get out! Get out!' Ginny rushed towards her, holding her back. Jessie came to the door, pushed him away.

'You'd better leave.' She wasn't angry, just sad for her friend. He could see the compassion in her eyes as she gently forced him out into the corridor.

'Tell her I'm sorry, Jessie. It was meant to be a surprise.' It was a feeble excuse, a lie, but words had failed him. He had hurt her, somehow he had hurt her, but he would put it right. He would insist Ruby came to Cleethorpes, or he would come on his own.

Chapter 19

On the morning of the talent show Jessie received a telegram from her agent, Bernie Blackwood. Things were moving again and the impresario, Vernon LeRoy, had been in contact, offering her a supporting role in the production at the Adelphi. It wasn't what she'd been expecting, but things had changed. He hoped she'd understand that. Jessie handed it over to Grace.

'Well, darling, only you can decide.' Her mum's voice was level, betraying nothing of her opinion one way or another. 'It's your life, your dreams.' Jessie had expected her to be more helpful.

'But what about you and Eddie? I feel I've brought you here and now I'm thinking about abandoning you.'

Grace laughed gently. 'It's hardly abandoning. We're more settled than we've been in a long time.' She held out the telegram and Jessie took it, folding it in half and tucking it with the others behind a chipped china plate on the dresser. It was what she'd wanted, but everything had changed, and not only because of the war. She leant against the dresser.

'I don't know what to do …'

Grace picked up the sock she was darning for Eddie, pushing the heel onto a wooden mushroom, easing it into place. 'You don't have to take the first thing that's offered, darling.'

'As I did when I came here?' She watched her mum take up her needle, thread it with grey wool. Grace looked up, smiled. 'It all worked out perfectly. But it's a good thing to bear in mind. Concentrate on what you really want, Jessie. What will make you happy?'

She wanted so many things, that was the trouble. To be with Grace, to be with Harry – only that was impossible, as it was for so many others. Once she'd longed for success, but things were all up in the air lately and she couldn't find the solid ground she needed.

'I'm scared,' she blurted out, her thoughts so knotted she thought she would burst.

'Of the bombs?' Grace stilled her hand.

'Partly.' She sat down on the chair beside Grace. 'But not wholly.'

'Then what else?' Grace reached out and Jessie took her hand, clasping it, feeling her mum's firm grip that belied her frail appearance. She was much improved, her strength returning. It was comforting. Jessie needed to find that same strength within herself.

'I know there hasn't been the bombing we expected. Perhaps they might never come.'

Grace inclined her head. 'Let's hope so, for all our sakes.'

Jessie blew out her breath, letting her shoulders sag. 'It's all been so confusing, Mum. I wanted to be successful so that I could bring us all together.'

'And you've done that,' Grace said, shaking her hand gently. Jessie wanted to do so much more. It was all right lodging here, with Geraldine. She looked stern but she was kind really, and generous. She'd been an absolute angel when Jessie had arrived with Grace and Eddie, her unexpected and unprepared-for lodgers, making room for them both. It had been under Geraldine's watchful eye that they had nursed Grace back to health. She knew Grace enjoyed the companionship of the older woman and was certain it was reciprocated. But Jessie wanted Grace to have a house of her own, to have the lovely things she deserved. And Jessie wanted to be a star.

'It's a good opportunity,' she said eventually. It wasn't the stellar trajectory she'd dreamed of, but it *was* the West End.

'It is.' Grace was non-committal.

'You're not helping,' Jessie said, trying not to smile.

'It's a big step. Coming here was one thing, London's another matter entirely. And we weren't at war then.' Grace let go of her hand and stroked Jessie's hair. 'You know how hard it is, Jessie. More so since you came here. Alone. You've done it once. Alone. And you made a success of it. Does it still make you happy?'

It was hard to know. These last few weeks had been strained, the colour that accompanied the summer variety show sadly missing. Vernon LeRoy coming along and offering her the moon had lifted her far beyond what she'd dreamt of for herself. She should be elated, but it was as if all the stuffing had been knocked out of her.

Frances rushed in from her shift at the pub, stuck her head around the door.

'Wait for me, Jessie, if you will. We'll walk together? Afternoon, Grace.'

Jessie said she'd wait and Frances thundered up the stairs, coming back down again within a few minutes. The night at the theatre had shaken her to the core but she'd refused to talk about it, only saying that it had caught her off guard, that she was frightened that she'd made a fool of herself. Jessie knew it was more than that, but also knew better than to push. When Frances came down again she'd unpinned her dark hair and was flicking it about her shoulders. 'Time for a wash?'

Jessie looked at the clock. 'If you're quick. Cold water.'

'Warm?'

'I'll wait.' Jessie got her gas mask and bag ready, got her jacket from the hall and pulled it on while she waited for Frances, who rubbed at her face with a towel, pulled at her hair with her fingers and decided to do the rest at the theatre.

'Enjoy yourselves, girls.' Grace said. Jessie leant forward and kissed her cheek.

'We'll do our best.'

Grace held her gaze. 'That's all you have to do.'

Ginny was already in the dressing room when they arrived. She'd brought a couple of photos and old postcards and was pinning them around her mirror when they walked in, the two of them slinging their gas masks in the corner. She hadn't yet put on her make-up and in the glare of the white light from the bulbs she looked gaunt and angular.

'That's a good idea, Ginny. Makes it look more homely.' Frances drew out her chair, pulled off her shoes. 'Still being sick?'

'Not so much.' Ginny leant forward, pushing another pin into the wall. In the mirror Frances saw her wince, tense herself. Frances opened her make-up box. 'Dolly said we've got quite a few booked for tonight, which is good. Let's hope this wind blows a few our way.'

Jessie pulled her dress over her head, shook her hair, wrapping her dressing gown about her. 'It will be good to have a few more bums on seats. It's like pulling teeth some nights.'

'That's showbiz, Jessie. Unless, of course, you're at the Palladium but if they don't like you there, it's even worse.' Frances spat into the small block of black eyeliner and pulled the brush over her eyebrows. There was a knock on the door and Chip, the new call boy, stuck his head around it. His grey hair tufted wildly about his ears and he was slow on his feet. He'd retired but Mike had called him in to work the tabs – pulling the curtains in and out needed a slow hand so he was well-suited to it, and as Jack was trying to run everything on a shoestring, many of them were doubling up on what needed to be done.

'This is your half-hour call, ladies.'

'Thank you, Chip, darling.' Frances winked at him and he grinned, showing his big yellowing teeth. He moved aside to let Annie, Jack Holland's assistant, into the room and left them to it. She was holding a sheaf of index cards with the names and talents of eager participants who had already put their names forward. Annie was all smiles. 'Seems to have got the locals out, girls. All the eager future stars have brought along their families, so we've sold quite a few tickets. It's the best day we've had in weeks. Who's going to take charge of these?' She held the cards up and Jessie came forward and took them from her. She flicked through them. 'Mostly singers,' Annie said.

'I think people are getting used to the blackout and gaining more confidence – the houses are getting better.' Jessie placed the cards on the dressing table.

'Or they're getting bored,' Annie said as she left.

'This could be fantastic. Or it could be a ruddy disaster,' Frances said when they heard Annie go up the steps to the stage.

'It's going to be fun, Frances. Don't be such a grump.' Frances ignored her.

'I wonder what idiots we'll get up tonight, thinking they're Gracie Fields or George Formby.' She ran her lipstick over her lips, pressing first, then moving them back and forth to even out the colour. She sat back in her chair, her long black hair brushed and tamed, pushed away from her face and held in place with Kirby grips.

Her words irritated Jessie. 'It doesn't matter, does it? They're people with dreams. We all have dreams, *all* of us.'

Frances wondered what Ginny's dreams had been. Had they been similar to her own? Perhaps not. The girl had already said she was doing it for her mother. It wasn't the same as doing something for the love of it, like Jessie and she had done. But they were all doing it for someone else in the end. Perhaps they weren't so far apart after all. Frances picked up an emery board and drew it over her nails.

'All right then, Shirley Temple. Let's hope we've got something to look forward to.'

Jessie grinned and Frances found herself smiling too. The girl was forever putting her foot in it, but she was an optimist – and optimism had been in short supply lately.

'Speaking of which ... have you heard from Bernie?'

'A telegram came today. Not what was planned, something else, but it's been so long that I'm not sure whether I want to go now.' She was hesitant. 'They'll surely bomb London first.'

'You don't know that. We thought they would bomb us all from the off, but they haven't, have they? There's been nothing in the papers.'

'They're not going to put it in the papers, are they?'

Jessie shrugged. 'I don't know, do I? None of us do. It could happen tomorrow. Here. Anywhere. But I think I'd rather be with Mum and Eddie. If we go, we go together. I can't help thinking of all those poor kids gone to strange places they've never heard of. They must be so frightened and their parents worried sick. I mean, they could be with anyone, couldn't they?'

Frances's forehead prickled with sweat. At least she knew Imogen was with kind people. How many other parents could be sure of that? But what if bombs did come along? She'd want to be with Imogen too.

'We must be brave,' Ginny said quietly.

'They won't know the gravity of it, Ginny. Most of the ones I saw lined up the other week were oblivious, looked like they were going off on some grand adventure. And their mothers holding back the tears.' She didn't want to talk about it but felt she needed to, to speak of her fears. 'Some of those parents might be in here tonight, hoping to think happier thoughts. We need to make sure they do.'

Frances dipped her head under the table, pretending to rummage in her handbag. The metal clip snapped as she opened it and when she felt the tears that threatened had gone, she reached in for her handkerchief, discreetly dabbing at her eyes, pretending to blow her nose. It would be so much easier if she could talk to them both, be upfront about her past, her relationship with Johnny, especially after her outburst the other night. She decided against it. Ginny might think it a way forward, and much as she loved Imogen, she wouldn't advocate her situation as being suitable for anyone else.

'I think we'll have to work hard to hold it all together,' Ginny said, standing up and slipping off her robe. She took the red dress that Dolly had worked on from the hanger and put it on. She turned her back and lifted her hair for Jessie to do up the zip. 'At least you won't have to play the piano tonight, Jessie. It'll be fun, the three of us holding the show together. Haven't we come a long way?'

Frances got into her own costume. Grace was a superb seamstress and the costumes were lovely, with fitted bodices and skirts that flared out when they danced but otherwise draped in folds. Unfortunately for Ginny, the design accentuated their small waists, but Dolly had been able to finesse them with waistbands. She had come up with an idea to make the three of them slightly different so as time went on she could let Ginny's out without attracting too much attention.

Annie knocked on the door.

'I'm going to get the contestants to come through the pass door at prompt side. If one of you can come with me when you're ready, we'll bring them backstage and then you can have a chat, put them at their ease, find out what they're going to do. I've sorted a running order with Mike so we're almost there.'

'I'll do it.' Jessie looked to the other two for agreement; Frances wasn't bothered and Ginny was doing as little out front as she could get away with. She left with Annie and when Frances heard their footsteps on the stairs that led to the stage, she turned to Ginny.

'How are you feeling?'

She shrugged. 'I'm trying not to feel, Frances. I'm trying not to think about it.'

Frances understood completely. How could she tell her that it didn't work, that at some point you had to feel, had to let the pain break you?

'I know it's a ridiculous way to behave. I know I've got to think about what will happen afterwards, but that's a long way off, isn't it?' She sank down into the easy chair, careful to smooth her skirt as she did so. 'My head feels like it's full of wool and I'm so tired when I've finished at the laundry. The extra money for the shows is a godsend, but it's exhausting, and I don't know if I'll be able to do both. The panto will be a welcome boost for my savings and I'll have to give up my job at the laundry to do it. But what will I do when the panto ends? I don't expect the laundry will have me back. Not that I want to go back there, but . . .' Her voice faltered.

Frances squatted down beside her and held her hand. Ginny hung her head.

'Don't be nice to me, Frances. I don't want to cry.'

Frances gripped her hand. 'You're not on your own, Ginny. There are places you can go when the time comes.'

They realised that Jessie had come back in and Ginny looked up, brushed a tear from her cheek. Frances got up and Jessie wafted the cards in her hand.

'Eight hopefuls, so far. I've put them in the old band room. Ron's having a quick fag by the stage door then he'll come and talk through what they want him to play, if anything.'

'Well, I hope he plays fewer bum notes than he did last time,' Frances said. She made one last check in the mirror. 'Welcome to the glamour of showbiz!'

The band room was crowded with eager hopefuls, some smiling, energised, others looking apprehensive now that they had their chance. Some of them had brought their own music and Ginny took it, matched it against the running order, and got it ready for Ron. An elderly woman with erect posture came sweeping in, dressed in a long black velvet skirt embroidered with flowers. She glared at a young, red-cheeked boy, who looked terrified and sought refuge behind a man carrying a ukulele.

'She wouldn't look out of place in the 1890s,' Frances whispered to Ginny, who suppressed a chuckle.

'I'd like a chair please, when I go on,' she commanded. 'Would you arrange that for me, my dear?'

'Of course,' Jessie said, dropping a curtsey, then turning to grin at the other two. 'Does she know it's the Empire Cleethorpes and not Hackney?' Ginny nudged her with her elbow before dashing out of the room.

A mother came in holding the hand of a little girl, all blonde girls and smiles. 'I know you,' Jessie said and went over, 'Hello, Julie.' She squatted. 'Are you going to be a

Variety Girl tonight?' She took a penny from her pocket. 'Remember this? You gave it to me on my first day in Cleethorpes.'

The child nodded. 'On the train. You shared your cake with me. Your mam made it for you.'

It seemed so long ago and things had moved so fast that she'd forgotten. Jessie's first tentative steps back into the theatre had been taken then, fuelled by anger at her aunt, her petty rules and regulations. She wasn't doing so badly, when all was said and done. It had only been weeks, not years. There was still so far to go. 'It's my lucky penny. Do you want to hold it and make a wish on it?'

'Ta, I will. I want to win.' She kissed the penny and handed it back to Jessie. 'Do you think it will work?'

'I hope so. Just have fun when you go out, that's the secret. Having fun.' That was something she'd needed reminding of herself.

The child leant close to Jessie, her hand guarding the side of her mouth, and whispered, 'I want to buy Mam a new coat. An' a hat. When I win.'

Her mother looked anxious. 'She should be in bed, but she would insist. She heard me and me sister talking about the show and said she wanted to come. And there's no harm in it, is there?' She pulled at Julie's arm. 'I said she can do her bit, then we can go home. Bit of experience for her. Best to start young.'

Dolly peered into the room, searching for one of the girls. She spotted Jessie and came over. 'Jack sent me down to help.' She looked about her. 'It's a good assortment. Not just singers, thank goodness. At least the audience will get a bit of variety.'

Chip called Overtures and they left Dolly to chaperone the acts and went into the wings. Jessie peeped through the spyhole.

'Not a bad house, three quarters at least.'

Ginny took a turn. 'Oh, there's something about the excitement waiting for a show that makes me feel so happy!'

Jessie rested an arm on her back. 'I know what you mean. Gives me butterflies every time, but it's so much better with a good audience.'

'We don't know that they're good, yet,' Frances said.

'Misery guts,' Jessie chided.

The girls opened with 'When You're Smiling', hoping to encourage the audience into doing as instructed. They were receptive, in a good mood, and the girls went down well. Jack was waiting in the wings and applauded them when they came off.

'Wonderful, girls. All that lovely energy you've put out there. That's what we need.'

Jessie walked back out on stage to introduce the first act. They'd decided the woman they called Madame should go on first, followed by Julie, so her mum could get her off to bed. A chair had been found that met Madame's approval and she swanned onto the stage, Frances coming up at the rear with a spoonback chair on which the woman placed her generous bottom. Madame made a great drama of getting herself settled for her dramatic outpouring and played her accordion to accompany a dismal, dreary song that went on far too long. Just when they thought she'd finished she decided there was another verse, and then another. The girls huddled in prompt corner, waiting for her to end with a flourish that never came. Mike leant in, his face sinister in the blue light.

'We'll have to do something. She'll be on all night at this rate.'

Frances stepped in. 'Give the signal for the tabs, Mike. Jessie can walk on applauding and introduce the next contestant and when the curtains are closed, I'll get her off.'

Mike agreed.

'Fair call. Even I wouldn't argue with Frances.' Frances raised her eyebrows at him and he pretended to cower. She laughed. He gave the signal for Chip to close the curtains and Jessie marched out, her smile wide, clapping with her hands held high.

'Wasn't that wonderful, Ladies and Gentlemen? Thank you, Eglantine Powell.' Jessie continued applauding, smiling at the audience, who had become restless. The sounds of Madame's protests filtered through the curtain and she only hoped that Frances had arms strong enough to propel her into the wings. With any luck Julie and her curls would charm them. Jessie introduced her, encouraging the audience to applaud as she walked out, hoping their hands hadn't gone to sleep. Julie strode towards her, her golden curls bouncing as she walked. Jessie grinned. The child squinted out into the audience, the lights on her little chubby cheeks.

'I need that chair too,' she announced.

Jessie smiled to the audience. She could tell they had relaxed a little. 'What's your name?'

'I told you me name before, downstairs. Have you forgotten?' There was a ripple of laughter in the theatre.

'I've not forgotten but the people out there don't know it, do they?'

'Oh.' She looked out into the theatre again. 'My name is Julie, but Mam sometimes calls me buggerlugs.'

The audience roared with laughter.

Jessie glanced into the wings to see Julie's mother shaking her head, her hand covering her mouth. Jessie bit her lip to temper her own laughter.

'What are you going to do for us tonight, Julie?'

'I'm going to sing and dance and do acrobatics.'

'Marvellous.' Jessie squatted down so she was eye to eye with the child. 'Would you like me to stay here with you?'

'No, ta. I'm perfectly all right on me own.' The girl tossed her head and her curls bounced about her face. Jessie looked out into the audience. The first few rows were smiling broadly in expectation and she knew the rows behind would be too.

'Oh, that told me.' There was a warm burst of laughter from the audience and Jessie leant forward to speak to Ron at the piano. 'Teddy Bears' Picnic, low as you can,' she said and walked off to stand at the side of the stage.

The girl took a big breath, her little chest puffing out like a pigeon, and started to sing. As she did so, Ron began to play, keeping the piano quiet. She danced and skipped about the stage, holding out the skirt of her dress, smiling confidently out into the darkness of the auditorium. She came to the chair, put her hands on it and climbed up; she wobbled and there was a collective gasp as the audience caught its breath. She stood on the chair, smiling out into the auditorium, and waited with all the poise of a prima donna, then jumped off the chair, did a roly-poly, stood up and curtseyed. The audience cheered and Jessie walked forward, clapping and laughing, shaking her head. What a child she was.

'I think we can safely say this little girl is going to go a long way!'

The audience cheered and Julie bowed then waved as she left the stage holding Jessie's hand.

'I was good, wasn't I, Jessie?' she said as she walked into the darkness of the wings and to her mother.

'You were wonderful, Julie. A true star.'

Her mother was smiling, half-embarrassed. 'I could've died, the little madam.'

'Wait while I bring on the next act, will you?' Julie's mother said and Jessie went off to introduce the male baritone and hurried back to the wings.

'You were wonderful.' Jessie leant in. 'It could have been a disaster if she hadn't gone on when she did. Made them all laugh, made them smile. One day you'll be a star, Julie. We'll all be watching you.' Julie preened and her mam smiled at Jessie.

'You're a dear. Thank you, ducky. I'll take her off to bed now, though I doubt she'll sleep.'

They left and Jessie watched the baritone go through his act. He was good, which was a relief. She peered at the judges. Jack, the Mayor, and Jimmy Baker, the comedian from the Royal. Jimmy was a local man who had stepped in when Billy Lane had upped and left for stardom during the summer variety show. She wondered what Billy was doing now. Bernie had promised him work on the wireless, but they hadn't heard anything, not that she'd been watching out for news of him, but she was sure Ginny had. She peered across the stage into the darkness of the wings on the far side. Chip was leaning against the pros arch, watching the singer, moving his head in time to the music. Ginny was standing behind him with two boys who would sing and dance, the Lister Brothers. Their hair was slicked back and they were in their best shirts and ties, their cheeks rosy. One of them had glasses, the other red hair and a face full of freckles. They skipped onto the stage when Jessie introduced them and went into a Flanagan and Allen routine that was a hit with the audience. They had them singing along as if they were the real thing. Frances came and stood beside her.

'There will always be a line of young hopefuls queuing up to take our place, won't there?'

'Let's hope so, for all our sakes. In a few years, if the war lasts, they'll be fighting on the front lines. Doesn't bear thinking about.' She thought of her brother. Grace was scared too, she knew that from the way she looked at Eddie; she was trying not to show it, but it was there all the same. How could she go to London and leave Grace to more worry? She looked again into the wings. Ginny was bent over, holding her stomach, her other hand on her forehead. She wobbled and staggered into the darkness.

'Oh!' Jessie exclaimed, slapping her hands across her mouth. Frances dashed behind the backcloth to the other side of the stage and Jessie could just make her two friends out as the boys strolled along the stage. Chip looked across to her, his hands splayed. She leant into the light so he could see her and mouthed, 'All right?', making her mouth wide to give him visual clarity. Chip gave her a thumbs up.

The boys ended their act on a flourish and Jessie skipped on again, covering for Frances. She would guide them off herself and bring on the next act. As the boys took an extended bow, Frances appeared in the wings, her face flushed. Jessie smiled to the audience and Frances came onstage with Edgar, an elderly man who was going to play the whalebones. Frances walked casually back to opposite prompt before disappearing into the darkness again. When the applause died down, the man went into a long introduction to the origins of the whalebones, what he was going to play, why he had chosen the particular song, what it signified. Jessie's heart sank.

Frances returned and stood beside her. 'Ginny doesn't feel too well. I've made her lie down in the dressing room. We'll have to do the rest between us.'

'Is she all right?' The girls watched Edgar rattling his bones.

'So far.' Frances leant back to Mike. 'Looks like we've got another one, Mike. Let's get him off and the last act on. Some people don't know when to get off. When will they learn that you can have too much of a good thing?' She touched his shoulder. 'Not that he was a good thing in the first place!'

The girls went into action as they had done before, taking off the errant performer with winsome smiles and a flash of the legs; their skirts swirling as they spun on stage. The old man didn't stand a chance and the pair of them grinned at each other. When he was safely returned to the wings, Frances went to check on Ginny.

The last act was introduced. A barrel of a man walked on with his ventriloquist dummy, which he perched on his arm, although it looked more like he was sitting on the man's generous belly. He had a thick moustache which gave him the appearance of a rather fat walrus. When his dummy spoke, the moustache came into its own, concealing any movement that might otherwise have been obvious. He was saved by a fabulous repertoire that had the audience rolling in their seats with laughter.

Frances reappeared. 'Dolly's looking after Ginny. She sent her dad over the road for a hot water bottle and she's tucked Ginny up in the chair in the dressing room.'

'That doesn't sound good.'

Frances looked towards the stage, the light softening her dark features. 'What will be, will be.'

The girls worked together to finish the show. All the contestants were called back and stood beneath the spotlights. Jack came on stage to represent the judges and gave their verdict and the ten-pound note to the winners – the Lister Boys.

Frances and Jessie went back to the dressing room, but Ginny had gone.

'I'll check the lavvy. You ask George.' Frances scanned the room. 'Her bag's gone.'

Jessie ran up the steps to the small office at the stage door. 'Have you seen Ginny, George?'

'Left not five minutes since. Didn't look too well either; wanted to get off home.'

Jessie dashed back down the stairs, pulling off her costume, kicking off her shoes, Frances doing the same. Dolly came in and they could hear Jack placating Madame through the open door. 'Ginny's left. Could you hang our dresses up, Dolly? Sorry to leave you with this!' They handed her the dresses that she and Grace had so lovingly made.

Dolly paled, taking the dresses and draping them over her arm. 'Is she all right?'

Jessie was forcing on her shoes. 'I don't know. I don't likc to think of her on her own.'

'Let me know!' Dolly called after them. They dashed down the corridor and into the dark street, thankful that the moon was half decent, that it was Saturday and the streets were still busy with people out for the night. It seemed strange that things had gradually returned to a sense of normality, albeit a dark normality as they hurried through the marketplace and turned into St Peter's Avenue. There was no sign of Ginny; a young woman alone would have stood out among the men and couples that were idling along. They stopped, catching their breath for a second, making their way to Bowling Lane. The street narrowed, darker still, the bricks uneven beneath their feet. As their eyes adjusted, they saw her leaning against the wall, bent over, clutching her stomach. Jessie got to her first, putting an arm about her, trying to help her upright. A man with a tin hat and an ARP band on his arm hurried towards them.

'All right, ladies? Can I be of assistance?' Ginny groaned and Frances stepped forward, blocking the man's view of Ginny.

'Food poisoning. She's already been sick once. We're quite all right, but thank you for your offer. We're not far from home.'

Ginny groaned again and Jessie gripped her, holding her up.

The warden didn't seem inclined to move. 'If you're quite sure?' He stopped. 'Where are your gas masks, ladies? There's a fine, you know.'

Frances took him by the shoulder. 'We've only just come out. We were going back to get them.' He shone his torch and the narrow beam flicked over Ginny's face.

'Where do you live?'

'Kew Road.' Would he leave them alone, for God's sake?

'All of you?'

'Yes, all of us. Please, let us get her home?' Frances pleaded. 'We shouldn't have come out.'

He tilted his head. 'All right, I'll let you off this time. Seeing as you're so close to home.' He turned away, heading towards the main road. Frances rushed forward and took hold of Ginny's arm, hauling her upright. Jessie almost lost her footing and stumbled a little before regaining her composure.

'Walk,' Frances ordered and they slowly moved forward until they heard the man's boots clip the pavement as he turned down Glebe Road. Frances ordered Jessie to turn around.

'What?'

Ginny pointed with her hand. 'Wrong way. I'll. Be. Fine.' She drew in a long breath, pulling herself up, and they loosened their grip slightly.

'Course you will,' Frances said smartly. 'You're coming back with us.'

'I can't. I won't.' She was speaking through gritted teeth. Frances gripped her tightly.

'Don't talk cobblers, Ginny. You either come with us or we call an ambulance. Which do you prefer?' Ginny cramped again and moaned. It sounded hollow and painful and Jessie just wanted to do something, anything, to relieve the girl's pain.

'Us. Come on, Jessie, let's get her back to the Avenue.'

They held on to Ginny and struggled back onto the main road, propped her against the wall of a shop, Jessie hanging on tightly. Frances saw the white-painted wheel arches of a car and stepped into the road.

Jessie screamed, 'Frances!'

There was a loud screech as the car hit its brakes and Ginny sank to the ground.

Chapter 20

Frances was shaking as the driver got out, shouting merry hell at her.

'What a damn fool thing to do!' He came rushing forward, leaving his door wide and a middle-aged couple dashed towards them, the woman peering close into Frances's face. Frances's legs were weak, her head swimming, but she must think straight. They had to get Ginny back to Barkhouse Lane. The woman was close, in her face, shaking her arm gently to get her to respond.

'Are you hurt? Show me where it hit you.' Frances looked up; the woman's husband was at her side. She managed to speak.

'It didn't hit me. It's my friend.' She moved her head to draw their attention to the pavement. The woman looked across to where Ginny was slumped. The moon was showing enough light to let them see Jessie bent over her and a thickset man and a young chap helping Ginny to her feet. 'We need to get my friend home, she's ill.' The driver removed his hat, running his hand through his sparse black hair. His face was white too. He was right, it was foolish, but she'd achieved the result she'd wanted. The men picked Ginny up and carried her to the car. Jessie got in beside her and the driver gestured to Frances to get in the front.

He started the engine again. 'I doubt I've enough petrol to get you to the hospital.' He sounded apologetic.

'Not the hospital, ' Frances managed to croak. 'Barkhouse Lane, off the Kingsway. Please.'

He turned the car around and slowly headed back towards Oxford Street. Ginny was still groaning and the man looked through the rear-view mirror.

'Are you sure?'

Frances nodded. 'I'm so sorry,' she said. She inhaled deeply, blowing out a thin stream of air, her breath clouding in the coolness of the night, and drank in the dark shapes of the trees, the silhouette of the church, the blackness of the world.

The man turned into Barkhouse Lane. 'What number?'

'Here will be fine,' Frances said. He stopped the car and helped them get Ginny out. Her face was wet with tears and Jessie looked like a wraith. Frances had recovered somewhat, her breathing steady. 'Thank you. I'm sorry, I didn't even ask your name?'

'It doesn't matter.'

'It does to me. To us.'

'Clive. Clive Barrow.' Frances held out her hand and he shook it. 'Thank you, Clive. For rescuing we damsels in distress.'

He tipped his hat to her. 'Pleased to be of service.' He replaced his hat, walked back to his car and stood by it. 'Next time, take out your hanky and wave. I could have been taking you to hospital as well as your friend.' He got back in his car and drove away. Jessie was already battling down towards the house and Frances caught up with her, put her arm under Ginny's as they struggled the last few yards.

Jessie fiddled about for her key, opened the door and guided Ginny into the room that led to the kitchen, where she sat her on a chair, Frances supporting her.

Grace had heard them and came into the room in her dressing gown, her hair in a net. Ginny hung her head.

'What on earth is the matter, girls? Oh, Ginny!' Jessie bit at her lip. She was terrified for Ginny but what could she tell her mum? Frances saved her the trouble.

'It's complicated, Grace.' Frances held onto Ginny's arm. 'Is it OK if we take her upstairs and get her to bed? We'll look after her.'

Blood was seeping through Ginny's skirt and Grace looked at Frances. 'Quick as you can. Let me get some hot water for you to wash her.'

Ginny sobbed, said, 'I'm so sorry, Mrs Delaney.'

'Hush now, Ginny. No need for you to apologise.' Grace stood up and pressed a gentle hand on Ginny's shoulder.

Ginny was distraught, fighting to stand. 'I shouldn't have come.'

'Nonsense!' Grace was brisk but kind. 'Can you girls manage?'

Jessie helped Ginny to her feet. 'We can. Thanks, Mum.' It was all so awful. Frances opened the door, switched on the light and led Ginny upstairs.

'My room,' Jessie said in a loud whisper. She saw Geraldine at the top of the landing in her nightwear.

'Dear Lord, are you girls all right?' She stood back on the cramped landing, looked at Ginny's face. 'Oh.' Jessie felt Ginny's body sag again. Poor girl, this must be mortifying. 'Get her to bed. I'll help. Let me get my dressing gown. Is your mother awake?'

'In the kitchen.' They steered Ginny down the small corridor to Jessie's room at the back of the house.

'I'll find some towels, old sheets,' Geraldine called as she went downstairs.

They settled Ginny on the small spoonback chair in the corner of the room and Jessie turned back the sheets, wondering what else to do now that they had got her here. Frances removed Ginny's clothes, covering her with the blanket Jessie always left at the end of the bed. Grace came in with a bowl of water, soap and a flannel and Jessie rushed to take it from her. 'You should have called, Mum. I would have fetched it.'

'No matter,' Grace said quietly, brushing her hand down her dressing gown. 'Would you like me to take over, Frances?' Ginny seemed to fold in herself and Frances twisted to Grace. 'We'll be fine, thank you, Grace. Jessie, would you get the enamel pail from under the sink, give it a good clean and bring it up for us?'

Jessie pressed her lips together, tears pricking at her eyes. She felt so damn useless. Grace placed her palm on her back.

'It seems Frances has everything under control, Jessie, and I'm sure everyone is in need of a good hot drink. Come and help me, darling.' It took Jessie all her energy to move. Ginny was in such obvious pain. Thank God Frances knew what to do. But how did she know? She couldn't move, watching Frances, so calm, so contained, not the shivering wreck she was herself. Grace touched her shoulder, stirring her to action, and she bundled up Ginny's soiled clothes. She stopped at Eddie's door. Could he hear? Grace put her hand to the small of her back, pushing her forward.

'Don't worry, Jessie. That boy would sleep through an earthquake.' Would he? It felt like an earthquake as she made her way slowly down the stairs and into the kitchen. As she helped her mum she heard Ginny's moans filter through the floorboards. Grace handed her the kettle. 'Don't be afraid, darling, Ginny will be all right.' Jessie filled it with water and put it on the cooker as Ginny let out a blood-curdling howl. She burst into tears with the shock of it and Grace opened her arms and held her, stroking her hair.

She was never going to have children, Jessie thought. Never.

Frances washed Ginny as best she could, mopping her head with a cool flannel. Through the worst of it she rubbed her back, talking her through the pain, not wincing when Ginny gripped her hand so tightly that she felt the blood had stopped pumping through it. Jessie, white-faced and red-eyed, had brought up the pail and some old towels and stood by the door but Frances had urged her to go back downstairs. There was nothing she could do, the girl looked terrified, and she, Frances, needed to concentrate. Besides, Ginny seemed more comfortable when it was just the two of them.

'I know it's for the best, Frances. It's what I prayed for,' Ginny gasped.

Frances moved a strand of hair from her face that was red with effort and pain. 'It doesn't make it any easier though, Ginny.'

'No.' She bit down, panted through the pain as Frances had shown her to do. Frances pushed the open window higher, trying to cool Ginny down, then pulled on one of Jessie's cardigans as the room became colder. Where was Billy Lane now? Asleep, or in some bar, another girl on his arm. At least Ginny hadn't got stuck with him, for he would have broken her heart, sooner or later. Men walked away but the women couldn't. She breathed in the cold air, her eyes adjusting to the darkness, the middle hours of the night holding the stillness. She heard a thump as a cat landed on a dustbin in next door's yard, the rattle as the lid fell to the ground, its hollow echo ringing out. Ginny would forget Billy in time, but Frances had Imogen and would always be reminded of Johnny. She'd been shocked when he turned up at the Empire, furious when he sprang the dance on her.

But when they danced, everything was so right. She hadn't wanted to look at him but couldn't look away. She tugged the cardigan tight about her.

'Close the window, Frances,' Ginny said through clenched teeth. 'I'm fine.'

'Course you are, darling.'

Throughout the next hour Frances sat with Ginny, holding her hand, wiping her brow, rubbing her back, crooning. Ginny made loud grunts and groans, walking about the limited space, holding onto the wall, pressing her hands against it until she felt gravity working in her favour. Frances went to her side. 'This is the hardest bit. In a few minutes it will all be over.'

Afterwards, Frances drew a cloth over the pail and crept downstairs with it. Grace was sitting at the table, her eyes closed, Geraldine reading a book by the light of the small lamp on the dresser. Jessie had dropped her head onto her arms but sat up when Frances entered the room, looked at the bucket then at Frances, fear evident upon her face. Geraldine got up and took the pail from her.

'I'll take that.' Blood had dried on Frances's hands and she went through to the kitchen, rubbing the bar of soap over her hands, up her arms, washing them in the cold water. It made her feel more awake. She filled a pan of water and put it to boil as Geraldine came back into the room.

'How is she?' Jessie ventured, her voice croaky.

'Exhausted. I'll wash her again, then she can sleep. We all need to get to bed. It's over, and there's nothing more we can do.'

Jessie followed Frances upstairs with a fresh bowl of warm water with which to bathe Ginny. She looked haggard and drawn, but she was peaceful, no longer in such pain. Jessie took hold of her hand. Ginny's voice was weak.

'I'm so sorry to put on your mum and Geraldine like this. What must they think of me?'

Jessie smoothed her fingers over Ginny's hand. 'They're worried about you. We all are.'

Tears ran down Ginny's cheeks and she drew her hand across her face.

'I'm not crying because I'm sad – honestly, I'm not. I'm tired, that's all. Just tired.' The girls washed her, working quickly but gently, Jessie found a clean nightdress and they laid a towel over the sheets and placed her in the bed, pulling the blankets up to her chin. Jessie bent forward and kissed her cheek. 'We'll be next door, Ginny. Call out if you need us.'

While Frances dispensed of the water downstairs, Jessie collected her own nightclothes. She listened at Eddie's door as she passed but heard nothing. Eventually Frances came upstairs and the two of them got into bed.

'Will she be all right, Frances?' Jessie's voice was small.

'She'll recover, if that's what you mean.' Frances turned on her side. 'Now, go to sleep.'

Jessie fidgeted, and Frances waited, knowing what would come next.

'How did you know what to do, Frances?'

Frances stared at pale shadows slicing through the gap in the curtains. 'I knew a girl, Pamela. In the same situation. There was an older woman there and I helped her, watched what she did.' She had been terrified, just as Jessie had been earlier, but she had remained at Patsy's side. She wondered where Pamela was now.

'But you were so calm.'

She turned onto her back. 'I might have looked calm, Jessie, but I wasn't, not inside. We all put on a brave face, don't we?' Ginny would put on a brave face, carry on; so many girls did. If they survived.

'It was more than that, Frances. It was the way you—'

Frances interrupted her. She was tired, she might say more than she intended. 'I'm used to babies, Jessie. I have sisters, brothers – all older than me. There was always someone having a baby … or losing one.' She tugged the sheet up to her chin. 'Now, go to sleep.'

Jessie didn't say any more, even though Frances knew she was awake. It was quiet now, the drama over, but the morning would have to be faced and there would be more questions.

Frances was first out of bed. She tiptoed into Ginny's room and gently lifted the bedding. The bleeding seemed to have stopped, the towel between Ginny's legs red, but not too much. As she lowered the sheet, Ginny opened her eyes.

'Thank you, Frances.'

Frances touched her hand.

'You're welcome, darling.' She sat down on the side of the bed. 'We need to get a doctor to check you over. I think everything came away, but better safe than sorry. We don't want you getting an infection.' Ginny wept silent tears. 'The worst is over, Ginny, honestly. I know you feel you'll never recover from this, but you will. Trust me.'

'I didn't want it, Frances, but now it's gone I feel …' The tears came again and she caught them with her fingers, wiping them away. 'I thought I'd have someone to love, someone who would love me.' She rubbed her face with the back of her hand. 'Ridiculous, isn't it? I'd have had to give it away and that made me sad too, to think that a part of me was somewhere out in the world and I would never know where it was.'

There was nothing Frances could say. If it hadn't been for Patsy she would have had to do the same.

'Can I get you a drink?'

Ginny gave her a weak smile. 'I've put you to so much trouble …'

'Not at all. No one else is awake so we'll share a nice quiet cuppa.'

'Can I share too?' Jessie put her head around the door.

Frances got up. 'You can stay with Ginny. I'll bring them up.'

After the tea Frances changed the towel and settled Ginny back to sleep. She gathered the soiled cloths and went downstairs and out into the garden, where she unhooked the tub from the nail on the back wall and ran cold water from the outside tap, dropped in the towels, swirling them around with the wooden tongs, then refreshed the water. When the water ran less pink she added soda that had been diluted in hot water and left them to soak. She would wash them tomorrow, before she went to the pub. There was a sharpness in the morning air, the north wind pinched her face and her hands were raw from the cold water. She pushed them to her waist and leant back, easing into the aches of her body. The soil was turned, the cabbages Geraldine had planted gaining strength, and under the cloches the tops of carrots showing green against the brown. Her breath billowed in clouds and she hurried back into the house, wanting to warm herself by the stove while more water boiled. Grace was in the kitchen.

'I've lit the gas fire in my room. Come and sit down, Frances, you must be exhausted.'

She didn't argue, she *was* exhausted, but with emotion more than fatigue. She went into Grace's room at the front of the house, settling herself in the small easy chair. Grace ousted her, making her move to the high-backed chair that was more comfortable. The fire was welcome, the warmth it gave out more so. She shivered and Grace took a small blanket from the end of the bed and gently draped it about

Frances's shoulders. It made Frances think of her own mother and she suddenly felt vulnerable. Her thoughts skipped to Imogen, longing to hold her child. She stared at the bricks glowing red on the gas fire, the hissing sound like air leeching from a tyre.

Grace returned carrying a tray. She passed Frances a mug then pulled out the toasting fork, fixing a thick slice of bread on it and held it in front of the fire. Frances watched Grace checking the bread for colour before turning it over. As she buttered the first slice, Geraldine came in with cups of tea for herself and Grace and placed them on the small table between the chairs at the window. She slipped behind Frances's chair and drew back the curtains to let in the morning light.

'How is she?' Geraldine sat on a hard chair she'd brought in from the room next door while Grace took the small chair opposite Frances. She was a gentle woman but her slight frame belied her inner strength. She had been so ill when Jessie had first brought her here, but she had recovered well. Ginny would recover too, in time.

'Sleeping.' It was all Frances could offer. Grace put the buttered toast in front of her and she bit into it, savouring the comfort.

'Poor child,' Grace said, passing another slice of toast to Geraldine. Jessie came in, settled at her mother's feet and took charge of the toasting fork. Grace ran her hand about Jessie's face and Frances felt a lump swell in her throat. She put down her toast, unable to eat.

'It's a sorry state to be in so young but a blessing nonetheless.' Geraldine bit down on her toast and the noise set Frances's teeth on edge. She took up her mug and sipped at her tea, enjoying the warmth, the taste of things familiar. Jessie peeled the toast from the fork and twisted, glancing at Frances. Her face was red from being close to the fire.

'Another?'

Frances shook her head. She closed her eyes and eased back into the chair, let the warmth envelope her, the sounds of the room fade away. Imogen would be awake now and images of her sleepy little face washed before her …

'Imogen?'

Frances snapped her eyes wide. Jessie was staring at her.

'I-I imagine,' she stammered, fumbling for words, 'that Ginny will sleep most of the day.' She forced herself to look more awake than she felt. She mustn't slip up; this was not the time to say anything. But when would it ever be? She drank more tea, emptying the mug, returning it to the table.

'It's a lucky escape your friend has had. She'll be able to get on with her life, sadder but wiser, I hope,' Geraldine said and picked up her cup and saucer. 'It must have been a worry for you, Grace, Jessie young and away from home.'

Jessie was indignant. 'That's a bit unfair, Geraldine. I was perfectly safe.'

'Well, I *was* worried, Jessie. A mother always worries for her child.' Grace was calm, soothing. 'But you had Frances here, watching out for you.' She gave Frances a grateful smile that made her wince. If she knew about Imogen, would she think the same?

'Even so,' Geraldine observed, 'Ginny is not the only girl to get caught out.'

Frances snapped. 'It's always the girl's fault, isn't it? Men get off scot-free. No one needs to know anything about *their* indiscretions!' She felt anger building in her. Johnny had walked away and then come breezing back into her life as if nothing had happened. 'Why is it always the girls who carry the blame, get the bad reputation?'

'Because they are the ones who get pregnant, Frances.' Geraldine replied. 'It's as simple as that.'

'But it's not, is it? Simple, I mean?' She was on her feet now, tiredness cast off like an old cloak. 'And what about Bi—' She stopped, calmed herself. 'Ginny was seduced, enticed; she was – *is* – a lonely girl.'

'We're all lonely, Frances. It doesn't mean you have to give yourself to any chap that spins a yarn.'

'Speak for yourself, Geraldine. I'm not lonely at all.'

They stared at her. The gas fire hissed. How could she have been so spiteful?

Geraldine didn't deserve that, none of them did. Jessie got up and came over to her. Frances sank down into the chair.

'Please forgive me, Geraldine. I didn't mean it.'

Geraldine rubbed her hands on her thighs, got to her feet. 'You're tired, Frances. I know you didn't mean it.' She stared into the distance. 'Even so, I *am* lonely.' Frances was sick to her stomach but there was nothing she could do to take back her words. 'Work to do.' Geraldine picked up the chair and left the room. Jessie sat on the arm of the chair next to Frances, who hung her head in shame. Jessie would never understand her outburst, none of them would. She was surrounded by people who thought it was Ginny's fault – and they would think it was her fault too. They were both soiled, like the sheets soaking out in the yard, with stains that would never go away …

At eight, Frances pulled on her coat and got ready to leave. She flicked her hair out of her collar and pulled on her beret, checking herself in the mirror in the narrow hallway. Jessie came out to her, closing the door, whispering, 'Where are you going?'

Frances smoothed her hair, tucked it behind her ear. 'To Patsy, Jessie. The same as I always do. It's Sunday.'

'But what about Ginny?' Jessie looked up the stairs, then back to Frances.

'Ginny will be fine.' She mustn't get into a conversation; mustn't be delayed. Tiredness hung heavy on her and it would be heaven to go back to bed, to sleep away the day, but she wanted to be with her child more than ever, to hold her, feel her warmth. She turned from the mirror. 'Remember to call the doctor.'

The fear was plain on Jessie's face. 'What do I say to him?'

'Jessie, your mother is here, as is Geraldine. And Ginny will have to speak up for herself. There's nothing more I can do for her.'

'But she's our friend,' Jessie pleaded, following her to the door. Frances sighed heavily, too tired to explain. 'Is Patsy more important?' Frances pulled the door open. She must keep her head, keep up the façade. She gave Jessie a smile, touched her shoulder.

'I'll be back this evening. As usual.'

Imogen was waiting at the window with Colly. They waved when they saw her at the gate and Frances felt her heart swell with love, her tiredness fall away as she strode up the path. The front door was flung open and Imogen ran towards her, Colly close behind. She threw herself into her mother's arms and Frances swooped her up, swinging her around, the child laughing as she planted kisses all over her face. She knew what Ginny had meant when she'd said she wanted to be loved. No matter how difficult things had been, Imogen had been worth every moment. She nuzzled into Imogen's neck before settling her child down onto the path. Imogen took hold of one hand, Colly the other as Patsy welcomed them at the front door.

'You look rough,' she said, taking Frances's coat and gas mask and hanging them by the door.

'Thanks!' Frances grinned and Imogen dragged her into the front room, where a fire burned in the grate. Frances warmed herself by it as she recounted events of the previous night.

Patsy was sympathetic. 'It's for the best, in the circumstances, but tough on the girl. She must have been in agony.'

Frances closed her eyes, Ginny's pain foremost in her mind. 'She was. But she's still here, and that's a blessing.'

Sufficiently thawed, she settled on the sofa. Imogen disappeared briefly and came back with a book of fairy stories and handed it to her mother. Frances opened the cover, ran her hand over the page as Imogen leant close. She put her arm about her and the child snuggled closer still. Frances planted a kiss on her head. She smelled clean and pure; it was a comfort. 'It reminded me of Pamela. Do you remember?'

Patsy plumped up her cushion, sat back. 'I haven't forgotten any of those girls. Nor the ones no longer with us. Such a waste of their young lives.'

Frances agreed. She turned the page and began to read.

Later, as they busied themselves in the kitchen preparing vegetables, the children drew pictures at the table.

'Colin away again? Did he get his call-up papers?'

'No, he's fishing.'

'Is that better or worse?'

Patsy leant on the sink and stared out over the garden. The trees were bare now, the apples stored on racks in the shed, the soil on the vegetable patch freshly turned that morning. 'I have no idea, Frances. Fishing is a hard enough way to make a living. I'm always relieved when his ship docks.' She paused. 'But I don't think he's just fishing, not these days.'

'What else can he be doing?' Frances twisted, checked on the children.

Patsy shrugged. 'Who knows? He won't say anything but he's back and forth to Norway, I do know that.' She ran water into the pan and put it on top of the cooker. 'I reckon Colin thinks the less I know the better, but I hate being kept in the dark. I'd rather know – wouldn't you?'

Frances considered it. Would she rather her imagination run away with her? Or would she want to know the truth, however bleak? She took off her apron, hung it on the back of the pantry door and joined the children at the table, admiring their masterpieces.

'Who's this?'

Colly pointed out his family, little round bodies and stick arms. He'd included Imogen as part of it. It should have made her happy, but she felt a flicker of regret.

'Mine, Mummy! Look at mine.' Imogen put her little finger on the figures. 'That's me. And that's Colly. And this is you. And this is my daddy.' She twisted to look at her mother and Frances felt her stomach lurch. 'Where is my daddy, Mummy? Is he at sea on Uncle Colin's ship?'

Frances clutched at her throat. It was the first time she'd asked. 'Sort of, darling. He's not on a ship but he's a long way away.'

Patsy came and stood beside her, studying the children's pictures, saying quietly, 'She's growing up, Frances, and the questions are just beginning. How long can you keep everyone in the dark?'

Imogen picked her crayon and started drawing a big fat sun in a cloudless sky.

Chapter 21

Johnny leant forward, shuffling the papers spread out on the coffee table. The print was small and reading through the countless pages had made his eyes sore. He rubbed at them, easing himself back into the chair. It was quiet without Aunt Letty, but she'd left her mark. The flat was more homely, made so by the plump cushions she'd purchased at Liberty's and the Aubusson rug beneath his feet that had arrived soon after she'd left. All the family photos had been unpacked and were arranged around the room so that wherever the two of them looked there were memories of shows, of meeting their idols – the Astaires – and, most importantly, of their parents.

He got up and went to the mantel, took down a photo of his mother. What a beauty she had been when she was young! Ruby was so like her in looks, but not in temperament. Was he doing the right thing? Finding Frances again, being with her, had coloured everything. It wasn't only about Ruby any more. He replaced it, turning his attention to another. Mother was in the centre, holding their hands, a child either side, he in his smart shorts and jacket, Ruby in a white dress, a huge white bow in her hair. What a happy child she'd been, bubbly, effervescent. America had ruined her and it was his fault. He'd promised his mother he would take care of her. Getting out of London was the right thing to do, if only temporarily, and Aunt Letty, although doubtful, had been in full agreement in the end. He'd told her of finding Frances again, asked her not to say anything to Ruby. Aunt Letty hadn't been happy about that.

'Don't keep it from her too long, my boy, not if you harbour any hope of her being happy again.' He hadn't been thinking of Ruby's happiness, not then.

He replaced the photo on the mantel. 'I will take care of her, Mother. I promise.'

The doorbell rang. He shook his head, smiling. 'She's forgotten her key again, Mother. What will I do with her?' Ruby was scatterbrained of late. He went to the door, a smile on his face which disappeared when he found Mickey Harper there.

'Hey, Johnny, I've come for your sweet little sister.' He peered over his shoulder. 'Is she here?'

Johnny stood in the frame, making himself as large as he could to block his view. 'She's not, Mickey.' How the hell did he know where they lived? And what was Ruby doing with him?

'Odd.' Mickey smirked. 'She said she'd meet me. Didn't she tell you?'

'Must have slipped her mind.' Johnny held onto the door, pulling it close to his back.

Mickey jangled the change in his pocket. 'Shall I come in and wait?'

'At any other time that would be no problem, Mickey,' Johnny said, hoping to stymie him, 'but I'm on my way out.' He rolled down his sleeves while Mickey leered at him. 'It's a good job you interrupted me, or I'd be late.' Johnny was about to close the door. Mickey leant on the jamb.

'I'll walk with you.'

Johnny bit the inside of his cheek. Now he would have to leave. He lifted his jacket from the chair in the hall and slipped it on as they waited for the lift. Mickey looked about him.

'Smart place.'

'Yes.' Johnny willed the lift to go faster, wanting to give the loathsome man as little of his time as possible. They heard the clang of the mechanics as it arrived on their floor, the jolt as it settled. Johnny drew back the grille and they got in, both facing forwards. Mickey took out a cigarette, tapped it on the packet, offered one to Johnny. He put up a hand in refusal. Mickey took an expensive gold lighter from his pocket and lit up as soon as the lift arrived on the ground floor. He caught Johnny looking and held the lighter in his hand, admiring it. 'Beautiful, isn't it? A gift.' He pushed his shoulder to Johnny. 'One of my lady friends.' The muscle in Johnny's cheek twitched.

'Crazy girl, Ruby. Such a party girl, and great fun. But then, you know that.'

Johnny merely smiled, pushing open the grille and holding it. Best to get the man out and away before Ruby got back. What on earth was she doing hanging about with the likes of Mickey Harper?

The room was small and dark, for little light came in from the window at the front of the shop. The fat man was bent over his desk that was cluttered with items, small screwdrivers, bits of broken jewellery, a calendar that hadn't been turned since the fourteenth of May. The entire room was cluttered with boxes and old newspapers that tottered in piles about the floor.

'Take a seat,' he offered. She looked about her. A large grey cat was curled on the chair and it eyed her; she wasn't going to chance moving it. A boy clattered about in a small workshop to the side and she caught him looking as he went about his business. She pulled her collar higher, hoping to hide her face. He smiled and she felt uncomfortable, her heart hammering. Why couldn't the man hurry up so she could leave?

'I can't offer any more than four hundred and fifty pounds,' the jeweller said, removing his eyepiece. He sat back in his chair, waiting for her answer, pushing his bottom lip forward. He held the brooch out to her, his big hands dark with grime, nails black with dirt.

'But I need five hundred. It's not enough.'

'Then take it somewhere else, see if you can do better. I'm doing you a favour as it is, no questions asked. I don't know where you got it, do I?'

He placed the brooch on the desk. It wasn't the most expensive piece she'd ever owned, but it was the most precious. What on earth was she thinking? No matter how desperate she was, that it should come to this. It was as though she were selling her mother. The rest of her jewellery had gone to pay debts and, latterly, Mickey Harper. There was nothing left to pay him off with. She put her fingers on it. Her mother's brooch. The man was watching, waiting for her to decide. He didn't care what it meant to her, did he? It was a business transaction. The same as Mickey Harper. Men controlled everything. Women could only use what they had. She could tell that the dealer wouldn't fall for needy and she didn't do simpering. Was her desperation evident? She heard her mother's voice, felt the anger, the disappointment. She tossed back her head. 'I know it's worth far more than that.'

The man clasped his hands together, resting them on his belly. 'Last month, maybe, last year definitely, but I've got too much stock on my hands these days.' The door opened, setting the bell tinkling over the door. Ruby picked up the brooch, slid it into her bag.

'I'll think about it.'

'Up to you,' he said, looking over her shoulder at the man who had walked into the shop. He had his back to her, which was a relief. 'You know where I am if you change your mind.'

Outside, she blinked at the brightness of the light and hurried down the alleyway until she was back on main street. Buses whooshed by and she felt unsteady, unsure of where she was, and pretended to look in a shop window to compose herself. She was already late for Mickey and she didn't have the money. She gripped at her bag. He'd threatened to tell Johnny. He had photos of her in various stages of undress: sprawled on a bed, a thin sliver of a satin sheet, covering very little; another with no sheet at all. She shuddered. She vaguely remembered going into a room, in a club, somewhere off Piccadilly, drunk as she so often was. Mickey had introduced her to one of his friends, who had seemed nice. Respectable. A photographer, Mickey said. An artist, the man had corrected. Odious little man! She had been so damned stupid. They had flattered her and she had preened, enjoying the adoration. It wasn't her fault, was it? Mickey had taken everything else. All she had was her mother's brooch and her own good name. Johnny would be furious. She knew she pushed him to the limits, but he would always be there for her; the knowledge comforted her. They weren't two people, they were one: The Randolphs. She looked up at the sky. Was her mother up there, watching?

'Send me a sign, Mother. Help me,' she whispered.

The barrage balloons drifted with the wind over Trafalgar Square. Protecting. Shielding. People pushed by her and she slowly came to her senses, made her way down the Strand. A nippy showed her to a table in the Lyons tea shop, where she'd arranged to meet Mickey, and she sat down, ordered tea and waited, nauseous. Drink had got her into this mess so she would stick to tea. She would try and be more like her mother, who certainly wouldn't behave like this. Aunt Letty had been kind, strong, like Mother, like Ruby could be. If she wanted to. Yes, she could be a better person. The door opened and she tensed. It wasn't Mickey. People came and went and there was no sign of him. Perhaps something awful had happened to him. She hoped it had. She left change on the table, picked up her bag and hurried home. What a mess it was. She had resisted so far, but if the only escape was Grimsby, then so be it. They would be earning again and she could pay her way out of it, start afresh. Yes, that's what she would do.

She was feeling more positive as she turned into the street, happy to be almost home, a plan forming in her head. It would all work out. She took her key from her bag, dropped it, bent to pick it up and as she did so, heard a familiar voice; one she didn't want to hear.

'Well, whaddya know? Ruby Randolph,' Mickey said loudly. 'I thought you'd forgotten our little meeting.'

Ruby looked up, seeing first Mickey, then Johnny. Johnny was furious. He was managing to contain it, but only just and she tried to control her tremors, forcing herself to act brave. Would Mickey make a scene in the street? Would he tell? He wasn't carrying the photos. Had he already given them to Johnny? A quick glance at her brother told her that no, he didn't know. Not yet. She plastered on her sweetest smile.

'No. No, I hadn't. I got held up. I was with Shirley, Shirley Grant.' She was agitated; did it show?

'Have you got that thing I asked for?' Micky said. He wasn't being outright, he was being cautious. It was a chance and she had to take it.

'No, Shirley couldn't get hold of it.'

'Hold of what?' Johnny asked.

Ruby felt the heat rise in her neck. What could she say? Mickey was enjoying this.

'Oh, some photographs,' Mickey said. Ruby rushed forward, took hold of Johnny's arm. 'Movie stars, you know the thing. Get them in cigarette packets. Collector's items, aren't they, Ruby? Ruby said she had a friend who had a special edition.' He looked up at the flat, then to her, raising his eyebrows. So, he knew where to find her. Had he followed her home? She was so drunk sometimes she wouldn't have known if he had. Mickey laced his arm around the rail at the front of the mansion block, puffed on his cigarette and blew out the smoke, tilting his head to one side. Ruby felt as if she would faint if she had to stay there any longer. They moved to one side as two soldiers walked past. One of them winked at Ruby but she couldn't even offer him a smile.

Johnny pulled her close, wrapped his hand over hers. It reassured her and she felt less afraid.

'Thank heavens you came back,' he said, briskly. 'We'll be late for our meeting with Bernie if we don't get a move on.' He turned to Mickey. 'Sorry to dash off, old chap. Good to see you and all that.'

Mickey tipped his hat. 'Don't let me hold you up.'

Johnny started walking and Mickey called after them, 'Don't forget the photographs, Ruby.'

Ruby looked over her shoulder. Mickey was standing in the middle of the pavement and he waved at her, grinning. She turned back, furious. Johnny was silent until they rounded the corner.

'I didn't know we had a meeting with Bernie?' She was almost running to keep up with him, his strides were so long.

'We haven't. That vile man came to the flat, looking for you.' He skipped up the steps to the hotel and she waited at the bottom. He knew their flat! He would come back and he would keep coming back. 'I wouldn't let him in. Did you tell him where we lived, Ruby?'

'No, I would never do that. I don't know how he knew.' She followed him up the steps and they waited while the doorman opened it.

'Mr Randolph. Miss Randolph.' He bowed his head as they walked in.

'Afternoon, Victor.' Johnny said, pressing a coin into his hand. 'While we're here, we might as well have a drink – and you can tell me about Mickey Harper.'

Ruby linked her arm in his; people recognised them and smiled. Ruby smiled back.

'Oh, let's not spoil the afternoon with talk of him. We've something to celebrate.' He stopped and turned to her. 'I've changed my mind. I *will* come to Grimsby.' She pulled him closer, flicking at his lapel, patting at it with the flat of her hand. 'Reluctantly, of course, but I know it's the right thing to do.' He was taken aback. Was it enough to delay talk of Mickey, if not distract him altogether? 'You're right, Johnny, we need to invest in the future. And if the future is in Grimsby, then that's where we'll go.'

Chapter 22

As November drew to a close it brought with it a sense of hope and excitement. The Empire was showing *The Three Musketeers* starring Don Ameche and the Ritz Brothers and the houses had been good in spite of the colder weather. It was great news for Jack, but the girls had found it a slog, trying to keep optimistic, hoping the Empire would hold on long enough for them to be able to ditch their jobs and start work on the pantomime. Grace was assembling the ingredients to make a plum pudding on stir-up Sunday and Christmas cards had appeared in the shops. Frances had put a doll by for Imogen, paying off a little each week. She was certain Imogen would love it. These little things, the anticipation of her daughter's joy, made the sacrifices worthwhile. They would be together on Christmas Day and she hoped, for Patsy's sake, that Colin would be home too.

On a misty Monday morning the cast of *Aladdin* had gathered in St Peter's Church Hall and knuckled down to work, wanting to make the most of the rehearsal time before the show opened on the eighth of December. They had seemed nice enough and, in the first awkward days, threw themselves into getting to know each other. The festive appearance of the room had added to the atmosphere, giving them something to talk about, to break the ice with the newcomers. Paper chains were draped across the ceiling and a large tableau of the Nativity ran the full length of one wall. It had been created by the Scouts and Brownies who used the hall throughout the year. A donkey with uneven legs was carrying a smiling Mary towards a small wooden shack made of sticks, a scowling Joseph leading the way. Cotton-wool sheep dotted the hillside and a gold foil star hung high above them all.

'It doesn't seem so long ago I was at school doing the same,' Jessie said, pointing out the host of angels made from paper doilies.

'And making icicles from newspaper, cutting out the little holes,' Ginny added. 'It always seemed like magic to me.'

Frances smiled. She had spent the Sunday doing exactly that with Imogen, Colly and Bobby. It had brought back happy memories of sitting at her mammy's kitchen table. It was important to remember the happy times. Christmas wasn't for sadness, not any more.

On Wednesday, as they took a break, the girls walked round to Joyce's. Dolly joined them, bringing a letter from Rita that had arrived for Frances at the theatre. After leaving the Empire, she'd joined ENSA and told the girls if they needed an audition to get in touch.

Ginny handed Rita's letter back to Frances. 'Well, she did say she wasn't going to sit around and wait for anything when she left at the end of the summer season.' She gazed out of the window. 'That's what I'm going to do. In fact, if I hadn't already committed to the panto, I'd go now. ENSA might be the fresh start I'm looking for. It'll be steady work and the money's OK.'

Frances folded the letter and put it back in her handbag.

'Well, I'm glad you are committed, Ginny. We'd miss you,' Jessie said. Ginny hadn't left Barkhouse Lane since the night of her miscarriage. Geraldine had insisted, as long as the girls were in agreement and it was an easy decision to make. At the earliest moment she'd given up her loathsome job at the laundry and Jessie hers. Only Frances held on to her job at the Fisherman's Arms, helping Lil when she could. She smiled at Ginny. 'I suppose that means I can have my bed back.'

'That will be a relief,' Frances said.

'For me or for you?' Jessie nudged her with her elbow.

They left it until the last minute before rushing back to rehearsals, preferring the warmth of the café to the chill of the hall. The rest of the cast were sitting about, scripts in hand, waiting for the next session to start. It was the sitting about that Jessie found the hardest. She needed to be doing.

Frances looked about her. Don Roper, the dame and director, was talking to Joe Taplow, a long and thin chap with sandy-coloured hair and glasses. They were sitting side by side on the wooden chairs that were dotted about the hall, Joe leaning forward, looking at the floor as if all the answers to life's problems were there. Don was talking and gesticulating and Joe was nodding his head. Basil Morgan, the genie of the lamp, was reading Proust, his script discarded. He was a thick-set Welshman with dark hair and a black moustache. An actor, not a 'turn', he kept himself to himself and the others left him to it. If he thought himself a cut above, then so be it. Over in the corner the double act, Bailey and North, were practising their moves. Sid North had his hands on his hips and was bending forwards and backwards while Bailey tried to take a swing at him with his fist. They worked hard at getting the timing right so that as North bent forward and back Bailey missed him every time.

'We might join ENSA too, mightn't we, Frances?' She heard her name but nothing else.

As Jessie repeated her question, Frances rubbed at her arms to try and warm herself. All this sitting around was mind-numbingly boring. She stood up, needing to move, to generate warmth. Grey clouds moved across the windows and the room grew darker. Someone turned the lights on and it helped lift her a little. Jessie was waiting for her answer. What could she say? She had no thought of what she would do after the panto ended.

'I don't know …' She sat down again, put her coat over her shoulders. 'I might stay here, work at the pub with Lil, see what else Jack can offer me. I can get another job. Or two.' She turned to Jessie. 'Anyway, you won't be joining ENSA anytime soon. I thought Bernie had news?'

'He has and I'm glad I waited. But I don't know whether I want to go to London now. It's a big step.'

'It's *all* a big step, Jessie.' Frances sighed. 'Life is one big step after another. We wobble, we fall down, but we pick ourselves up and carry on.' They watched Bailey and North, who had perfected their move.

'Clever, aren't they?' Ginny said. 'Apparently they've been together since they were kids. You can tell, can't you?'

'Only because they've worked hard, Ginny.' Frances admired their dedication. 'Their timing comes of practice. We can all learn from it.' Johnny and Ruby were the same. She knew first-hand the hours they put in, rehearsing routines over and over again until they were faultless.

They continued watching. Don slapped Joe on the back and got to his feet. He walked over to Bailey and North and the three of them stood chatting.

'I've never been abroad before,' Ginny said. 'Rita's going to France so I might get to go too.'

'Not sure that it's a good time to go, Ginny.' Jessie was cautious.

'Bit of a Hobson's choice.' She picked at her fingernails. 'At least I won't have to think about anything that reminds me of the summer.'

'Or of us.' Jessie was light-hearted but Ginny was horrified.

'Of course not. I will never be able to thank you two enough.'

Kitty Bright dragged a chair forward and joined them. 'Thank 'em for what?' She rolled the chair round and sat astride it, leaning forward and resting her arms on the back of it. Her hair was red as rust, harsh, not like the glorious deep copper of Ginny's; nor did she have Ginny's soft features. Frances had met her type before, nose in everyone's business and eager to spread it around – along with everything else she possessed. She pitied Jessie having to play Princess to Kitty's Aladdin.

'Finding her digs,' Jessie said quickly. 'Ginny's been staying with us these last six weeks. Managed to escape a creepy landlord.'

'I'd 'ave 'ad him by the short and curlies, sharpish.' Kitty reached out and demonstrated with a clawed hand and a menacing look. Jessie flinched and Frances laughed.

'Too right,' she said. 'Although I've not tried it myself.'

'Soon stops the buggers,' Kitty said, sitting upright.

'We'll bear it in mind should we need it, won't we, girls?' Jessie's eyes grew wide and Frances bit down on her lip to stem her laughter. It wouldn't go down too well with Kitty.

'So you was all togevver 'ere for the summer, then stayed on. An' you all live togevver?'

'Something like that.' Frances glanced over the woman's shoulder. Don Roper was peering over the end of his glasses, looking at the girls and beckoning with his hand for them to come over. 'Looks like we're wanted.'

The afternoon was long and tedious and, as the girls only had small parts, there was a lot of hanging around. Frances picked up her knitting. She was making a jumper for Patsy's little boy, Colly, a Christmas present, and Jessie was reading a magazine. Ginny contented herself with watching the other actors go through their lines and scenes. She felt sorry for Joe Taplow – he seemed a gentle sort and not at all suited for the part of Abanazar, Aladdin's wicked uncle. Bailey and North hadn't said much but were cheerful, not brash like Billy.

'Poor Jessie,' Ginny said. 'Kitty's very commanding, isn't she?'

Frances stilled her hands. 'It will be good for Jessie to work with her, even though she might not think it. I know Jessie was disappointed about not getting the title role but Kitty has more of a name and people know who she is.'

'For a lot of reasons.' Sid North came and sat beside Frances. 'She's got a reputation for rubbing people up the wrong way – in more ways than one.'

Frances sat back so that he could become part of their group. His partner joined them and they watched Don give direction to Jessie, who listened intently.

'I think Jessie finds Kitty a bit overwhelming,' Ginny whispered to Frances.

Frances agreed. 'That's nothing. Kitty's holding back. Even old Twankey will have a job topping her when she's got an audience in front of her.' She started knitting again. 'Jessie'll have to get used to it if she really is thinking of going to London on her own. And she'll have to toughen up, or she won't last five minutes.'

When he was satisfied with their performance Don dismissed them and Jessie came back to her seat.

'I've a lot to learn,' she said, ruefully. 'I need to be more forceful.'

'No, you don't, Jessie. Then you'd be like Kitty – and Lord, we don't want you to be like that.' Sid patted her on the shoulder. Kitty had turned her attention to Joe, who looked terrified. 'Be yourself. That's the key. Be original. Be you. There's no one else like you and that's as it should be.'

Don put his hands on his hips, called around the room, 'Abanazar, where are you?' Joe Taplow sidestepped Kitty, relief clear on his face.

'From the top then, Joe. Give it a bit of oomph this time.'

Joe shuffled forward and delivered his line.

Don Roper raced forward. 'Dear God! Not like that, laddie. You won't scare the mice at that rate. Here...' He snatched the script from Joe's hand, lifted up his glasses to read, then made him himself bigger by sweeping out his arm then dragging it forward as he clinched the line. He leant out towards the strip of tape on the floor that served as the front of the stage. 'More effort, much more. You're like a wet weekend in Filey, Joe. We need to scare the little buggers witless. Try it again.'

Joe did his best and the girls looked at each other. There was still a long way to go. Don stepped quickly towards the girls; he was a round, heavy little man but very light on his feet. He took hold of Ginny and pulled her onto the stage. 'Watch me, my boy.'

He grabbed Ginny by the arm and drew her towards him, grimacing menacingly into her face as he delivered Joe's line. He was short and Ginny was tall, even without her heels, but he did look scary and Ginny trembled accordingly. He let her go and Ginny rubbed at her arm. 'Grab her wrist. You try it.'

Joe gently took hold of Ginny, apologising as he did so, and she smiled to reassure him. He was far too gentle to play the baddie.

Don threw up his hands. 'It's called acting, ducky. Pretending, remember?'

Joe wrung his hands. 'I'm sorry, Mr Roper. I'm a magician. I'm not used to speaking.'

Don tapped his hand to his forehead, shaking his head in frustration. 'Damn that bloody Hitler! Look what dregs I'm left to work with.' He put his hands on his hips, swirled them from side to side and Ginny tiptoed back to her seat. Don was well into his seventies and knew every trick in the book; if Joe paid attention he would learn a lot from the old man. For the next twenty minutes Don put him through his paces, trying the line over and over until Joe finally got mad enough for Don to call a halt.

He put his hand to his brow. 'We'll have to move on to the next scene or we'll never get done.'

They were dismissed at five, Don keeping Joe behind to give him extra lessons.

'Do you think the boy will survive an hour with the old queen?'

'He's already white with fear; how the hell Don's going to kick him into shape is anyone's guess.'

Bob Bailey held open the door that led to the small hallway before they stepped out into the December darkness. He was taller than his partner, thicker-set, and always immaculately turned out, even for rehearsals. The two of them always wore suits, removing their jackets and rolling up their sleeves to get down to work. Bob brought a packet of Woodbines from his pocket and offered them around. He took a cigarette himself, lit it, blew out the smoke. 'Where's the best place to go in town for a bit of company, girls?'

'The Café Dansant's your best bet,' Ginny offered. She stuffed her hands in her pockets and stamped her feet to keep warm. 'They have dances. It's along the promenade near the open-air bathing pool.'

'Opposite that place with the dome roof, Olympian?' Cigarette smoke billowed about his face. Jessie coughed, stood back.

'Olympia,' Ginny corrected him.

'Fancy showing me some fancy steps?'

Ginny was quick to say no. 'Not tonight, perhaps another time.' Frances sensed her discomfort. Ginny wasn't going to make the same mistake twice.

'I'm going home to write a letter to my fiancé,' Jessie said, swiftly. Bob was deflated.

'What about you, Irish? Will you come and keep me company?'

'What a smooth talker you are, Mr Bailey.' She pulled her scarf up about her chin. 'The name's Frances – don't forget it.'

'I won't.' He grinned and she did too. 'Frances.'

She tilted her head. 'Sorry to disappoint you, but I'll be working.'

'What? After the day we've had.'

She opened the door to the street where they assembled in the winter darkness. A choir was rehearsing in the church over the road and they listened as they sang the last verse of 'In the Bleak Midwinter'. The moon was low with only minimal light to guide them and Frances switched on her torch. 'I work in a pub. I like it. Lil the landlady's a darling and I'll be sad to leave her in the lurch while the panto's on.'

Bob shoved his hands in his pockets, waited for Sid to join him on the step.

'Seems we'll see you all tomorrow, then. Night, girls.'

The girls walked around the corner to Cambridge Street.

'Nice, those two, aren't they?' Jessie said.

'They seem so,' Frances said as they linked arms. 'Come on, girls, don't shilly-shally! I need something to eat before I go back to work. I'm famished.'

They decided to walk up through Sea View Street, wanting to peer in the shop windows using the light of their torches. The displays had been suitably decorated for the season and ideas for Christmas gifts given prominence: gloves and scarves, fine handkerchiefs and cosy slippers. Jessie pressed her finger to the window. 'That's not unlike the handkerchief my old boss, Miss Symonds, gave me as a parting gift when I came to Cleethorpes.' She rooted around in her pocket and pulled it out. The girls compared it.

'A lovely gift. And one you've used often, Jessie.'

Jessie ran her fingers over the initial J Miss Symonds had embroidered. 'She was a lovely old woman. I hadn't thought I would miss her as much as I do.' She put it back in her pocket. 'That whole life feels as if it belonged to someone else.'

Frances put her arm about her. 'Well, it didn't. It was part of your life that you've left behind. We all have to do it if we are to move forward.' She patted Ginny on the shoulder. 'The past is behind you too, Ginny. Leave it there. Don't let Billy win.'

Ginny bristled. 'I don't know what you mean.'

'Sure you do. I've watched you give all the men a wide berth. Even Don, and he's no threat to you at all. It's Joe who needs to keep a lookout from what I've seen.'

Jessie blushed. 'Frances! How do you know?'

They walked on. 'I've been around a lot longer than you two have. You learn these things. And Don's not at all subtle.' She shook her head, grinning. 'No, not at all.' Frances hugged Ginny close. 'Be brave, darling. Not all men are like Billy Lane.'

A woman with her head down against the wind and a basket over her arm pushed past them. Ginny tucked herself to one side.

'But how will I know?' Ginny's eyes glittered with moisture, but it was hard to tell whether they were tears or because of the bitter cold.

Frances reached for her again, took her hand in hers. 'You have to let go of your fear, darling, little by little, and open your heart to love someone.'

'Like you?' Jessie challenged. 'And Johnny Randolph?'

'That's different,' Frances said, curtly. 'Completely different.' The Randolphs were already in Grimsby; the local paper had made a great deal of their arrival. And the flowers hadn't stopped coming, nor the letters. She hadn't responded, too afraid to go forward, preferring to stay where she was, where she felt safe. They walked quickly up to the pub on the corner. Fudge was sitting on the doorstep.

'Sweet little dog.' Jessie crouched down and rubbed him under the chin. The dog stretched his neck and Frances scanned the street.

'Don't know where Artie is. Must be in the off-licence.' She checked her watch. 'Mercy me, I need to get home and grab a quick sandwich and be back for Lil. I said I'd help her put up the Christmas decorations if it was quiet. Why don't you come in later? We could sing a few carols. It will be fun.'

The girls hung their bags and gas masks in the hall and when Jessie opened the door to the sitting room the smell of beef stew drifted out of the kitchen. A fire was in the grate, warming the room, and a strong gust of wind blew down the chimney, sending out a small cloud of smoke. Grace wafted it away with a newspaper. Her cheeks were rosy and over the last few weeks she seemed to have put on a little weight. It suited her. Jessie kissed her.

'Something smells good. I'm famished!'

'How's it going?' Grace flapped the newspaper again. The smoke caught in Jessie's throat and she coughed.

'All right, I suppose.' Geraldine bustled in and held out the cutlery to Grace. Jessie intercepted it and began laying the table. 'A lot of hanging around.'

'Make the most of it.' Grace put the newspaper on top of the wireless. 'Panto's hard work from start to finish. You'll be longing for it to be over by the end of January.'

'Oh, Grace, we haven't even started yet,' Frances groaned. Geraldine stood in the doorway to the kitchen, wiping her hands on a towel.

'Shall I save you something, Frances?' Geraldine asked. Things had been cool between the two of them since the night of Ginny's miscarriage. Her words had stung and left Frances more guarded than ever. 'Wouldn't want you to miss out.' Geraldine smiled, Frances did too.

There was banging in the yard and Eddie came in the back door and went to the sink, his hands dirty. 'Chain came off my bike.'

Grace went to the kitchen. 'Working late, Ed?'

'Every little helps. I was fixing old man Fisher's pump, down at the yard. It needed a new washer.' He patted his pocket and change jangled. 'More for the pot.'

Frances laughed. 'By, lad, you'll be buying yourself a car before you can drive it.'

'My bike will do for now.' He leant over and kissed his mother, sat down at the table. 'I'm saving for the future. And Christmas.'

Frances left them talking of Christmas and went upstairs to change her clothes and freshen up. What kind of Christmas would it be with so many people away from their loved ones? She picked up Imogen's photo. At least *they* would be together. She would leave for Patsy's the minute the curtain came down on the Saturday before Christmas Eve.

Frances pulled her coat collar up around her ears and wrapped her scarf about her mouth as she hurried down to the Fisherman's Arms. A thick fog descending, the temperature had plummeted in the last hour. Lil had already opened up and Frances hurried through to the bar, glad of the warmth and welcome. Boxes of paper decorations and pine cones were stacked on one side and Lil, her arm resting on one of the pumps, was looking at Fudge, who was curled up in his usual spot.

Frances unwrapped her scarf and took off her hat. 'Where's Artie?'

'Copped it,' Lil said sadly. 'Blackout caught him out, poor old sod. Didn't see the bus coming.'

'Oh, no!' She put her hand to her mouth. 'Poor Artie! I saw Fudge waiting outside earlier. I thought Artie was … I didn't imagine …' She sighed. 'How sad.'

'Aye, it is. Them Germans haven't dropped a ruddy bomb yet and I reckon we're popping more off without his help. Ruddy ridiculous!'

Frances lifted the bar flap and went and sat beside the dog that was resting his head on his paws. He looked at her with chocolate brown eyes and whimpered as she ran her hand over him. 'He looks so sad, Lil.'

'Aye, he does. Do you want to take him home with ya?'

Frances glanced up, still rubbing the dog's neck. 'Isn't there a Mrs Artie?'

'Not that I know of, not one round here anyways. He was on his own, was Artie.'

The dog lifted his head and rested it on Frances's lap. 'I can't take him back with me, Lil. The house is full.' Much as she loved dogs, he was way down on the list of priorities.

Lil patted the counter. 'Guess I'll have to take him until I can find a home for him. I can't have him sitting on me doorstep day and night.'

Frances was cheered. 'Did you hear that, Fudge? Lil is going to look after you.' The dog wagged his tail but otherwise stayed where he was. Frances got up, went behind the bar and washed her hands. 'He'll be company for you, Lil.'

'Not the sort of company I was hoping for, lovey. But he'll do.'

Lil held fort at the bar while Frances unpacked the boxes, decorating the high shelves at the back of the bar with pine cones and holly. She cleared the narrow shelf above the till and placed a small wooden stable with the nativity figures on it, tucking a sheet of cotton wool around the edges to represent snow. Would they have snow this winter? She hoped it wouldn't be too bad if it did come. It would make getting out to Waltham difficult but it would be fun making snowmen with Imogen and the boys. She watched Lil talking to Big Malc through the mirror. What was Lil doing for Christmas? She hadn't even asked.

As the regulars came in, Fudge invited comment and talk of Artie, customers chipping in bits and pieces until they built up a picture of his life.

'Well, for a quiet man we knew plenty about him after all,' Lil said. 'Just goes to show you.'

'Show you what?' Frances was at the optic getting a double whisky. She handed it over, got the money and rang it in the till.

'How we give little bits of ourselves away, even if we don't know it.'

Chapter 23

It hadn't been as bad as he'd imagined it would be. Ruby's change of heart had flummoxed him for a time – would she change her mind again? But she hadn't, and she'd been swift to pack, eager to rehearse. They had put together a show using many of the routines they'd done in America and Jack Holland's secretary, Annie, had secured them a house in Park Drive. For the first time in months he'd felt a glimmer of hope that Ruby would finally settle down and the sense of unease at bringing her to Grimsby abated. They spent the days developing new routines, Johnny trying to find the delicate balance of keeping Ruby busy without overworking her. It had been a huge success so far and they were playing to packed houses almost every night, which helped. His primary concern had been to get this show up and running and after Christmas he would audition for his replacement.

He found Ruby sitting on a bench in the rear garden, a blanket over her shoulders. The late winter sunshine was low in the sky and the warmth from it was enough to be able to enjoy it for a while. She was drinking tea from a china cup, leaning her head back so that the sun could kiss her face. He was pleased that she looked less haggard lately, was more of her old self. Mrs Frame, the housekeeper, was wonderful, a surrogate mother, and there was a sense of home, of peace about the place. He joined her on the bench, stretching out his legs, resting his hands between them.

'This is the life, eh,'

She opened one eye. 'Are you being sarcastic?'

He nudged her. 'Be truthful, Ruby. It's not as bad as you thought it would be.'

'You have no idea what I thought it would be.' She closed her eyes again. 'That godawful smell of fish makes me sick, but I've got used to it.' She opened her eyes, placed her cup down on the small table to the side of her. 'I suppose you can get used to anything – eventually.' A robin hopped about and she tossed crumbs from her plate.

'I'll take that as meeting with your approval then.'

'Don't push it, brother.' A sudden gust set stray leaves rolling along the lawn like pennies.

'Nice to have a garden, isn't it?' It was a luxury they seldom had. America had been non-stop city to city, travelling on trains from state to state, staying in high-rise hotels and apartments with no time to enjoy the parks and open spaces. The garden at Park Drive was long, with trees and mature shrubs filling the beds along the fences that separated the house from the ones on either side of it. Here, there was dogwood, red against the brown, and a gnarly old apple tree with bare branches. Leaves lay in drifts along the beds where the green shoots of bulbs pushed through and the long droopy branches of weeping willow fell to the ground.

'It's all barren; the trees have no leaves and there are no flowers.'

'It still has colour, Ruby. Can't you see it?' Had life dulled for her so much? She was quiet. He stood up, held out his hand. 'Time we got ready.'

She pouted. 'Do we have to go? Really?' She took his hand and he pulled her to her feet.

'Yes, we do. I promised Jack we would be there for the beginning, if not all of, the opening night. Well, opening afternoon.' They walked up the small steps and through the French windows into the sitting room. 'Not sure whether people will come out this early, but these are not normal times. I admire Jack for even trying. But he's been successful so far.'

'Let's hope it stays that way. For our sakes.'

Johnny put an arm about her shoulder. 'Trust me, Ruby, it will. Jack and Bernie are good partners. We couldn't have better.'

'You hardly know them,' her voice was softer now, the fear leaking from the gaps in the brittle shell she hid behind. 'How can you tell?'

He shrugged. 'I know how many sharks there are out there. I'd rather have Jack and Bernie at my side.' He thought of Mickey Harper. 'You have to tread carefully, Ruby. We have a reputation to protect. You must know why it was better for us to come – for the time being.' He tried to encourage her. 'I'm working on getting a show at The Savoy; Bernie has the backers lined up and things are looking more settled, people are taking a chance again. We need to take a chance too.' He hadn't broached the subject of enlisting since that night at the flat with Aunt Letty because Ruby was still volatile – that was her nature. In time he would go, whether she liked it or not. And then there was Frances. After his disastrous visit she had refused to see him. He still hadn't told Ruby, but what was there to tell?

They walked through to the hallway and Ruby went upstairs. The door to the kitchen opened and Mrs Frame came out. She was wearing her little blue hat as she always did. Said it kept her head warm.

'Are you to be having something before you leave, Mr Johnny? I've got some soup on the go.'

'That would be wonderful, Mrs Frame. We'll eat in the kitchen, if that's not too troublesome?' Johnny looked up the stairs to his sister. Ruby leant over the rail.

'Thank you, Mrs Frame. I won't be more than ten minutes.'

Johnny raised his eyebrows. 'Make that thirty.'

He walked back into the sitting room and closed the doors into the garden. The house had been let fully furnished. It was decorated with heavy fabrics that kept out the cold and the sitting room had a gas fire so that it would be warm when they came in from the theatre. Thankfully, Mrs Frame had stayed on as housekeeper. He wrote to Aunt Letty and told her of their good fortune. She had warned that Ruby might relapse into her former behaviour but so far, he tapped the wood of the easy chair, she was improving daily. He picked up the paper and tried to read the headlines but couldn't concentrate and lowered it onto his lap, closed his eyes. He planned to slip backstage at some point and see Frances. She'd ignored his letters and they had been too busy rehearsing for him to ask her to dinner, but he must speak to her today. He got up and went back to the French windows. The sun was dropping below the tree line and golden fingers of light filtered through the gaps between the branches. How would Ruby react? She might be waspish, but she would surely have some sense of control in public. He hoped she would be civil.

Ruby slipped off her dress and threw it in the general direction of the chair. She would wear the red this afternoon. Festive, cheerful. She went to the window and looked out across the park where a scattering of children were running along the paths, weaving between the shrubs and chasing each other. It wasn't too bad here and she loved the garden – not that she would let Johnny know that, not yet. She had felt the darkness of the last few weeks dilute. London was so far away – and so was Mickey Harper. Christmas was on the horizon, the New Year close behind. She gripped the windowsill, put her head against the cool glass. Maybe next year would be kinder to them ... She went over to the dressing table, patted her cheeks with rouge, coloured her lips. Johnny was right. The show was going well and she would die rather than admit it to him, but she was enjoying every minute. She reached across and picked up the Christmas card Aunt Letty had sent. A snow-covered scene, children pulling a sledge, their faces shining with happiness. There had been a letter too, telling her to be strong, to look to the future that would be bigger and brighter – and what their mother wanted for them. Mother. Her jewellery box was open and she took out Mother's brooch. She had almost sold it. What on earth had she been thinking of? She clutched it tightly, finding new resolve. Next year would be better, she would make it so.

They waited in the hall for the taxi. Ruby was irritable but she'd at least made every effort to look the part. Her fur stole was wrapped about her and she pulled it high on her shoulders so that it accentuated her small face, her pointed chin. It was fastened with their mother's brooch, the diamonds catching the light, and she fiddled with it constantly, putting her hand to it, holding it.

Johnny was glad when the car arrived. He tugged again at his cuffs, ran his finger around his collar.

Ruby turned to him. 'Are you nervous?'

'What makes you ask?'

She looked to his cuffs. 'You keep tugging at them. You always do that when you're nervous.'

He placed his hands in his lap and looked out of the window as they turned to travel up the hill towards the main road. He should have told her ...

'Who else is in the show? Anyone we know?'

'You haven't been the slightest bit interested before. Why now?'

'Boredom.' She grinned. 'Might be someone we can have fun with.'

Where should he start? 'Bailey and North are the Chinese policemen; Kitty Bright is the title.'

'Ugh. *That* tart!' She put her hand on the seat in front. 'If I'd have known she was in it, I'd have stayed at home.'

'It's nice to think you're taking an interest. We could do with your input and flair.' She sneered as the car pulled up outside the theatre and he rested his hand on her arm. 'People are having a tough time, Ruby. It's our job to make life a little more bearable, help them forget their troubles.'

'I know. You don't have to remind me, I'm doing my best.' He took her hand, squeezed it. In her own way she was doing what she could. Most nights she would spend an hour or more at the stage door after each show, chatting to the chaps in uniform who waited in the cold for her after every performance.

A doorman rushed forward and opened the taxi door. Ruby stepped out, followed by Johnny and people gasped and nudged each other. He held back, letting her have her moment. It made her happy – and the happier she was, the better she'd behave. A boy rushed forward with his autograph book and Ruby bent lower and signed it for him. At least she could still be professional. He watched her chatting, smiling, signing autographs with a grace she didn't show to him.

She stepped into the foyer of the Empire and people stood back while she swept in, shoulders back, head held high. She could hear her mother, telling her to be professional, to be something special for people, and she wanted so much to be special. The foyer was full of families, eager children, the pitch of their excitement ringing in her ears. Oh, to be a child again, with all the magic … Her heart shrank. There was no more magic. She heard her mother again, berating her. Up went her head again. *'Smile, my darling, smile.'* She tugged her stole, clasped her hand over her brooch, gaining strength. She could do this. It was easy to pretend. Smile! Eyes, teeth, *smile*.

Jack Holland weaved through the crowds towards them. 'Johnny, Ruby! So glad you could come.'

Johnny put out his hand and Jack took it, shaking it vigorously. 'We won't be able to stay until the end, Jack, but we wanted to be here for the opening.'

'Glad you got here at all.' He slapped Johnny on the back and turned his attention to Ruby. She was enchanted. Jack was tall and dark and the scar on one side of his face made him appear rather dashing, a little like Errol Flynn though perhaps not so naughty. Shame! He shook her hands, holding hers in both of his, and she saw what Johnny had described: an honest man, one possibly too nice for this business. A striking, haughty woman was heading their way and Ruby couldn't decide whether she was smiling or sneering as she sashayed towards them, looking as if being at the theatre was beneath her.

She held out her hand and Ruby took it, admiring the jewellery on her arm. The dress was expensive too. She must have a fabulous seamstress or gone to London. It had to be the latter.

'My dear, so lovely to have you here! I've so admired you and your brother. Like our very own Astaires, weren't they wonderful? Did you ever see them on the London stage? No?' She tilted her head, not waiting for Ruby's answer. 'Perhaps not. Far too young. Come, my dear. We have a private room upstairs. I managed to secure a bottle of champagne.'

Ruby looked over her shoulder and pulled a face at Johnny in the hope that he would rescue her. He wiggled his fingers in a small wave, listening to Jack. The bastard! She followed Audrey upstairs.

Jack led Johnny into the auditorium, where the early birds were taking their seats. There was a bubble of happiness in the air as lively children wriggled along the rows, shushed by mothers and aunties. What men were among them were in some sort of uniform, mostly army, but a lot of what he now recognised as the Naval Reserve. One of the stage crew at the Palace had told him that most of the fishermen had signed up and were manning the minesweepers. He wished he had a little of their bravery now and berated himself his cowardice. What was the matter with him? He wasn't at all sure who he was more afraid of, Ruby or Frances.

They went through the pass door at the side of the stage. Jack gave a nod to the chap at the stage door and led Johnny downstairs, where a cluster of babes were listening to instructions from their chaperone. Johnny smiled, it brought back memories of when he and Ruby were small, getting the adrenaline rush of being on stage before the curtain went up. He still had it, to a degree, but it wasn't the same. More the pressure of not disappointing these days.

He waited as Jack knocked on the first door and introduced Johnny to the older dancers. Costumes spilled from the hangers and rails and the girls were sitting in front of a long line of mirrors, getting themselves ready for curtain up. The girls smiled and fluttered their eyelashes and while he wanted to be gracious, he wanted to see Frances more. He checked over his shoulder. With luck, Audrey would commandeer Ruby until curtain up. Jack walked on and the girls waved at him. He heard their excited giggles as they moved on to Don Roper. The elderly man was sitting in front of his mirror that was festooned with Christmas cards. His make-up was already in place, his gaudy costume hanging from hooks on the wall behind him. His wig, an ornate affair in black with plaited hoops and a large bun in which were threaded knitting needles, was to the left of him on a stand. In his hand he held a teacup half-filled with an amber liquid Johnny knew was not tea. He looked up, frowning at first, and then got to his feet, all smiles, the tiredness disappearing from his face.

'Young Johnny Randolph!' He took Johnny's hand, gripping it fiercely, shaking it with vigour. Johnny laughed Don stood back, his hands on his hips. He was wearing his underclothes, a less-than-white vest and pants, black socks held up with suspenders. His legs were raddled with varicose veins and angry purple patches gathered about his calves.

'My, look at you now! You were but a slip of a boy the last time we met. You were with your father, a dear, dear, man. Sad we lost him so young. What a talent he was.' Don held out his hand to the empty chair by the wall. 'Sit down, my boy.'

Johnny declined. 'Not before curtain up, Don. I know you need to prepare. But we will catch up – perhaps one afternoon when neither of us have a matinee?'

'That would be terrific. Don't forget old Don, will you?'

Johnny promised he wouldn't and turned back to the door. It was hard when you got old, watching those with youth and exuberance coming up behind you, left treading water, hoping you didn't drown. He blew out a long breath as Jack knocked on another door. Jessie opened it and he could see Ginny staring at him. Frances was standing behind her and she wrapped her dressing gown over her costume, tied the belt with an exaggerated tug.

Jack stepped to one side to allow Johnny to walk forward. He hesitated. Someone knocked on the door behind them and they turned.

'Chip?' Jack said.

'You're wanted front of house, Mr Holland.'

Jack spread out his hands. 'Will you excuse me, girls. Johnny?'

Jessie signalled to Ginny with a tilt of her head and the two of them left. Johnny stayed by the door. Behind him small children hurried down the corridor, their chaperone hissing at them to 'walk'.

'Can I come in?'

Frances shrugged. God, she was so beautiful! He wanted nothing more than to sweep her into his arms and kiss her hard, damn hard. Instead he said, 'You haven't answered my letters.' He longed to be closer; to touch her hair, her face, and feel the warmth of her breath, the taste of her lips.

She sat down in front of the mirror, her back to him. 'I didn't see the point.' She picked up her black and spat on it, rubbing it with a small brush, and drew a line at the edge of her lids, sweeping it up sharply towards the end. 'And I wanted you to know what it felt like.'

'To know what *what* felt like?' He leant against the doorframe, not understanding.

'To be ignored.'

He stepped into the room and she stilled her hand. He stopped.

'*I* haven't ignored *you*! It was you who didn't write, though you said you would.' He paused. 'I thought we had something special.'

Chip came back down the corridor, calling the fifteen minutes. Frances took out her rouge and brushed it over her cheeks, her skin milky-white and her dark eyes glittering in the bright lights. 'So did I, Johnny. So did I.' She was fierce, her anger visible but restrained. Frances wouldn't make a scene, not like Ruby. They were as different as night and day. His heart was racing, wanting to talk, knowing how limited their time was. He had to do something. He leant forward to take a step nearer, but she looked at him and he knew not to go any further. Her eyes were full of sadness and he could see she was hurt. Could she see his own hurt too – was it as obvious?

She took out her lipstick and ran it over her lips. He wanted to kiss them, wanted to drag her from the chair, pull her around to face him properly, hold her in his arms and kiss her. People moved down the corridor and Johnny leant out, checking for Ruby; he didn't want a drama, not now, and Jack might bring her back. He should have warned him; he should have done so many things. Jessie and Ginny were loitering at the end of the corridor and a sense of urgency made him braver.

'Frances, I don't know what happened, but believe me, I wrote.' He was pleading now. 'So many times. And the ticket?'

She twisted in her chair, looked at him, her chin high. 'Ticket?'

'For your passage to America.'

She laughed, really laughed, and it incensed him. 'I didn't get anything from you, Johnny, just the cold shoulder. Here's mine now.' She turned away and he felt someone tap his back. It was Jessie.

'I'm sorry, but we have to get ready.' She was apologetic and he appreciated the girls consideration. They squeezed past and Frances picked up a magazine, ignoring all of them. He tapped his hand on the doorframe, wondering what to do next. He didn't want to go. He wanted to stay, just to look at her, and he would have done, had he not heard the commotion in the corridor as Chip walked down calling overtures. He made to move but Kitty Bright stepped out of her dressing room as Ruby came down the stairs. The dancers tumbled out, followed by the babes, a sea of satin in bright jewel colours, red and yellow, surging down the corridor like a wave, bringing Ruby ever closer. He pressed himself against the wall, letting them pass, hoping that Ruby would wait too, but she was oblivious, forcing herself against the flow. He tried to move but couldn't, and then he didn't want to, understanding that Ruby would have to find out some time. He braced himself. She swept up beside him and peered into the room, smiling benignly at the girls until she registered Frances.

'Oh! *You*.'

No one spoke, no one moved.

'Frances O'Leary. Well, well...' Ruby turned to Johnny. '*Now* I understand.'

Johnny sucked his cheek.

Frances got up. Her feet were bare, her toenails painted bright red. 'Ruby! How lovely to see you again.'

Johnny put his hand on Ruby's shoulder. 'Good to meet old friends, isn't it, Ruby?'

She shrugged his hand away. 'Old friend? It was a little more than *that*, wasn't it, Johnny? Mother knew, you know. And she didn't like you, Frances. Not one bit.' Ruby was shaking her head from side to side. She turned to him, her jaw jutting forward. 'Now I know why we came to this dead-end dump of a place.'

'Ruby! Don't. Please don't.' He grabbed her arm. Frances hadn't flinched but the shock was clear on the faces of the two girls standing close to her. Ruby tried to free herself, but it only made him grip more tightly. They could hear the musicians taking their places in the orchestra pit.

'The curtain's going up,' Jessie said quietly.

'Bright little thing, aren't you?' Ruby spat.

Johnny put his hand under Ruby's elbow. 'Please excuse us, ladies. We came to say break a leg, didn't we, Ruby?'

Before she could reply he guided her out into the corridor and though she stumbled, he kept forcing her on, pushing their way past Kitty Bright and Don Roper, who were enjoying the spectacle. Ruby was trying to wriggle free but he drove her forward, up the stairs and out onto the street. It was raining and George stepped out, offering them an umbrella. Johnny took it, holding it over her.

'You sly, crooked bastard! You liar! You b-brought me here ...' She was breathing hard and fast, clenching and unclenching her fists. He braced himself, knowing what would come next, and she rushed at him, slapping his chest with the flat of her hands, over and over again, and he stood there, letting her release the fury, the disappointment. When she stopped, he gently took hold of her with his free hand. What had he expected? That she would be happy for him? What a fool he was.

'I'm sorry, Ruby. I should've told you Frances was here.' He should have been braver. It would have saved her this. 'I love her, Ruby. I have *always* loved her.' She slapped him one last time with her free hand, half-hearted, her rage ebbing.

'You know Mother didn't like her!'

He let his shoulders drop. 'Mother didn't like anyone, Ruby. Not if she thought they'd come between us.'

She stopped, pressed her lips tightly together. Tears pricked at her eyes and she looked away from him. A man passed by on the other side of the street, his head down. Ruby turned back, sadness etched on her face.

She stared down at thc pavement, quieter now. 'I want to go home. Back to London.'

He felt the cold rain running down the back of his neck soak through his jacket. 'We can't, Ruby. This is our future.'

'*Our* future. Or yours?' Her eyes narrowed and she tilted her head to one side.

'*Ours*, Ruby. Ours. The Randolphs.'

A tear ran down her cheek and she quickly pushed her finger to the corner of her eye to stem the flow. 'I thought you'd come here for us, for me.' She was biting back tears. 'It was for her all along, Johnny. Frances. You just wouldn't admit it to yourself.'

He let her hand drop. He couldn't argue. They could have gone anywhere in the country; they could have stayed in town. Shows were opening up again, he could have waited.

She scrutinised his face. Pouted. 'I was right. The truth hurts, doesn't it, Johnny?' She turned on her heel and marched off. He hurried up beside her.

'Where are you going?'

'Home. Wherever that is. London. Anywhere but here.'

He grabbed at her arm, pulled her back. 'You can't, Ruby. I need you.'

She looked down at his hand, peeled it away from her sleeve. 'I thought you did, but I was wrong.' Her voice quivered with emotion and he took her arm again, gentler this time, touched her hand.

'Come back in, Ruby. Please. We'll talk later, I promise.' The rain had stopped, and he withdrew the umbrella. She looked pale, her nose red from standing outside in the cold. Their breath clouded and intermingled. 'We can't let people down. It's not who we are.'

Rain clung to the fur on her stole. She stared at him and he knew she would do as he had asked; there was something in her eyes, the fire had gone from them.

Outside the Empire Ruby powdered her nose and refreshed her lipstick while Johnny opened and closed the brolly to shake off most of the rain. It was dreary and grey, the sea churning as it crashed along the walls of the promenade. He walked to the door, held it open for her. She hesitated. He held out his hand and after a second or two she took hold of it. It was light and warm inside the theatre and he felt as if a window had opened. No more secrets.

Chapter 24

Jessie turned up the volume on the tannoy so they wouldn't miss their cues. They would have at least ten minutes before any of them were due on stage – Jessie as the Princess, Ginny her handmaiden, and Frances as the Slave of the Ring. The overture ended and they heard a warm burst of applause.

'Oh, Frances! What on earth have you done to upset Ruby Randolph?' Jessie pushed the door shut and leant against it.

Frances had expected Johnny to turn up at some point but hadn't bargained for Ruby. She had seen the shock on her face and it was obvious that he hadn't told her Frances was in the show. 'Who knows? Breathed the wrong way? I have no idea.'

Jessie came away from the door. 'No, you're not going to get away that easily. She was fine until she saw you.'

Frances sighed. She might as well tell them more. Ruby's outburst couldn't be explained away as nothing. 'I was competition. I was her understudy. And Johnny loved me.' She lowered her voice. 'Don't you dare breathe a word of this to anyone. Promise?'

Jessie put her hand on her heart. 'Promise.' Ginny did likewise.

They heard a roar of laughter as Bailey and North made their entrance as the Chinese Policemen. There was a brief flicker as the audience response registered with the girls. Patsy was out there somewhere with Colly, Bobby and

Imogen. Would she enjoy the show? Jessie and Ginny were waiting for her to speak.

'Once upon a time Johnny and I were engaged.' The girls gasped. 'He bought me a ring and I truly thought we would be together for always. He asked me to keep it quiet until he found the right time to tell his mother and Ruby.' She gave a small laugh. 'Not that there was ever a right time for either of them. But I trusted him. *Big* mistake.' They heard someone walk along the corridor. The tannoy system crackled, the audience laughing and applauding. 'Sounds like a good house.'

'And?' Jessie ignored her attempt to distract them.

'They went to America and he forgot all about me.' She thought of Imogen, out there, so close to her father . . .

'But he loves you. You can tell from the way he looks at you. It's as if he can't see anyone else in the room.'

'And neither could Ruby,' said Ginny, getting into her costume, urging Jessie to do the same. 'I'll bet his sister has something to do with keeping you apart.' Ginny fixed her headdress on with pins, leaning into the mirror to fiddle with the loose strands of her hair.

'She's her mother's daughter,' Frances said, shrugging. There was a knock on the door and Chip gave them their cue. She got up, took off her robe. 'It will always be his sister – and I can't afford to battle with her. And I have—' She was about to say she had Imogen to think of but checked herself.

'Have what?' Jessie put her foot on her chair, fastened the strap on her shoe.

Frances swallowed, trying to think of something. 'Yet to meet Mr Right.'

'Perhaps you've already met him,' Ginny said, as she walked out into the corridor. Jessie followed her, leaving the door ajar.

Frances sat in the dressing room, glad to be alone, to gather her thoughts. She glanced at the photo of Imogen. Nothing would come between them, not like Johnny and Ruby. She got herself ready and went up into the wings. Jessie was on stage, falling in love with the forbidden Aladdin. Joe was waiting in the wings, dressed in black and silver, an extravagant turban on his head. His dark eyebrows had been thickened and shaped under Don's instruction and he looked menacing, even though he'd confessed to not feeling it. They had all worked hard in rehearsals, Joe most of all, learning to be bad when it was against his nature. Frances peered through the spyhole, watching the audience. Ruby was scowling, seated between Johnny and Jack, while two rows behind them, Imogen sat with Patsy, enchanted, her face aglow as Princess Jessie sang 'Someone to Watch Over Me'. When the song ended, she clapped her little hands together in delight and Frances wished for all the world that the make-believe could last forever.

When the curtain came down at the interval, Johnny and Ruby were led from the auditorium, Audrey walking alongside Ruby, obviously enjoying the attention that celebrity engendered. People were hurrying down towards the stage to queue for ices and cigarettes, children were being dragged to the lavatory, where a line was forming outside the door. Johnny was relieved to see that Ruby was playing her part. She smiled and waved, signed autographs, blew kisses, transforming the energy of her rage into being larger than life. It was what people expected of them: to be happy and gay all the time, not a care in the world – for how else could they entertain if they didn't hide their own sadness?

Out in the foyer, Jack stopped by the stairs. 'I'm so glad you could make it today. And we'll see you again tomorrow at the Town Hall. You know, the usual – drinks and a few canapés.'

'We'll be there, Jack.' He turned to check where Ruby was.

'I should have given you the official invitation,' Jack continued, 'but we've all been so busy. It's in my office. Let me get it.' Johnny hurried up the stairs after him, leaving Ruby chatting with Audrey.

In Jack's office Johnny said, 'Have you got a pen and paper?' Jack passed them over and Johnny wrote a note. He handed it to Jack. 'Could you make sure Frances gets this?' Jack took the folded paper from him, pushed it into his breast pocket, gave Johnny the invitation in return. It would be another chance to be with Frances and he planned to grasp every opportunity that came his way. He almost skipped down the stairs into the foyer. Ruby's face was a tight smile as Audrey introduced her to a rather round woman and her equally round husband. He was sweating profusely, mopping his head with a handkerchief. Ruby gave him a limp handshake and she flashed her eyes at Johnny, who swept in to rescue her, taking her by the elbow.

'Sorry to steal you away, little sis, but we need to leave for our own show. Would you excuse us?' He beamed at the couple, said goodbye to Audrey and hurried Ruby outside to where their car was waiting. Johnny opened the door and Ruby slid onto the seat. He hurried round to the other side and got in beside her.

'Thank you, Ruby.'

She stared out of the window. 'What for?'

'Staying.'

When they arrived outside the Palace they waited in the car until the driver opened the doors. Ruby stepped out onto the pavement. The air was full of smoke from the factories around them and the odious stench of fish. She'd thought she'd got used to it, but now it stank stronger than ever and at that moment she hated it. Johnny was waiting by the stage door. Well, he could wait a little longer. Her head was spinning, trying to make sense of it all; she'd hardly watched the panto, wouldn't be able to tell anyone what she'd seen, the songs she'd heard. Seeing Frances had been such a huge shock that she hadn't been able to find the words, any words, good or bad. That after all these years he had found her, here, of all places; had chosen this place because of her. She pulled her stole about her, held onto the brooch, their mother's brooch. How she wished Mother was here: she could tell her how frightened she was, frightened of Mickey Harper, of Frances, of losing the last person in the world who loved her. She studied him as he waited, so patiently. It was dark but she could make out his features by the blue light over the stage door. She breathed in, hating the smell, looked down at the pavement, at her shoes that glittered with diamante. It all felt so stupid here, so false, and she was keenly aware of how ridiculous she was, how out of place. But where *did* she fit? She lifted her head and stepped from behind the car, made her way to where Johnny was waiting and stood with him for a moment, understanding now when she hadn't before. There had been something different about him and now she knew what it was. She gave a slight nod of her head and he opened the theatre door. Stepping inside, she ignored Jeff at the stage door office, her heels echoing in the emptiness. They were early – it hadn't been worth going home – but where *was* home? Nowhere and everywhere …

'Miss Randolph, your mail,' Jeff said, as she opened the door to the corridor. How could she have forgotten? She turned, ashen. Jeff was holding a large brown envelope and a few smaller white ones. Johnny had the key to their room and reached up to take them, but Ruby moved quickly, snatching them from Jeff's hand. The handwriting on the large envelope was one she'd come to recognise. Her fingers were trembling and she couldn't breathe; her legs couldn't hold her up. Johnny swept forward, taking her by the elbow and hurried her into their room, where she collapsed onto her chair, still gripping the envelopes tightly. Johnny went to take them from her, but she managed to pull her hand away. The smaller envelopes fell to the floor and when he bent to pick them up, she slid the brown envelope face down on the dressing table, fighting to compose herself.

'What happened?' He tossed the letters onto the dressing table. Her breath was coming hard and fast, and she placed her fist on her breastbone. It hurt. He went to the sink on the back wall, brought her a glass of water, watched as she sipped it.

'I don't know,' she lied. 'I suddenly felt faint. Thank you for looking after me.' He gave her a gentle smile; he was confused, she could tell.

'This is all my fault. It's the shock. I should have told you about Frances, but there never seemed to be the right time.' She gave him a small smile and he ran his hand over her cheek, pushed her hair back from her face. She reached up, rested her hand on his. There was never a right time for bad news, was there? 'I didn't want to hurt you, Ruby. Please believe that. I should have been braver.'

She should be brave. She should tell him about the photos, the letters. Why had her mother made her save them? She'd never understood. Was she going to give them to him at some point? Is that what she was meant to do? It was too late to ask. Nausea swept over her and she leant forward, her hand on the dressing table, saw the envelope again. She looked at Johnny through the mirror.

'I need something to eat. Would you get me something, a cracker? Something small?'

'I don't like to leave you …' He squatted beside her, gently taking hold of her hand. She bit down on her lip. 'Oh, Ruby, what are you doing to yourself?'

He wouldn't care so much if he knew about Mickey, about the debt. He would get Frances to take her place. Frances knew the routines, was a better dancer, even Ruby knew that. What was such a talented girl doing in that little theatre by the sea?

'Please go.' She forced herself to smile at him.

He picked up some change from the table, hesitated. 'I'll be as quick as I can.'

She waited until the door clicked shut then stood with her back to it. Her fingers trembled as she tore at the envelope. Inside were two photographs of Ruby, one where she was laid on a bed, naked, save for a sheet that was pulled across her middle. She was smiling, drunkenly she supposed, for she couldn't remember exactly where they were taken, or when. In the other photograph she was minus the sheet. She looked in the envelope again and withdrew a note in Mickey Harper's hand. *Enjoying your time at the Palace? Coming up for a few days. Would be lovely to see more of you.*

Her hands were shaking uncontrollably as she pushed it back in, along with the photos. Johnny must never see, must never know. He would hate her, loathe her for what she had done. She didn't deserve to be happy. But he did. And he had found Frances. Was there anything left for her at all?

The entire company assembled on stage for the finale, the bright satins and sequins shining under the lights as the audience called and cheered their approval. The girls bowed again and again, and Don Roper stepped forward, taking his applause, boos resounding loudly as Joe took his turn. Don clapped his protégé; the kids had hated him more as the show progressed and Joe fought to hide his discomfort. Ginny smiled reassuringly and he winked at her. Frances and Jessie exchanged knowing looks as they bent forward to bow again. Don walked across the stage, holding out his arm against the cast, encouraging the audience to keep going with their appreciation.

Frances peered out into the auditorium. Imogen was standing up from her seat, she and Colly side by side, clapping, jumping up and down. That was what panto was all about, setting off on a magic carpet ride to a land of dreams, where good conquers all. If the only bad in the world were people like Joe Taplow, there would never be a war. Joe was acting, and doing his best, but the evil they all faced was always in the shadows. People like Harry and Pete were up in the air, out on the ocean, in the darkness, with no light, no magic to guide them. An image flashed in her mind of the children lined up in the station. Were they safe? Who was tucking them up in bed at night? She hoped they had someone like Patsy watching over them. Jessie stepped forward with Kitty Bright, centre stage. Imogen stopped clapping, her little face shining in the soft light and Frances felt her heart swell with happiness. As the curtain came down for the final time, she hurried off stage, eager to get out front to be with her before they caught the bus back to Waltham.

In the dressing room, Jessie flung herself into her chair and Ginny stepped out of her finale costume and hung it up neatly, everything slow and measured. Jessie hadn't even taken her costume off and Frances was at the door.

'You're in a rush to get to the bar all of a sudden.' Jessie picked up a rag and dipped it in the cream, wiping off her dark make-up, thick black and orange appearing on the cloth.

'I want to say goodbye to Patsy before she leaves.'

Frances hurried out the pass door and through the auditorium. Patsy was waiting in the foyer as arranged and Imogen and Colly rushed forward, throwing their arms about her. She caught hold of them and ran her hand over Imogen's hair. Imogen tipped up her head and smiled, her eyes shining, and Frances yearned to leave with her, to leave everything behind and walk into another life, one in which she was always with Imogen. Patsy and Bobby stood back as people pushed past them to the exit.

'It was wonderful, Franny.' She took hold of Colly's hand. 'The kids loved it.' Frances held on to Imogen, the small hands warm in hers, and squatted down beside her.

'Did you have fun, my darling? I could see you from the stage. You were laughing at the funny men. I saw you singing when Widow Twankey had the big song sheet at the end. Did you like it?' Imogen nodded excitedly, nestling close to her mother. Frances ran her hand around her child's face but Imogen looked beyond her, eyes shining, her smile growing wider still. She held her arm out and pointed.

'The princess!' Frances froze then struggled back to her feet, turning to find Jessie, who couldn't take her eyes off Imogen.

'Jessie!' Frances stepped towards her, hoping to hide Imogen, knowing it was already too late. Jessie handed over a piece of folded paper, stared at Imogen, then Patsy, Bobby and Colly in turn. Patsy took Imogen's hand in her own. People pushed about them, wrapping themselves up before they stepped out into the cold street. There were icy blasts as the doors were opened and closed. Frances felt she could almost see Jessie putting it all together; they had to get out.

'Jack was looking for you. A note. I said I'd make sure you got it.'

Frances pushed the paper into her pocket. 'Thanks, Jessie. This is my friend Patsy – and the children.'

Patsy took the children's hands. 'Lovely to meet you, Jessie, but we must dash or we'll miss our bus.' Patsy turned her back and was off through the door, pulling the children with her.

'Ow, Mum!' Colly called out as she jostled them through the doors, pushing past a couple of old ladies who were blocking the doorway. Imogen turned her head, smiling at Jessie with admiration. Jessie watched them as they went out into the darkness, rooted to the spot. Frances galvanised herself.

'I'll see you later, Jessie. In the bar.'

Jessie nodded mutely and Frances hurried through the doors, thankful to be out in the street. It was freezing and she pulled her cardigan closed, wrapping her arms around herself, and dashed across the road to join Patsy at the bus stop.

'Oh, God, she knows!' Her stomach was churning and bile rose in her mouth. Jessie would be like a dog with a bone. The queue grew longer, people stamping their feet and beating their arms about them for warmth.

Patsy reached out to her. 'Is that a bad thing?' The bus was coming down the hill, the thin slits of the headlamps showing as it made its way towards them.

Frances blew out a long breath. 'I don't know.'

Jessie walked through to the bar and pushed herself to the window, stepped through the curtains and pulled them behind her to keep out the light. Over the road Frances had her back to her and she watched her squat down in front of the little girl, touch her face, hold her. Then she stood up, kissed the top of her head. The little boys said something and she knew from the way Frances moved her body that she was answering them, but Frances didn't kiss them. Patsy reached out and pressed Frances's arm and Frances leant forward and hugged her. The bus drew up and they were gone from sight. Jessie stepped back into the bar. The girl she'd just seen was the same child in the photo on her bedside table. Imogen, the girl Frances had said was her niece. But it was a lie. It wasn't Patsy who was so important every Sunday. It was the girl . . .

The bar was warm and welcoming. Most of the cast were in there and Jack and Audrey were moving through the crowd, chatting, smiling. There was much shaking of hands and slapping of backs. Frances stood by the door, peering from side to side until she saw Jessie and Ginny over by the curtains. Ginny waved to her and she eased her way through the crowd. Someone grabbed her hand.

'Can I get you a drink, Irish?' Bob grinned. 'Sorry, *Frances*.'

She pulled her hand free, pressing his arm. 'Another time.'

'Sure.'

She hadn't meant to be abrupt, but she needed to get to Jessie. She pushed through the throng and Jessie handed her a glass. 'Got you a stout.'

'Thanks.' Frances held her gaze. Ginny's attention was elsewhere. Frances and Jessie looked in the same direction. Joe Taplow was leaning against the wall, staring into his pint, gangly, awkward, out of place. Ginny looked back at them, blushed. She picked up her drink.

'He looks as if he would rather be anywhere than here.' He looked up and saw them and Frances waved him over. It was a cowardly thing to do, but it would stop Jessie asking any awkward questions. She sipped her drink. Jessie would save it until they got home. Joe pulled up a stool and sat beside Ginny. Bob Bailey had been watching and he walked over, stood next to Frances.

'Where's your partner?' Frances tried to be relaxed but knew she was overcompensating, trying to give the impression there was nothing untoward. But Jessie knew. How much longer would Imogen be a secret now?

'Giving me a wide berth.'

'Oh?'

He shrugged. 'Something we don't see eye to eye on. Nothing much. Can't be mates all the time, can we?' Joe drew another stool close and Bob sat down. Frances moved up a little. They chatted about the show, could hear Kitty Bright's laughter ringing around the bar.

'No ignoring her, is there?' Bob said sarcastically.

'Some things you just can't,' Jessie agreed. Frances looked at her, then away. 'What was the note about?'

'Note?'

'From Jack.'

She took it from her pocket to read it. 'Johnny wants to meet.' She screwed it up, tossed it into the ashtray. It had all been too much – Ruby, Imogen ... Jessie picked up her glass.

'His divine little sister is going to love that.'

Frances gave a small laugh. 'Perhaps she'll come too.' She wouldn't put it past her. He was sending a car. Well, she couldn't ignore him forever – and she knew she didn't want to. It was exhausting, keeping everything a secret, and now it was only a matter of time before it all came out. At least this way she would have a modicum of control.

Jack came over and Bob and Joe got to their feet. He gestured for them to sit down.

'I'm in a bit of a fix. I know we've all been invited to the town hall tomorrow ...' Bob groaned and Jack grinned. 'You might like this, then, Bob. The children's home in

Grimsby have been in touch. They usually have films for the kids on a weekend but their projector's broken and can't be fixed. They've asked around, and ours is too large for them to use, but when I heard about it, I thought – well, I hoped, as it's almost Christmas – we could do something a bit special for them.'

'I'll go,' Frances said, sensing escape.

'Me too.' Jessie agreed. 'We can do something together?' Frances could hardly refuse and when Jessie smiled, it made her relax a little.

'Can't let these girls go unaccompanied, Jack.' Bob said. 'I'll go and Sid will too. I'll make sure of it.'

'That's good of you, especially at such short notice.'

'Not at all,' Jessie said. 'I count my blessings that I've got my mum and my brother. Even more so at Christmas.'

Frances looked away, over her shoulder. Kitty Bright was throwing back her head with laughter, her red hair like a flame in the room. Frances ran her finger around the collar of her dress, suddenly hot. 'I'm going home to get an early night. Busy day tomorrow.' She put her glass down on the nearest table and Jessie did the same, slinging her bag over her shoulder.

'I'll come with you.'

Frances wrapped her scarf around her face, pulling it up over her nose. She breathed into it, the warmth taking the chill from her cheeks. Jessie shoved her bag up to her elbow, held her arm out to link with Frances and Frances took it, neither of them speaking, just keeping close to each other as they walked up the incline towards the Cliff Hotel. Jessie didn't say a word until they got into bed. It was cold and they layered themselves in jumpers and woolly socks over their pyjamas. Frances turned off the bedside lamp.

Grace had put a hot water bottle into the bed and they got in, feeling the warmth on their feet.

'God bless your mam,' Frances said, when her teeth had stopped chattering. Jessie's silence unnerved her. They lay in the darkness until eventually Jessie said, 'Why didn't you tell me?'

Frances shifted in the bed.

'The girl in the photograph, the one on your bedside table, at the theatre. Your niece?'

'Jessie, I . . .'

Jessie sat up, leant across Frances and put the lamp back on. She picked up the photo that Frances kept by her bed and scrutinised it. 'The little girl at the theatre. With Patsy. She's not your niece is she, this little girl?'

Frances sat up, pulling the blankets up to her chin. Her breath was a cloud.

'Imogen is my daughter.' Her voice caught with the pain of it, with the lie of it. It had been a whisper that sounded like an explosion, but Jessie hadn't flinched. Frances reached out for the picture and Jessie handed it over, looking at her friend. She could see the hurt in her eyes.

'Why did you keep her a secret? Why?' Jessie shook her head, not understanding.

Frances studied the photo. Her darling innocent.

'To protect her.' It was that simple. And that complicated. She put the photo back on the bedside table.

'Are you going to tell me?'

There was no point in holding back anymore. 'I will,' Frances said, and Jessie listened as she told her of how Johnny had gone off to America promising to send a ticket that never came; of how she discovered she was pregnant, had hoped and prayed that a letter would come but nothing ever did. Talking about it reawakened the fear.

'How on earth did you manage?'

'Some of the time I didn't. If it hadn't been for Patsy and Colin …' She stopped, finding it hard to express what they had done for her. It seemed such a small thing to say, kindness. But it was everything. 'They've been angels. I can never repay them for all they've done for me.'

Jessie clasped her hand.

'One day you will, Frances. We all get our turn.'

Chapter 25

It seemed she had talked half the night and lain awake the rest of it, for when dawn broke Frances was exhausted. She watched a shaft of cold morning light filter through the gap left in the curtains. It was a habit she couldn't break, for somewhere in the darkness there had to be the hope of light. A new beginning. Her nose was cold and she hunched the blankets up about her shoulders. She'd expected to feel relieved that Jessie knew but instead she felt afraid. As if she was losing control. Jessie was full of good intentions, always wanting to fix things, but she could be reckless. Could she be trusted? She sat up on her pillows, adjusted the blanket. Jessie groaned, turned away from the wall.

'Are you awake?'

'Uh uh.' Her voice was croaky. She coughed, scratched her head, pulled herself upright, tugging the bedclothes about her. 'It's freezing.'

'We're a pair of daft beggars, aren't we? Me and you scrunched up in here and Lady Muck, Ginny, getting a bed to herself.' Jessie yawned, stretching her arms out of the blankets. She shivered, tucking them up to her chin again.

'You could swap.'

'Never,' Jessie yawned again, and Frances did the same.

'She's doing OK isn't she?' Frances said, thinking of how Ginny seemed to be finding her way again. Grace and Geraldine had been kind, although Geraldine couldn't help voicing her disapproval in small ways. Would they be so kind to her? She gripped Jessie's arm. 'Please don't say anything. About Imogen.'

'I won't.' Jessie frowned. 'I promised. Although I think you're wrong. Mum and Geraldine would get used to it. I think they'd be more cross that you've struggled on and kept it from them. I know I am.'

Frances couldn't bear it; this was what she had been afraid of. She threw back the blankets, wanting to move not think … She pulled on her dressing gown.

'I know you're angry, Jessie, but there never seemed to be a right time.' She couldn't go over and over the same thing. What was done was done.

'There is never a right time. For anything. Only time.'

'That's a bit profound this early in the morning.' Frances drew back the curtains. The sky was heavy with dark clouds and rain ran from the gutters.

Jessie slid to the side of the bed. 'Who knows how long any of us have got, Frances? We can't sit on the sidelines any more.' She wiggled her feet into her slippers. 'I used to think I had all the time in the world to do all the things I wanted to.' She stared towards the window. 'I'm frightened for Harry every day, every single minute. I think of all the time I've wasted already.'

Frances picked up her washbag, wrapping the cord around her fingers. 'I can't say anything to comfort you.'

Jessie got up. 'It's the hardest thing, isn't it? Having no words of comfort.'

Frances opened the door, leant against it. 'Sometimes just being there for each other is enough.'

The fire was lit in the room downstairs. Eddie was sitting at the table with a mug of tea and Grace was standing at the cooker, Ginny was washing her smalls in the kitchen sink.

The pair of them looked up when the girls came in. Frances put her washbag on the dresser and stood in front of the fire, warming her hands. She turned her back to it, letting the warmth hit her legs. Grace placed two boiled eggs in front of Eddie and Jessie fetched the plate of toast their mother had made for him and put it on the table, taking a slice for herself. She pulled out a chair next to the fire and slumped into it.

'I'll be finished in a minute,' Ginny called out, emptying the dirty water into the sink.

'You look tired, Frances,' Grace said. 'Bad night?'

Frances rubbed at her face. 'No more than usual. Probably the tension of opening a new show.'

Ginny was wringing out the washing. She came into the room, her hands red from the cold water. 'I should move out and let you have your bed back, Jessie. It was only meant to be temporary.'

'Don't be daft,' Frances said quickly, 'Jessie and I keep each other warm. Better be gone by summer, though.'

'I'll be gone long before then.' Ginny went back to the bowl, calling through to them, 'I've applied for ENSA.' She raised her voice over the noise of the tap as she ran more water into the bowl. 'Once the panto's finished I'm going down to London to audition.' She turned off the tap, swirled her underwear in the bowl, looking down at it. 'A fresh start.'

Frances moved to the kitchen. 'I was only joking, Ginny. We're fine. Honestly we are.'

Ginny looked up. 'I know you are. But I need to move on. From everything.'

Frances understood the need to leave bad memories behind. How could she tell her that it didn't work, that the memories came with you wherever you went?

They were all quiet until Grace spoke.

'What time do you have to be at the children's home, you two?'

'One.' Frances was glad to break the silence. 'We're going on the bus so we won't have chance to come to the Town Hall with you. Will you be all right, Mum?'

'Of course I will. I'll have Ginny with me.' Ginny lowered the pulley from the ceiling and draped her underwear over the wooden bars. Eddie glanced her way then quickly concentrated on his egg. He still hadn't got used to a house full of women.

'I'll look after your mum, Jessie. Not that she needs it. She'll be looking after me.'

'Aye, and you'll be taken up with Joe Taplow if he has half a chance.'

Ginny turned her back on them. 'I'm sure I don't know what you mean.'

Frances grinned at Jessie, shaking her head. 'Don't tease.'

'*You* did.'

The front door opened and Dolly's voice rang out, 'Cooee!' An icy blast accompanied her as she hurried in and closed the door. Her nose and cheeks were red and her eyes were watering with the cold. She unwrapped her scarf and pulled off her gloves, taking a note from her pocket, which she handed to Jessie.

'I didn't think you'd want to wait. Mike took a phone call at the theatre. He popped it over to Dad.'

Jessie opened it. 'Harry's got leave!' She flung her arms around Dolly. 'Oh, darling Dolly, thank you so much for thinking of me.' She did a little dance in the room and Frances laughed. Eddie stuffed the last piece of toast in his mouth, got to his feet and took his jacket from the back of his chair.

'Do you think he'll come in his car? He might not be able to get petrol.' He took his cap from the dresser behind him and pulled it hard on his head.

Jessie read the note again. 'I don't care if he comes in his plane and lands it on the beach!' Grace was smiling and Frances could see the love and pride shining from her face. How lucky they were to have their mother close.

'I think that's a bit extreme, Jessie love.'

'That's me all over. Extreme. And I don't give a fig.' Jessie laughed. 'Just to see him again. It's the best Christmas present ever.' Eddie leant over to kiss Grace and as he did so she pulled his cap over his ears.

'Scarf?'

He pulled it from his pocket, grinning, wrapped it around his neck. 'I can't kiss you with it on, Mum. I can't move my neck.' He called goodbye to Ginny and waved, said the same to the other girls. Jessie gave him a playful punch on the arm as he passed. They heard him whistling as he opened the front door and went out into the street.

'When is Harry's leave?' Grace got up and began clearing the table.

'This weekend. He's hoping to be here later tonight.'

Dolly walked with them to the theatre. It was hard to tell whether it was colder outside than in. The forecast had said snow was on the way, but they hadn't seen any sign of it yet. The shops along the main road had put in extra effort with their decorations, hoping to entice people to throw caution to the wind and spend on their loved ones, forget they were at war. The three of them stopped briefly to admire a scene; a sleigh piled with gaily wrapped presents and a tailor's dummy dressed as Father Christmas. Imogen was getting excited and the boys too. They had come home from school with little gifts they'd made, pictures they'd painted.

Imogen would be ready for school soon, something else she needed to think about. There would be no more travelling for a while. Not for her, anyway. Inside the dressing room they removed their scarves and hats but kept on their coats as they gathered their things together.

'Which costumes should we take? I can't make up my mind.'

Dolly went through the garments on the rail.

'Take this one.' She held out a lilac full-length dress that shimmered with diamanté and sequins. 'The kids will love all the jewels. It makes you look like a proper princess.' Frances recalled Imogen's little face at the panto. It had been Jessie that she'd fallen in love with; at the bus stop she could talk of nothing else. Frances began putting her make-up into a vanity case.

'Shall we share?' Jessie came over, adding her sticks of greasepaint to Frances's. 'We might as well make it as easy as we can for ourselves.'

Dolly covered the costumes with cloth and helped Jessie fold them into a suitcase.

'This is going to be awkward,' Frances said, as the pile accumulated by the door. 'By the time we've got our bags and gas masks we'll look like a couple of pack horses.'

'We could go in our costumes,' Jessie offered, grinning.

'Well, good luck with that. *I'm* not going in chiffon harem pants and bare feet. I'll get chilblains.' The three of them laughed and once their things were organised they sat down to wait for Sid and Bob to arrive.

'Have you heard from Pete, Dolly?' asked Jessie. 'I'm so sorry I didn't ask. It was thoughtless of me.'

'No, it wasn't. You were excited.' Dolly put her hands behind her and leant against the wall. 'No more letters. They come in threes and fours now, half-covered in black lines, but I suppose they can't say much.'

'No,' Jessie said. 'Harry's are the same.'

'I sent him a parcel. He wanted some fags and stamps, little things. Mam made him some thick socks and I got a tin of biscuits. A little bit extra for Christmas.'

'Will he be home for Christmas, Dolly?' Frances was leaning into the mirror. The dark circles under her eyes would need some concealing.

'I don't know. Shouldn't think he does either. He hasn't been home for weeks. His mam's worried sick about him.'

Frances turned away from the mirror. Behind Dolly's brave face she was as worried as Pete's mam.

'The troops are already in France,' Jessie said, 'but nothing's happening.'

'It will, though.' Dolly's voice was flat. 'They're not out there for nothing. It's only a matter of time.'

The sun had escaped from behind the clouds when Grace and Ginny left Barkhouse Lane and turned into Humber Street. It was a short walk to the Town Hall and it was good to feel the gentle warmth that came from the sun. Grace put out her arm and Ginny linked hers into it. Grace patted her hand.

'Good to have a little sun on our faces, isn't it, Ginny?'

Ginny looked up at the sky as if to check that the sun was still there. 'Summer seems such a long time ago, doesn't it?'

'Years and years,' Grace replied.

'In many ways I wish it was.'

'Don't live a life of regrets, Ginny. Learn from your mistakes and move on. Be brave.'

'That's not being brave, Grace. Bravery is fighting the enemy.'

A cyclist passed and Grace stepped out onto the road, looking about her until they reached the safety of the pavement. 'Sometimes the enemy is ourselves, Ginny. You deserve happiness. It's what your mother would want for you.' They unlinked their arms and Grace took hold of the rail to walk up the stone steps of the Town Hall entrance. Inside it was warm and Grace peeled off her gloves, unwound the scarf from about her neck. She folded them neatly and left them in the cloakroom, along with her hat and coat. The two women checked themselves in the mirror and went up the wide steps to the floor where the party was being held. A tall Christmas tree was placed at the centre of the large window on the half-landing, the stairs dividing and sweeping up either side of the light and airy hall, decorated with brightly coloured baubles and ribbons. She stopped for a moment to admire it. It would be the second Christmas without her beloved Davey and she thought how swiftly the time had passed, how piercing the pain that lingered. She smiled at Ginny and patted her hand as they made the turn on the stairs.

They were guided through the heavy oak doors and into the council chambers by an elderly gentleman in a suit who introduced himself as Councillor Alfred Talbot. Many of the cast were there already, the dancers huddled in a group, trying their best to appear as if they did this every day of the week. Grace waved and they waved back. A table had been set at one end, a pristine white cloth over it, glasses set out in rows. Another table abutted it, laden with sausage rolls and sandwiches. Don Roper was slowly moving along, a plate in one hand on which he was balancing an assortment of food. He reached out for a glass of sherry and moved over to chat to Basil. In one corner a huddle of children waited silently as a woman spoke to a man sitting by the piano. They were wearing their coats, woolly hats and scarves, holding lanterns as if they were about to wander the streets. The woman moved towards the children; the pianist played the introduction to 'Deck the Halls' and the children started to sing. It was a treat to hear their voices, so pure and clear. It had been worth coming for them alone. Jack and Audrey were standing in front of the canopy at the opposite end of the room, chatting with the Mayor and Mayoress. She saw Jack make his excuses and hurry towards them. Audrey followed him with her eyes, seeing Grace without acknowledging her. Grace smiled but it wasn't returned. She hadn't expected it. Jack put out his hand.

'Good to see you, Grace, Ginny. Did the girls get off all right?'

'They did, thank you.'

'It's me who should be thanking them. I'm sure the kids are going to enjoy every minute of it. Especially Jessie's beautiful voice. Let me get you ladies a drink.' He guided them over to the table. 'Sherry?'

'It's a little early but as it's a celebration ...' Ginny was scanning the room and Grace smiled to herself. The girls had been teasing earlier but they were right.

Grace raised her glass: 'To the Empire.' Ginny chinked her glass and Jack took a sip. 'It looks like she won't be able to soldier on much longer.'

'Why's that, Jack?'

He lowered his voice, leant into Grace. 'The government want to requisition the building. I've managed to hold them off. They've agreed to let me run to the end of the panto, but after that?' He shrugged. 'I don't know.'

'You fought on.'

'It's not the fighting others are doing.'

She pressed his arm. 'But it's fighting all the same, Jack. Fighting to put on a show, to spread happiness. We need it more than ever.' Audrey swept over and Grace withdrew her hand.

Jack took a step back. 'You remember Grace, Audrey? Jessie's mother.'

Audrey shot Grace a fake smile.

'Will you excuse us.' It wasn't a request. She put a hand on Jack's shoulder. Her nails were perfectly manicured and Grace unconsciously rubbed at the hard patches on her fingertips. 'Graham was asking for you, darling.' She turned her back and took Jack over to the Mayor.

'First-name terms. Audrey will like that; she's that kind of woman,' Ginny said wryly. As people moved about the room, Grace spotted Joe Taplow hunched in a corner, reading the neat metal description plates under the portraits that hung around the room.

'Go and rescue him, Ginny.' Ginny reddened. Grace nudged her. 'The poor boy looks as if he's drowning. Go on,' Grace urged. 'Be brave, remember?'

Grace found herself a chair at the edge of the room and watched. She much preferred it that way. Kitty was preening, checking to see who was paying her attention, and when a couple of boys in uniform walked in she hurried over and drew them into her circle, led them to the table with alcohol and handed them a beer. They looked suitably adoring. Kitty waved at her and Grace raised her glass. Kitty Bright would never need to be rescued.

Ginny wished she'd stayed where she was, but Grace had said to be brave. And poor Joe, he looked so lost. She knew how that felt. He was admiring a portrait of a woman wearing a blue dress, a fur stole draped about her generous shoulders, a kindly expression on her face. Joe moved slightly, saw Ginny, smiled awkwardly, and turned back to the picture. She was being kind, she told herself, that's all it was, she didn't want anything else but friendship and he looked as though he needed a friend.

'I wonder who she was ... is?' Ginny said eventually. He didn't reply and Ginny answered her own question. 'She looks nice, whoever she is.'

'How can you tell?' Joe said, his brow furrowed. He peered at the portrait.

'It's the eyes.' Ginny pointed. 'See how the artist has captured them. And the way her hands are on her lap.' She looked at him, but he continued staring at the woman. She thought of Billy, the twinkle in his eyes. He hadn't loved her, she'd known that, but she hadn't wanted to acknowledge it. Would he have stood by her? Joe turned to her.

'It's lost on me.' He shrugged. 'Half my trouble.'

'What is, Joe?' He had nice eyes, blue grey. Wise, her mother would have said; quiet, gentle colours.

'Not understanding. I can't read the signs.' He turned to face the room. 'I notice things. All the little things, but I can't seem to assemble them into any sense. It's all . . .' He seemed to have trouble finding the right word. He looked at her. 'Very black and white. I can't see the colour. Do you understand?' He looked embarrassed.

'Sort of . . . I suppose.' It didn't matter, did it?

He fiddled with his cuff, brushed at his jacket.

'Would you like a drink, Joe?'

'I would.'

She smiled. 'Come with me then. We can get something to eat while we're there.' She led the way, grinning, puzzled. He was strange but she liked him. He was gentle and so unlike anyone else she'd ever met. They filled their plates, she piling what she fancied on the plate while Joe asked questions of the waitress and slowly placed sandwiches in a neat pattern on his own. He adjusted the triangles until he was happy.

'Would you like a sausage roll, sir?' the girl asked, holding tongs above the plate. He froze, looked at Ginny, his eyes pleading as if suddenly overwhelmed.

'We'll come back,' Ginny said. He smiled and it was as if the clouds had parted and the sun had come out.

Encouraged, she became more confident. 'Let's go and sit down, Joe. It will be more comfortable over there. Easier than juggling a plate and a drink.' She led the way and they sat under the portrait of the woman with the kind eyes.

'I'm not very good at this.' He picked up a sandwich. 'I'm not very good at anything, really.' He took a bite.

'Oh, but you are, Joe. You're good at magic. You're good at being Abanazar.'

'Only because Don worked with me.'

'But you learned, Joe. You learned quickly.'

He stared down at his plate.

'I'm good at deceiving people,' he said. She was taken aback. He noticed, panicked. 'What I meant was, that's all magic is, you know, sleight of hand, misdirection. It's making them look where you want them to look, see what you want them to see.'

She was relieved, unsure of what he had been about to say.

'Oh, I see. You had me worried there.' She laughed.

'Did I?'

Ginny saw the puzzlement on his face. 'Confused is a better word. I should have said confused.' He nodded, understanding. They ate in silence.

The atmosphere in the room changed when Johnny and Ruby Randolph arrived. Audrey quickly detached herself from the Mayor and his wife and hurried towards them. Grace watched as she fussed and preened, her fluted laughter slicing through the conversation. She'd seen the Randolphs briefly at the Empire and Jack had given Grace tickets for herself and Geraldine to see them at the Palace. They'd been meaning to go but Geraldine was at work most of the time and Grace was busy with WVS duties when she wasn't at the theatre.

Ruby flitted about the room like a butterfly, giving everyone a small portion of her time, as did Johnny. They were an elegant couple, well versed in the politics of show business. Grace had known both Randolph parents over the years, before and after they were married. The father had died in an accident when the children very young – it had been in all the papers. Such a tragedy. She watched Johnny as he guided Ruby, protective, gracious. Audrey made attempts to monopolise them and Ruby was bored though she hid it well. Over in the corner Ginny was chatting to Joe, who was listening closely. Even from this distance she could see that he was entranced. She rubbed at her wedding ring; how she wished her Davey were here. It was lonely without him. She closed her eyes, thought she smelt his cologne. It was a comfort.

'Grace?'

She snapped her eyes open, startled. Johnny Randolph was standing before her. 'Oh, I am so sorry, Mrs Delaney, I didn't mean to disturb you.'

She shook her head. 'I closed my eyes. I was …' She smiled, remembering '… somewhere else.'

He sat down beside her, looked to his sister. 'Is your talented daughter not here?'

'Some of the cast went to the children's home in Grimsby, to put on an impromptu show. She went with Frances.' He was disappointed, though he fought to hide it. 'They'll be sorry they missed you and Ruby.'

He rubbed his hands on his thighs. 'They made the right choice. These things can be very dry.'

'They can indeed. I expect you've done many of them over the years?'

He sat back, clasping his hands in his lap, looking and yet not seeing. 'Too many.'

'And at your age,' she smiled, 'many more ahead of you, you poor things.'

He laughed.

'Part of the job.' Audrey wiggled her hand at him, wanting to introduce him to a well-dressed, well-fed couple. 'Here we go again.'

'You have my deepest sympathies,' she said as he got to his feet. She heard him laugh again as he made his way over to Jack. She watched them for a time; she could easily have slipped away but Ginny kept seeking her out and so she stayed, enjoying the interactions as people came and went. Don Roper was talking to the dancers, his face getting redder with the drink. He was making shapes with his body, making them laugh, but he looked tired and old. It was a hard life. Ruby Randolph sat down next to her. She bent down and ran her finger around the heel of her shoe.

'That woman is such a snob!' She sat up, leant into Grace, whispering, 'I can't abide snobs, can you?'

'I try to avoid them if possible.'

Ruby put out her hand. 'Ruby.'

'Grace.' She took her hand and held it. Ruby crossed her long legs. 'Are you in the panto?'

Grace laughed. 'Dear me no, not at all. I'm in Wardrobe. My daughter Jessie is. She's playing Princess.'

Ruby scanned the room. 'She's not here?'

'No, as I told your brother, some of the cast are entertaining at a children's home today.'

Ruby sought her brother out. He had been hooked by Kitty Bright, who was leaning far too close and pressing her breasts into him. He looked uncomfortable and gave her a signal that meant he wanted to be rescued. She raised her glass and turned her back to talk to Grace.

'Do you need to go?'

Ruby shook her head. 'Let him suffer, that's what I say.'

Grace laughed. 'He doesn't deserve it.'

Ruby quaffed her white wine, tipping back her head. 'He doesn't. He's one of the good guys.' She sounded sad. She looked back at Grace. 'Jessie's very talented. She'll go a long way. The top.'

'Perhaps.'

'Don't you want that for her?' Ruby tilted her head on one side. She was an attractive girl, beautiful almond-shaped eyes, her brown hair a cascade of waves.

'I want her to be happy. It's what every mother wants for their child.'

Ruby looked down in her glass and as she crossed her legs a couple of thc soldiers glanced her way, admiringly. 'Jessie's lucky to have her mother with her.' Ruby's voice cracked; she drank again. A waitress came around and she held out her glass. The waitress topped it up.

'How's the show going at the Palace? I've heard good reports. Wonderful reports, in fact.' She'd also heard of the rumpus Ruby had caused at the theatre.

'It's going well.' She sipped, looked at Grace and forced a smile. Grace felt she could almost touch Ruby's sadness.

'It's not everything, is it, Ruby?'

'No, indeed it's not, Grace. It's pretty damned lonely, I can tell you.' Ruby looked down at her lap. A teardrop fell from her cheek onto her dress, deepening the colour of the satin. The girl drew a hand over her cheek, tossed her head back.

'I've made such a mess of things.' She sniffed. Grace passed her a handkerchief and Ruby thanked her. 'I shouldn't drink so much. It's not good for me.'

'It's not good for *anyone*,' Grace countered.

Ruby returned her handkerchief. 'That's what my mother would say.' The girl's lips trembled and Grace gave her the handkerchief again. Ruby gave sad little laugh and Grace touched her arm.

'We all make mistakes, Ruby. Which is fine as long as we learn from them.' She paused. Over by the window Joe produced a sixpence from behind Ginny's ear. She took it, smiling. Grace took hold of Ruby's hand. 'How many mistakes do you make with your dancing before you get it right? But no one sees the mistakes, the hard work. They only see you gliding across the stage. That's the art of it. Look around you.' Ruby did so. 'Everyone's enjoying themselves, yet they all have their secrets and their sorrows, every single one of them.' She patted Ruby's hand. 'We have to keep going, one step at a time. Little by little, first there's a glimmer of light and then the sunshine.'

Jack raised a glass, tapping it with a spoon to quieten the room. The Mayor, standing there in his striped suit with his matching hair, looked like a smart badger.

'May I have your attention?' He cleared his throat. 'The Mayor has suggested that we open on Christmas Day to give an afternoon performance for our military personnel. Those boys and girls that are away from their homes, their families, much as you are. With your agreement, we'll go ahead.'

'That's great, Jack. Count me in.' Kitty was standing with two boys in naval uniform. They put their arms about her and she smiled coyly. The room was in full agreement and when Jack finished speaking the volume of voices rose as they discussed the change of plans.

Ruby remained next to Grace, watching people come and go. Grace was cautious, not wanting to speak out of turn. 'Shouldn't you mingle a little, Ruby?'

Ruby drained her glass. Held it up. A waitress hurried over and replenished it. 'I can't, Grace. Not any more. Johnny is much better at it than I am. He's so much better at everything.' She leant her head back against the wall. Grace caught Ginny's eye and beckoned with her finger. Ginny got up immediately and crossed the room to Grace.

'Let me get you something to eat, Ruby.' She sent Ginny for sandwiches, hoping they might soak up the alcohol. Johnny came over.

'Come and join in, Ruby.' He hid his irritation well.

'I'm tired, Johnny.'

'I think she's unwell, Johnny,' Grace offered. 'She might be better at home?'

He understood immediately. 'I'll get a cab.'

He disappeared for a moment then returned with his sister's fur stole. Grace helped wrap it about Ruby's shoulders, then got to her feet.

'Let me come with you. To say goodbye.' She took hold of Ruby's hand and Johnny swept his sister to her feet. They walked out of the room and down the staircase without mishap and Grace stood on the stone steps with Ruby while Johnny went to summon a taxi over. The wind was sharp and Grace, without her coat, tried not to shiver.

Ruby adjusted her stole, touched her brooch. Grace admired it.

'It was my mother's.'

'It's quite beautiful.'

Ruby couldn't find the words. Tears fell again.

'She'd want you to be happy.' Grace gripped Ruby's hand with both of hers. 'Remember that. Happy.'

Ruby tried to smile but her mouth wouldn't move properly.

Johnny opened the door and Ruby got in the cab. She watched as Johnny shook hands with Grace then got in beside her just as Ginny came down the steps with Grace's coat and put it over her shoulders. Grace pulled it about her, waving at Ruby as the car drew away.

If only she had her mother here, Ruby thought. She would know what to do, as Grace knew what to do. What had Grace said? One step at a time. The pain inside Ruby expanded until she felt it would burst from her skin. Johnny took hold of her hand but she couldn't look at him; instead she leant her head against the car window. It was cold and it helped. The sky was heavy with dark clouds. One step at time. And then the sunshine.

Chapter 26

Frances pushed the bell and the four of them waited in the porch of the children's home. They'd managed to avoid the rain but would certainly meet it on the way home and at least they weren't bedraggled before the show, that was the main thing. A woman came to the door, hurrying them inside.

'I can't thank you enough for stepping in like this.' She was tall and smartly dressed, her grey hair set in curls and brushed away from a broad forehead. 'Mr Holland has been beyond generous. You all have. This is a special treat indeed. Oh, Irene Lewis.' She held out her hand and they shook it in turn. She was brisk and efficient and reminded Jessie of Miss Symonds again. She was going to come and see the pantomime with Norman and Beryl. Would Aunt Iris come too? No, definitely not. Aunt Iris thought the theatre and its people lacking in morals. What would she have thought of Ginny? And Frances …

They followed Irene into a large room with parquet flooring and a small raised platform at one end, the high walls decorated with Christmas murals the children had created. Heavy dark curtains hung at the high windows and a walnut piano that had seen better days was pushed against the wall. Jessie walked over to it and played a few notes. She grimaced.

'I know. It's a bit flat.' Irene raised her eyebrows.

'Doesn't matter.' Jessie was cheerful. 'We'll sing louder and Bob has his ukulele. Although what Christmas carols sound like on a uke is anyone's guess!'

'You'll soon find out,' Bob said with a smile.

Sid went to the end of the room, hopped up onto the platform and jumped up and down to test the floor. He walked over to each side, taking in the space they had to work with. Irene checked her wristwatch, holding the face with thumb and forefinger.

Frances held up her case. 'Any chance of somewhere to change?'

'You can use my room,' Irene said and took them back to the entrance where a typist was working in a reception office. The woman looked up and said hello. Jessie was so glad she'd escaped the typing pool; she wasn't planning on going back if she could help it.

'Can I get you a warm drink?' Irene asked. 'It's very cold out there. Tea?'

'That would be lovely.' The girls put down their bags and pulled off their scarves and hats. Frances removed her gloves, rubbing her hands while Jessie peered out onto the street, then settled herself down on the sofa. Sid sat next to her. Bob was reading the certificates on the wall.

'This brings back some memories. None of them good ones.' Sid was looking about the walls, which were decorated with long photographs of children who were lined up outside the building, some sitting cross-legged on the floor. Above the desk hung a portrait of King George.

'Were you in an orphanage?' Jessie was curious.

'In and out.' He folded his arms. 'When my mum couldn't keep us, we went in. When things got better, or she got another fella, we came out again. Bit like the 'okey-cokey.' He smiled and Jessie did too, wondering why comedians always had to make a joke of things, even if they were painful. But perhaps that was what kept them going. 'Did it a few times. She did her best, bless her, but times were tough after the last war.' He put his chin to his chest and Jessie wondered how many people that would happen to this time around? She glanced at Frances. Is that something she'd had to do, with Imogen? How little she knew about her friend.

Irene had returned with a young girl, bringing with them trays of tea and biscuits, and overheard.

'Many of our children are true orphans, Mr North. Although we do have some children who are in similar circumstances.' The girl poured tea and offered it around. Jessie sipped it, grateful for the warmth of the cup and its contents.

'I'm afraid the children are rather excited.'

'Don't apologise.' Bob put his empty cup on the tray. 'That's exactly how we want them to be. It will make it easier for us.'

'Although not easier for you when it's time for bed,' Frances said before biting on a custard cream.

'We can cope.' Irene left the plate of biscuits on her desk. 'I'll leave the teapot with you. There's hot water and shout out if you want anything else. Janet will bring whatever you need.' She touched the girl on the shoulder and she followed Irene out of the room.

They took it in turns to use the mirror to put on their make-up, using a lighter hand than was needed in the theatre. They heard the children lining up outside, the sound of excited chatter, someone barking at them to shush, then silence, save for the sound of shoes as the children walked on. Sid and Bob stripped off and got into their policemen costumes. They were both wearing long black socks and their blue trousers were wide and stopped below the knee. Their jackets were blue with gold braid – the overall look an oriental take on a British bobby. They put on their red silk mandarin hats with single long black pigtails fixed to the backs.

Jessie applied her make-up. 'I'm glad we came here instead of the town hall, aren't you, Frances?'

'You've missed out on all the alcohol,' Sid said. 'They won't be drinking tea up there.'

'Don will be drinking most of it.' Bob pulled on his shoes, tugging at the laces. 'We wouldn't get a look in.' He messed up his hair then put on his hat. 'His nose will be flashing like Rudolph's when he gets on stage tonight.'

'It's not funny. It's sad.' Jessie said.

'I know,' Sid agreed. 'Funny is the bottle of EMVA Cream he keeps in his room for his guests. You ever seen any guest in his room, Bob?'

She had to smile; after all, it was the truth.

Bob and Sid jumped up and down, limbering up, pulling faces, sticking out their tongues to make their faces more mobile. The girls called, 'Break a Leg' after them as they left the room and finished getting ready themselves. Out in the hall they sat on chairs meant for visitors and waited for their turn. Sid and Bob were working the kids to a crescendo, the sounds of laughter coming in waves that got bigger and bigger.

'Nothing can beat that sound, can it, Frances?' Jessie peered through a gap in the door. The children were sitting cross-legged on the floor, boys on one side, girls the other, teachers on chairs along the sides of the room. They were all laughing, some of them wiping away the tears from their eyes. She smiled, remembering how her father always told her that entertainment lifted people away from their problems and miseries, allowed them to forget how bad things were. She put her hand to her heart. Another Christmas without him. At least she remembered him, would always remember him. And they had Mum. She looked at the laughing faces, heard real belly laughs as Sid pretended to bash Bob over the head. They tumbled and rolled and sprang straight back up as if they had springs on their feet. It was as though they were made of rubber. Sid turned his back on Bob, who became squat, sticking his tongue out, putting his hands to his ears and wiggling his fingers. A little boy almost fell onto his friend, he was laughing so much.

'The kids are loving it.' Jessie let go of the door and sat down.

Frances was pacing up and down. 'I can hear.'

Jessie's smile disappeared. What an idiot she was. Frances was thinking of Imogen, wasn't she? It was the laughter. Frances sat down next to Jessie. 'Why don't you bring Imogen to Barkhouse Lane?'

'Don't, Jessie. Please.' Frances got up and resumed her pacing.

'I'm only thinking of you – and Imogen. You should be together. It would be easier.'

'Easier for who?' Frances stopped. 'I have to think about what's best for Imogen. That's my first, last and only thought.' She sat down again. Bob sounded a hooter and the children squealed with delight. 'Imogen is safe where she is. Settled. I don't know what I'm going to do after the panto.' She began wringing her hands. 'If I sign up with ENSA, it'll mean going away again and I'll have taken her away from Patsy for nothing. And she'll need to start school at some point.' She sighed. 'You wouldn't understand.'

Jessie was affronted. She folded her arms, staring at the entrance doors. The rain was coming down now, beating against the windows. 'How patronising.'

'I didn't mean it to be, Jessie.' She sighed again, more heavily this time. 'You can't possibly know how it feels.'

'Maybe not.' Jessie sat up. 'But I know what it is to miss a parent. One that you can never have back. I know I'm older, but it's still the same – we all want our parents.'

'We do.' They were silent. Thoughts tumbled in Jessie's head and she was shocked. Surely Frances had told her parents? She turned to Frances, who was looking at her, almost as if she knew what Jessie was going to ask next.

'They don't know,' Frances said. 'I couldn't go back to Ireland. It would break their hearts.'

'But it . . .'

Frances was shaking her head as if to deflect the words. 'Don't, Jessie. Please don't tell me how lovely it would all be. How the roses would be around the door, the sheep gambolling in the fields. It's not like that.'

'They write to you all the time. Your brothers, your sisters – do none of them know?'

Frances looked down the long dark corridor. 'No one.'

'But . . .'

Frances put up her hand to silence her. 'I'm not talking about it any more. We need to concentrate.'

Jessie sat on her hands and stared at the floor. She couldn't bear to think of Imogen without her mum. It had been bad enough leaving Grace in the summer – and she wasn't three years old.

It was a wonderful afternoon. The children were delightful; they listened when Jessie and Frances sang songs from the pantomime and then Jessie sat at the piano and encouraged the children to join in with Christmas carols. The sight of their happy faces as they sang 'Rudolph the Red-Nosed Reindeer' was one Jessie would never forget. What kind of Christmas would they have here? How lonely they must be and they were all so young. Frances was singing her heart out and Jessie wondered what was going through her mind.

Irene gave a lovely thank you speech at the end of the performance. She led the children in three cheers and the hoorays nearly lifted the roof off. They walked back into the office, applause ringing in their ears, and got changed. Bob sat in his vest and trousers, sweat still leaking from his chest and back, dripping down his temple.

'Beats the town hall any day of the week.'

There was no dissent.

Johnny left Ruby to sleep, asking Mrs Frame to make sure she ate something when she awoke. He took his heavy coat and hat from the stand in the hall and wrapped his plum cashmere scarf about his neck. The temperature had dropped these last few days and he pulled up his lapels, head down against the rain as he headed for the children's home. He took a shortcut through the park. It was empty, the lake still, no brightly coloured yachts, no wooden battleships patrolling today. Staying in Grimsby had made him fully aware of the battles that were already taking place. The army was heading south, but the boats and ships had already suffered losses. He didn't even want to contemplate how cold it must be in the North Atlantic. He turned onto Welholme Avenue. It was cold here but not as cold as New York. They had been there the Christmas after Mother had died and it should have been a triumph, but it had been bleak. Was that the start of it?

He crossed the road. A Christmas tree was set up in one of the bay windows, bright and cheerful. He should get a tree for the house, he thought, there might be decorations in the attic. He would ask Mrs Frame. It might cheer Ruby a little. He pushed his hands in his pockets, he had no idea what to do any more. The only thing that gave him any kind of hope was Frances – and she'd not been there today. He couldn't let her go, not a second time. The sky grew darker and he heard a distant rumble of thunder and quickened his pace. He stopped in front of the children's home, the rain running off the brim of his hat. Lights were on in the office and he pulled the front door open and walked into the lobby. Kids were being led out of a hall, a long line of boys looking straight ahead. Quiet. He knocked on the open door marked Office, saw Frances through the door leading to another room. She saw him, looked away. Jessie leant forward, said something to Frances he couldn't hear and came out to him. She was fastening the buttons on her coat.

'She'll be out in a minute.'

Irene came from the hall. She furrowed her brow. Johnny was used to the expression, the sudden recognition that they knew him but not from where. He held out his hand.

'Johnny Randolph. I'm a friend of the girls.'

'Of course. Would you like to sit down?'

He shook his head. 'I'll stand, if I'm not in the way.' He didn't want to have Frances slip past him. Jessie went back in, came out carrying cases.

'Can I help?'

She grinned. 'I wish you could.'

Bob and Sid followed, Frances lagging behind. 'Johnny.' Sid shook his hand with vigour.

'Good fun?' Johnny asked.

'It was. The kids were great. How was the town hall?'

'Not fun.' He looked at Frances. Bob stood close to her. Were they a couple? He couldn't tell. Not from Frances, but he guessed Bob would like it to be. Jessie stepped in.

'I'll take the bags to the bus stop, Frances, if you two need to talk.' Frances glowered at her but Johnny could have kissed the girl. At least she was on his side.

'Here, let me.' Bob took the case from her and the three of them made to leave. As they opened the door, Frances called out.

'I'll catch you up.'

'Thanks for staying,' he said, knowing it was under sufferance. God, it was exasperating and it wasn't as if it was his fault. There was no one to blame, was there? He couldn't fathom why she was so angry. Ruby was the same. He didn't understand women at all.

Frances shrugged. 'I didn't want to embarrass myself.'

He put his hands in his pockets to stop himself from reaching out and touching her.

'I thought you'd be at the town hall.'

'This was more important to me.' She wound her scarf around her neck and adjusted her beret. He waited while she put on her gloves.

'Frances, I know you're angry with me and you've every right to be if you thought I didn't reply to your letters.'

Irene was walking towards them.

'Not here.' Frances smiled at Irene. 'Thank you, Irene. It's been a wonderful afternoon.'

'It should be me thanking you. Although, as you said before, getting them to sleep later might be a challenge.'

Frances put the strap of her gas mask box over her shoulder and Irene returned to her office. He could hear her telling the secretary about the show. He wished he'd been there too – and not because of Frances. The town hall had been business and it was superficial, sometimes, glad-handing people, but these things were important all the same. Their reputation was hard-earned and he had to do what he could to maintain it. Frances started walking towards the door and he rushed ahead, held it open. She shivered as she stepped out into the air, pulling her scarf up about her face so that he could only see her eyes. Had she expected him to kiss her? She waited, watching the retreating backs of her friends as they headed for the bus station. The rain had steadied into drizzle and droplets fell softly; she dipped her head.

'Have supper with me.'

He touched her arm, as gently as he could, hoping, praying that she wouldn't draw away. She glanced up at him and he held her gaze, staring into her dark eyes. He loved her. But did she love him? He couldn't tell any more and it was infuriating. 'Please, Frances.' His breath swirled about him as he waited for her to answer.

'What about Ruby? She won't like it.' There was no hint of anger in her voice and for that he was grateful.

'It's not about Ruby, Frances. It's about *us*.'

'There *is* no us,' she said flatly. A bus drove past, its engine slurring as it slowed, the brakes squealing, exhaust fumes filling the air as it passed.

'But there was. And there can be again. I want it to be. Do you?'

She stared down at the pavement.

'Can we talk about it, at least?' He took hold of her gloved hand. 'Have dinner with me, tonight, after the show?' She withdrew her hand, put it in her pocket, looked up into his eyes. Could she see how much he loved her?

She nodded abruptly, then turned away, walking towards the bus stop. It felt as though his heart would burst and he hurried beside her. 'I'll call the theatre, send a car.'

'Will you?' She didn't believe him. Well, he'd prove her wrong. Something had happened, he didn't know what, but the only way to find out was to talk about it.

'The car will be there, I promise.' She waited at the kerb, looked both ways and crossed. Another bus went past, briefly obscuring her. He remained where he was as she joined the others and he watched them get on the bus, Bob and Sid taking the cases. They moved along the aisle, took seats. She was sitting by the window. He could make out Jessie nudging her, then Jessie waved. He took his hand from his pocket, held it up to her, turned around and headed home.

As the bus moved off, Frances pulled the scarf from her face. It had been so hot she could hardly breathe, but it had been a shield. Jessie tugged at her arm.

'Well, what did he say?' she whispered. Bob and Sid were sitting behind them.

'He asked me to supper.'

'That's good, isn't it?'

Frances didn't know. She rubbed at the window. There was nothing to see but shadows, sketchy outlines of people hurrying along the street. The bus braked and they lurched forward. Frances gripped the rail.

'Ruddy cyclists!' the conductor said. 'Sorry, folks.' The bus moved on and the conductor strode down the aisle to the front.

Jessie sat back. 'Please tell me you said yes?'

'I did.'

Jessie let out a long breath. 'Well, thank the Lord for that!'

Chapter 27

Ruby had slept for the rest of the afternoon. Mrs Frame had hovered around like a mother hen while she ate. She cleaned her plate and regretted it. Johnny came in.

'Where have you been?'

'To the children's home.'

'For the children?' She stared at him. Would he tell her the truth?

He sat down opposite her. 'To see Frances. I'm having supper with her tonight.'

Ruby was silent. Johnny was talking but she couldn't hear what he was saying. She shouldn't have eaten anything. She got up. Her stomach churned and she could feel the acid pumping into it, burning her insides.

'I need to get ready for the show.' She pushed back her chair, ran upstairs to the bathroom and locked the door. Her heart was pounding so hard that it hurt her chest and she knelt in front of the lavatory and stuck her fingers down her throat. The relief it offered was welcome and when it was over, she sat with her back to the cold tiles. The emptiness felt good and she remained there until she felt able to move, hauling herself up using the bath for support. She ran the cold water, cupping her hands to drink, splashing it over her face, then went to her room.

Despite everything, the show went well. She concentrated hard, feeling light, as if she was floating. The audience was warm and giving, and she felt loved, really loved. The applause was like a balm, soothing, nourishing, and she wished it could last forever. Johnny took the bows and they came back for three encores. He wasted no time getting changed.

'Jeff will call a car when you're ready to go home, Ruby.'

She sat in front of the mirror, listening but not comprehending. She watched his lips moving, his reflection in the mirror, agreeing, not knowing if it was the right thing to do. He splashed himself with cologne, leant down and kissed her cheek. She could see the excitement in his eyes and, for the briefest of moments, she hated him for being so happy. He put his hand on her shoulder, standing behind her, and she reached up and took hold of it. It was warm and strong and safe and she wanted him to stay. She thought of Grace, of her mother wanting her to be happy.

'I hope it goes well.'

He squeezed her hand. 'Thanks, Ruby. That means such a lot.' He adjusted his tie and reached for his coat then he held his hat in his hands, turning it by the brim. 'Are you sure you'll be all right?'

'Of course I will.' She blew him a kiss as he left.

She sat for a while. The room seemed bigger than normal and she listened to the footsteps as other members of the cast and crew called out as they left the theatre. She scrutinised her reflection. How ugly she was, inside and out. Reaching into her bag, she took out a half-bottle of gin and drank it back. It warmed her throat, then her stomach. She pulled a rag from the pile, taking off her face, her smile smearing against the white linen.

She rubbed and rubbed until the cloth was black and her skin was clear of its mask. Naked. Someone knocked on the door and she called for them to come in. Jeff put his head around the door.

'Old friend here to see you, Miss Randolph.' He stepped back – and Mickey Harper walked in, putting out his arms.

'Ruby, darling!' He came towards her, embraced her, and she tensed her body, trying to make it smaller, hold it away from his embrace. She smiled over his shoulder at Jeff, who was waiting by the door.

'Thanks, Jeff.' She pulled away from Mickey, hating the smell of him, the sight of him. 'How lovely to see you.' She gestured for him to sit down on the battered sofa. Jeff closed the door as he left and Mickey sat back, his legs spread wide. He looked about the room.

'Not your usual standard, eh, Ruby? How's it going?' She sank into her chair, her back to the mirror, fearing her hammering heart would break her ribs.

'What are you doing here?' She struggled to keep her voice steady, as if she didn't care.

He spread his arms along the back of the sofa. How dare he make himself comfortable!

'I waited till Johnny left. I don't think he likes me.' He checked his nails, picked at his thumb.

'I wonder why?'

Mickey titled his head, leering. 'He might not like you, either, if he knows what you've been up to.' She twisted away from him and began putting on fresh make-up.

'He won't find out.'

Mickey sat forward, let his hands hang between his legs. 'You've got the money, then?'

She patted powder on her nose. She mustn't let him see how scared she was.

'Almost.' She took out her lipstick, applied it. 'You'll just have to wait a little longer.' He got up and stood behind her, his hands on her shoulders, and she wanted to be sick.

'I can't wait, Ruby. It's cost me to come and find you and Christmas is coming.' He laughed, baring his teeth. 'Did you think you could run away and hide?' He shook his head. 'Tut, tut, tut, poor little Ruby!' He pulled an envelope from the inside pocket of his coat. It had Johnny's name on it. 'Pity he wasn't here to collect it himself. Perhaps tomorrow?' She snatched it from him and he shrugged his shoulders. 'Plenty more where they came from. Shame you haven't got the money. You could have had the negatives.' He fastened his coat. 'I'm at the Blenheim. Two days. Sweet dreams, gal.'

When she was certain he'd gone, she stumbled to her feet, ripped off her robe and got into her dress, shaking uncontrollably. She rummaged in her bag for the gin; emptied the bottle. Jeff would get more from the Palace Buffet next door. She sank back onto her chair. Her make-up was ruined and she reached for another cloth; there was nothing she could do but start again …

A car pulled up outside the hotel and the driver hurried round and opened the door for Frances. It was a far cry from earlier that day when they'd struggled on the bus to the children's home. She got out and walked towards the entrance, paused. She didn't have to go in, but she had to go forward. A liveried doorman opened the door and she hurried inside; he pulled the heavy curtain behind her. It was bright in the foyer and she blinked until she became accustomed to the light. On the right, a girl in uniform waited at the reception desk and Frances walked past her to the cloakroom, where she handed over her thick coat. The woman gave her a ticket, which she put in her bag. Her coat didn't need a ticket – it stood out against the furs and the expensive camel coats that hung in neat lines. She took a deep breath and walked to the dining room. It was fairly quiet – most of the diners would have eaten long ago and were either in bed or drinking at the bar – and she was glad. She gave her name to the man at the restaurant entrance and was led to a small booth. Johnny got to his feet.

'You came!' He seemed surprised. The waiter pulled out the chair and she sat down.

'You didn't think I would?' The waiter gave them a menu and she opened it, watching Johnny's face.

'I wasn't sure.'

She read the entrées. 'That I'd keep my word?'

He didn't answer, looked at the menu. He asked Frances what she'd like, ordered the wine, asked her opinion. He was so courteous. She'd forgotten. Or had she been so angry that she'd pushed it all away? The good memories lumped in with the bad. The waiter poured the wine, waited for Johnny to approve, then slipped into the background.

She looked about her, taking in the opulent surroundings. Other diners glanced discreetly in their direction. They would recognise Johnny. What were they thinking of her?

She felt cheap, her clothes not equal to the quality of her surroundings, and she shrank a little. He raised his glass and she did likewise. 'To the future,' he said. She clinked her glass to his but didn't say anything.

He put his glass down, touched his knife and fork. 'Who knows what kind of future that will be. For any of us.'

'Indeed.'

He was silent and she felt uncomfortable. He hesitated, opened his mouth to speak, stopped, started again. Eventually he said, 'Is there anyone else?'

She took a sip of her wine, which was rich and smooth on her throat. There would always be someone else, but that was not what he was asking.

'Bob?'

She laughed. 'No. No one else.' His shoulders softened, he gave her a gentle smile.

'And you?'

He toyed with his glass. 'There were girls, of course there were girls. I don't want to lie to you, Frances. I wouldn't. But no one special.' He paused, held her gaze. 'No one like you.'

He'd have to work harder, rolling out cheesy lines like that. She didn't want to be loved and left again; she wasn't sure she wanted to be loved at all. It hurt too much.

They talked and it got easier. She enjoyed his company and she'd missed it. He asked her what she'd been doing since they left and she told him parts, but not all. She asked of America. He told her of Ruby.

'Is that why you came back? I'd thought you'd been gallant and returned to fight for King and country.'

'Ouch!'

She was embarrassed, spoke quickly. 'I wasn't being rude. I couldn't think what else it could be. War has been on the cards for a long time and America's safe. For now, at least, and you were successful.'

'I intend to enlist.'

He looked ashamed and she hadn't meant to make him feel small.

'You don't have to explain.'

He wiped his mouth with his napkin. 'But I do. Mother died and Ruby took it badly. Very badly.' He paused. 'Well, you know Ruby.' His smile was sad. It had obviously been a painful time for them both. At least she still had both her parents and she could go back – one day …

'That's why we're here. Well, one of the reasons.' He gazed into her eyes. 'I've invested with Bernie and Jack; in theatres. Then, if the show flops or if Ruby gets worse, I can make sure she's looked after. If anything should happen to me …'

There was so much she wanted to say to him. Where could she start?

The waiter took the plates away and they ordered coffee. He sat back in his seat, smiling at her. It had been a wonderful evening; it all could have been different … She thought of the picture Imogen had drawn at Patsy's.

'Does Ruby know you're here with me?'

He took out his cigarettes, offered her one and she took it. 'She does. I told her. No more secrets.' He sparked his lighter, held it to her and she leant into the flame, then sat back.

'You're deep in thought,' he said.

She fiddled with her napkin on the table. How she wished she could turn back time! He leant forward and took her hand; she let him. It felt so good to touch his skin, to be so close, and she knew it would be easy to let down her guard, to let love in again. He was earnest and she couldn't think of anything to say, wanting to hold onto the moment with nothing of the past to spoil it.

'Marry me, Frances.'

She was taken aback, astonished that he could even think it.

'I asked you once before and you said yes. Things haven't changed.'

She tugged her hand away. '*I've* changed.'

He screwed his cigarette in the ashtray, looked beyond her. He was about to speak again but there was a disturbance in the foyer and heads turned. They could hear a woman's voice. Johnny got up.

'Ruby!' He scrambled to his feet as Ruby staggered in, swaying wildly. One of the female attendants was trying to talk to her but she swung out her arms, catching the woman on her cheek. Johnny rushed forward. Ruby's fur coat was falling from her shoulders and she hunched it up, losing her footing. Johnny caught her before she fell. Frances came up beside him, unsure of what to do. The pain in his face was unbearable.

'Oh, darling, Johnny.' Ruby's words were slurred and she was dribbling. Johnny hauled her upright and Frances moved forward and took her other side. 'Ha! I knew it was you.' She wiggled her finger at Frances. 'All along, I knew. He loves you. Did you tell her you love her, Johnny? Did he?' She went limp like a rag doll, her legs collapsing. People were coming into the lobby, collecting their coats, staring at the three of them.

'Let's get you home, Ruby,' Frances whispered quietly, soothingly, coaxing her like a child. Between them they managed to get her to a leather sofa and Frances sat with her, trying to quieten Ruby's incoherent ramblings while Johnny went to organise a car. He returned, grave-faced, and sat down beside his sister. Frances got up to claim her coat, pulled on her beret, stuffing her scarf in her pocket, and went back to them. Johnny was holding Ruby's hand, talking to her in a low voice, their faces close, and she realised then that it was all hopeless, that Ruby would always come between them.

The doorman came forward.

'The car's here, Mr Randolph.' Johnny put his hand in his pocket and tipped him. How could he think of it, at a time like this? He turned back and between them they helped Ruby to her feet. The girl behind the reception desk was trying to keep her head down but she caught Frances's eye and gave a small pitying smile. Frances sighed, linked her arm through Ruby's, and Johnny did the same, and together they walked her to the car, made sure she was safe inside it. She was sobbing, inconsolably.

'Forgive me, Johnny.' She was reaching out for his arm. 'I didn't know. I had no idea.' Her cheeks were stained with black rivers as her mascara ran. Johnny talked to her, his voice soft, soothing, stroking her face. He leant forward, asked the driver to wait and closed the door. Frances put on her scarf, her woollen gloves. The temperature had dropped and ice was forming on the windows. Johnny came to her, caught her arm.

'I'm so sorry, Frances. I can't let her go home alone.' It was embarrassing for him and she didn't want to make it worse.

'Ruby needs you. No need to apologise.' He took her hands and she looked down at her woollen gloves. His hands were mottled with cold. She looked into his eyes, his sadness evident, and she was surprised how much it hurt her. 'It's been a lovely evening, Johnny. Thank you.'

'It hasn't ended the way I wanted it to.' He glanced at the car, turned back to her.

'Take her home,' Frances urged. 'Look after her.' He let out a long sigh, as if he wanted to let go of a huge burden. He put his hand under Frances's chin, tilted her face towards him.

'I love you, Frances. I have always loved you.' He kissed her and his kisses were light, then fierce, and she gave in to him, the warmth of his body so familiar. It was as if time stopped and the years fell away in the darkness and she longed to stay there, not thinking, only feeling, never wanting it to end. Another car drew up beside them and Johnny released her, kissed her again, briefly this time, the longing clear, and she bit her lip to stop herself from wanting more. Johnny stepped back, moved towards the car and opened the door. She got in and he closed the door. She wound down the window and he caught her hand again. 'I won't let you go. Not a second time.' He leant in, kissed her again – and for one wild moment she believed him.

The driver helped Johnny get Ruby into the house. He turned on the gas fire, pulled the easy chair close to it and sat Ruby in it. She was incoherent, babbling then terrified, sobbing, wailing. She'd never been as bad as this, never. When she had calmed, he laid her on the sofa and covered her with a blanket, propping her head with cushions.

'You won't let him hurt me, will you?'

He put his hand on her head. 'No one will hurt you, Ruby. I'm here.' She caught his hand. Her nails dug into him.

'I haven't got the money.'

'What money? Ruby, what money? For who?' He wanted to be angry with her, but he couldn't. It was his fault she'd got this bad. He should have bought them out of the contract, come home.

'Don't let Mickey get me. Please. Don't let him.' She was confused. It was the drink. Why else would she say such things?

He stroked her forehead; she was sweating now, her hair damp, and he sat down beside her. 'Mickey's not here, Ruby. You're quite safe.' He kissed her temple. Their mother had done the same when they were small. If only she were here. Ruby seemed to settle as he held her hand, crooning to her, hoping to be of comfort.

'Oh, Johnny,' she whispered. 'I'm sorry. Truly, I am.'

At last she slept and he sat on the floor, his back against the sofa, watching the flames in the fire. Things had been going so well, Frances had been like her old self – the girl he remembered, the girl he loved, had always loved. He was sure she loved him still. If Ruby hadn't come in when she did would Frances have said yes? His proposal had taken him by surprise, but being her with her, after all the years of loneliness, made everything else seem small and insignificant. Ruby moaned and he reached up and took her hand in his. In the morning she would be sober and he would find out exactly what she was frightened of.

Chapter 28

Jessie clasped Harry's hand as they walked along the promenade. He looked so smart in his uniform, his dark blue overcoat belted against the wind. He'd arrived late last night and they had talked into the small hours. Neither of them had slept much – although Harry was in dire need of it.

He leant on the rails. Barbed wire lay in coiled spirals along the sand and the steps were barred with wooden planks, warning signs forbidding them from going any further. Gulls pecked for worms in the sand. The tide was out, way out, but the day was clear and they could see the lighthouse at Spurn Point on the other side of the river.

'It's a far cry from summer, isn't it?'

'A world away, darling.' She moved closer to him, making her teeth chatter with exaggeration. He nudged her and she laughed and kissed him. He was so glad she was his girl. They started walking again and he put his arm about her shoulder. She leant into him, happy to be close, and they made their way down towards the pier, taking in the long walkway that seemed to stretch over the sea. 'Remember when we danced on it, Harry?'

He nodded. 'We were supposed to be dancing in the ballroom, not on the walkway.'

'It was fun though, wasn't it?'

'It was.' And so different from the way he spent his days now. Being up in the air was exhilarating; it still took his breath away, to soar above the fields and towns, the land that he loved, the land they were fighting for. But Jessie

– she was his whole world. He pulled her towards him again. Seagulls soared high above them.

'It seems such a long time ago, Harry, and it isn't. Not really.' She sounded wistful. He moved his arm, took her hand in his. It seemed like a lifetime. All he had worried about then was Jessie – did she love him or would she fall for someone else's charms? He knew now that he'd been wrong to doubt her and it was a comfort. There was far worse to worry about these days. Like staying alive. She smiled and it made him forget.

'Shall we catch the bus then? Or keep on walking down memory lane?'

He kissed her nose, grinning.

'What?'

'Your nose. It's like kissing ice.'

'Better warm me up then.' They stopped and he pulled her to him. She wrapped her arms about his waist and he touched her face; her eyes were sparkling, her ears as red as her nose. If only it could still be summer … He kissed her, their lips warm. A car tooted as it passed them and they both smiled, still kissing. He pulled away, took her hands.

'We're wasting time.' He put his arm back around her.

'I like wasting time that way,' she said, resting her hand on his chest. 'Don't you?'

'I do, but we've a ring to buy. I have no idea how long it will take you to make up your mind.'

She batted her hand on him, laughing. 'I'm getting much better at it.'

'Glory be! Wonders never cease!'

The bus was full and they made their way to the back, delighted to find an empty seat. She sat by the window, pointing things out to him as they headed for Grimsby – the football ground, the cinemas and theatres along the route, the Globe, and the Palace where she told him the Randolphs were appearing. When they reached the town hall they got off and walked along Victoria Street, looking in the windows, holding hands. They stopped outside a jeweller that had its name across every window in gold lettering: A. C. Pailthorpes. He studied Jessie's reflection in the glass as she pointed to rings, her eyes shining, wanting to burn her happiness into his heart so that he could carry it with him. Sprigs of holly and ivy were placed among the display and glass baubles in bright colours sat amid swathes of gold satin that wound about the trays of diamond rings.

'It looks a little like Aladdin's cave, Harry. Do you think I'll get three wishes?'

He kissed her again, laughing. 'I only want one.'

He guided her inside and she gripped his hand, her excitement palpable. He couldn't stop smiling at her delight as the cases were brought from the window and she tried rings on. She held out her hands, tilting to let the stones catch the light, asking for his opinion. He liked them all – because they were on her finger and she wanted him. Only him.

They settled for one with three diamonds. It fitted perfectly. He put it on her finger and she kissed him. 'Happy?'

Jessie stretched out her arm, splaying her fingers, admiring the ring. 'Deliriously.' She bobbed up and down on her toes with excitement.

'You don't want to change your mind?' He took out his wallet.

She shook her head. 'About the ring?'

He grinned. 'Or me?'

She kissed him again. 'Never. I've wasted too much time already, darling Harry.'

Jessie left her gloves off, wanting to keep looking at her diamonds. He laughed. 'I'm glad I made you happy, Jessie. It means everything to me. *You* mean everything to me.'

She linked her arm in his as they left the shop. 'I never knew just how much.'

Jessie led him down an alley between the jewellers and the bank and stepped into a café, tucked away from the main street. A waitress led them to a table and they sat down and removed their coats, Jessie taking every opportunity to admire her ring, then look at him. He adored her. They gave their order and he took her hand in his to get her attention, covering the ring so that she looked at him.

'So, what's been happening? The show good?'

'Fun. The kids are great and I get to act. Although I have to kiss Kitty Bright on the cheek every night and marry her.'

He laughed. 'As long as it's only pretend. It will be our turn soon. For real.' The waitress brought their order and they tucked in. She asked about his work and he told her as much as he could, as much as he dared. 'We've been night flying.'

She frowned. 'It's dangerous. I can tell from your face.'

'It's all dangerous, Jessie. You have to pay attention. Or . . .'

'Or what?' She gripped his hand. 'I want to know. Good and bad.'

He explained about having to rely solely on instruments, that you couldn't use the landscape for markers, that it was cold and tiring, made your eyes sore, your brain hurt. 'But I'm good at it, Jessie. Don't worry, darling. All those hours cooped up in the solicitor's office at your Uncle Norman's has stood me in good stead. My powers of concentration are immense, thanks to him.' It didn't comfort her, he knew it wouldn't, but he couldn't make out it was all a bit of a lark. It was war and he'd already lost friends. Mistakes, careless mistakes, a lapse in concentration, an idle thought . . . He wanted to talk about something else. 'Ginny looks well. Happier. She's over Billy? And that other stuff?'

Jessie looked about her, leant forward. ‘I wasn’t meant to tell.’

He leant into her. ‘Don’t worry, I won’t tell a soul.’ He took her hand, holding it. The diamonds caught the light and she grinned, then was suddenly sombre. ‘What?’ He was confused.

‘I hate secrets. And I don’t like having secrets from you, Harry. It’s not right. But . . .’ She drained her cup. ‘Shall we walk back to the bus? I don’t feel we can talk in here.’ He paid the bill and picked up his cap. He held the door for her and once again she linked her arms in his, this time resting her hand on his arm, wiggling her fingers. He kissed her temple and she told him about Frances. ‘Please don’t say I told you, Harry. No one else knows, not Mum, Geraldine – no one. It’s been such a burden. I have no idea how Frances managed all these years.’

Frances was making up the fire in the bar when Johnny walked in. Ben and Fred were playing dominoes at their table by the window; they looked up briefly when he entered then resumed their game. She raked the coals, put another offcut of timber and a few lumps of coal on. The wood spat and crackled as the flames took hold. Fudge was sitting on his usual seat, his head turned towards the heat, and she ruffled his head. Johnny walked towards her, sombre in his dark overcoat. He didn’t look as if he had slept. She went behind the bar and rinsed her hands at the sink below the counter, dried them on a towel. He took off his hat and placed it on the bar.

‘I came to apologise.’

‘You have nothing to apologise for.’

Lil stuck her head around the door that led to her backroom.

‘Are you all right, lovey?’

She turned to her. 'I am, Lil.' Lil went back in her room. The landlady had been suffering from a cold and Frances had told her to rest, saying she'd call if she needed her.

'How is Ruby?'

He blew out a breath. 'Can I have a drink first?'

'That's what I'm here for.' She got him a whisky.

'Far too early in the day, really.' He sipped at it, put the glass down and stared into it.

'That bad, eh?'

He looked up. 'Worse. Ruby is being blackmailed.' He lowered his voice and told her all he knew. 'I got it out of her this morning and had to get the doctor in the end. When she sobered up, she was hysterical.'

Frances leant in close to him. 'You haven't left her alone?'

'No, we have a housekeeper, Mrs Frame, who's old but tough – you know the type.'

Frances grinned. 'I do. She sounds like Lil. The landlady here.'

Ted came in with a tray of pies and she took them from him, signed the chit and carried them through the back way. She returned with some of them arranged on a plate and placed them on the counter. Johnny was rolling his glass around, staring into it. She watched him, understanding how lonely he must be, for all his fame and money. He was no different from Artie, God bless him, or Big Malc or any of the other men who came through the doors of the Fisherman's Arms, looking for company. She asked him what he was going to do.

'Pay him. What else can I do?'

She leant on the counter and he leant in towards her; she didn't move away. 'It doesn't seem right, to let him get away with it.'

Lil walked in, blew her nose, stuffed her hanky up her sleeve. 'Who's getting away with what?' She narrowed her eyes. 'Johnny Randolph?' She looked at Frances, raised her eyebrows. Frances did the same. Lil leant on the beer pump, one hand on her hip.

'You can trust Lil,' Frances said. 'She won't tell a soul. Will you, Lil?'

'My lips are sealed,' she said and Johnny told her. 'Well, the ruddy snake!' She smacked her hand on the counter. The domino players glanced in their direction. No one liked to upset Lil. 'Franny's right. You can't let the bugger get away with it.'

The door opened and Jessie walked in with Harry. They were holding hands as they came to the bar and Frances was glad that Jessie was bringing some happiness with her. Jessie reached her hand over the counter and Frances took hold of it; her fingers were freezing but Frances totally understood why she'd removed her gloves. She admired the ring, then Lil took over: 'Lucky girl!'

'I'm the lucky one.' Harry put his arm about his beloved and she snuggled into him, her face beaming. He glanced around the pub. 'Drinks all round to celebrate my good fortune!' The chaps playing dominoes voiced their thanks and, as Lil poured, Harry took their drinks over to them and stayed and chatted a while. Jessie looked at Johnny, flashed him a smile and leant across the bar to talk to Frances.

'I didn't get chance to talk to you last night and we were out early this morning.' She grinned at Johnny then back at Frances. 'It obviously went well?'

Frances pursed her lips.

'Oh.' She reddened. 'Have I put my foot in it? I saw you and Johnny and thought, well . . .' Her voice trailed off. 'Me and my big mouth.'

Johnny pulled up a bar stool and settled himself on it. He looked truly miserable. Defeated, Frances supposed, and she didn't think it was about the money or the photographs. It was the damage Ruby was doing to herself that was hurting him most.

'I'll tell you about last night later,' Frances said and glanced at Johnny, 'but it's up to Johnny what else gets told.'

His tale was punctuated by Jessie's angry outbursts. 'How could anyone do that! It's *wicked*?'

'There are wicked people everywhere, Jessie. We can't always tell them from the good guys.'

Harry had come back and stood next to Jessie, listening.

'You can't pay him.' Harry said. 'It's blackmail and that's illegal.'

'If I involve the police it will make it a huge scandal. I'd rather pay him off and keep him quiet.' Johnny took a swig from his glass.

'And let him get away with it?' Jessie was shocked.

'To protect my sister, yes. I'm not thinking of him.'

The door opened and Ginny walked in, followed by Joe. They made a space for them at the bar and Jessie quickly brought them up to speed with the conversation.

'Surely between us we can do something to help?' Harry said and Jessie looked at him, adoringly. It made Frances smile. Harry was Jessie's hero and she hoped he would never let her friend down.

Joe and Ginny got their drinks and went to sit down by the fire. Jessie and Harry joined them and when Joe moved up the banquette, Fudge growled.

Lil shouted across to them, 'You can't sit there. That's where Artie used to sit. Fudge still thinks he's gonna come back one day. He might be a little dog but his bite's sharp enough if you upset him.' She took over in the bar, urging Frances and Johnny to sit among their friends.

'But you're not well, Lil.'

She shrugged it off. 'I'm right as ninepence. I'll only sit back there feeling sorry for meself. Get out there with your mates for half an hour.' Lil winked at Johnny, who waited until Frances had come from behind the bar then walked with her to where the others were sitting. They dragged more stools over and Jessie and Harry made room for them. Harry slapped Johnny on the shoulder.

'We're trying to find a way to help. We can't let that scum get away with it.'

'Can't you do something, Joe?' Ginny asked. 'With all your magic.'

'It's not magic. It's misdirection.'

Harry leant in close. 'Sounds exactly what we need.'

Frances went back behind the bar, not wanting to take advantage of Lil's generosity. It had been good to sit there, with her friends, with Johnny.

'You make a lovely couple,' Lil said. 'He clearly adores you. He's got all that worry and the only thing that keeps him going is looking at you.'

'Don't, Lil.'

Lil touched her arm. 'Life's short, lovey. You might not get another chance. He seems a nice boy. And he obviously loves his sister.'

'He does.' Frances watched him. He shook hands with Harry and Pete across the table and came back to the bar.

'By, lad.' Lil sneezed and rubbed her nose. 'You look better than you did when you walked in.'

'I didn't know I had friends then.' He pulled the bar stool across and sat down. 'And I didn't have a plan. Now I do.'

He filled Lil and Frances in on the details.

'That's everyone in agreement, then. And you're sure you don't mind us using the pub, Lil?'

She shook her head. 'I'll bat him round the lughole meself, if I get chance.'

Johnny laughed. 'Then it's all down to Ruby. Let's hope she's able to hold her nerve.'

Chapter 29

Ruby sat on a stool opposite the fire, her back to the door. Lil was behind the bar, polishing glasses, overseeing her empire. Harry sat on the banquette seat, his arm round Jessie, and Joe was playing dominoes with Ben and Fred, the perfect spot in which to observe his prey. Big Malc had been recruited in case they needed a bit of muscle and he was chatting to Lil at the bar. It all looked so normal. Frances left them talking and went through the door to the backroom, leaving it ajar so she could hear what was happening. Johnny was sitting at the small table and Fudge was laid out in front of the gas fire.

'How's Ruby?' He was strained. It had been hard convincing him that they could pull it off, but Harry had said that it was worth a try. And why give in to bullies? Wasn't that what their country was fighting for?

'She looks OK and I think she'll be fine. It's easier when you know you have friends.'

He cleared his throat. 'We don't deserve this, not me anyway. I barely know any of you.'

'But it's the right thing to do, Johnny. Too much thinking and not enough doing doesn't get you anywhere.'

'When did you get so wise?' It wasn't really a question, but she wouldn't have answered it anyway. It would have taken too long and they needed to concentrate on pulling this off. They'd had a practice run-through before the pub opened, making sure everyone knew exactly what was expected of them. It was the oddest rehearsal she'd ever done. She heard the pub door open, then Lil coughed and spluttered, blew her nose like a raspberry. 'That means he's in.' He got up and took her hand.

'Thank you, Frances. For helping.'

'Isn't that what friends are for?'

'More than friends, I hope.' She didn't answer but picked up the dog lead.

'Ready for your starring role, Fudge?' she whispered as she fastened it to his collar. As she stood up, Johnny came close, kissed her on the lips, touched her hand.

'Break a leg.'

She pulled away. 'I'll do my best not to.'

Mickey Harper was wearing a black wool coat and he slid onto the banquette seat opposite Ruby without removing it. The fire was roaring in the grate, giving out a fierce heat. Her own coat was draped over the other stool, her bag underneath.

'Why, that coat makes you look almost respectable, Mickey,' she said.

He smirked. 'That's what success does for you, Ruby. And you should know. You can dress things up how you like, but underneath we're all the same, aren't we?'

She didn't comment, only watched as he settled himself, removed his hat and gloves.

'Nice little place.' He leant forward. 'Quiet.' He sat back. 'Going to get meself something like this back in town. A pension for me old age.'

'When you've run out of women to prey on?'

'Now, now, Ruby! That's not the attitude, is it? It's not my fault if you like a drink or two.'

'No, but it's your fault for taking advantage.' She gritted her teeth to stop them chattering. The heat from the fire was hot on her face and she wanted to move her chair but couldn't. Joe had to have a clear view. 'How did you get those photos?'

'A friend of mine. Lots of rich little girlies know how to party so there's a room at the back of the club. Oh yes, we've got a nice little thing going.' He leant forward again and she wanted to push him into the fire. 'You're not the first, Ruby. And you won't be the last.' He sat back.

'Where are the negatives?' She still doubted whether he had them with him. He enjoyed the control he had over her, liked the power. Would he really relinquish it? She was beginning to tremble, but she took a deep breath and steeled herself. She must carry on; must remember that she wasn't alone. Not any more. She could almost sense the kindness of the other people in the pub, protecting her, and yet she hardly knew them. Or they her. Why were they helping, especially Frances? She didn't owe her anything. Quite the opposite. She mustn't let her mind wander, she must concentrate.

Mickey leant forward. 'Have you got the money?' She reached into her bag, showed him the thick envelope. He reached out to take it, but she held it tight, opening the flap to show they were real notes, then replaced them inside her bag.

'You can have it when I've actually *seen* the negatives.'

He pulled an envelope from his inside pocket and she relaxed a little. Joe would have seen clearly which side it was. Her heart started beating a little faster and she held out her hand.

'I want to check they're the right ones.'

He raised his eyebrows. 'I'm impressed. Didn't have you down as being that smart.' He took out one strip of negatives and showed it to her. She held it against the light of the fire and wanted to be sick. She handed it back and he put it in the envelope with the others.

'I've learnt a lot because of you, Mickey. Or should I say, *thanks* to you. Because it's a business transaction at the end of the day.'

He was smug. 'That's the way to look at these things, Ruby. Business.' They swapped the envelopes, Ruby putting hers into her bag, he slipping his into his pocket. It made her feel a little calmer. She had the negatives, so they were halfway home – and she was surrounded by friends. It gave her courage.

'Shall we have a drink on it? Isn't that what you do when you complete a deal, Mickey?'

'I like your style, Ruby.' He got to his feet. She had clearly surprised him, as had been her intention. 'What are you having?'

'Port and lemon.'

He went to the bar and Ruby heard Lil deliver her line perfectly. 'You're not from round here, are ya?'

'Here on a bit o' business.'

'Oh, aye? What can I get you and your good lady?' He gave his order and Lil got it for him. He returned to his seat, a drink in each hand, and was about to sit down when the door opened and Frances walked in and let go of Fudge's lead. He bounded over to Mickey, barking, then biting at his ankles. Mickey's beer slopped over the glass and all over him so that his coat was covered in best bitter. Oh, the satisfaction it gave her.

'Ruddy dog! That's me new coat. Look at it!' He raised his fist. 'Why you little—' Ruby got up, knocking over her stool, and as Jessie rushed towards the bar, Lil threw her a cloth.

Harry stepped forward. 'Can I help?'

Frances fussed around, pretending to grasp for Fudge's lead, calling sorry, the dog jumping up and down, barking furiously. Jessie rubbed at Mickey's coat and Joe got up and took the cloth from her, patting it harder, apologising to Mickey as he did so.

'It'll take more than a tea towel to sort this mess out, sir.'

It was pandemonium and Mickey had had enough. Ruby threw back her head and began to laugh. It made him furious. Joe went back to the dominoes.

'You can wipe that smile off your face, you little trollop!'

It made her laugh even more; she was hysterical with the tension of it all. Big Malc turned from the bar and stood next to her.

'Is this man bothering you, miss?'

'He was.' She fought to control herself. 'But he isn't any more.' She stood as tall as she could, though her legs felt hollow. Mickey pulled his coat about him and strode towards the door, swearing under his breath. He left it open, letting the cold air rush in, and Fudge lifted his head and whimpered. Joe got up and closed it, then walked towards the fire and rubbed his hand over Fudge's back.

'Good dog. There's a *very* good dog.'

Johnny came from behind the bar and hugged his sister. Jessie was behind him and she picked up the stool that had fallen over and Johnny sat Ruby down on it. His hands were firm and she felt safe. She hadn't felt that way in a long time. She was trembling all over, her teeth chattering, and she was suddenly cold despite the fire so close. Frances fussed over Fudge and he jumped up and sat in his place. He put his head between his paws and stared at her, his little chocolate brown eyes bright and it was all too much. Ruby burst into tears and Frances crouched down beside her.

'It's all over now, Ruby. All over.' Jessie produced a handkerchief and Ruby wiped at her eyes. Johnny took the negatives from the envelope and threw them into the fire. Ruby watched as they curled and twisted in the heat. How could so little do so much damage?

Ginny dashed over to Joe and kissed him. He was clearly taken aback and Frances hid her smile. 'The hero of the hour!' It was Joe's turn to blush. He took a brown envelope from under the table and gave it to Johnny.

Johnny pulled out the notes.

'When do you think he'll realise that he's gone home with a wad of newspaper, Joe?'

Joe put his hand in his pocket. 'Probably about the same time as he goes to look at his watch.' Joe held up a wrist-watch and they all burst into laughter.

Harry got the drinks in and they waited to see if Mickey would return. He didn't.

'That sent him off with a flea in his ear,' Lil said, triumphant. 'You kids did a grand job.'

Frances brought them mugs of tea from the backroom and Ruby stared into the flames. There was no trace of the negatives, not one shred. The boys got up and stood at the bar. Frances was chatting with Jessie and Ginny was sitting with the shy magician, whose sleight of hand had made sure that they didn't lose their money. She owed them so much, especially Frances. She had wronged her all those years ago and had no idea how she would ever make it up to her. But she would try. Johnny came over, put a hand on her back.

'Feeling better, Ruby?'

She touched his hand. 'I feel so tired, Johnny. Dreadfully tired.'

'It's the shock,' Frances said, kindly. 'You'll probably be tired for a few days. But it will get better. You'll feel like the sun has come out, even if it is the middle of winter.'

Tears rolled down the girl's cheeks when she'd thought she had no tears left. It reminded her of what Grace had said. *And then the sunshine*. Could she ever see the sunshine again? Feel its warmth?

'I don't know how to thank you, Frances. You and your friends. I don't deserve it.'

Frances took her hand in hers, wrapping her own around it. 'It's got nothing to do with deserving things, Ruby. No one should be treated that way.' She smiled. 'Look on it as an early Christmas present.'

She was dreading Christmas. There was no magic any more. 'I was mean to you.' The words caught in her throat, but she had to say something, make a start. One small step at a time. 'When we were in London.'

'It's in the past, Ruby. Leave it where it belongs.'

Ruby closed her eyes. If only it were that easy.

Chapter 30

The girls were sitting at their table in the window of Joyce's café, waiting for Jessie to join them. She was red-eyed when she did.

'He's gone?' Dolly moved up a chair so that Jessie could sit down.

She nodded, tears starting again. 'I've never been this scared for him. I think it was better when I didn't know anything. I can't stop thinking about him, up in the air, in the dark.' She closed her eyes. 'I only ever thought of him soaring in the blue, between the clouds, like the seagulls, free as a bird.' Tears rolled down her cheeks as she took off her coat and hung it over the back of the chair.

What could any of them say to comfort her? He'll be safe, He'll be back soon? None of them knew, did they, not for sure, how the days would pan out. Jessie sat down and Dolly rubbed at Jessie's arm to comfort her.

'You have to keep thinking good thoughts, Jessie. Imagine him safe, coming back to you. Don't let the bad thoughts win.'

It was good advice for anyone. How many times had she thought the worst when times were hard? Dolly understood more than anyone. She was in the same boat as Jessie – or Pete was. Out on the water, God knows where. And Colin too. Out in the dark and the ice and no warmth, no family to comfort them. How did Patsy cope, and all the women like her? Frances got up and went to the counter. Joyce was reading the *Grimsby Telegraph*.

'By, them buggers are rum 'un's!' She was poking at the paper with her forefinger.

'What buggers might they be?'

Joyce let the paper drop and Frances saw the headlines: another ship lost with all hands. Joyce shook her head in despair.

'What can I get you, lass?'

'Another tea and four teacakes please, Joyce. We're in need of something sweet.' Joyce looked over to the table. 'Harry's gone back to his squadron.'

Joyce sighed. 'Poor lamb. By, it's hard on you young 'uns.' She picked up a teapot and held it under the hot water urn. 'I never thought we'd have these times again. Not after the Great War, but here we are. Broken hearts.' Her eyes watered and she sniffed. 'Reckon I've got a ruddy cold coming.' She rubbed at her nose with the back of her sleeve and turned her back in the pretence of needing something from the kitchen. She came back empty-handed and began slicing through the teacakes. 'Pop back to your friends, Frances. I'll sing out when they're ready.'

Jessie had dried her tears when Frances returned, although they shimmered near the surface, ready to fall again. She hated being so impotent. Bad thoughts had a habit of coming to the surface all too often these days.

'Let's have another look at that beautiful ring of yours, Jessie. I didn't really get chance, earlier.' Jessie held out her hand and Frances took it. 'How lovely it is, Jessie. Did you set a date?' Could she help her to think of happy things? Jessie shook her head.

'It all depends on his leave. But if we make a start, get things in place, we can get married any time, can't we?' She leant forward, admiring her ring as the diamonds caught the light. 'It's not what I'd dreamt of. I always thought I'd have a church wedding, but I don't care about the dreams any more. I just want to be Mrs Harry Newman.' Her voice faltered.

'A change of plans, that's all it is, Jessie,' Frances said, hoping to comfort her. 'A change of plans.'

Joyce brought over a tray with the tea and teacakes on it, which she put down on the table next to them. Ginny put her hands up to take the cups as Joyce passed them over. She placed the teacakes in the centre of the table.

'Chin up, you lasses. The lads need to see your smiling faces, not your tears.' She put her hand on Frances's shoulder. 'I know it's hard, ducky, but you've got to be strong like they're having to be strong.' A lump formed in Frances's throat. She thought of Pete out on the minesweepers. He was only eighteen. But Dolly smiled and seemed to lift herself.

'You're right, Joyce. Us sitting here worrying doesn't help anything, does it?'

'No, it doesn't, sweetheart. We've got to make sure everything keeps ticking along just as it always has, make sure they've got something worth coming home for.'

Jessie took out her hanky and dabbed at her eyes. 'Forgive me, Joyce. You're absolutely right.' She sipped at her tea and though tears brimmed on her lower lashes, she kept smiling. They would *all* keep smiling.

'That's the ticket, girls.' She held the empty tray to her chest. 'I hear you're doing a special show for the lads and lasses in the forces on Christmas Day?'

Frances stirred the pot then poured the tea. 'We are.' She'd been looking forward to spending the day with Imogen and it had been a blow, initially. But she counted her blessings. Those boys in the audience were someone's children, someone's father, brother, all of them far away from home. It was the very least any of them could do.

'I think it's wonderful. And I want to help. So, Vi and I are going to cook Christmas dinner for you all after the curtain comes down. We've all got to do our bit to keep up morale, haven't we? And well, that's my little bit.'

Jessie got up and hugged her. 'You've got a heart of gold, Joyce.' Joyce wriggled, uncomfortable with Jessie's show of affection, and Frances smiled. Jessie either didn't notice or didn't care. Her emotions were all up front and Frances loved her for it.

'I know you've got your mam here, Jessie, but I was thinking of you lasses and the rest of the cast. None of you will be able to go home till the New Year.' She turned and went back to the counter.

They stayed until it was time to go back to the Empire. Dolly waited at the door.

'I'll pop and tell Mam about Christmas Day. She'll want to help. See you in the theatre.' She hurried down the street and disappeared into one of the terraced houses.

'I wished I hadn't blubbed.' Jessie rubbed her hands. 'Dolly's bloke has been out on those minesweepers for months.' Frances didn't mention the newspaper headline.

'I'm sure Dolly sheds a tear or two, but she has her mammy and her daddy close by, and her sisters too.' She linked her arms in Ginny's and Jessie's. 'And we've got each other. We're lucky. Some people don't have anyone.'

George was settled in his chair in his small office at the stage door, reading the paper when they walked in. He let it drop and got up, handing them their keys and their mail. Ginny hurried downstairs.

'It's good to see her happy again, isn't it?' Jessie said.

'It is,' Frances agreed. There was a letter from her parents, a postcard from her brother. More Christmas cards. She put them in her bag. 'It's nice to think she found some magic at last.'

Jessie laughed. 'We all need a little bit of magic in our lives.'

In the dressing room Frances dropped her bag on the table in front of her chair and put her hands on the radiator. It was scarcely warm enough to make much difference. 'Sometimes I wish I had a magic wand, or a magic lamp. I could make everything all right. For everyone.' She looked at Frances through the mirror.

'Or three wishes, Jessie?'

'I'd need more than that to put the world to rights, wouldn't I?' She took off her coat and hung it up on the back of the door alongside Frances's. Her eyes were still red, matching her nose. Thank God they had plenty of make-up!

Jessie sat down in front of the mirror. There was plenty of time before they needed to get ready. 'It's good of Joyce to do Christmas Dinner, isn't it? I'm glad we're doing a show because Harry won't get leave, and Dolly's Pete might still be away. At least Ginny will have Joe – and you will have Johnny.'

'Nice try.' Frances took off her dress and pulled on a thick dressing gown she'd brought from home before sitting down and brushing her hair away from her face, twisting it in a knot at the back of her head. 'The Palace is doing a show for the troops as well, at six o clock, so everything will clash. If we do see each other, it will be brief.'

Jessie hesitated, then said, 'I know you think I'm nagging, Frances.'

'That's because you are, Jessie dear.' She was irritated but didn't want to show it. Jessie was still upset about Harry and searching for happy endings.

But Jessie wasn't to be distracted. 'Time's running out. Johnny'll be gone again soon.'

'It's been so rushed; all the drama with Ruby hasn't helped.' She took out her post and ran her thumb through the envelope, withdrew a card. 'I can't bring Imogen into a life like that. It's not fair.'

'You'll run out of excuses, Frances. Best to get it over and done with. Think how wonderful Christmas will be.'

Frances ignored her and began applying her foundation with a sponge. Ginny opened the door but didn't come in. The girls turned to her. She looked worried.

'There's a call for you, Frances. Someone called Patsy. George says she sounds distressed.' Frances flung down her greasepaint and ran down the corridor, barging past Kitty, who was leaning against Don's open door. Frances heard her shout, 'Manners!' as she pounded up the stairs to the phone. There was no time to apologise. It must be serious if Patsy had called the theatre. George held out the phone and she pressed it to her ear. Jessie came up and stood beside her, her face wreathed with concern.

'Patsy?' It was difficult to hear above the babble the babes were making as they made their way to the dressing rooms and Jessie told them to shush. Frances turned her back and stuck her finger in her ear to block out the noise.

'Oh, God, Frances!' Patsy's voice was tight. 'It's Imogen. And Colly.'

'What?' Her heart was pummelling in her ribcage. 'What's wrong, Patsy, are they ill? Have they been in an accident?' Her mind was racing, the blood thrumming in her ears. *Not Imogen, please, not Imogen . . .*

'Th-they're missing.' Patsy's voice faltered. 'I th-think they've come to you.' She explained that she'd found Colly's money box empty on the bed. 'I can't find their coats and outdoor clothes.' She could tell that Patsy was trying to stay calm but there was the unmistakable tremor of fear in her voice. Jessie was beside her and Ginny had come, Joe too. George moved people away. 'Mrs Bramley said she saw them waiting at the bus stop.'

Frances let the phone drop.

'What is it, Frances? What's wrong?' Jessie's voice was getting higher. Why were *they* here in the light and the warmth? It was so cold outside. And so dark. Jessie shook her and it moved her to action. 'It's Imogen. Patsy thinks she might be coming here.'

Ginny frowned. 'Who's Imogen?' It was an innocent enough question, but it sounded damning now. It was her own fault. She made for the door, tugged at the handle but Jessie stopped her.

'Think first, Frances. You need help. Us, your friends.' Frances let her arms fall. Jessie was right. She turned to face the people who had gathered in the lobby. Her friends. Friends she had deceived. She looked to Ginny.

'Imogen is my daughter.' Her voice faltered and she cleared her throat. Tears were pricking in her eyes and she blinked them back. This was no time to be weak. Imogen needed her. She quickly relayed what Patsy had told her. 'Imogen and Colly, Patsy's boy, came to the panto. Imogen was obsessed with it, the princess and the jewels, the colour, the pretty lights.'

'How old are they?' Joe asked. He stood head and shoulders above them all, and Bob and Sid crowded about her, Basil and Kitty, Don Roper, with his red nose . . . She wanted to laugh but her heart was hammering. Dear God, let them be safe. 'Imogen is three.' Her voice broke and she balled her fists. 'Colly's almost six.' Joe took charge.

'Ginny, go to front of house and alert them. What do they look like?'

Jessie came forward. 'Imogen looks like a small version of Frances, dark hair, dark eyes. Colly's got sand-coloured hair. They're about this tall.' She demonstrated with her hands and then Joe divided them into groups and gave them instructions.

'They won't go far. They'll stick to what they know. And it's dark.' Frances caught a sob in her throat.

Jessie held her hand.

'We'll find them, Frances. We will.'

Frances wished she could believe her. This was her fault. Thinking she could control everything, have it the way she wanted. This was her punishment. It was what she deserved. But not what Imogen deserved. She barged past Jessie, pulled the door open and ran out into the street. It was black as pitch and she blinked to get her vision after the light inside the theatre. It was cold, icy cold, and as she turned into Market Street she felt the full blast of the wind. It was black right down to the pier, down to the water. It would be freezing. Stop, stop! She wouldn't go there, not to the sea. No, she wanted the princess. Colly was a good boy, a clever boy, he would keep Imogen safe. He loved her. Frances loved her. She pulled her dressing gown about her. Her hair was falling from the pins and blew about her face; she pushed it back and Jessie caught her, stopped her. They heard voices calling, 'Imogen! Colly!' over and over again. She couldn't bear it; she saw people hurrying along Alexandra Road and in the shadows she could make out one of the stage crew talking to the conductor of a bus that had pulled up at the stop across the road. The passengers were lit by the blue lights, shaking their heads, looking out into the street. Some of them got off and joined the search.

A car pulled up and Patsy got out of the passenger side. She saw Frances and ran to her, Bobby following close behind. 'Oh, Frances, I am so sorry!' Sobs caught in her throat and they hugged each other, Patsy fighting to stay calm. Now people were walking towards them.

'Not a sound. We should call the police. The wardens might have seen something.'

Frances was shaking with cold and fear.

Jessie caught her arm. 'Let's get you inside.'

They went into the busy foyer and Frances blinked at the brightness of the lights. People were coming into the show and taking their seats. Dolly was in her usherette uniform and she forced the programmes into her colleague's hand and rushed over to Frances and Jessie.

'Any luck?' Jessie shook her head, gripped Frances's hand. Frances held on as if she was holding on to life itself.

'I've had a thought.' Dolly smiled at Frances, but for once Dolly's smile wasn't the sunshine it normally was. What if it was too late? They could be lost, anywhere. In the cold. She couldn't bear it. She wanted to run out in the street and scream.

'What thought, Dolly?' Jessie was taking control. God bless Jessie …

'They could be inside the theatre already.'

The other usherette came to stand beside Dolly and Frances looked away. She couldn't stand the pity.

'We would have seen them,' the other girl said, 'two little kids on their own.'

'Not necessarily,' Dolly said. 'We wouldn't notice two little kids. We wouldn't check their tickets. We'd be looking for the parents – and when everyone comes in together you don't notice so much. We'd have thought they were coming back from the lavatory.'

Frances pulled away from Jessie, who rushed after her. She hauled the door open to the stalls, ran down, looking frantically down the rows, up into the circle. Where would they be? She saw a sea of faces staring back and she pulled her dressing gown about her. Though what did it matter? Nothing mattered! She could see Dolly walking steadily down the middle aisle, the other usherette at the far side, asking, checking. She heard a voice. Was it Imogen? She hurried towards the sound. A woman was standing in the middle of the aisle, talking to small children; she couldn't see; why wouldn't the blasted woman move? Frances called out, 'Imogen!' The woman turned.

'I'm afraid they're in the wrong seats.'

Frances cried out, almost fell as she pushed herself forward. 'She's here! Oh, my God, she's safe!'

People were huffing and puffing at her outburst but she didn't care. Imogen was there, and Colly, sitting in the same seats as they had before, waiting for the show, waiting for the magic to start. The woman stood back and Frances swept Imogen into her arms, hugging her so tightly, kissing her head, crying, laughing. She would never let her go again.

It took a while for things to calm down, but when the curtain went up it was only a few minutes late. Seats were found for Patsy and the children and for the neighbour who had driven Patsy to the Empire. The performance was a blur; Frances managed to get through it, but was glad when it was all over. The overwhelming fear followed by the exhilaration of finding Imogen safe had left her feeling wrung out and exhausted. And now she was left with the reality. No more secrets. Everyone knew – well, almost everyone. Jessie had been wonderful, filling Ginny in with the details. They had both been so considerate, but Frances felt Ginny deserved more of an explanation.

'I'm sorry I didn't include you before, Ginny. Jessie found out by accident and I swore her to secrecy.'

'Poor Jessie. Piggy in the middle. It wasn't so long ago I did the same.' Ginny unpinned her hair, shook it free and began brushing it into smooth waves. 'I don't think I could have done what you've done, if things had been different, Frances. I think you're very brave.' Ginny started to get changed into her outdoor clothes. They could hear the babes being herded out of the dressing rooms, their footsteps as they raced up the stairs. 'What about her father? Does he help?' Jessie looked at the floor. Frances paused: her secret was out and the world hadn't ended. It would all come out soon enough.

'Johnny. Johnny's her father.'

Ginny was shocked. 'Johnny Randolph? And he didn't help you?' She frowned. 'I thought he was really lovely.'

'He is. He doesn't know.'

Ginny leant against the dressing table, her face revealing her obvious shock.

'I know,' Jessie said. 'And she hasn't told him.'

'But I will,' Frances said, quickly.

'Will you?'

Frances nodded. 'But first I need to tell Grace and Geraldine before they find out from someone else.'

Frances carried Imogen all the way back to Barkhouse Lane and Ginny and Dolly walked with them. Ginny was going to stay with Dolly for the remainder of the panto – George and his wife had already aired the bedroom for her. Everyone had been wonderful, fussing over Imogen and Colly. She regretted holding back so long.

Jessie went inside the house and knocked on her mother's door and Grace called for her to come in. Jessie went in first, then stepped to one side to let Frances pass, Imogen asleep in her arms. Grace let the newspaper drop to the floor and got to her feet.

'Glory be! Frances, put the child on the bed.' She did so and Imogen moaned a little and turned on her side but didn't open her eyes. Grace looked at the child and then at Frances. 'No need to ask whose child she is!'

France's throat was thick with pain. There was such compassion in Grace's eyes that Frances wanted to cry, but she didn't. Tears had never helped.

'I'll get my things,' Ginny said.

'I'll put the kettle on.' Dolly followed her out of the room. Frances sat on the bed, holding Imogen's hand, watching her sleep, stroking her head, wanting more than anything to lie down beside her, hold her, sleep. Now that they were safe she felt depleted.

Grace put her hand on Frances's shoulder. It gave her a little strength. 'Get Geraldine, Jessie,' Grace said, quietly and Frances twisted as Jessie left the room. 'You don't want to have to tell your story twice, Frances. You look exhausted.'

'I am.' Frances stood up. The room was cosy and warm, the gas fire low, the lamp soft. Safe. Imogen was safe. And she was here, with Frances. It was what she'd wanted for so long.

'Oh, Grace, I'm afraid of what she'll say.'

'Say about what?' Geraldine came in, wearing her dressing gown and slippers, a net over her hair. She looked severe with her hair drawn back.

Frances moved away from the bed. 'My daughter. Imogen.' The child murmured at the mention of her name, sucked at her thumb.

Geraldine gazed at the child. She peered down her nose at Frances. Frances straightened her shoulders. If she wanted them to go, Lil would have them. It didn't matter. Someone would take them in, or she could go back to Patsy.

'Your child?' Geraldine said, quietly. She paused. 'I can't tell you how disappointed I am, Frances.'

Frances held firm. 'I knew you would be.'

'And offended,' she continued, 'that you thought so little of me. That I would judge you harshly, without asking questions.'

Dolly came in with a tray of hot drinks and hovered in the doorway, unsure as to whether she should stay or leave.

Geraldine turned. 'How kind, Dolly. Now, sit down beside your beautiful daughter, Frances.' She took a mug from the tray and handed one to Frances, and to Grace, then took one for herself. The two older women took a seat in the window and Frances sat down on the bed. Jessie came in and sat on the floor by the fire with Dolly. 'Right,' Geraldine said, not unkindly. 'Begin at the beginning, Frances. We are all ears.'

When she had finished, they all agreed she had indeed been brave – and silly not to trust them.

'But the day war broke out, you were quite damning about the type of girls in the theatre, Geraldine,' she said.

'A sweeping statement. Forgive me, for I'm as much to blame with my careless words. If I'd have known the effect they'd have had I would have bitten off my tongue.' She got up and walked over to Frances, rested a gentle hand on her shoulder and gazed down at the child. 'Quite a beauty, like her mother! I'm looking forward to getting to know the latest addition to our household when she wakes.'

It was too much for Frances. She swallowed down the hard lump that had formed in her throat. 'So it's all right if we stay?' Her voice cracked.

Geraldine gave a slight nod of her head, seemingly unable to find the words, and she looked so sad that Frances felt even worse. 'We are all being judged, Frances. And we judge in return. I was wrong. So were you.' She clasped her hand. 'Now get this child upstairs to bed and we should all do the same. We start afresh tomorrow.'

Chapter 31

It was the Sunday before Christmas, a Sunday when Frances didn't have to leave the house early. She would never have to do that again, not as long as they all lived at Barkhouse Lane. The vegetables for dinner had been peeled as they always were, the dinner cooked and cleared away, and for once she and Imogen had been a part of it. Eddie had returned from caddying for Mr Archer at the golf club and was now sitting on the floor in front of the fire in Grace's room, helping Imogen complete a puzzle. Grace was sewing in her chair by the window, lit by the sun as it dropped low in the sky, and Geraldine was reading. In the bay window, between the chairs, the girls had placed a Christmas tree and Imogen had delighted in helping to decorate it. Frances sat with Jessie on Grace's bed, pillows against their backs, making paper chains.

Jessie leant close and whispered, 'When are you going to tell Johnny?'

'Oh, let me enjoy this time with her.' It gladdened her heart to see Imogen so content.

Jessie took a strip of paper and looped it, dabbing paste on the end and pressing it tight until it held. Frances passed her another strip.

'But time is running out. The Randolphs will be leaving soon, Frances.'

She knew Jessie was right, that Johnny deserved to know, but for the first time in her life she felt a sense of ease, that life was uncomplicated. 'I *will* tell him, Jessie. But I have to do it in my time, in my way.' She moved the paper chain over her lap. 'I could face it if he left me again, but not Imogen.'

'Surely you trust him?' Jessie whispered.

It was difficult to know whether she did or not. She wanted to, but something inside her couldn't let go, a small voice that said, 'Hold on.'

'I trusted him before and he let me down. How do I know he won't do the same thing again?'

'You don't.' Jessie was thoughtful. 'You're afraid.'

'I am not!' It rankled. Jessie knew nothing of what she'd been through, *they'd* been through. 'I've managed.'

'That's not what I meant.' She watched Imogen put the final piece inside the jigsaw, clap her little hands. 'You're afraid of being happy.'

Frances looked about her. 'I *am* happy, Jessie. I have my child, good friends. The only thing I'm afraid of is that I'll have too much …'

For the first time in years Frances was filled with hope for the future. The last performance on the Saturday before Christmas Eve had held a special magic, and she had left the theatre with Jessie, anticipating the joy that tomorrow would bring. That Christmas Eve fell on Sunday made it all the sweeter, being able to spend the whole day with her child, her friends. The excitement, the build-up, and being able to leave presents at the foot of Imogen's bed. That night, while she played Mother Christmas, the grown-ups gathered downstairs, the kitchen full of the smells of the season, pickled onions and smelly cheese, the rich scent of Christmas pudding. Afterwards, she'd lain awake, her child at her side, watching the dawn creep through the gap in the window, knowing she would never receive a better gift in all her life.

In the morning they gathered in Grace's room, the fire aglow, the presents set under the tree. They had come together at Barkhouse Lane only months before but now they were as tight as any family. Eddie had been working hard, saving hard, and had delighted Jessie with the gift of a guitar.

'There isn't room for a piano, but this is the next best thing.'

Jessie was thrilled and sat on Grace's bed, strumming Christmas carols while Imogen played with the doll Frances had bought her. She'd felt extravagant, spending so much, but it was worth the celebration. Geraldine sat on the floor with Imogen, helping her to dress the doll in the woollen coat and bonnet that Grace had knitted.

Imogen put the doll's bonnet on and Geraldine tied the bow under its chin. 'Are you going to give her a name?' she asked.

'I'm going to call her Jessie, because she's a princess.' The child said, beaming and Frances felt as if her heart would burst with the warmth she felt inside.

Frances picked up the book that Geraldine had given to Imogen, *A Thousand and One Tales of Arabian Nights*. She had written inside, *So that you always have a bedtime story.* Everyone had been so kind.

The clock on the mantel chimed the hour.

'Time we were leaving.' Geraldine got up, peering through the nets at the window. 'No sign of snow, Imogen. Not yet. But it will be cold, so we need to get wrapped up warm before we leave the house.' She left to get herself ready, as did the others, and they all appeared in the street in their best clothes, wrapped in newly knitted hats and scarves that had been Christmas presents from Dolly.

They called at the pub to wish Lil, 'Merry Christmas!' Big Malc was in his usual place at the bar, Fudge on his seat by the fire, and a few of the lads in uniform had called in on their way to the theatre. Lil lifted the flap and came out to them. She kissed Frances and Jessie, touched Imogen's head, admired her doll.

'What a Christmas it is, eh, Franny? Bet you never thought it would turn out the way it has.'

Frances felt tears prick at her eyes. Happy tears. Lil had been so generous, in her heart and spirit. She had been there for them all, in some small way. And here was her pub, filled with friends.

'Lot of lonely people out there, Franny. All them boys away from home, their loved ones. I'm glad you're doing this show.'

'You will come to Joyce's when you've locked up?'

'I might. I'll see how I feel. Might just want to put me feet up.'

'But it's Christmas, Lil,' Jessie cried. She took her hand, squeezed it. 'Please come.'

'We'll see.'

Frances knew she wouldn't. Lil didn't need anyone. And there was always Big Malc if she did.

They walked along Alexandra Road, down towards the Empire. People were wrapped up warmly against the cold, kids on their bikes, a lad walking on stilts. It all seemed so normal – and it would have been, save for the absence of all the young men, the fathers who would be over in France. Frances thought of Harry: where would he be? And Pete? At least Johnny was here, somewhere. He'd said he would sign up once he knew Ruby was safe. But now she was . . .

The troops were already milling around the theatre, lorries and trucks parked along the road. They parted at the stage door and Geraldine, Grace and Eddie went to Joyce's while the girls and Imogen went into the theatre.

George was already in his office and he came out when he saw them.

'No need to guess what Father Christmas brought for you, Imogen.' She held up her doll and he bent down, admiring it. He brought out a parcel, wrapped in jolly paper. 'A little gift from me and the missus.'

Frances kissed his cheek. 'That's so kind of you both, George.' They skipped down to the dressing rooms, wishing everyone 'Merry Christmas!' Ginny was getting ready, Dolly seated in the easy chair. Imogen hurried towards them to show them her doll and the girls grinned when they found out her name. 'Is she a naughty dolly, or a good dolly?'

'Oh, a good dolly,' Imogen said, her face serious. 'She's a princess.'

'So she is.' The girls laughed and Jessie cradled her namesake while Frances removed Imogen's coat, hanging it up beside her own. It looked so small and she squeezed the cloth, patted it as if it were her child. When she turned back, Dolly was holding a length of red ribbon.

'Would you like Mummy to put this in your hair, Imogen?' She took a narrower strip. 'And one for your Jessie too, so you can be the same?'

Imogen beamed and Frances lifted her onto the chair, telling her to stand so she could see herself in the mirror. Frances threaded the ribbon through her fingers and began to brush Imogen's hair, smiling at her child's reflection as she did so. There was a knock at the door and Jessie went to open it, the doll in her other hand. The room fell silent as Ruby swept in all smiles, her arms full of gifts.

Frances stopped brushing, her hand trembling. She began to brush again, trying to appear as composed as she could, as if little girls came into the dressing room every day to have their hair brushed. She could be anyone's child.

Anyone's. Ruby placed the presents down on the dressing table, staring at Imogen through the mirror. Frances tried to tie the ribbon, all fingers and thumbs, her hands shaking. Her heart was pounding and she was at a loss as to what to do. Ruby held her gaze, opened her mouth to speak then closed it again, smiled at Imogen.

'Oh, Ruby, you really shouldn't have!' Jessie dashed forward, gabbling, trying to counter the tense atmosphere that had been created when Ruby walked in. Frances felt as if she were made of stone, didn't want to speak in case she broke the spell. Ruby was almost in a trance but she shook herself, smiling at Jessie, at them all.

'It's a thank you, for what you did for me.'

'We did it because it was the right thing to do, Ruby.' Ginny said, standing up and coming closer to Frances, 'You don't need to say thank you.'

Ruby was looking at Frances and back to Imogen. Frances could almost see her brain clicking over, working it out.

'I need to say so many things.' Ruby took a deep breath. 'And I have to start somewhere.' She handed over the boxes. Frances put down the brush and Ruby handed her a small parcel wrapped in expensive paper. Whatever it was would be over the top. Imogen was mesmerised by the sparkling diamonds in Ruby's brooch.

'Pretty,' she said.

Ruby came close, studying the child's face, then she reached out, touched her hair. 'Do you like it?' Imogen said she did. Ruby held it closer to Imogen and as the light hit the diamonds, it sparkled brighter still. Imogen ran her fingers over it, her face alight with pleasure.

'My mummy gave it to me,' Ruby said. 'It's very precious. As you are precious to your mummy.' Imogen let go of the brooch and Ruby stepped away. She went to the door. 'I came to Grimsby thinking I would hate it.' She took a deep breath and her voice quivered as she spoke; she looked directly at Frances. 'I'm glad I came.' She wiggled her fingers at Imogen. 'Merry Christmas, girls!'

Everything was frozen for a few seconds, the girls staring at Frances, wondering what to do. She threw down the brush and ran after her.

'Ruby!' Ruby stopped, turned. Tears glistened in her eyes and for a moment Frances didn't know what to do. Sid and Bob came down the corridor, wished Ruby 'Merry Christmas', kissed her cheek. She was warm with them, gracious, and Frances admired her for it.

'Is Johnny here?' Ruby nodded, biting her lip, shaking her head to shake away the tears. 'Please let me tell him myself?'

Ruby looked small and afraid. Beyond the make-up Frances could see that she was weary. The last few months must have taken their toll but it was over now. Ruby swallowed.

'Of course. I'm so sorry, Frances. Truly. For everything.'

She left, her head down, and Frances hurried back to the dressing room. Dolly had fastened the ribbons and the girls stopped talking when Frances returned. She took Imogen down from the chair.

'Will you take her to Joyce's, Dolly?' Dolly didn't ask any questions, simply took Imogen's hand in hers and left the room.

Frances began getting herself ready, fighting to stop herself shaking. Would Ruby keep her word?

Jessie asked, tentatively, 'What did she say?'

'Nothing – but she knows.' She checked her reflection. Fear had bleached the colour from her face.

'Oh, Frances!' Jessie opened her present. It was an expensive bottle of perfume. 'She didn't have to do that. It's too much.'

'That's all Ruby knows how to be.' Frances steadied her hand. 'And Johnny's here.'

'Tell him.' Jessie urged. Frances didn't reply.

She was ready when the knock came on the door and Johnny peered around it. His plum scarf was loose about his neck, his coat dark on the shoulders with spots of rain.

When Jessie and Ginny made to leave the room he stopped them. 'I seem to scare you two away!' He grinned and Jessie fumbled. 'We thought you'd want the privacy.'

Frances couldn't bear it.

'Ordinarily I would,' he said. 'But we have to be back at the Palace. We're hosting a dinner there for some of the Naval Reserve chaps. Then the show and, well, like you, it will be a long day, but worth it.' He looked at the gifts on the dressing table. 'I see Ruby beat me to it. She'll never forget what you three have done for her.' He smiled. 'And neither will I.' He withdrew a square box from his coat pocket and handed it to Frances. 'Happy Christmas, Frances.' She took it from him, her hands still shaking, her heart still pounding and managed to smile. It was easier to be merry than happy, but she was happy, now that she had Imogen.

'Should I open it now?'

'It's up to you.' He wasn't pressing her to do anything and she relaxed a little, knowing Imogen was safe with Joyce. The girls were right: she should tell him, but not now, not this moment. She undid the paper, her fingers awkward, opened the box. It was a necklace, a single tear-drop diamond. She lifted it out. 'Do you like it?'

'It's – it's beautiful.' She tried to open the clasp, but her hands were shaking and she fought to steady them.

'Here,' he said, 'let me.' She lifted her hair and he placed it about her neck, fastening the clasp. Jessie and Ginny admired it and she turned to him, aware the girls were watching. He touched her face, kissed her cheek and she longed to take his hand in hers, to lead him away and tell him everything. Would she ever find the right time? 'I must leave.' He looked to Jessie and Ginny. 'Good to see you, girls.'

'I'll come with you. Say goodbye.' She followed him down the corridor and up the stairs, out into the street. It was cold and she wrapped her arms about her for warmth.

'I didn't get you anything.' There hadn't been time, nor the money, for every spare penny had been spent on Imogen.

'I didn't want anything, Frances. I wanted you. That's all I ever wanted.' It began to snow, soft flakes that landed on her hair, on his coat collar, and she reached up to brush them away. He caught her hand, kissed her fingers, pulled her to him and she let him. He held on to her hand. 'The answer was "yes" once. If I asked you again, what would it be, I wonder?'

She looked across to Joyce's café. Vi had made paper snowflakes and stuck them on the window and one of them was peeling away. It didn't matter now, they seemed to have the real thing. She looked up into his eyes. He was kind, generous – and she loved him. But she didn't need him … Ruby came out of the stage door.

'Oh, there you are.' She glanced at Frances and reddened, knowing she had interrupted something special. 'Sorry, Johnny. We need to leave. The car's at the front.' Ruby went back inside and, as the door closed, Johnny swept Frances into his arms and kissed her so hard that it took her breath away. She held back for a fraction and then gave herself to him, for his kisses were like life itself and she felt something awaken in her that hadn't been there before. Was it happiness? At last? She pulled back, catching her breath.

He kissed her again. Her lips, her cheeks, her forehead, and she laughed as the snowflakes fell and melted in the warmth of their breath.

'I must go. I'll call.' She let go of his hands and he went inside. She remained on the pavement, watching the snowflakes swirl and fall in the quiet street as they settled on the ground. She hoped Ruby would be true to her word, but if she wasn't, there was nothing she could do about it any more. She could feel the chains she'd held onto so tightly begin to fall about her feet.

It was fun on stage that afternoon, a totally different experience, playing to an audience devoid of children. They had worried whether the lads would join in with the 'He's behind you!' nonsense but it had been needless. They had joined in wholeheartedly, and when Joe came on shouting, 'New lamps for old!' a wag in the audience shouted, 'Put that ruddy light out!' It brought the biggest laughter of the afternoon.

When the curtain came down the cast went out front in their costumes, chatting to the lads and lasses who were out there in their uniforms. Autographs were signed, publicity photos handed out – and many of the lads left with lipstick kisses on their faces. When the last one had gone, they went back to their rooms, changed and headed over to Joyce's. The smell of roast beef greeted them when Jessie opened the door.

Grace and Geraldine were red-faced, their sleeves rolled up to their elbows. They stood with Joyce, passing plates over the counter, which Eddie and Dolly took, weaving between the tables, serving the cast and crew. Joyce had pushed some of the tables together so that no one sat on their own. Kitty Bright had squeezed herself between Bob and Sid, while Don and Basil sat opposite. Ginny took a seat next to Joe. She picked up her cracker, held it out to him. They tugged, she won. She unfurled the paper hat and placed it on his head. Jessie smiled; he deserved to be crowned. It was his ideas that had made sure that Ruby had a better Christmas than she would have had. Vi was at the girls' table at the window, nursing baby Frank, and Imogen was nursing her dolly. Jessie and Frances sat down with them and Imogen held her baby close, crooning a little song that Geraldine had taught her. When everyone was served Grace, Joyce and Geraldine took off their aprons and sat down to join them. Don got up, glass in hand.

'I hope you'll join me in a toast. To the wonderful Joyce and her lovely assistants. Thanks from us all, and a very Merry Christmas!'

They raised their glasses.

'To Joyce and her helpers – Merry Christmas!'

After a small and appropriate silence there was a clatter as knives and forks were taken up and the feast began. There was a lull while Eddie and Dolly cleared the plates and Kitty led them in singalong of carols. Everyone was quiet while Imogen sang 'Away in a Manger', rocking her baby from side to side. Tears rolled down Frances's cheeks and she wasn't alone. The little girl glowed at the rousing applause.

Joyce placed a dish of pudding in front of them and they leant back while she drowned it in cream.

'That'll put hairs on your chest, lasses!'

'Good lord, I hope not, Joyce! I'll be auditioning for the circus if it does,' Jessie said, laughing.

It was hot and it was loud, and laughter filled the room. Frances felt so very blessed. Jessie pushed her empty bowl to the centre of the table and leant back in her seat. She turned to Frances, whispering, 'Do you think Ruby will keep her word and not tell Johnny?'

'I want to think she will.' Something told her Ruby would.

'She doesn't look well, does she? I thought she was very thin.'

Imogen came to her and she pulled her on her knee. She couldn't recall a Christmas like it. She kissed the top of Imogen's head. 'Perhaps she'll get well now that she's got Mickey Harper off her back. It must have been dreadful.' The girl had tortured herself. More so keeping it from Johnny.

As if catching her thought, Jessie said, 'Secrets aren't good for anyone, are they?'

Chapter 32

As Christmas Day drew to a close, Ruby was empty but for the memories of a job well done. The audience had been pretty special, those young men who would be leaving their loved ones behind to fight for what they believed in. It had been good to see people so happy, to give something and want nothing in return more than smiling faces. They had finished with a sing-song, something they'd added for the occasion, and she had led them in a medley of songs, conducting them with her outstretched hands. There had been rows and rows of smiling faces, boys some of them, away from their families. It broke her heart to think what many of them would face in the days to come. They didn't deserve it and it was the least she could do. It felt good to do something.

Johnny had grasped her hand as they took the applause, the boys cheering and stamping their feet in appreciation. He pulled her to him, hugged her. Every time she looked at him, she saw the child, Imogen. In the end she stared past him, not being able to bear the overwhelming sense of hatred and loathing she felt for what she had done.

It was long after midnight when they got back to the house. Johnny poured them both a drink and when Ruby stretched out on the sofa, he tucked a blanket over her legs.

'You made a lot of people happy tonight, Ruby.' She stared into the fire so that she didn't have to look at him. He put a record on the gramophone and they listened to Christmas carols until her eyelids were heavy and she fell asleep. He woke her, helped her upstairs and she lay on her bed, the curtains wide, looking at the stars in a crisp black sky. Puffy white clouds floated across. What would it be like to climb on one and float away, far, far, away?

She heard him come upstairs not long after, humming to himself. The sound of his voice was comforting. He was happy. He would be happy with Frances. And Imogen. Oh, God, what had she done? Her stomach was hollow. He knocked on her door.

'Goodnight, Ruby. Sweet dreams.'

She managed to call out. 'Goodnight.' Her voice felt as if it was coming from somewhere else. She lay there a long time, afraid, wondering what she could do, playing out scenarios of what Johnny would do when it all came out. He would never forgive her. Not for this. She hauled herself up, felt the rug under her bare feet, brought the letters from the wardrobe. Why had her mother done it? Why hadn't she opened them? Was it too late now, to put things right? They didn't belong to her, they belonged to Frances. She found some paper, wrote a letter; wrapped everything with Christmas paper. Somehow, she would make it right. One step at a time. And then the sunshine.

The day after Boxing Day Frances went into the theatre to discover a gift on the dressing table. Jessie hung up her coat, peered at it.

'Lucky you.'

Frances checked the label.

'It's not from Johnny. Not his hand.' She undid the string, peeled the paper away to find a battered shoe box. She removed the lid; inside was an envelope with her name and, underneath, more envelopes. She ran her fingers over them. Her letters to Johnny, others with her name on so obviously from him. She sank down into the chair, her hand to her mouth.

'What?'

Ginny hurried to her side and Frances looked up into the mirror and saw them staring. 'My letters! *Our* letters!' She looked through them again. 'And a ticket for America – in my name. My ticket ...' Her hand was shaking as realisation dawned on her.

Jessie gripped her shoulder. Frances had the white envelope in her hand.

'Ruby?' Jessie said. Frances nodded. 'So, Johnny was telling the truth. He *did* send for you. He wanted you all along.' Jessie pulled her chair close, sat down beside her, pressing her hand on Frances's arm. 'Aren't you going to open it?'

Frances swallowed. She didn't know if she dared. It was all too much. She felt waves of anger and rage sweep over her, followed by a surge of happiness and hope. Yes, it was hope, because Johnny was the man she'd thought he was all those years ago, he had kept his word. Tears fell and she put her hand to her mouth, her body racked with sobs she tried so hard, so very hard, to hold in. Jessie pulled her hand away, hugged her, held her like a child.

'Let it all out, Frances. Let it go.'

Free at last, Frances did.

Frances handed the letter to Jessie. The handwriting was erratic, loopy, parts of it incoherent. It took them a while to decipher the words. Ruby explained that her mother had thought Frances was after Johnny's money, his fame. She'd convinced Ruby that Frances wouldn't settle for just that, once she got her claws into Johnny. She would want to take Ruby's place too. Not only in his life, but in their act. And what would Ruby have left then? How would she manage? She had been terrified, had done exactly as her mother had asked. She had made sure she was always at the theatre first to get the post; always offered to take the mail. Johnny hadn't suspected a thing. He had trusted her.

'Will you tell Johnny?' Jessie gave the letter back to Frances.

'It's not my tale to tell.' Her eyes were red, sore. 'Ruby has respected my wishes. She obviously hasn't said anything to Johnny.'

'And you still haven't told him?' Ginny raised her eyebrows.

'I couldn't find the right time. Or the courage. We're having dinner on Sunday. I'll tell him then. It has to be right.'

Jessie was not convinced. 'Delaying hasn't worked for anyone. Not for Ruby. Not for you. Sunday is New Year's Eve.'

'A fresh start,' Frances said. 'It's the right time.'

It had been five days since Ruby had sent the letters. Five days and nights when she had waited for Johnny's anger, his rage. She was prepared for that but not this silence and keeping the knowledge of his child from him was unbearable, the time ticking away on the clock, but she mustn't say anything. She'd promised Frances and she owed it to her. Ruby hung her dress in the wardrobe. What had Aunt Letty said about tidying? That it would help tidy her thoughts. She gazed about the room. It was all neat. Tidy. Everything where it should be. She ran her fingers over her silver-backed brush and mirror, sat in front of her dressing table, brushed her hair. Everything felt lighter; she felt as if she could float. Like a fairy, an angel, a cloud.

Johnny knocked, came into her room.

'Are you sure you don't want to come with me? It's not too late to change your mind, you know. A woman's prerogative. Especially tonight.'

'Quite sure.'

He stood behind her, kissed the top of her head. 'Make sure you get something to eat. We'll be back home soon. Not long now.' She reached up for his hand and he clasped it in both of his.

'I wish you'd let it all go, Ruby,' he said, 'leave it in the past where it belongs.' She flinched. Frances had said the same. Would she still think it now? There had been no word from her . . .

'I love you, Johnny, you know that, don't you?'

He squatted down beside her. 'Of course I do, silly girl! I love you too.'

Her heart felt as if it had crumbled to pieces. When she heard the front door open and close she went to the window, watched until he disappeared out of sight. The sky was heavy with snow and she looked over to the park, where the trees were black witches, fingers splayed against the grey of the sky. Tomorrow it would be a New Year, a new beginning. Would she be on her own? Without Johnny? She went to the dressing table, picked up her mother's photograph. 'I tried to make it right, Mummy. I tried to be happy. To make Johnny happy.' She returned to the window. Snow was starting to fall and she could see lights on the other side of the park. It looked cosy, inviting, and she didn't want to wait. She slipped out of the house, leaving the door open. She wouldn't be long, she just wanted to be where the light was.

Johnny turned the corner; sleet was beginning to fall. He shouldn't have left Ruby on her own, not on New Year's Eve. He should take her with him; Jessie would be glad of the company and Ginny. It would be better if she was with people, kind-hearted people. He looked up at the sky, more snow on the way. He checked his watch. He would only be a few minutes late and Frances would understand, the weather was slowing everything down. He pictured her waiting for him at the Dolphin Hotel across the road from the Empire. They had met there before and it had been her choice. He patted his pocket. The ring was still there. Would she say yes this time? He hesitated then turned back, hurrying through the snow. A woman was crossing the road over to the park; astonishingly, she wasn't wearing a coat. He peered, the sleet coming faster now, and realised it was Ruby.

He shouted, 'Ruby!' but she didn't stop and he ran, slipping in the slush under his feet, his heart pounding, calling her name, the snow catching in his mouth. 'Stop! Stop!' Could she hear him? Damn the wind, the snow! She must stop, she *must*. He ran through the park gates. His brain didn't want to register what his eyes were seeing as she walked into the water. He ran faster, slipping, stumbling. She fell and he lunged forward, grasped at her arm, held on, fell onto his knees in the water. It wasn't deep but it was cold and he gasped at the shock of it, pulling her up, dragging her to the edge, crying her name: 'Ruby! Oh, my God, Ruby!'

Her eyes were closed, her face white. A couple ran towards them and the man tore off his coat and put it over her, helped Johnny take her in his arms.

Johnny's teeth were chattering. 'Over there.' He indicated with his head. The light was shining out from the hall and the man helped him carry her across the park and into the house, his wife following. Johnny settled Ruby on the sofa, then eased off her clothes and covered her with a blanket as the man turned his back and turned up the fire.

The woman came to him. 'Let me get help.' He managed to garble Mrs Frame's address and the pair of them left the room. He was talking to Ruby, shaking her gently, rubbing warmth into her body. God, if anything happened to her, he'd never forgive himself.

It was busy in the hotel dining room. The staff were milling around getting things ready for the evening's entertainment. As Frances watched the last diners left and the staff swept in to clear the tables and reset them. The cutlery and wine glasses glittered in the light of the chandeliers as they were placed on the tables. It looked gay and inviting and she almost wished she would be seeing in the New Year here, with Johnny. She checked her watch. Was it fast? Yes, it was a little. No matter. She sipped at her wine.

Musicians came in and started setting up their instruments. The drummer placed the cymbals on stands, the sound of them ringing out as he fixed them in position. The sense of anticipation was all around her. She checked her watch again. Imogen would be at the Empire now, with Grace and Geraldine because Jack was throwing a party for the cast. Lil and some of the customers had been invited and Joyce and her family would be there, other friends they had made. She could picture them gathering, walking up the stairs to the top of the building, just as she could picture Johnny meeting his child for the first time. This was the best time to tell him, the cusp of the year and a sense of new beginnings.

She sipped again. Her glass was almost empty.

Ruby opened her eyes.

'Thank God!' He was smiling, he was crying. Her big brother was crying. She reached up, touched his face. He caught hold of her hand.

'I'm so sorry, Johnny.' Her body was trembling and she tried to will it to stop but she couldn't; it made her tired.

The room was hot. She saw faces, strangers. Who were they? Then a woman, older, she tried to focus. Mummy? Her heart shrank with the disappointment.

'Oh, Ruby, what a thing to do!' Mrs Frame squeezed Johnny on the shoulder. 'Get out of those wet things, Mr Johnny. You'll catch your death.'

'You silly, silly girl.' He kissed her hand, kissed her forehead, sat back stroking her hair. She took her hand away from his cheek.

'Frances knows.'

'Frances knows what, darling girl?'

Tears began to fall, she didn't think she had any left but still they came. Big fat tears that were warm on her face.

'I gave her the letters.'

'She's rambling.' Mrs Frame tugged at his arm. 'Go get changed, my boy, or you'll be ill yourself.'

He got up. 'I must thank the couple who helped.' The clock chimed seven. 'Oh, Lord, I was meant to be with Frances! Will you wait while I see her, Mrs Frame? I won't be long, but I can't let her down. She'll never forgive me. Not this time.'

'Get changed. I won't be leaving. My old man will come here to see the New Year in. Off you go. I'll take care of Ruby.'

The doctor came into the hall as he gave his thanks to the couple who had helped so much, then called for a taxi.

'I've given her a sedative, but I'd advise you to seek specialist help as soon as you possibly can if you want your sister to get well.'

The taxi made its way slowly into Cleethorpes. The snow was coming in drifts now and the car kept sliding across the road. In the end it was quicker to get out and walk. He strode up Isaac's Hill, pulled his scarf up about his face, held onto his hat. He hurried straight into the dining room, hoping she would still be there, but the room was empty save for the staff and a few musicians warming up. He walked away, desolate. He was too late. He looked up, saw her putting on her coat.

'I almost missed you.'

She didn't smile as he had thought she would. 'Forgive me, Frances. Please let me explain.'

He looked haggard, his eyes so sad. It had to be Ruby. Had she told him? Had they had a row? He ordered a large whisky and a waiter showed them to a table in a quiet corner. Johnny told her what had happened.

'Is she all right?'

'She is. She will be.' He didn't sound convinced. She reached for his hand. He looked afraid. 'I thought I was doing the right thing, getting her away from London. I didn't know about Mickey Harper.' He grasped her hand. 'And I was selfish. I saw you that day when I came with Bernie Blackwood and I thought there might be a chance. I wasn't thinking of Ruby then, at all.' He took her hand. 'She told me.'

Frances held her breath.

'About the letters. I had no idea. She offered to post them. And my mother too. I didn't think anything of it.'

'She was afraid,' Frances said. 'We all make mistakes when we allow fear to take over.' He would understand that's what she had done, let fear colour her judgement. She and Ruby were the same.

'She's not strong, like you, Frances.' Frances swallowed, bit at her lip. She hadn't been strong at all, but she'd had to find it within her, for Imogen. Ruby would find hers. Perhaps she had already begun to find it. He kissed her strength hand, let it go. 'We'll be leaving tomorrow.'

'What about the show? Haven't you got another four weeks?'

'We won't reopen.' He sipped at his whisky. 'I'll be taking Ruby to stay with Aunt Letty – I should have done that in the first place – but I thought work would help her. It helped me, when I thought I'd lost you.'

'Don't hold it against her, Johnny. What she did, she did because she loves you. We all do what we think is right at the time.' She took her hand in his, clasping it tightly, feeling the warmth, the strength of it. 'I have so much and Ruby is lost for the moment. But she will recover. She has been hiding a terrible burden and now she can let it go.'

'I had a ring.' He patted at his pockets. 'It's in my other suit.' He laughed, a sad laugh.

'They all say that.' She smiled, hoping to lift him somehow. She knew now how much he loved her. In his sadness, it shone through.

He took her hand. 'This is not what I wanted it to be like.'

'Not everything goes the way we want it to. But we get there in the end.'

He touched her fingers to his mouth, his breath warm on them. 'Will you wait for me, Frances?'

'I will.' He leant across and kissed her and she closed her eyes; a pool of sadness filled her, for him, for Ruby, for all the lost time.

She got up. 'My friends are waiting for me and you need to go back to Ruby.'

He walked her to the theatre and they stood on the steps, the world white, snow illuminating the dark night. He took her in his arms and kissed her. 'I'll be back as soon as I've got Ruby safe. Do you believe me?' He held her around her waist.

'I do.' How could she be so happy, and so desperately sad?

'If only I had that ring.'

She laughed. Snowflakes fell on her lips and he pulled her to him and kissed them away and she didn't feel the cold or see the darkness any more.

A taxi was waiting by the front of the theatre. He stood by it and she held onto his hand. Could she bear to let him go again? She pulled him away, towards the theatre, up the steps and into the foyer. He was laughing, his eyes sparkling, and she stood close, put her hands either side of his face, kissed him. They'd both waited too long – now it was Ruby's turn to wait. She led him up the stairs, past the dress circle and onto a small landing.

'Wait.'

He waited, bemused.

The room at the top of the Empire was cosy, the fireplaces at either end burning bright with logs. She moved through the crowd to where Grace was sitting with Geraldine. Imogen was asleep, her dark curls falling onto Grace's lap. Jessie came over.

'Where's Johnny?'

'On the landing.' She scooped Imogen into her arms, woke her gently with kisses. Imogen blinked at the light, smiling sleepily. Jessie went ahead, making a path for her, clearing the way. Frances was talking to Imogen, whispering, watching the child's eyes as they widened with delight and anticipation. Jessie opened the door and Frances stepped out into the darkness of the hall, down to the landing. Johnny looked up, stepped forward. She let Imogen down gently, holding onto her shoulders as she faced her father. Time seemed suspended as he looked to the child. Their child.

'I couldn't tell you before.' Tears dropped onto her cheeks, happy tears. The struggle was over, at least for her. She didn't have to think about Ruby. Not tonight. The night belonged to the three of them, a family at last. Johnny squatted down and she managed to find her voice, the lump in her throat so big, so wide. 'Imogen, this is your daddy.'

Johnny opened his arms and Imogen ran into them. He swept her up, standing, laughing, kissing, and laughing again. He held her for a long time, burying his face in her small body, disbelieving, bewildered. He put out his arm to Frances and she went to him, and he wrapped it about her shoulder, pulling her close. She placed her hand on his chest, feeling his heart beating, so strong. He kissed her head and she looked into his eyes.

'How? Why?'

She placed her finger on his lips. 'Not now. There'll be time enough later. But it's New Year's Eve and our friends are upstairs. Will you stay?'

He brought her to him, kissing her face. Imogen giggled and Frances smiled, Johnny too. 'How could I ever leave?'

The room was a sea of happy faces when the three of them walked back in. Lil was dancing with Big Malc, Fudge lying so close to the fire he might melt. Don Roper was entertaining the stage crew with stories from his repartee and George and Olive waved as they passed, their faces rosy from the heat. Geraldine got up, making a place for Johnny to sit down with Imogen. He held her on his lap, talking to her. Imogen showed him her dolly and Frances went to get drinks. Bob was topping up Audrey's glass and flirting with her. Her trilling laughter could be heard in all four corners of the room and she was sweet and gracious to everyone gathered there, regardless of their position.

'Make the most of it,' Sid said to Jack out the side of his mouth. 'She'll have one hell of a head on her tomorrow.' They slapped Jack on the back and he laughed so hard, it set him off in a coughing fit. They were surrounded by friends, seeing out the old. Soon it would be time for new beginnings.

At five minutes to midnight Jack tapped on his glass with a spoon. He waited for the noise to die down before he spoke.

'I'm glad you could make it tonight, friends – or should I say family?' A cheer went up. Audrey was smiling, red-faced, and Jessie giggled. Frances nudged her. Dolly and Ginny came close. Over in the corner she could see Imogen fast asleep, Johnny holding her tight. Jack continued, 'There's no such thing as the good old days. The best day we have is now. Let's enjoy it while we can.'

Johnny laid Imogen down on the chairs and came to Frances and together they joined the circle, their arms crossed, hands held, and as the clock chimed the hour they sang 'Auld Lang Syne'. As it ended, Johnny broke free, drew Frances to him and kissed her lips, her cheeks, her hair. She pulled away, laughing, and they were swept into a joyous round of hugging and kissing to welcome the year.

When the celebrations died down, Johnny went back to Imogen, took her onto his lap. Frances left him, just for a moment. There was so much catching up to do, so many lost moments, but there would be new ones to grasp hold of from now on. She joined with Jessie, Ginny and Dolly and they took their drinks and went downstairs to the dress circle, opened the balcony doors and stepped out. The moon was bright, leaving a silver path along the water, ships silhouetted on the horizon. The snow had stopped and a blanket of white covered the road, the pavements. Out on the street people called out the New Year. There was a sense of promise in the air.

'It's a different kind of looking forward, isn't it?' Jessie said. 'Now that we're at war. Who knows what the year will bring? For any of us.'

Frances linked her arm in Jessie's, held out for Dolly and Ginny to do the same.

'Whatever it does, we'll be ready for it.' Frances pulled them close. 'We're the lucky ones. We have each other.'

She thought of Ruby, of how she must feel, alone on this of all nights. She could forgive her and Johnny would too. But for the moment she wanted to celebrate. She had friends, good friends, she had Johnny and Imogen – and at last she knew what happiness was.

ACKNOWLEDGEMENTS

It was a strange experience working on the edits of *Christmas with the Variety Girls*. It opens when the theatres are closed, and during the early months of 2020 theatres were closed once again – except none of us knew for how long. It has been an odd time, a time of people pulling together – much as it was during WW2 – and a strong sense of community was forged that we were perhaps lacking before.

Once again it was entertainment that made us forget our troubles and provided some welcome relief. And this time everyone had a chance to entertain. My niece Roxie is a nurse in ICU in the UK. The coronavirus updates came on TV at 5.00pm, leaving some low and perhaps fearful, and she wanted her children to have something to cheer them before they went to bed. She set up *Sing at Six*, where people could post their videos singing the chosen song of the day. And for a brief part of the day there was fun and much laughter. My sister, Dianne – Roxie's mum – joined in wholeheartedly and emerged from her garden shed each night dressed as everyone from Judy Garland in *The Wizard of Oz* to little orphan *Annie* (my particular favourite). Dianne was doing it for her daughter, to make her laugh while she was on shift at Diana, Princess of Wales Hospital, Grimsby. It did what she set out to do and entertained many others in the process. It seems that in such times of trouble we find many ways to support each other and spread a little happiness.

This is what the Variety Girls are all about, making people forget their worries if only for a short time.

Lil the landlady is of my imagination and partly of my experience. On Cleethorpes station there is a small pub, Under the Clock, and years ago Nelly, the landlady, would often have a sing-song when the fancy took her. I was thinking of her when Lil dances about the pub, holding the hem of her skirt. Pubs are full of characters and as my parents managed and owned pubs and nightclubs I met many of them at an early age. In fact, living in the pub opposite Cleethorpes Pier left me ideally placed to meet an abundance of characters and entertainers over the years. It was as if it was all there waiting to be released into the pages of *Variety Girls*.

All the places in my story exist – the Empire, the Dolphin, the Fisherman's Arms and so on – but the interiors and characters are fully imagined. And as always, any mistakes are my own.

So many people helped me get this show on the road and I'd especially like to thank Vivien Green, who has guided, directed and encouraged me the whole way.

Gillian Green, my magical editor whose skill and insight made the *Variety Girls* sparkle all the brighter on the page.

Dan O'Brien, the magician's assistant, and the team at Ebury who worked so hard on my behalf – especially Anni Shaw, who got the word out and was always so enthusiastic. And to Amandeep Singh who so wonderfully stepped in to make sure *Christmas with the Variety Girls* made it to curtain up.

The special talents of Kati Nicholl for her copy edits. Thank you so much for your eagle eye and skill in tightening my wobbly timeline.

Once again, my everlasting thanks to the superlative Margaret Graham. I am one lucky woman to have her in my life.

Helen Baggott for Mondays, antlers and ambushing Gulliver's Bookshop, Wimborne, on one of our many 'meetings'.

To Jess and her team at Waterstones, Grimsby, who hosted my book launch and joined in wholeheartedly – and to all the family and friends who came along to make my day extra special. Thank you for travelling far and wide to support me.

It goes without saying that I owe so much to my mum and dad, Tom and Joan Lee, who loved me and my sisters, Dianne and Taryn, beyond measure. We really were the richest kids in town. Family was first, last and everything in the middle – it always will be, no matter what that family is made up of.

To my children – all six of them – because we don't do in-laws. I love them dearly. They are my greatest happiness, my grandchildren my greatest joy. I feel so very blessed to have them.

And I had to leave the top of the bill until last. To Neil, who left me alone to write even though he was bursting to interrupt; for all the teas placed quietly on my desk, and for a million other things, for the endless laughter – I always get 100 per cent entertainment value – whether I like it or not! It's never been a dull moment even though many times I have longed for a quieter life – but the everyday tumble of life is where the stories are.

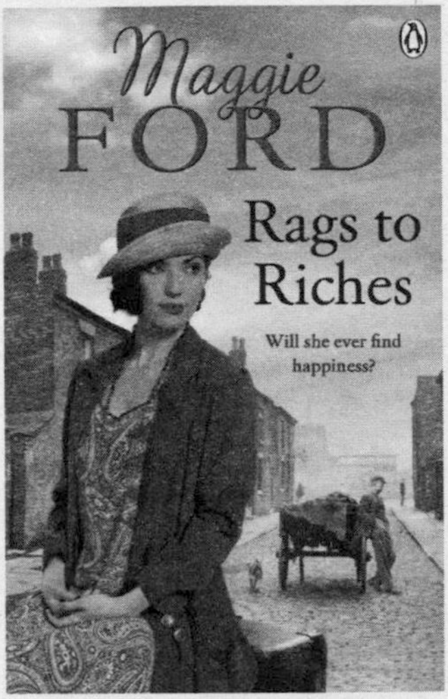
Maggie
FORD
Rags to
Riches
Will she ever find
happiness?

In the 1920s, nobody is safe from scandal…

Amy Harrington leads a privileged life out in London society. Her maid, Alice Jordan, lives in the poverty-ridden East End. But when a disgraced Amy is disowned by her parents and fiancé, Alice is the only person she can turn to…

Forced to give up her life of luxury, Amy lodges with Alice's friendly working class family. But while Amy hatches a plan to get revenge on her former love who caused her downfall, Alice finds herself swept into the glittering society her mistress has just lost. And when Amy meets Alice's handsome older brother Tom, they can only hope that love can conquer all…

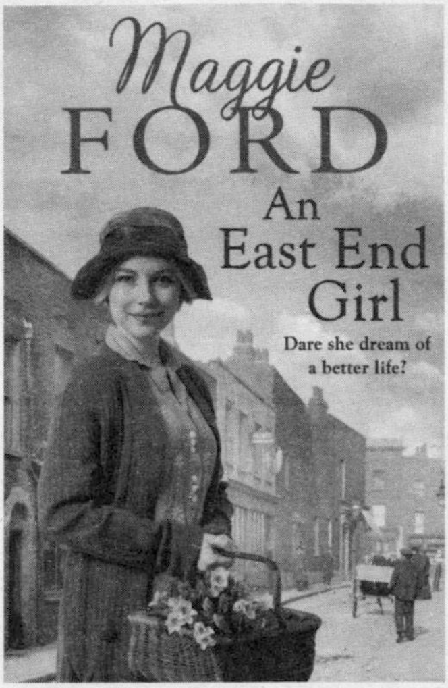

Will she ever be anything more than an East End girl?

Cissy Farmer longs to escape her life in London's Docklands where times are hard and money is tight. And when she meets the debonair Langley Makepeace, her dream seems within reach.

But the price of belonging in Langley's brittle, sophisticated world could be much higher than Cissy ever imagined. Torn between Langley and her gentle childhood sweetheart, Eddie Bennet, she is forced to gamble on her future chance of happiness, a decision that will change her life forever…